# all the Darkest truths

All The Darkest Truths © 2025 Avelyn Paige



Cover Designer: Simply Defined Art

Editor: Breathless Lit

Page Edge Designs by Painted Wings Publishing

This is a work of fiction. Names, places, characters and incidents are either the product of the author's imagination or are used fictitiously, and any resemblance to any actual persons, living or dead, organizations, events or locales is entirely coincidental.

# Dedication

To the mess that is my life,
and the deadline that watched me drown with a stopwatch.
May you both step on Lego.

# Trigger Warnings

**Trigger Warning (or: A List of Reasons Your Therapist Might Finally Quit on You)**

Welcome to this absolute dumpster fire of a love story, where morals are optional, consent is complicated, and the only safe word is *laughter through tears*. If you're here for emotionally stable characters and healthy relationship models, friend... you have taken a *very wrong turn*. There's still time to back out. Maybe go read a cozy mystery. One with cookies. And *no severed limbs*.

Inside, you'll find anxiety attacks so intense you'll think your Kindle is vibrating, blood and gore in amounts that violate at least three Geneva Conventions, and body horror that might have you reconsidering your physical form entirely. There's a boating accident (because apparently land wasn't deadly enough), breath play, edge play, and a murder or ten—because what's a little light homicide between morally bankrupt soulmates?

Oh, and let's not forget the charming little extras: attempted rape, attempted sexual assault, kidnapping, torture, forced marriage, abortion, infertility, and involuntary pregnancy—because nothing says "romance" like reproductive trauma and a total loss of bodily autonomy.

Also included are: non-consensual medical procedures performed by people who really shouldn't have licenses, drugging, emotional abuse so sharp it cuts through your spine, and organized crime that makes the Sopranos look like a church choir. Sprinkle in some PTSD, a touch of sex trafficking, and the kind of psychological damage you can't fix with yoga, and you've got yourself a five-course meal of "what the actual hell."

So, if you're ready to be emotionally wrecked by fictional criminals with questionable ethics and surprisingly good hair, grab your emotional support beverage and dive in. Just remember: this book doesn't pull punches. It stabs. Repeatedly. With feeling.

🖤 Good luck out there. You're gonna need it.

**Full List of Trigger Warnings:**
Anxiety and Anxiety Attacks
Blood and Gore
Body Horror
Boating Accident
Breath Play
Edge Play

Captivity and Confinement

Death

Dismemberment

Drugging

Emotional Abuse

Forced Marriage

Infertility

Involuntary Pregnancy

Kidnapping

Loss of Autonomy

Murder

Mutilation

Needles

Non-Con Medical Procedures

Organized Crime

Post-Traumatic Stress Disorder (PTSD)

Pregnancy

Sex Trafficking

Sexual Assault

Sexual Harassment

Torture

Attempted Rape

Attempted Sexual Assault

Abortion

# Play List



*Brought to you by Sleep Token on heavy rotation, caffeine fueled chaos, and the unrelenting need to suffer beautifully.*

"Battlefield" – SkyDxddy

"Reflections" – Melrose Avenue

"Thumbs" – Sabrina Carpenter (aka the quiet scream)

"Too Much" – Dove Cameron (file this under 'Vesper, probably')

"Ordinary" – Alex Warren

"The Summoning" – Sleep Token (a religious experience, honestly)

"Provider" – Sleep Token

"The Apparition" – Sleep Token

"Give" – Sleep Token (emotional support song)

"Break In (Feat. Amy Lee)" – Halestorm (for *that* scene—
you'll know)
"Save Yourself" – My Darkest Days

# Rossi Family Tree

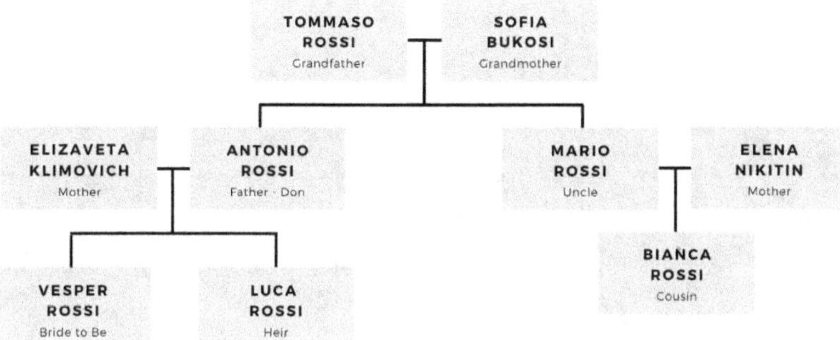


# Petrov Family Tree

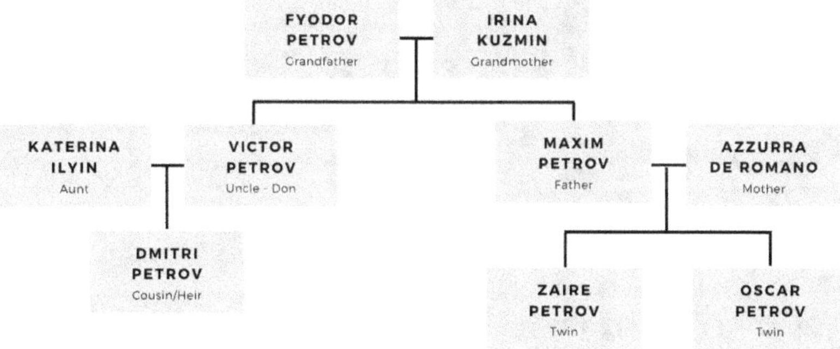

# Chapter 1

## VESPER

I KILLED HIM.

I killed my uncle.

"No, no, no!" I rush to Mario's slumped form in my father's leather chair, his blood soaking into the expensive upholstery. My hands grip his shoulders, shaking him violently as if I could rattle the truth from his lifeless body. "Where is he? Where's Luca? Tell me where the Collector is, you bastard!"

Mario's head falls back, eyes vacant, mouth frozen in a half-smile that mocks me even in death.

"Where is my brother?" I scream. My fists pound against his chest. "You don't get to die! Not until you tell me!"

Strong arms suddenly encircle my waist pulling me away from Mario's corpse. I fight against them, clawing, kicking.

"He's gone, Vesper." Oz's voice cuts through my hysteria, steady but strained. "He's dead. He can't tell us anything now."

"No!" I twist in his grip, tears streaming down my face. "He has to! He's the only one who knows where Luca is!"

My legs give out beneath me, and Oz lowers us both to the floor, holding me against his chest as I shatter completely. The sobs wrack my body, violent and uncontrolled. My fingers clutch at Oz's shirt, twisting the fabric as if it could somehow yank me away from this gruesome reality.

"What have I done?" I choke out between gasps. "I've lost him. I've lost my brother. It's all my fault."

Oz's arms tighten around me, his heart beating steadily against my back. "We'll find him, Vesper. This isn't the only way."

But it feels like the end. Mario's blood soaks into my father's imported rug, the sharp, coppery scent saturating the air. My uncle lies dead by my hand, and with him went our most direct link to Luca. Our only link.

I barely register the movement behind us, the sound of footsteps approaching.

"Zaire," Oz's voice vibrates through his chest against my ear. "Take her. Get her out of here."

My fingers tighten reflexively in his shirt. I can't leave. Not yet. Not with Mario's corpse still warm, not with the answers I need turning cold with his body.

"I'll take her," Talon offers.

I feel Oz hesitate, his arms still wrapped protectively around me. Then, with a reluctant sigh, he loosens his grip.

"Just until we clean this up," Oz says, his words meant for me as much as Talon.

Talon replaces Oz, strong and steady as he helps me to my feet. My legs tremble beneath me, threatening to give out with each step toward the door. I can't look away from Mario's body.

"Take her home, Talon," Zaire orders. "Now."

I try to pull away from Talon's grip. "No. I can't leave. There might be something in his office, files, his phone—"

"There's nothing you need to see," Zaire says, his voice firm, allowing no space for argument. His features soften just slightly as he turns toward me. "We'll handle this, Vesper. We'll find whatever information he had."

"But I—"

"This isn't a debate." The finality in his voice cuts through me like a blade. "Talon, go."

Talon's hand on my lower back urges me toward the exit, and I'm too exhausted to fight anymore. My body moves on autopilot, one foot in front of the other.

The warm afternoon air slaps against my skin as we step outside. The sun above is offensive in its brilliance, the world continuing to spin while mine has crashed to a halt. I glance down at myself and freeze.

Mario's blood is everywhere—dark stains blooming across my dress, splattered on my hands. The evidence of what I've done screams in color. My breath comes in short, painful gasps. My uncle's blood. It's *everywhere.*

"Hey, hey, look at me."

I can't look up. I can't *breathe.*

"Vesper." The urgency of Talon's tone finally pulls my attention upward. His eyes lock with mine, steady and grounding. Without hesitation, he shrugs out of his jacket.

"Arms," he commands gently.

I comply without thinking, letting him drape the heavy fabric around me, hiding the worst of the evidence. The jacket envelops me in warmth and the subtle scent of his cologne. It's too big, swallowing my frame, but I clutch it close with trembling fingers.

"Come on, sweetheart." His hand returns to the small of my back. "Let's get you home."

He steers me toward the black SUV parked at the curb, his body angled to shield me from the world around me. My legs move mechanically beneath me, each step feeling disconnected.

When we reach the passenger side, Talon opens the door and gently guides me inside and fastens the seatbelt across my body, the click oddly final in the silence between us. I stare straight ahead, barely registering the movement as he secures me like I'm something fragile.

Maybe I'm more broken than I thought. Maybe, deep down, the Rossi blood in my veins is rotting me from the inside out once and for all.

He closes my door with a soft thud that reverberates through my hollow chest before circling around to the driver's side. I watch him through the windshield, his movements purposeful, controlled—everything I'm not right now.

When he slides into his seat, the engine purrs to life, and I flinch at the sound.

"You're safe now," he says. "Just breathe, Vesper."

I try, but each breath feels like swallowing glass. My brother is still missing. The Collector still has him. And I've just killed our only lead.

"He deserved it," Talon says, eyes fixed on the road. "Mario deserved to die for what he did. To you. To Luca."

I stay quiet, my throat closing around words I can't force out. Of course my uncle deserved to die. He'd arranged my brother's kidnapping—mine too. He'd created life using my body, betrayed our family, and sold himself to the Collector.

Deserving death is one thing. But delivering it myself? That was something else entirely. That made me judge, jury, and executioner.

"You may not believe it now, princess, but you did what you needed to do."

"I didn't mean to kill him," I manage. "I just wanted answers."

"Sometimes your body reacts before your brain can process what's happening," he says after a moment. "Your instinct to protect yourself and Luca took over."

A dry, bitter sound escapes me—something too broken to be called a laugh. "And how did that work out? My brother's still in the hands of that monster..."

"We'll find Luca." His grip tightens on the wheel, the

tension creeping up his forearms. His voice stays calm, but every muscle in him says otherwise. "There are still threads to follow. We just haven't pulled the right one yet."

I shift toward him, watching the lines carved into his expression, the stubborn set of his mouth.

"What if we're already too late? What if he's been sold? Like I was?"

"We got you out, Vesper. We'll get him out too." His head turns just enough to check on me before facing forward again, jaw clenched like he's bracing for war.

"You don't know that."

"I do." His response is immediate, unwavering. "Because I won't stop until we find him. None of us will. It took us two years to find you. We'll find your brother, too."

"What if—" I swallow hard. "What if he's already dead?"

Talon's hand leaves the steering wheel, finding mine where it rests on my lap. His fingers intertwine with my blood-stained ones, not hesitating for a second.

"He's not," he says firmly. "Your brother is the heir to the Rossi family. He's not going to kill him. He's worth far more alive."

God, I hope he's right. For Luca's sake, and mine.

"Trust me, princess. When Oz, Alex, and Zaire finish at the mansion, they'll bring whatever they find home," Talon continues, his thumb brushing over my knuckles in gentle circles.

"If there's information to be found, Alex will uncover it. The man can extract data from a brick if he must."

I want to believe him. God, how I want to believe that this wasn't all for nothing. But the image of Mario's lifeless body keeps flashing in my mind—his mocking half-smile, the hole in his forehead, the blood dripping from his face. Dying with the secrets I desperately needed.

# Chapter 2

ZAIRE

I WATCH from the window of the office as Vesper disappears when the car pulls away. My chest feels like someone's wrapped barbed wire around it and keeps pulling tighter the farther away she gets from me.

"She'll be okay," Oz says, but his voice lacks conviction. My twin knows better than to lie to me.

I turn back to the still warm body of her uncle in the desk chair. "No, she fucking won't. We just got her back. We're going to lose her all over again."

Oz doesn't argue with me. His blue eyes, mirrors of my own, flick toward the body and then back to me. It has taken us both to get her this far. Taking a life, it changes you on a cellular level. Marks you in a way that redefines you. You either learn to live with the taint on your soul or you crumble.

"We're not losing her again."

"Keep saying that to yourself, Oz. She fucking collapsed after she killed the bastard. The stains from her tears are still on your shirt."

"I know, Z. I was there. Now is not the time to argue. We need to clean this up before his guard or his staff show up."

"We should have just—" My words cut off as the door swings open.

Alex kicks his way in, arms loaded with plastic sheeting, bleach, hydrochloric acid, and black garbage bags. His usual smirk is plastered on his face, like this is just another Tuesday for him.

"Found everything we need. They've got a whole closet dedicated to this shit downstairs. It's giving me some ideas for the basement. *Murder Supply Closet* has a nice ring to it." He dumps the supplies on the floor with a clatter that makes me wince. "Makes you wonder how many bodies the Rossi family have buried in their garden over the years, eh?" He grins, like we're discussing the weather and not standing in a room with the cooling corpse of Vesper's uncle.

I stare at him, jaw clenched so tight my teeth might crack. "Shut the fuck up, Alex."

His smile falters. "Just trying to lighten the mood."

"There's nothing light about this," I snap, gesturing to Mario's corpse. "Vesper just killed her uncle. So excuse me if I don't find your gardening jokes fucking hilarious right now."

Oz steps between us, always the mediator. "Z, he's just trying to help."

"Then he can help without the commentary." I snatch a roll of plastic from the pile.

Alex has the decency to look chastened as he pulls on latex gloves. "Sorry, man. I know you're worried about her. We all are, but until we get Mario out of here, and cover our tracks, this takes priority. The sooner we clean up, the sooner you get back to her." He pauses, looking over the scene in front of us. "Let's get him bundled up. It'll be easier if he isn't bleeding all over the place."

"You're the expert," Oz remarks.

We work in tense silence, wrapping Mario's body in the blood-soaked rug from under his desk, and layers of plastic. The bullet wounds have stopped actively bleeding, but dark crimson still seeps through his expensive suit. All clean shots. I shouldn't feel proud of that, but some dark part of me does.

"What are we going to do with him? Talon took the SUV."

"Already covered. Drag him out back. I'll go pick something out for us," Alex orders before slipping back outside the office door.

Oz and I exchange a look. It's not the first time we've had to dispose of a body, but there's something different about this one. This is the man who sold Vesper to The Collector, who paid for her torment for years. And now he's nothing but dead weight in plastic. He deserved so much worse than this for what he's done.

"Let's move," I say, grabbing the wrapped corpse under

the arms. The smell of copper and death fills my nostrils as we lift him.

Oz takes the feet, and we shuffle awkwardly out the office door and down the ornate hallway. Every step feels like we're carrying Vesper's innocence further away from her. She'll never be the same after this. None of us will.

"You think she'll forgive us?" I ask as we maneuver through the doorway of what turns out to be the kitchen.

Oz grunts. "For what? Letting her pull the trigger or for cleaning up after?"

"For all of it. For bringing her into our world."

My brother looks up at me over the plastic-wrapped bundle, something fierce and unshakable in his expression. "She was always in our world, Z. She's just not prey anymore. She's a predator like the rest of us."

I spot the door at the rear of the kitchen, shifting us towards it. The warm air hits us like a slap as we shoulder through the back door. A small patio with neatly pruned hedges extends into a manicured lawn and expansive garden. The same one Oz and I used to cover our tracks to sneak into Vesper's bedroom years ago before her life went to shit.

"Where the fuck is Alex?" Oz mutters before a limo appears around the edge of the building and drives toward us. The limo's tinted windows gleam in the afternoon sun as Alex pulls it to a smooth stop just yards from where we're standing with Mario's body.

"You've got to be fucking kidding me," I growl, staring at

the sleek black vehicle. "A limo? Could you be any more conspicuous?"

Alex kills the engine and hops out, looking pleased with himself. "Relax. It's Mario's personal car. Everyone knows he uses it. No one will question it leaving the property." He pops the trunk. "Plus, plenty of room for our cargo."

"And when someone reports it missing?" Oz asks, shifting his grip on our burden.

"By then it'll be stripped and at the bottom of the harbor," Alex replies, helping us maneuver the plastic-wrapped corpse into the spacious trunk. "Trust me, I've got a guy who specializes in making expensive cars disappear."

I can't argue with his logic, but I still want to punch the smirk off his face. "You never leave your fucking room, Alex. How do you meet all these so-called people?" I ask.

"I told you. The dark web isn't just a place to buy and sell kidneys. It's a community of like-minded individuals. You should try it sometime. You might find someone who has tips about how to get that giant stick dislodged from your ass, Z."

I lunge for Alex, but Oz catches my arm, jerking me back.

"Not now," Oz hisses, his grip tightening. "We need to finish this."

The rage pounds at the inside of my skull, but he's right. We're standing outside with a corpse in the trunk of a limo. Not the time for a pissing match.

"Let's finish cleaning inside."

Back in the office, Alex dives into Mario's laptop, scrubbing the security footage. Oz sprays down every surface with bleach while I collect shell casings, wipe the counters, and eliminate any sign Vesper was ever here. The sharp scent of blood mixes with the harsh bite of chemicals, burning the inside of my nose and throat.

"Found the security footage," Alex calls from behind the desk, fingers flying over the keyboard. "Wiping the last forty-eight hours now. I'm replacing it with a loop from last week." He looks up, his face tight with focus. "The cameras will show Mario leaving in his limo, alone and very much alive."

I nod and drop blood-soaked rags into a garbage bag. Every part of me wants to be with Vesper, not here cleaning up the aftermath of her first kill. The image of her—frozen, pale, completely shattered—won't stop replaying in my head. That expression, that moment, is burned into me.

"Z, you're spacing out," Oz says, nudging my shoulder. "Stay focused."

"I am focused," I snap, tying off the bag with more force than necessary. "I just want this done."

Oz's expression softens fractionally. "I know. We all do."

"How much longer on the tech shit, Alex?"

"Ten minutes tops," he answers.

"Make sure you get everything," Oz replies, scrubbing at a stubborn bloodstain on the expensive Persian rug. "We can't afford loose ends."

I pocket the last shell casing and move to the doorframe, checking for any stray blood splatter.

"Almost done," Alex responds. "Hey, you guys should see this. Mario's got some interesting files on his computer. Looks like blackmail material on half the east coast families."

"Download it," Oz says immediately. "Could be useful."

"Already on it. There's something else too. Files on Vesper. A lot of them."

My blood runs cold. "What kind of files?"

"Records of payments. Correspondence. Photos…" Alex trails off, and I know whatever he's seeing is bad.

"Save it all," I bark, my fists clenching. "Every last fucking byte."

"Z," Oz warns, recognizing the edge in my voice.

"No. I want to know everything he did to her."

"I don't think you do, Z," Alex declares.

I cross the room in three strides, looming over Alex's shoulder. The screen flickers with an image that makes my stomach turn. Vesper, younger, thinner, eyes vacant in ways that make me want to resurrect Mario just to kill him again. "I want names."

"You'll have them," Alex promises. "All of them."

The room falls silent except for the clicking of keys as Alex copies the files. Even he seems subdued now, no jokes falling from his lips as he works. I step away, unable to look at the screen anymore without putting my fist through it.

"We're going to hunt every last one of them. Every person in these files."

Oz doesn't argue. His expression has hardened into something I recognize—the cold, calculating look he gets when planning something lethal. "We will. But first, we finish this."

Ten minutes later, the office is spotless. No blood, no bullet holes, no evidence that Mario Rossi ever met his end here. Alex pockets the flash drive with all the stolen data along with Mario's laptop and his phone, which we find on the desk, and we do one final sweep before heading out to the limo.

"I'll drive," Alex says, jangling the keys.

"Like hell you will," I growl, snatching the keys from his hand. "You're in the back, keeping an eye on our cargo."

Alex opens his mouth to protest but catches Oz's warning glance and shrugs instead. "Fine. But if we get pulled over, I'm not the one explaining why we've got a corpse in the truck. That's all on you, Z."

# Chapter 3

## VESPER

I'VE ALWAYS KNOWN that blood washes off easier than guilt. I just never expected to experience it first hand.

I stare at my reflection in the mirror. A stranger stares back at me. Blonde hair plastered to tear-stained cheeks, mascara running in dark rivulets down my face. My uncle's blood spattered across my dress and exposed skin—a grotesque Jackson Pollock of violence.

I need to be clean. I need his blood off of me.

I reach for a washcloth from the neat stack on the corner of the counter.

"Fuck," I hiss, turning on the faucet. The water runs hot over my flesh as I hear Talon rummaging through my closet in the other room.

I press the damp cloth to my face, watching as Mario's blood dissolves into the white fabric. Pink water swirls down the drain, carrying away the physical evidence but leaving the stain on my soul intact.

"Is this okay?" he asks, holding out a pair of black leggings and one of Zaire's stolen t-shirts.

I nod, grateful for Talon's thoughtfulness. My voice feels trapped in my throat, like my vocal cords are coated in the same blood I'm washing away.

"Thanks," I finally manage.

Talon sets the clothes on the closed toilet lid and hesitates, his usually confident demeanor softened by his current concern for me. The golden boy of the Second Sons looks decidedly tarnished in the harsh bathroom light.

"Do you need help?" he asks gently.

I shake my head, not trusting myself to speak again. What I need is something no one can give me—absolution.

He backs away slowly. "I'll be right outside if you change your mind." The door begins to close behind him, but the idea of being alone right now terrifies me.

"Talon?"

His retreat stops instantly as he shifts, the door opening wider until his face appears around the edge.

"Stay," I request.

I stare at my reflection again, fingers fumbling with the zipper. My hands are shaking too badly to manage even this simple task. The tears start again, hot and relentless.

"Let me," Talon says, stepping forward. His fingers brush mine aside, carefully working the zipper down my back. He doesn't rush, doesn't make me feel exposed despite the intimacy of the moment. "Arms up," he instructs gently.

I comply, allowing him to peel the ruined fabric from my skin. He turns away, giving me space as I slip out of my dress, left in nothing but my underwear.

"Shower," he suggests, reaching past me to turn the knobs. Steam begins to fill the bathroom as water cascades down. "It'll help."

I nod numbly and step toward the glass enclosure. To my surprise, Talon removes his handgun and cell phone from his belt, setting them carefully on the counter before following me into the shower, still fully dressed in his shirt and pants.

"What are you doing?" I ask.

"Making sure you don't collapse," he says simply, closing the door behind us. Water immediately soaks through his clothes, plastering the fine fabric to his muscular frame. His hair darkens under the spray, rivulets running down his face.

"Your suit—" I begin.

"Is just fabric," he interrupts me. "You're more important to me than threads and cotton, princess."

I sway beneath the water, too numb to protest or even properly feel the heat against my skin. The water swirling at my feet turns pink, then red, as Mario's blood washes away. My uncle's blood. The blood I spilled.

"Turn around," Talon says softly. "Lean your head back."

I comply without thinking, too empty to resist. His fingers thread through my hair, working methodically from roots to ends. The scent of lavender fills the steam-clouded shower as he massages shampoo into my scalp. His touch is unexpectedly tender, each stroke deliberate and soothing.

"Close your eyes," he instructs, tilting my head further back to keep the suds from running down my face.

I surrender to his care, letting my lids fall shut as his fingertips work small circles against my scalp. The gentle pressure draws a sigh from my lips.

"That's it," Talon encourages, his thumbs pressing lightly at the base of my skull where tension has knotted my muscles. "Just breathe."

He works the lather through my hair, massaging away the physical remnants of what I've done. If only he could wash away the memories as easily.

"I keep seeing his face. Does it...does it ever get easier?" The question feels like poison on my tongue.

"It shouldn't. The day taking a life becomes easy is the day you've lost something essential. I wish I could tell you it will fade with time, princess, but it won't. The first life you take will always stick with you."

"Who was your first?"

"Someone who stole from my father."

"Did you mean to do it?"

"Yes. Unlike yours, mine wasn't an accident." His jaw tightens. "My father handed me the gun and told me to prove my loyalty to the family. It was his little test to see if his bastard son was worthy of his last name."

"Did it hurt you? After?"

"For a long time." He reaches for the conditioner, squeezing a dollop into his palm before working it through my hair with the same careful attention. "But the difference between you and me, Vesper, is that I knew what I was getting into. This life wasn't forced on me the way it was on you."

"I'm sorry," I mumble.

"Never apologize for doing what is necessary, Vesper."

Talon's hands pause in my hair as he notices me trembling beneath his touch. The water has gone lukewarm, but that's not why I'm shaking.

"You're freezing," he says softly, reaching behind me to turn off the shower. "Let's get you dry."

He steps out first, grabbing a plush towel from the rack and wrapping it around me before I can even register the cool air hitting my wet skin. The tenderness in his touch makes my throat tighten. He grabs another towel for himself, quickly running it over his drenched clothes before draping it around his neck.

"Better?" he asks, his voice low, searching for something in my face.

I manage a small nod, clutching the towel tighter around my body. My teeth have started chattering despite every effort to keep them still. A sharp knock at the bedroom door makes us both turn. Talon's demeanor shifts instantly—shoulders tightening, his jaw setting with silent resolve.

"Get dressed." He pauses in the doorway, glancing back. "Will you be alright for a minute?"

"I'll be fine," I lie, the words like ash on my tongue.

Talon gives a single nod—hesitant, clearly unconvinced

—but says nothing else. The door clicks shut behind him, leaving me alone with my reflection once more.

The leggings cling uncomfortably to my damp skin, but Zaire's T-shirt drapes over me like armor. What used to be playful—wearing his clothes, stealing them for fun—now feels like my only defense. At this rate, his closet might be empty soon.

Through the bathroom door, I catch the low hum of voices—Talon and Oz, speaking in hushed tones.

I press both palms to the cool sink, grounding myself in the steady, solid chill of porcelain.

When I finally step out of the bathroom, Talon stands by the door, his soaked shirt plastered to his chest and arms. The light from the hallway catches the planes of his face as he turns, tension carved into every angle.

"That was Oz. They're back from the mansion."

"Did they..." I trail off. I already know. They were cleaning up what I left behind. Getting rid of the body. The truth slams into me all at once, crushing the air from my lungs.

"Vesper."

Talon crosses the room in three long strides. His touch is gentle.

"Breathe with me."

He lifts my hand and places it over his chest, letting me feel the strong, steady rhythm beneath my palm. A silent reminder that life keeps going—mine included.

"Feel that? Match it," he instructs. "In through your nose, out through your mouth."

Gradually, the vice around my lungs loosens, and the room stops spinning quite so violently. Talon's heartbeat steadies me, the rhythmic thump-thump like a lifeline I cling to with everything I have.

"That's it," he encourages. "You're doing great."

"I don't know how to do this," I confess. "How to live with what I've done."

Talon's expression softens, something like understanding flickering across his features. "You survive it one breath at a time, Vesper. That's all any of us can do."

The door swings open abruptly, and Zaire strides in with a commanding presence. His attention snaps to Talon's hands, still clasping mine, then drops to take in Talon's drenched clothing, water dripping onto the floor.

"Out," he orders Talon.

Talon doesn't move. "I don't think that's what Vesper needs right now."

"I wasn't asking," Zaire's voice cuts like ice through the room. The silver in his stare has turned to steel, with that dark, stormy edge that only surfaces when his control begins to fray.

I step back from Talon's grip, wrapping my arms around myself. "It's okay," I tell him softly. "I'm okay now."

The two men face off in silence, tension thick enough to choke on. I expect Talon to push back, but instead, he gives a slight nod before turning to me. "I'll be just down the hall if you need me," he says softly.

As he passes Zaire in the doorway, their shoulders brush —neither man giving ground.

When the door clicks shut behind Talon, Zaire's sharp edges fracture. In three swift steps, he's in front of me, hands trembling slightly as they hover just shy of my skin—uncertain if touch will soothe or shatter.

"Vesper," he breathes.

Before I can respond, his mouth crashes into mine—raw, aching, desperate. I taste salt, though I can't tell whose tears they are. His touch finds my face, cupping it with a gentleness that defies the urgency of his kiss. This isn't just a kiss—it's grounding, claiming, making sure I'm still here. Still his. Still real.

When we finally part, he studies me without speaking, scanning my expression for something only he understands. His thumbs brush over my cheeks, wiping away tears I hadn't noticed falling.

"Don't disappear on me. Not again."

"I'm here," I promise, though my voice trembles. "I'm not going anywhere."

Zaire leans in until our foreheads touch, our breaths mixing in the small space between us. "What happened tonight...it should've been me pulling the trigger."

"No," I pull back slightly. "Don't say that."

His jaw clenches, a muscle twitching beneath his skin. "It's my job to protect you, Vesper." His words come rough and uneven, full of a wounded pride I've never heard before. "I'm supposed to be the one who does the ugly things so you don't have to."

I can see it now—the pain he carries isn't just about

Mario's death. It's about me being the one who pulled the trigger.

"You hate that I killed him," I say, the realization dawning with sharp clarity. "Not that he's dead, but that I was the one who took his life."

Zaire's silence is confirmation enough. He drops his forehead to mine again, his breath warm against my lips.

"I'm supposed to be your monster." His grip tightens at my waist. "I can live with taking another life. I can't live seeing you shatter again. It will kill me this time, moya koroleva."

His confession hits like a punch to the chest. I press my face against him, leaning into the warmth of his skin, into the steady rhythm of his breathing. My fingers twist into the fabric of his shirt.

"I'm still here," I whisper, pressing my palm to his cheek. "Nothing has changed."

But even as the words leave my lips, I know they're a lie.

The woman who woke up this morning no longer exists. In her place stands someone who understands exactly how much pressure it takes to end a life—who has watched the light vanish from a man's face.

Zaire studies me in silence, his features drawn tight with grief and knowing. He doesn't speak, but the small movement of his jaw—a tick, then another—says everything.

He knows I'm lying.

He's always known.

"What do you need from me right now?" he asks instead.

I exhale slowly, grateful for the reprieve. "Sleep."

I let him guide me to the bed, my body suddenly heavy with exhaustion. He pulls back the covers and helps me settle against the pillows. The tenderness in his movements nearly breaks me again—this dangerous man is treating me like I'm made of glass. I would expect it from Oz and Talon, but not Zaire.

"Don't leave," I demand, reaching for his hand. The thought of being alone with my thoughts terrifies me more than anything else.

Zaire's expression softens. Without a word, he kicks off his boots and lowers himself onto the bed beside me. He doesn't get under the covers, just stretches out on top of them, creating a barrier between me and the world. His arm drapes protectively over my waist, his body a solid wall of warmth against my back.

"Never," he vows with a fervor that sears the air, his breath hot and urgent against my neck. "No one will ever tear you away from me, Vesper. Not even the God himself would dare to try."

# Chapter 4

## OSCAR

SLEEP IS a luxury I've never been able to afford, especially when it comes to protecting what's mine. I've been staring at Vesper's closed bedroom door, mapping every crack in the wood grain.

"You're going to burn a hole through the door if you keep glaring at it like that."

I don't jump at Talon's voice behind me—a testament to my exhaustion rather than my composure. The familiar scent of freshly brewed coffee fills my nostrils before I see the mug he's extending toward me.

"Thought you could use this," he says, his voice subdued in the pre-dawn quiet. "It's been what...thirty-six hours since you last slept?"

I accept the steaming cup, letting its warmth seep into my palms. "Something like that."

I take a long sip, letting the bitter liquid burn down my throat. It's not enough to chase away the bone-deep weariness, but it helps sharpen my focus. I move away from my position at her door and drop onto the worn leather couch in the living room, stretching my legs out on the coffee table.

Talon follows, settling beside me with his own mug. For a few moments, we just exist in the quiet, both watching the steam rise from our cups.

"How was she?" I finally ask, keeping my voice low. "In the car, after..." I don't finish the sentence. We both know what happened at the mansion.

Talon's jaw tightens, the muscles working beneath his skin. He's never been one to soften blows, and I brace myself.

"Fucking wrecked, Oz." He sets his mug down with a dull thud. He runs his fingers through his hair, loosening the bun. "She thinks killing Mario means Luca is gone."

My stomach clenches. I suspected as much, but hearing it confirmed makes it real in a way I wasn't prepared for.

"Mario deserved worse than what he got," I say, the words coming out like gravel.

"I wish I killed him."

"I think we all do, Oz," Talon admits. "Anyone but her."

I take another sip of coffee, but it tastes like ash now. "She shouldn't have had to pull that trigger," I mutter, setting my mug down with more force than necessary.

Talon leans forward, elbows on his knees. "You know she

wouldn't have let us take that from her. Not when it involved Luca."

He's right, and that knowledge burns worse than the coffee.

"We need to find Luca," I say instead.

"Please tell me Alex found something at the mansion."

"Mario had files on Vesper." I pause, my voice dropping lower. "There are...photos and videos."

Talon's head snaps up, expression sharpening. "What kind?"

"The kind that's going to make my brother even more insufferable and protective than he already is," I say, rubbing at the stubble on my jaw. "I didn't look at them myself. But Zaire did."

"Fuck," Talon mutters, leaning back against the couch. "That bad?"

"Bad enough that Zaire wanted to resurrect Mario just to kill him again." I lean back against the couch, staring at the ceiling. "Alex had the same reaction."

Talon sets his mug down carefully. I recognize the controlled movement. It's what he does when he's fighting the urge to break something. While things seem settled between Z, Vesper, and I, Talon's place in her bed is unclear. He cares for Vesper, that's plain enough to see, but he's still figuring things out.

"You think there's something in those photos that could lead us to Luca?" Talon asks, his voice deceptively casual—but the way his fingers tighten on his knee betrays him.

I shake my head. "Alex is combing through everything. If there's a connection, he'll find it."

"Why don't you go get some sleep? I can take over watching her door."

My eyebrow raises.

"Yeah, that's what I figured. Good thing I stocked up on coffee."

A soft click draws both our attentions to Vesper's bedroom door as it opens.

Zaire emerges from Vesper's room instead of her, his clothes wrinkled like he'd slept in them. The tension radiating from him is palpable.

I straighten instinctively. My twin has always been more volatile than the rest of us, but there's something in his expression now that puts me on edge.

Without a word, he stalks over to where we're sitting, reaches down and grabs Talon's untouched mug. He tips his head back and downs the entire thing in several long gulps.

"Jesus, Z," Talon says, watching his coffee disappear. "There's a fresh pot in the kitchen. You didn't have to take mine."

My brother sets the empty mug down with a clink and wipes his mouth with the back of his hand. "Needed it more than you did."

I study him carefully. "How is she?"

"Sleeping. Finally." Zaire runs a hand through his disheveled hair.

The unspoken hangs between us—what happened in

that room, what comfort did my brother provide that I couldn't. It shouldn't bother me, not when we've already established where we he and I stand with each other, but something primal and possessive twinges in my chest. I push it down, focusing on what matters.

"Did she say anything?"

Zaire drops heavily into the armchair across from us, his body folding into itself, "Nothing we don't already know. She's convinced we won't be able to find Luca and that it's all her fault."

"But we don't know that," Talon interjects, leaning forward. "The Collector isn't going to kill him. He's too valuable."

"Try telling her that." Zaire's laugh is hollow, empty of any real humor. "She just kept saying the same thing over and over."

"She kept cycling between being convinced he's dead and certain he's alive." His voice catches. "She begged me to promise we'd find him."

"And?" Talon prompts.

"What the fuck do you think?" Zaire snaps, then immediately closes his eyes, exhaling slowly. "Sorry. I promised her we wouldn't stop looking until we found him—dead or alive. Has Alex found anything?"

"He hasn't emerged yet from his lair. The music is still going so he's working," I offer.

Alex and music go hand in hand. We can normally tell his mood by what he's playing. Metal when he's concentrating. Classical music when he's in the basement doing his serial killer shit. Pop for some reason when he's drunk. To be honest, he's a revolving door of musical tastes.

"Oz told me about the photos," Talon adds.

"Don't." Zaire's voice cuts like a blade. "Not now."

Talon shifts beside me. "If there's something in those photos that could help us find Luca—"

"You think I don't know that?" Zaire hisses.

"We're all trying to help her," I say, attempting to soothe the tension crackling between them. "We're all on the same side here."

"I know that, Oz. But, the last thing I want to do is drag her back down into the depths when we just got her head above water. Those fucking photos will take her back there. I'm not willing to risk losing her again. If either of you care about her, you wouldn't want that either."

"That's not fair," Talon snaps. "You don't have a monopoly on caring about her."

"She's blown you once, to my knowledge. Vesper having your cock in her mouth does not give you some moronic claim to know what's best for her."

"And just because you've fucked her doesn't mean you do either."

I stand before this can escalate further. "Both of you, stop. This isn't helping Vesper or Luca."

"We all fucking care about her. Don't turn this into a pissing match. Her choice, remember, Z?" My brother glowers at my use of his own words against him from when I am struggling with the idea of sharing her with him. He'd been right, of course. It is her choice. Vesper needs my brother, and I, Talon, too, it seems. Who am I to deny her happiness? With the three of us, she'll always be protected, and I can live with that even if I have to share her.

"You two done?"

"Hardly," Zaire mutters, but the fight drains from his posture. He slumps back in the chair, defeated in a way I've rarely seen him. "I can't lose her again."

Talon leans forward, resting his elbows on his knees. "None of us wants that. But we need to find Luca, and if those photos hold even a clue—"

"I know." Zaire's voice is hollow. "I fucking know."

"We need to be smart about this," I continue, pacing the small living room. "The Collector has Luca. We know that much. What we don't know is where he's keeping him, or what he plans to do with him."

"What about Ricky?" Z asks. "He knew about the auction. Maybe he knows more."

"He's a start," I admit. "But it's going to take more than a low life thug to get us to The Collector's doorstep."

"If we push him hard enough—" Talon starts, but the sound of a door opening cuts him off.

Alex steps from his room. All heads turn toward him.

"Please tell me you found something," I say, not bothering to hide the desperation in my voice.

He looks exhausted, dark circles smudging the skin beneath tired features, his usually meticulous appearance disheveled. He's been working nonstop since we got back. Running a hand through his hair, he nods slowly.

Zaire straightens immediately, every muscle in his frame coiled tight. "What is it?"

"The transactions I found in the file on Mario's computer were payments made to that fucking clinic."

A heavy silence crashes down on the room.

"The clinic?" I repeat the words like acid on my tongue. "The one where they—"

"Yes," Alex cuts me off sharply, shooting a glance toward Vesper's door. "That one."

Talon leans forward. "Mario was storing her eggs there. Monthly storage payments would make sense."

"This is about something else," Alex states. "These are transaction logs for harvesting procedures. And they're recent—within the last month."

"Shit, you don't think?"

My blood turns to ice in my veins.

"They're harvesting from Luca?" The words taste like poison on my tongue. "Taking his..."

"Sperm," Alex finishes, his clinical tone doing nothing to soften the horror. "Based on these payment records, they've been doing it systematically. The Collector...he's farming him."

Zaire explodes from his chair, pacing like a fuse lit too close to the flame. Every step is sharp, volatile energy radiating off him in waves as his fists clench at his sides.

"It makes a sick kind of sense," Talon comments. "If Vesper was valuable to them for her eggs, Luca would be valuable for the same genetic material."

I force myself to think clearly despite the disgust

churning in my gut. "This could be our way in. If the clinic is processing these...samples...then they have to have some record of where they're coming from."

"There's only one problem. We left the good doctor and his ass frozen to the exam table. That clinic is burned, figuratively. He'll have moved his operation."

"And you have no idea where it is?"

"Correct."

"Until we locate it, finding Luca isn't going to be easy."

A soft sound from the hallway freezes us all. We turn as one to see Vesper standing in the doorway of her bedroom, barefoot and hollow-eyed, wearing one of Z's t-shirts that hangs to her mid-thigh. Her hair is tangled around her face, and her face is pale, making her appear even more fragile than she already is. But it's the way she holds herself that stops me dead in my tracks.

"They're harvesting from my brother?" Her voice is soft but steady, devoid of the hysteria I expected. Something about her calm is more terrifying than if she'd been screaming.

Zaire moves toward her immediately. "Vesper, you should be resting—"

"Don't." She holds up a hand, stopping him in his tracks. "How long have you known?"

"We just found out," I say, rising from the couch.

She looks at each of us in turn. The broken woman from hours ago is gone, replaced by something harder, sharper. "So, the clinic is still operational."

"Different location, definitely different doctor," Alex confirms, his tone cautious. "But yes."

Vesper nods once, processing. "Then that's where we start."

Talon shifts uncomfortably. "Vesper, we don't know where—"

"We'll find it." She leaves no room for argument. She walks further into the room, her bare feet silent on the hardwood. "The doctor may be gone, but his clients aren't. Someone knows where he's set up shop. We just need to figure out who and get them to talk."

The four of us exchange glances. This isn't the fragile, traumatized woman who cried herself to sleep in Z's arms. She's stronger now. More confident, even. I don't dare to admit it aloud but it's as if taking a life has snapped her out of her victim spiral.

"Did you find anything else?"

"Yeah," Alex starts before Z's head snaps in his direction.

"No," Zaire's voice cuts through the room like a blade. "Absolutely not. We don't need to go there. Not now."

"She has a right to know," Alex argues.

"Know what?" Vesper interjects between Z and Alex's standoff.

"Mario had photos of you on his computer."

Vesper's head snaps toward him, her green eyes narrowing. "What photos? What is he talking about?"

The tension in the room thickens as Alex hesitates, his fingers tapping nervously against his thigh.

"Tell me," Vesper demands.

Alex exhales slowly. "When I was going through Mario's computer, I found a folder with your name on it. It contained photos of you...from your time in captivity. Intimate photos."

The color drains from Vesper's face, but her expression remains resolute. "I want to see them."

"Fuck that," Zaire interjects, stepping between her and Alex. "There's no reason for you to subject yourself to that."

She steps toward my brother, not backing down a single inch. "Those photos are of me, my body, my trauma. I have every right to see them."

"I know what happened to me, Z. Nothing in those photos can hurt me more than I've already been hurt. If there's anything in them that could help us find Luca, I need to see them."

I watch my brother's face contort with conflict—his need to protect her warring with his respect for her autonomy.

"Vesper," I say, stepping forward. "What if we look through them first? If there's anything we think could lead us to Luca, we'll show you those specific images."

"Would you trust us to do that for you, Oscar? If it were your body, your pain being passed around like trading cards, would you sit back?"

The question strikes me silent. She's right, and we all know it.

Talon clears his throat. "I think we need to trust Vesper to know her own limits."

"Thank you," she says, a flicker of warmth breaking through her guarded features as she looks at him before turning back to Zaire. "I survived it once. I can survive it again."

"Bullshit," Zaire snaps, the veins in his neck prominent as he struggles to contain his emotion. "I'm not letting you—"

"You're not allowing me to do anything," Vesper interrupts. "This isn't about you, Z. Or any of you," she adds, shifting her attention slowly across the room, each look deliberate. "This is about me reclaiming something that was taken from me. I need to do this my way." She turns to Alex. "Show them to me."

Without objection, Alex gestures for her to follow him into his room, and the two of them vanish through the doorway. I can only hope she emerges from his room the same way she went in.

# Chapter 5

VESPER

"SO, THIS IS YOUR ROOM," I say, trailing my fingertips along the edge of his pristinely made bed. The dark blue comforter is pulled taut, not a single wrinkle in sight.

Alex closes the door behind us with a soft click that seems to echo in the pristine space. "Nobody comes in here," he says, his voice lower than usual. "Except me."

"And now me," I add, turning to face him.

His lips quirk up at one corner. "And now you."

I move toward the desk, drawn to the command center of screens and keyboards. This is clearly where Alex spends most of his time—the heart of his operation. Each monitor displays something different: security camera feeds, lines of code, news headlines, and financial charts. I would imagine it's like looking directly into his brain.

"You could run a small country from here," I state, careful not to touch anything. "I practically do," he replies, coming to stand behind me. Close enough that I can feel his warmth but not touching. "Information is power, Vesper. And in our world, power is survival."

I turn my head to look at him, suddenly aware of how alone we are.

"Are you sure you want to do this, Vesper?" he asks. His eyes search mine. "The photos from your captivity—they're not easy to look at. Even for me. The videos I found...are worse."

I swallow hard, feeling my resolve waver for just a moment. Part of me wants to run from this room, pretend those days never happened. But I've never been one to hide from painful truths.

"I need to see them, Alex," I say firmly. "I need to know exactly what happened while I was drugged. What they did to me. What they recorded."

"Okay. But we stop the moment you say. No questions asked."

Alex pulls out the chair for me, and I sink into it, the leather still warm from his body heat. His fingers move across the keyboard.

"I've sorted them chronologically," Alex says, hovering over the *Enter* key. "There are sixty-four images total."

My throat tightens as he pulls up the file, and I watch his

reflection in the dark monitor as he starts to leave the room. Without thinking, I reach out and grab his wrist.

"Wait." My voice sounds smaller than I intend. "Don't go."

His eyes meet mine in the reflection of the screen, surprise evident in his expression.

"I thought you wanted privacy," he says softly.

I swallow hard. "I did. I do. But..." I trail off, struggling to articulate the rush of vulnerability tightening around my throat. "I changed my mind."

Alex nods once, pulling up another chair to sit beside me. Not too close, but close enough that I can feel his steady presence. He doesn't touch me, doesn't offer empty platitudes about how everything will be okay. I appreciate that more than he could know.

"You control the pace," he says, gesturing to the keyboard. "Left arrow to go back, right to advance. Escape to close everything."

I take a deep breath and press *Enter*.

The first image fills the screen, and I flinch involuntarily. It's me, unconscious, on what looks like a medical table. My clothes are still on, but my arms are strapped down with leather restraints. My hair spills over the edge of the table, and there's a bruise forming on my temple where they must have struck me.

"This was a week after they took you," Alex says quietly. "Based on the timestamp."

I nod, unable to speak as I press the right arrow key. The next photo shows a man in surgical gloves checking my pulse, his face carefully turned away from the camera. Smart. The third image has me stripped down to my underwear, still unconscious, with monitoring equipment attached to my chest and arms.

"They were monitoring your vitals while you were sedated," Alex explains, his voice clinically detached—a kindness, allowing me to process this as evidence rather than trauma. "Making sure you stayed alive."

"How considerate," I mutter, continuing through the images.

Each photo documents my captivity with meticulous precision. Some show me unconscious, others semi-conscious and slack jawed, clearly drugged. In several, masked men pose beside me like hunters with their trophy, though they're careful never to show their faces completely.

When I reach the twentieth image, my finger freezes over the keyboard. I'm awake in this one, frozen with terror, struggling against my restraints while a man holds what appears to be a branding iron near my exposed shoulder.

"They didn't," I gasp, my hand instinctively reaching for my left shoulder.

"No," Alex confirms. "They were staging it—psychological torture. Making you think they would brand you but never following through." Alex's voice remains steady, but I notice the slight tightening of his jaw. "The next photos confirm it never happened."

I press forward, my stomach churning as I see myself recoiling, tears streaming down my face as the branding iron hovers inches from my skin. My expression is raw, full of panic—but I have no memory of this moment. They'd stolen it from me.

"I look so…" I trail off, unable to find the word.

"Strong," Alex finishes. When I turn to him, doubtful, he adds, "Even drugged and terrified, you're still fighting. Your whole body is screaming defiance."

I study the image again but only see a terrified version of myself.

The next series of images shows men I don't recognize visiting my holding cell, each taking turns posing with me, some touching my hair or face with possessive gestures that make my skin crawl. "The Petrovs?"

"Yes, mid-level enforcers at best."

"What about…?"

"Dmitri never appears," I note, advancing through more photos.

"No," Alex confirms.

By the fortieth photo, I'm sitting upright in some images, clearly more lucid though still restrained. The timeline is advancing toward my rescue. In several shots, I appear to be speaking, my lips forming words I can't recall saying.

"Did they record audio?"

Alex hesitates. "Yes. But I haven't—"

"Play it," I say, my fingers digging into the armrests of the chair.

"Vesper, I don't think—"

"Play it, Alex." My tone leaves no room for argument.

He sighs, reaching across to type a command. A new window appears with an audio file. His finger hovers over the play button, his expression tight with hesitation, waiting for my permission. I nod, and he clicks.

Static fills the room, followed by a voice I barely recognize as my own, slurred and distant.

"My father will kill you all."

A man laughs, the sound sending ice through my veins. "Your father isn't going to be a problem. No one is coming."

My voice grows stronger. "He will come for me."

A slap echoes through the speakers, and I flinch involuntarily. Alex's hand moves toward mine but stops short, respecting the invisible boundary between us.

"You Rossis think you're untouchable," the man snarls. "But you're just merchandise now. A body that is going to make me a lot of fucking money."

I hit pause, feeling nauseous. "That's enough."

Alex immediately stops the recording. I can sense he's watching me, but I can't bring myself to face him. Not yet.

"They were right about one thing," I finally say, my voice steadier than I expected. "I was just merchandise."

"Vesper—"

"It was a business transaction." I push away from the desk, needing space, air. "My father arranged my marriage to Dmitri. Mario arranged my kidnapping and medical rape. Different methods, same result. I'm property to be traded."

Alex stands too, his movements careful as if approaching a wounded animal. "You're not fucking property. Not to the others. Not to me."

Something in his tone makes me look up. His expression

catches me off guard—there's anger, yes, but something else too. Something that makes my breath catch.

"What am I to you, Alex? Oz, Zaire, and…I know what I am to them. Talona and I…I don't know just yet. But you. I don't understand." The question slips out before I can stop it, hanging in the air between us.

He takes a step closer, close enough that I can see the flecks of silver in his icy blue eyes. "You're…" He pauses, searching for words. "You're the variable in my equation that I never accounted for. The glitch in my matrix."

Coming from anyone else, it might sound clinical, cold even. But from Alex—the man who lives his life in patterns and codes—it's practically a declaration.

"Is that why you're keeping your distance?" I gesture to the careful space he maintains between us.

Something flashes across his face—frustration, perhaps, or restraint. "I'm keeping my distance because you've been through hell, Vesper. Because you're still processing what happened to you." His voice drops low. "And because once I touch you, I'm not sure I'll be able to stop."

The confession sends a rush through me, unexpected and powerful. In this sterile room, surrounded by evidence of my victimization, I should feel anything but desire. Yet here it is, unfurling inside me like smoke.

"Then don't."

The words hang between us. Alex's pupils dilate slightly, the only visible reaction to my admission. His self-control is impressive—and suddenly, incredibly frustrating.

"You don't know what you're saying," he replies, voice tight. "The trauma, the images you just saw—"

"Don't tell me what I know." I step closer, eliminating half the distance between us. "I'm not confused about this, Alex. I'm not some fragile victim who can't distinguish between comfort and desire. I'm a fucking monster just like the rest of my family..."

"You're not a monster," Alex says, his voice low and certain. "A monster wouldn't feel the way you do. I've hunted them. Tracked them. Become them when necessary." His stare locks with mine, unflinching. "I know exactly what monsters look like, Vesper. And you're not one."

"Then what am I?"

He studies my face, his attention drifting to my lips before returning to meet me again. "You're a survivor. A fighter. And right now, frustratingly tempting."

I close the remaining distance between us, grabbing his shirt in my fists.

"Then stop resisting," I challenge him.

Something snaps in Alex. I see it—the exact moment his control fractures. In a blink, his fingers tangle in my hair, tugging hard enough to sting, sharp and addictive. Then his mouth is on mine, crashing into me with a hunger that leaves no room for doubt—only need.

There's nothing gentle about it. His lips claim mine with bruising intensity, demanding rather than asking. I gasp against his mouth, and he takes the opportunity to deepen the kiss, his tongue sliding against mine with skilled precision.

My back hits the wall—I don't remember moving. Alex is on me in an instant, all sharp edges and restrained power. One hand slides from my hair to my jaw, tilting my head to deepen the kiss. The other clamps onto my hip, fingers pressing hard. A spark ignites low in my belly, pulsing with every breath.

I'm drowning in him. Thought, memory—everything blurs. The images from my captivity, the sound of those recordings, my father's betrayal—it all dissolves beneath the relentless force of Alex's mouth. There's nothing but this: his body pinning mine, his lips claiming me like I belong to him.

When he finally breaks the kiss, we're both breathless. His eyes are dark, pupils blown wide, leaving just a rim of icy blue. He doesn't let go—one hand still cupping my jaw, the other gripping my hip like I might disappear if he loosens his hold.

"There are three other guys sitting feet away on the other side of that door who deserve this far more than I do."

"That's not for you to decide," I say, my voice hoarse with desire. "It's about what I want."

I pull him back to me, gentler this time, my lips brushing against his with deliberate slowness. His breath hitches, and I feel a tremor run through the fingers still gripping my hip.

"What about what you want, Alex?"

"What I want doesn't matter. Not when it comes to you."

"Why not?"

"Because you're—" He cuts himself off, pulling back slightly to look at me. "Because you deserve better than this. Than me. I'm not like the others."

"This isn't about them."

He watches me close, searching for any kernel of doubt —anything that would give him reason to pull away. He won't find it. My mind has never been clearer than in this moment, pressed between Alex's body and the wall of his sanctuary.

"What is it about then?"

I consider lying, saying something simple about desire or distraction. But the intensity in his eyes demands honesty.

"Control," I admit. "Taking it back. On my terms." Understanding dawns in his expression. This isn't about comfort or even just desire—it's about reclaiming what was taken from me. My brother. My son. My fucking life. All of it. Building the power to keep us all safe. To prevent what happened to me, and what is now happening to Luca, from ever happening again.

Alex's fingers tighten in my hair, and for a moment, I think he's going to kiss me again. Instead, he carefully releases me and takes a deliberate step back. The cold air rushes between us, and I instantly miss his warmth.

"I want to give you that. But not like this. Not with..." He gestures toward the computer screens still displaying the evidence.

I look at the images, and something inside me deflates. He's right. The timing is all wrong, and suddenly I feel foolish for pushing this now, here, surrounded by images of my darkest moments.

"I understand," I say quietly, smoothing down my shirt where his hands bunched the fabric.

"No, I don't think you do." He takes a deep breath. "This isn't rejection, Vesper. This is...postponement."

His locks onto me, and the intensity there makes my breath catch.

"I won't do this. I won't be your next distraction." He steps closer again, close enough that I can feel his words against my skin when he speaks. "It will be because you want me. Just me. Nothing else between us."

The promise in his voice sends a shiver down my spine. This is a side of Alex I've never seen before—commanding, certain, almost carnal. It's intoxicating.

"And how will you know when that time comes?" I challenge, refusing to back down despite the way my heart hammers against my ribs.

Because you'll tell me."

His finger trails along my jawline, barely a whisper of contact, but it sends a pulse of heat straight through me.

"I want to hear you say it," he murmurs, voice low and intimate. "When your mind is clear. When there's nothing left but the truth."

I swallow hard and give a small nod.

He steps back, creating the space we both need, but his gaze stays locked on me. The tension between us crackles like a live wire, sharp and electric.

"We should finish this," he says, gesturing to the computer screen. "If you're up for it."

I take a steadying breath and return to the chair. "I need to see it all."

Alex sits beside me again, careful not to touch me as I

continue through the remaining photos. The last images show me being moved, presumably in preparation for the exchange that never happened thanks to the guy's intervention.

When the final photo fades from the screen, I lean back, emotionally drained but somehow lighter. Knowledge is power, and now I know exactly what I'm fighting against.

"Thank you," I say quietly, turning to Alex. "For showing me. For staying."

He nods, his expression unreadable. "Are you okay?"

"No," I answer honestly. "But I will be."

The pictures of me strapped to that table make my skin crawl even after Alex closes the files on his computer. I feel dirty, exposed, like I need to scrub my soul with bleach and steel wool. Seeing myself like that, seeing what I experienced in that fucking torture chamber for two years like someone observing a caged animal at the zoo will haunt me. The only consolation prize is if they stir something from the dark recesses of my mind. The images flash behind my eyelids every time I blink—me unconscious, vulnerable, being prepped like a lamb for slaughter.

"I'll keep looking, Vesper. I haven't even scratched the surface of my capabilities yet. This won't have been for nothing."

God, I hope he's right.

# Chapter 6

VESPER

A LOUD CRASH comes from the living room, followed by arguing. "We might want to head back out there," Alex suggests as he shifts from his spot next to me. "I'm pretty sure Zaire is about a minute away from kicking down my door, and you're the only person who can diffuse that powder keg."

Another crash, this one followed by a string of Russian curses I recognize all too well.

"Z does sound pissed," I mutter, forcing myself to move toward the door.

"Can you blame him?" Alex smirks. "You didn't kick me out when you looked at the photos."

I shoot him a glare. "I asked you to stay."

"Tell that to your Russian bodyguard out there. Both of them. My conversational Russian is a bit rusty, but I'm almost positive he mentioned something about my dick, and a knife."

"Have they always been like that?"

"As long as I've known them," he shrugs. "But they're worse now. I think we both know what the common denominator is in that volatile equation."

"Me."

I sigh before following Alex through his bedroom door and back out into the hallway.

The others are waiting in the living room, tension thick enough to choke on permeating the air. Zaire's eyes lock onto mine immediately, something primal flickering in those silver depths. Before I can choose my own seat, he reaches out, pulling me onto his lap, like I'm his personal property. His arms wrap around my waist, holding me firmly against his chest.

"Really?"

"Yes, really, moya koroleva," he declares against my hair, his breath warm against my scalp. "You were gone far too long."

"Did you recognize anything?" Talon inquires.

I shake my head, disappointment settling heavily in my chest. "No. Nothing we can use. Just more evidence of what those bastards did to me."

Alex clears his throat from where he's settled into an armchair. "It's not a complete waste. I've got software running through the dark web looking for anything that matches the backgrounds in those photos. Architecture details, equipment models, even the lighting fixtures. Something might ping."

Hope flickers, small but persistent.

"I'll get started extracting the audio from the videos I haven't analyzed yet. We might not recognize the voices, but my recognition software might find matches if they're in any database—legal or otherwise."

Z's arms tighten around my waist. "It better find something. I'm not letting those fuckers breathe free air much longer."

"We need to move forward regardless," Oz interjects, his expression serious. "I need to find Ricky."

"Ricky?" I question. "Who is that?"

"Ricky Novak is an informant I've used for a few years," Oz answers.

"Do you think we can trust him?"

"No," Oz admits freely. "But he's the best shot that we have. He may be able to point us towards The Collector's new clinic. It's worth a shot."

"What makes you think this Ricky knows anything about the new clinic?" I ask, leaning forward despite Z's possessive grip.

"He knew about your auction and got us into it. Ricky is the reason we found you."

Something shifts in my chest at this. Ricky—a name I've never heard before—is part of the reason I'm sitting here instead of still being passed around like property. I glance at Oz, studying the tight line of his jaw.

"Then he knew I was there all along?"

"Not exactly," Oz clarifies. "Ricky deals in scraps of information from the underbelly. He heard rumors about a high-profile sale and caught wind that several of the major families were interested."

I shift in Zaire's lap, his possessive hold loosening just enough to let me turn and face the room properly. "And you trust someone who profits from human trafficking intel?"

"Trust is a strong word," Oz responds coolly. "I trust that he values his life and the money I pay him. Ricky has never fed me false information—not intentionally."

"He's a cockroach," Zaire comments against my back, his chest rumbling. "But cockroaches survive by knowing where the dangers are. They scurry between worlds unseen."

Alex interjects. "If he knew about the auction, he might know about other operations. The Collector doesn't work alone—he's got a network. Ricky may be a part of it or knows someone who is."

"When are we meeting him?" I ask, already knowing I'm not staying behind.

"We aren't meeting him," Oz says, emphasizing the 'we' with a pointed look. "I am. Alone."

Z's chest rumbles against my back. "Like hell you are."

"Ricky has only ever worked with me. He doesn't know about the Second Sons, or Vesper," Oz argues. "I'd like to keep it that way. He's been helpful in the past, but Ricky is the kind of guy who would sell out his own mother if he could make a quick buck."

"So, we send you in alone to meet a man who sells information to the highest bidder?" I ask, my voice laced with skepticism. "That sounds like a terrible plan."

"It's not ideal," Oz admits. "But Ricky's paranoid. One whiff that something's off and he'll disappear."

Zaire's fingers flex against my hip. "I don't like it."

"You don't have to like it," Oz counters, a familiar tension building between the twins. "But we need information, and Ricky's our best lead."

I shift in Z's lap, trying to process everything. "What if we compromise? Oz meets Ricky as planned, but we have backup nearby."

"Ricky checks for tails," Oz says, shaking his head. "He's survived this long by being careful."

"Then we'll be more careful," I insist, feeling Z's approval in the way his arms tighten around me once more. "I'm not risking losing anyone else."

"Fine," Oz finally concedes. "But distant surveillance only. First sign Ricky's spooked, you all back off."

"Deal," I agree before Z can argue further. "How do we get in touch with him?"

"I'll set it up. We usually meet at a bar on the southside."

"We'll be watching and listening the entire time."

Oscar pulls out his phone, typing quickly before sliding it back into his pocket with a sigh. "Message sent, but I wouldn't hold my breath for an immediate response. Ricky's nocturnal—probably just crawling into whatever hole he sleeps in right about now."

I rub my temples, exhaustion suddenly crashing over me. The adrenaline that's been keeping me upright is fading fast, leaving behind bone-deep weariness, and the phantom ache of memories I'd rather forget.

"So, what now?" I ask, unable to keep the fatigue from my voice. "We just wait?"

Talon, who's been unusually quiet, stretches his long limbs and yawns dramatically. "Now, we sleep. It's been a long fucking day." He looks at me, some of the edge in his voice easing. "And tomorrow's only going to be longer if Ricky actually shows. We need to be sharp."

He's right. My body feels like it's running on fumes, my mind foggy with exhaustion and the aftershock of seeing those photos.

"Sleep sounds..." I hesitate, wondering if I'll actually be able to dream without seeing myself strapped to that table. "Necessary."

Z's arms tighten around me protectively, as if sensing my unease. "You'll stay with me." It's not a question but a statement of fact.

"No." I push myself off Zaire's lap, standing on unsteady legs. "I'm sleeping in my own room."

Z's expression darkens, confusion and hurt flashing across his face. "Vesper—"

"Alone," I add firmly, wrapping my arms around myself. "I need space. Time to process everything."

The silence that follows is deafening. Talon's eyebrows shoot up, and Alex suddenly becomes very interested in his phone. Oscar watches me carefully, taking in every micro-expression.

"You shouldn't be alone right now," Z argues, rising to

his feet. "After what you just saw—"

"That's exactly why I need to be," I interrupt, meeting his intense stare. "Those photos...seeing myself like that...I can't just crawl into bed with someone and pretend it didn't affect me."

Zaire takes a step toward me, but Oscar places a hand on his twin's shoulder. "Let her breathe, Z."

"Funny. I don't remember you being the one with common sense when it comes to Vesper," Z snaps.

"About the time you became the irrational one," he mutters under his breath.

Z shrugs off his brother's hand with a sharp movement. "She shouldn't be alone after seeing those images."

"I'm not a child," I snap. "And I'm standing right here. Don't talk about me like I'm not in the room."

The brothers fall silent. I take a steadying breath, trying to center myself despite the exhaustion threatening to pull me under.

"Look, I appreciate the concern—all of you—but I need to sort through my own head. Alone." I meet Z's worried face. "Please, just give me this." For a moment, I think he might argue further, but something in my expression must convince him.

"Fine." The single word is heavy with reluctance. "But your door stays unlocked. And if you need anything—"

"I know where to find you," I finish for him, offering a weak smile that doesn't reach my eyes.

Talon clears his throat. "Well, this has been sufficiently awkward. I'm turning in." He stretches again. "Wake me if

Ricky responds or the world's ending—whichever comes first."

As the group disperses, Oz lingers. When the others have moved out of earshot, he approaches me with measured steps.

"You don't have to be alone to be strong, Vesper," he says quietly, his tone carrying none of his twin's intensity.

"This isn't about being strong. It's about..." I trail off, searching for words that won't come.

"Finding yourself in the aftermath," he finishes for me. There's understanding in his eyes that makes my chest ache. "I get it."

"Do you?" I challenge softly.

Oscar's lips curve into a sad smile. "More than you know." He reaches out, his fingertips barely grazing my arm. "Just remember that walls keep people out, but they also lock you in." He presses a gentle kiss to the top of my head, then turns and walks away, disappearing into his room— leaving me truly alone with my thoughts.

# Chapter 7

VESPER

I JOLT AWAKE, sweat-slicked and gasping, the phantom scent of copper and gunpowder clinging to my nostrils. My hands clutch at empty sheets beside me, and for one disorienting moment, I panic before remembering—I asked for this. I demanded space.

I'd ordered them to leave me alone. To allow me to think, and process killing my uncle, the photos, and finding out The Collector is medically raping my brother. Just as he had done to me. Since I put that bullet through Mario's skull, Z has been suffocating me with his protection.

But now, in the darkness of my empty bedroom, I almost wish he'd ignored me.

I pull my knees to my chest, trying to shake the images

from my nightmare—Luca strapped to a medical table, The Collector's wielding instruments that make him scream. And then the memory that wasn't a dream at all. Mario's face twisting in shock as I pulled the trigger, his body crumpling like a marionette with cut strings.

"Fuck," I groan, pressing the heels of my palms against my eyes.

A soft creak from the corner of the room makes me freeze mid-breath. I'm not alone. My head snaps up, scanning the shadows—and that's when I see him.

Zaire sits motionless in a chair by the door to my room.

"What the fuck are you doing here?" I hiss, but there's no real heat behind my words.

He looks terrible. His usually immaculate appearance is gone, replaced by a disheveled ghost of himself. His dark hair is a mess, and the shadows ringing his under eyes suggest he hasn't slept at all. He's still wearing the same clothes from the night before.

"Couldn't stay away, moya koroleva." His voice is rough, scratchy. "Not when I know what haunts your dreams."

I should throw something at him. Should scream at him to get out. Should remind him that I specifically told him to leave me alone. Instead, I clutch the sheets tighter, swallowing hard against the lump forming in my throat.

"You couldn't give me one day?"

The silence stretches between us, filled only by the sound of our breathing. Zaire stands there, hollow and worn, but his lips stay firmly shut.

"Seriously?" I push the covers away, suddenly too hot,

too confined. "All I asked for was one day to process the shit show that is my life, and you couldn't even do that."

He finally moves then, leaning forward with his elbows on his knees, hands clasped so tightly his fingers tremble. "I tried, Vesper. Then I heard you screaming."

Something in my chest constricts painfully. I hadn't realized I'd been screaming aloud.

"So, what, you've just been sitting there watching me sleep?" I push myself up against the headboard.

"Watching over you," he corrects, his voice soft but unapologetic. "There's a difference."

I want to be angry—I should be angry—but the raw honesty etched into his features makes it impossible. The fight drains out of me like water through cupped hands.

"Z..." I trail off, not even sure what I want to say.

He stands slowly, like any sudden movement might shatter the fragile air between us. "I'll go if you want. But I need you to know something first." He takes a step closer, then stops, respecting the invisible boundary I've drawn. "What happened with Mario, with Luca—none of it falls on you alone."

"I pulled the trigger," I remind him, the words tasting bitter on my tongue.

"And I would have done the same." His jaw tightens, voice steady. "Mario deserved worse than a quick death."

The mattress dips as Zaire sits on the edge of my bed, still maintaining distance, but close enough that I can smell his familiar scent—sandalwood and gunmetal. He reaches out, his hand hovering in the space between us, waiting for permission.

Against my better judgment, I place my hand in his. His fingers immediately curl around mine, warm and solid.

"Why me, Vesper?" Zaire's voice cracks slightly, his thumb tracing circles on my palm. "You've let the others close. Oscar, Talon—even Alex. But you're pushing me away. Specifically, me."

"Because your guilt is eating you alive, Z. I see it every time you look at me. You think you failed because you weren't the one to put a bullet in Mario."

His fingers tighten around mine, but he doesn't deny it.

"And now you're treating me like I'm made of glass." The words tumble out faster now, sharper. "Like I'll shatter if you turn your back for even a second. I hate it. I'm not some fragile doll that needs to be protected and coddled."

"That's not—"

"It is," I cut him off. "You hover. You watch. You barely sleep because you're too busy making sure I'm still breathing. And the worst part?" I pull my hand from his, the loss of his warmth instant and jarring. "The worst part is you're not looking at me—you're looking at someone broken. A victim."

Zaire's jaw tightens, a muscle ticking beneath his skin. "That's not true."

"No? Then why can't I sleep alone? Why are you fighting with the guys? You were ready to take off Alex's head because *I* asked him to stay with me about the photos."

Zaire's expression darkens at the mention of Alex. "That

was different," he snaps, his accent thickening with emotion. "He had no right to even tell you about—"

"To show me what they did to my body? I know what they did. I lived through it. For two years." I push back the tangled sheets further, sitting up straighter. "This is exactly what I'm talking about, Z. You can't keep doing this."

"You don't understand what it's like," he starts, "to see you in pain and know I could have prevented it."

"That's your guilt talking, not your heart." The words come out softer than I intended. "And I can't heal with you drowning in it beside me."

"I can't lose you again," he finally admits. "I saw you clinging to Oz on that floor, shattering all over again for killing that fucking bastard, and I lost it."

"You're not losing me." The words hanging between us like fragile glass. "But you're suffocating me. You love control, I know that. In the bedroom, I'm okay with that. In fact, I love it. But, when I am trying to make a decision for myself, you need to let me do it, and you need to respect it."

Zaire flinches as if I've struck him. His silver eyes swim with an emotion I rarely see—fear.

"I need to breathe, Z. I need to process everything without feeling your guilt pressing down on me, too."

"Tell me how to fix this, Vesper. Tell me what you need from me."

The sincerity in his question catches me off guard. I expected resistance, not surrender.

"I need you to trust me." I reach out to brush my fingers against his stubbled jaw. "Trust that I'm strong enough to face my demons. Trust that asking for space doesn't mean I'm pushing you away forever."

His hand captures mine, pressing it more firmly against his cheek. "I do trust you. It's everything else I don't trust."

"The world isn't going to collapse if you let go for a little while."

"So long as you are in my world, I will never be able to let go, moya koroleva. If you leave it before me, I will burn it down and go with you."

I inhale sharply at his words. The Russian endearment—my queen—both warms and frustrates me.

"That's exactly what I'm talking about. You can't keep—"

"I know." He cuts me off, surprising me. "I know what I'm doing, Vesper. I just don't know how to stop. My brain knows you're strong—fuck, you're the strongest person I've ever met—but my heart...it's another story." He pauses, taking a deep breath. "I've never loved someone as much as I love you, Vesper. I want to protect you from the world so that I know every day when I wake up, you're still here. Still safe."

I swallow hard, his confession hanging in the air between us. How do I respond to that level of devotion when it's both everything I want but not something that I can handle right now?

"We need to find a middle ground. Because I can't live in a gilded cage, Z. Not even one built by you."

He nods slowly, his thumb tracing circles on my wrist where he still holds my hand against his face. "What does that middle ground look like to you?"

It's a fair question, and one I haven't fully considered. What do I want? Space, yes, but not emptiness. Freedom, but not abandonment.

"I need you to let me breathe," I start, choosing each word with care. "I need you to be okay if I make a choice you don't agree with. And I need you to stop snapping at the others just because I asked them to stay close." I pause, meeting his guarded expression. "It's not just you and me, Z. Oscar, Talon, and Alex—they're part of this, too. Each of you is in my life in a different way, and I need all of you."

I take a breath, the next part heavier. "I know you respect what I have with Oscar—your brother. But I need you to extend that respect to the others, too. I can't keep holding us all together if you won't even try."

I hesitate, then push forward. "And I need you to work through your guilt...separately from me."

Zaire's eyebrows lift slightly at the last suggestion, but he doesn't dismiss it outright, which feels like progress.

"And what about you?"

The question catches me off guard. "What?"

"Relationships go both ways, moya koroleva. If I'm making changes, what are you offering in return?"

I open my mouth to protest, but the words die on my tongue. He's right. As much as his overprotectiveness suffocates me, my walls push him away just as effectively.

"I need to stop shutting you out completely," I admit, the confession sitting like gravel in my throat. "When things get bad, I retreat. I always have. But I can't expect you to give me space while keeping you completely in the dark."

Zaire's expression softens, the tension in his jaw easing slightly.

"I'll try to tell you when the nightmares come," I continue, "instead of pretending I'm fine. And I'll...I'll stop acting like I'm the only one who's hurting. What happened affected you, too."

His hand slides to the nape of my neck, his touch gentle yet grounding. "It did. But not in the same way."

"Pain isn't a competition, Z." I lean into his touch despite myself. "And I need to remember that."

The silence between us feels different now—less charged, more contemplative. Zaire's thumb traces slow circles at the base of my skull, and I fight the urge to close my eyes and surrender to the comfort of his touch.

"So where does this leave us?" he asks finally.

"Somewhere in the middle, I hope. I can't promise I won't need space sometimes. But I can promise not to use it as a weapon against you."

"And what about Oscar and Talon?" Z's voice changes, something sharper edging into his tone. "Do these same rules apply to them? Or is it just me you're pushing away?"

The question hangs between us, loaded with implications. I study his face, the way his jaw tightens as he mentions the other men in my life.

"This isn't about jealousy, Z," I say carefully, "But yes, the same boundaries apply to everyone. The difference is..." I trail off, trying to find the right words.

"The difference is they respect those boundaries without question," he finishes for me, a bitter edge to his voice.

I sigh. "The difference is they don't carry the same guilt you do. They don't look at me like I'm something broken they need to fix."

Zaire's expression falters, vulnerability flashing across his features.

"Oscar has his own demons," I continue softly. "And Talon...he processes things differently. Alex is well, Alex. But they don't try to shield me from my own choices the way you do."

"And that's what makes me the villain in this story. Because I can't stand by and watch you suffer."

I reach up, cupping his face between my palms. "You're not a villain, Z, but you can't be my savior either. Not in the way you're trying to be."

"Then what can I be?"

The raw honesty in his question makes my chest ache. "My partner. Someone who stands beside me, not in front of me."

"I can try to be that." Each word is deliberate. "But old habits..."

"Die hard. I know. That's why this is a conversation, not an ultimatum. We both need to adjust."

The corner of his mouth lifts in a ghost of his usual smirk. "You're being remarkably reasonable for someone who was ready to throw something at me ten minutes ago."

A surprised laugh escapes me, "Don't test me. I still might."

His smile grows more genuine, a rare sight these days that makes something flutter in my chest. "I wouldn't dare."

The tension in the room has shifted, no longer crackling with unspoken accusations but something softer, more manageable. I look at Zaire—really look at him—and see beyond the protective enforcer to the exhausted man beneath.

"When was the last time you actually slept?" I ask, noticing the way he sways slightly, fatigue evident in every line of his body.

He shrugs, deflecting. "I'm fine."

"That's not what I asked." I exhale slowly. "Lie down with me."

His eyebrows lift in surprise. "I thought you wanted space."

"I do. But you need sleep, and I..." I hesitate, then admit the truth. "I don't want to sleep alone with the nightmares again."

He hesitates only briefly before toeing off his shoes and stretching his body alongside mine. The bed dips under his weight, and I find myself instinctively turning toward him like a flower seeking sunlight. He keeps a careful few inches between us, respecting the invisible boundary we've just negotiated.

"This doesn't solve everything." I watch as he settles his head on the pillow beside mine.

"No," he agrees, his voice already softening with the pull of exhaustion. "But it's a start."

# Chapter 8

## OSCAR

THE BUZZ of my phone drags me from a dreamless sleep, the screen illuminating the darkness of my room like an unwelcome intruder. Ricky.

> 10 p.m.
>
> 1453 Blackstone Avenue. Apartment 3B.

I check the time on my phone. Six o'clock in the afternoon. We've got four hours until the meet up to prep. Groaning, I swing my legs over the side of the bed. My mouth tastes like death, and my head is still foggy.

I send off a quick text to confirm I got the message, then

head to the bathroom. The cold water I splash on my face does little to invigorate me, but the shower that follows helps. I dress quickly in a t-shirt and sweats before heading out of my room.

Talon stands at the stove, his back to me as he expertly flips what looks like a grilled cheese sandwich in the pan. His bun is slightly disheveled, a few loose strands falling around his face as he concentrates on not burning our dinner.

"Sleeping Beauty awakens," he says without turning around. "I was beginning to think you'd miss dinner."

I grab a bottle of water from the fridge and take a long swig before responding. "Got a text from Ricky. Meeting tonight at ten."

Talon slides the sandwich onto a plate and turns to face me, his expression carefully neutral. "Where?"

"Blackstone Avenue."

"Better make it a quick meal then." He places the plate on the counter. "We'll need time to prep."

I nod, already turning toward the hallway. "I'll grab Z. Alex is your problem."

"He's not in his room," Talon calls after me, his voice carrying a hint of amusement that makes me pause.

I turn back, raising an eyebrow. "Where is he?"

"Where do you think?" Talon smirks, cutting his sandwich in half with more force than necessary. "He's been in Vesper's room for the last two hours."

I roll my eyes, trying to ignore the twist of something uncomfortably like jealousy in my gut. He circled his wagons around her the second Mario's corpse was taken care of, and even with Vesper's request to let her sleep alone, he couldn't abide by it. And he called me the clingy bastard between the two of us.

"Of course he is."

"Don't worry. She read him the riot act before she let him stay."

"And you know this how?"

"Good hearing," he says with a nonchalant shrug, his lips curling into a slight smirk.

"You were standing outside the door, weren't you?"

"Can you blame me?" Talon takes a bite of his sandwich, talking around it without shame. "To be honest, I was surprised you weren't there with me. Your twin has been a royal ass since Mario. It's like the two of you Freaky Friday'ed."

"We didn't 'Freaky Friday,' you ass," I mutter, leaning against the counter. "I just know when to give a woman space."

Talon snorts, nearly choking on his sandwich. "Since when?"

"I can be considerate."

"Sure, Romeo." He pushes the second half of the grilled cheese toward me. "Eat. You look like shit warmed over."

I take the sandwich, suddenly aware of how hungry I am. "Thanks for the compliment."

"Always here to boost your ego." Talon wipes his hands on a dish towel. "So are you going to knock on her door, or am I?"

"Not it," Talon smirks. I start to head towards Vesper's

room when Talon clears his throat. "Can I ask you something, Oz?"

"Sure," I answer.

"How do you..."

"Share Vesper?"

"Yeah," he answers. "I know things between her, and I haven't progressed quite as far as she has with you and Z... but..."

"Jealousy is a bitch, isn't it?" I offer him a half-smile. "Look, it's not like there's a handbook for this."

Talon runs his hand over his face, dislodging more hair from his bun. "I didn't expect to feel this...territorial."

I've felt it too, more times than I care to admit.

"It gets easier. But I won't lie to you—sometimes it still feels like someone's twisting a knife in my gut when I see her with Z." I pause, choosing my words carefully. "But then I remember that whatever she gives to him doesn't diminish what she gives to me. It's different, but not less."

"Very philosophical of you, Oz," Talon says.

"To be fair, Z was the one who talked me off the jealousy ledge. It's ironic considering his recent caveman shit. But, when he comes back to reality, he'll be fine with whatever you have with Vesper."

"Which will be what exactly?" Talon asks, his voice dropping lower. "With you two, it's clear. You've got history with her. Z's got that whole intense protective thing going. But me? I feel like I'm playing catch-up in a game where I don't know all the rules."

I take another bite of the sandwich, giving myself time to

think. "There are no rules, man. That's kind of the point. Vesper's not a prize to be won or territory to be claimed. She could tell me she only wants Z, and while it would kill me, I'd respect her decision. She's had enough choices taken away from her. I won't deny her any kind of happiness."

Talon considers this for a moment. "Fair enough." He pushes away from the counter. "I just...I've never felt this way about anyone before. It's unsettling."

"Welcome to the club," I mutter, finishing off the sandwich. "Now, are we done with this heart-to-heart? Because we've got a meeting to prep for, and I still need to drag my brother away from our girl's bed."

Talon chuckles, heading toward the weapons cabinet disguised as a vintage armoire in the corner of our living room. "Good luck with that. Ten bucks says he growls at you."

"Twenty says he throws something," I counter, already moving down the hallway.

The door to Vesper's room is closed but not locked. I consider knocking, then decide against it. If Z is hovering over her like a Russian guardian angel with anger issues, it's better to catch him off guard.

I push the door open quietly, expecting to find my brother perched on the edge of her bed. Instead, I find her curled into his chest with his arms wrapped protectively around her. Both, sound asleep.

For a moment, I just stand there, taking in the sight. My brother's face is softer than I've seen it in days, the perpetual scowl replaced by something almost peaceful. Vesper's blonde hair spills across his chest, her hand curled against his heart. It's an intimate picture that makes me pause, feeling like an intruder.

Then Z's eyes snap open, instantly alert. He doesn't move, careful not to disturb Vesper, but his stare locks with mine in a silent warning.

"Meeting with Ricky at ten," I say quietly. "We need to prep."

Z's jaw tightens, but he nods almost imperceptibly. With careful movements, he begins to extract himself from Vesper's embrace. She stirs, murmuring something unintelligible.

"Shh, moya koroleva. Sleep a little longer."

I lean against the doorframe, watching as my brother gently tucks the blanket around her before pressing a kiss to her forehead. He rises from the bed with silent grace, crossing to where I stand. As he passes, I catch Vesper's scent clinging to him.

"I know what you're going to say," he says once we're in the hallway.

"You're an insufferable asshole who doesn't listen?" I fire back at him.

Z's lips quirk up in a half-smile. "She had a nightmare."

'And you just happened to be there?"

"I was checking on her." He shrugs, unapologetic. "She didn't kick me out."

"That seems to be a theme around here lately. You seem better," I remark. "You two talk it out?"

"Yeah," he admits.

"You good?"

"Getting there." Z rubs a hand over his face. "She's...patient with me. More than I deserve."

"How about you give Talon and Alex some of that patience? I believe it was you who told me that it's Vesper's choice."

Z's jaw tightens, the muscle working beneath his skin. "I know what I said."

"And yet..." I let the words hang between us, raising an eyebrow.

He sighs. "Fine. I'll play nice with St. James. But Alex? You don't think...?"

I shoot my brother a knowing look. "Have you ever seen him be that protective over someone in the entire time we've known him?"

Z carefully considers the question.

"I just want you to be prepared, if, and when, it happens. Try not to piss off the son of a serial killer. I do like having a brother around."

Z's jaw clenches. "Alex wouldn't hurt me."

"Not intentionally, no," I concede. "But we both know what happens when you push him too far."

My brother's silence speaks volumes. We've all seen Alex's darker side—the cold, calculated precision that emerges when his control slips. The genetics he tries so desperately to suppress.

"Fair point. I'll ease up."

"Miracles do happen," I mutter, clapping him on the shoulder. "You can wake him up then."

Z's lip curls. "I said I'd play nice, not perform a miracle."

"Your problem, not mine." I gesture toward Alex's closed door. "I've got weapons to prep."

Z narrows his focus on me, then stalks toward Alex's room like a man heading to the gallows. I don't envy him. Alex waking up is like poking a hibernating bear—never a good idea unless you're ready for the consequences.

I make my way back to the living room, where Talon has transformed our dining table into an arsenal. Handguns, knives, and various other lethal implements lie in neat rows on a black cloth. He's methodically cleaning a Glock, "Where's Z?"

"Getting Alex."

Talon winces. "Better him than me."

I pick up one of the knives. "I need to go in light. I never openly carry when I meet with Ricky. Small caliber. Easily concealable."

Talon nods, tapping a small Beretta on the table. "This should work. It'll fit in an ankle holster without showing."

I pick up the gun, checking the chamber and magazine out of habit. It's a beautiful piece—compact but built for damage. "This will work nicely."

Z and Alex join us. Alex yawns as he drops into a chair. "Address?" he asks, voice still rough with sleep as he pulls out his phone. I rattle it off as Alex types on his phone. "Looks like an apartment complex. Didn't you say that you usually meet him at Southie bar?"

"Yeah, this is the first time he's given a new place to meet up."

"Give me a cup of coffee and an hour, I can have a bird's eye view of the entire block," Alex offers, shoving from his seat and padding into the kitchen towards the coffee maker. "We won't be going in blind."

"Make the coffee strong," I tell Alex, already running through potential scenarios in my head. "We've got three hours to scope the place and position ourselves. I don't like this change in location."

"You think Ricky's compromised?" Talon asks, sliding another knife into a sheath.

"It's not out of the realm of possibilities. His information game may have caught up with him, and he's hiding out."

"What about Vesper?" He glances toward the hallway.

"What about her?"

"Is she coming with us?" Talon clarifies. "If she stays behind, one of us will need to stay here with her. It might be the safer option."

"She's not going to like being treated like a child who needs a babysitter either," I point out, though the idea of leaving her behind in relative safety appeals to me.

Z's expression darkens. "I'm not letting her out of my sight."

"That's not your decision to make," Alex says quietly, the coffee maker gurgling behind him. His tone is mild, but there's steel beneath it.

I shoot Alex a warning look. The last thing we need is another alpha standoff before walking into this meeting.

"How about we ask her what she wants?" Talon suggests, ever the diplomat. "Novel concept, I know."

"Ask me what?" Vesper's voice cuts through the tension as she appears in the doorway. She's changed into black jeans and a fitted dark blue top, practical and understated. Still utterly fucking breathtaking.

All of our attentions snap to her. I can't help but notice how she commands attention without even trying. A queen amongst wolves.

"Whether you're coming with us tonight," I answer, watching her reaction carefully.

Her eyebrow arches slightly. "And why wouldn't I be going?"

"It's not safe," Z argues.

"Middle ground, remember?" she replies back to him.

"Fine," he relents with a huff. "But you're staying back with the rest of us."

I share a glance with Talon, unsure what exactly "middle ground" means between those two, but I'm relieved Z isn't digging in his heels. Progress.

Alex appears at Vesper's side, offering her a steaming mug. "Black, two sugars." Their fingers brush as she takes it, and something passes between them—a look I can't quite decipher.

"Thanks," she says, accepting the cup with a grateful smile. Their fingers brush during the exchange, and I note how Alex watches her for a beat longer than necessary.

Interesting.

I clear my throat. "We need to talk about logistics. I think it's best if I arrive separately, but I want the rest of you in position by the time I get there."

Alex shows his phone to Talon.

"There's rooftop access at the building across the street. I can cover you from there," Talon states. "Do you have any drones we can use, Alex?"

"Do I have drones? What kind of question is that?" Alex's voice drips with mock offense as he takes a long sip of coffee. "I've got three in my room, including the new Phantom that can hover for four hours on a single charge."

"Alex on surveillance, Talon on the roof. Z, I want you to hang back."

"And me?" Vesper asks, her tone sharp as she looks at me over the rim of her mug, challenge written across her face.

"With Z," I reply, holding up a hand before she can protest. "Not because I don't think you can handle yourself, but because I need someone, I trust implicitly to keep watch on my brother. He won't pull something reckless if you're there."

Z snorts but doesn't argue. Vesper's expression tightens, clearly sensing the deflection, but after a beat, she nods.

"Fine. But I'm not sitting in a car six blocks away."

"Wouldn't dream of asking you to," I assure her, even though the idea had briefly crossed my mind. "You'll be close enough to hear everything."

Alex returns to his room and reappears minutes later with a sleek black case. He sets it on the table and flips it open, revealing a drone and an array of compact gear.

"This beauty has thermal imaging and can pick up conversations from fifty yards," he says as he assembles the parts. "We'll have full coverage on that building before you even get there."

"Comms?" I ask Alex.

"Here." Alex reaches for a small black case in the drone box and passes it to me. "Barely detectable unless someone is specifically looking for it. Just tap once to activate, twice to mute."

I slip it into my ear, adjusting it until it feels secure.

"Alright, let's move out in thirty," I announce, checking my watch. "We need to be in position well before ten."

We disperse without further discussion, each of us focused on our assigned role. Talon begins packing up the weapons while Alex continues calibrating his drone. Z heads toward his room, presumably to gear up, though he casts a lingering look toward Vesper before he turns away.

I make my way to my bedroom to change. Dark jeans, a black t-shirt, and a jacket that will conceal my weapon without looking obvious. As I'm pulling the shirt over my head, I hear my door open and close.

Vesper stands just inside my door, her arms crossed over her chest. She's changed into a dark hoodie, her blonde hair tucked into a bun at the nape of her neck. Her expression is carefully controlled, but I can see the worry under her skin.

"You're staring," I say, pulling my shirt down.

"And you're not telling me everything," she counters, taking a step closer. "What aren't you saying about this meeting with Ricky?"

"It's just...unusual. Ricky's particular about his routines.

Same bar, same booth, same drink order. This change of venue feels off."

"You think it's a trap?"

"I think we need to be prepared for anything," I answer, grabbing my jacket from the hook. "Which is why I need you with Z. He's still raw after Mario, and if things go sideways..."

"You need someone to keep him from going nuclear and to protect me," she finishes, closing the distance between us. Her fingers brush against my arm, sending electricity through my skin. "I get it. But I don't like that you are walking in there alone."

"I won't be alone. I'll have the whole team watching my back." I cup her cheek, my thumb tracing the soft curve of her face. "Besides, Ricky's my informant. He trusts me."

"And if he's been compromised?"

The question hangs between us, heavy with implications. I don't have a good answer, so I lean forward until my forehead rests against hers, breathing in her scent.

"Then I'll improvise."

Vesper's hands come up to frame my face, her touch gentle yet insistent. "Oscar," she says softly, using my full name instead of the nickname everyone else calls me by. "Promise me you'll be careful."

I turn one to press a kiss to her palm. "Always am, solnishko." She shakes her head, her fingers tracing the line of my jaw. "Just...come back to me, okay?"

"I promise." I lean in to capture her lips with mine.

The kiss is gentle at first, a mere brushing of lips, but quickly deepens as Vesper's fingers thread through my hair, pulling me closer. I back her against the door, one hand braced against the wood beside her head, the other cupping her waist. Her body melts into mine, familiar yet exhilarating, like coming home.

"Was that supposed to convince me you'll be careful?"

"No," I admit with a small smile. "That was just because I wanted to."

She laughs softly, the sound warming something deep in my chest. "Good answer."

A sharp knock on the door interrupts us. "Time to move out," Z's voice calls through the wood, followed by retreating footsteps.

Vesper sighs, reluctantly stepping away from me. "Remember your promise, Oz."

"Nothing will ever take me away from you, solnishko."

# Chapter 9

OSCAR

I'VE BEEN WATCHING the building for twenty-three minutes, and not a single soul has entered or left. That could be good or bad, depending on whether I'm walking into an ambush or a genuine meeting. The neon sign from the convenience store across the street casts an eerie blue glow across my dashboard, illuminating the gun resting on my thigh.

"Alex, you copy?"

"Loud and clear, Oz," Alex's voice crackles in my ear. "Perimeter's quiet. Too quiet, if you ask me."

I check my watch. Ten o'clock on the dot. "Heading inside."

The leather seat creaks as I shift, tucking the gun into my

ankle holster as I step my left leg out of the car. I adjust my pants to cover it. I've never openly carried in front of Ricky and keeping that fact I am armed to the teeth with knives sheathed under my jacket hidden from him will be hard.

The night air hits me as I exit the car, carrying the faint scent of garbage and cigarettes. I scan the street one last time, noting the blind spots as I walk.

"Got a couple of heat signatures in the building," Alex declares through my earpiece. "Only one on the third floor. Guessing that is your buddy, Ricky."

The building's entrance reeks of piss and desperation. The security door's lock broken long ago, hanging uselessly from its housing. I push through, finding myself in a dimly lit lobby with peeling wallpaper and a bank of mailboxes, half of them hanging open like broken jaws.

No elevator. Of course.

The stairwell echoes with my footsteps despite my attempt to move quietly. Each floor I pass has its own distinct scent –cooking spices on the first and marijuana on the second. By the time I reach the third floor, the scent has shifted to something chemical, acrid.

The hallway stretches before me, lit by dim fluorescents that cast sickly silhouettes across the faded carpet. Apartment 3B is at the far end. I approach cautiously.

Three sharp knocks on the door. I wait, counting my heartbeats.

Nothing.

I knock again, harder this time.

Still nothing. Unease crawls up my spine as I reach for

the handle, thankful for the leather gloves that will conceal my prints. The knob turns without resistance, and the door swings inward on silent hinges.

"Door's open. Heading in." I leave it cracked behind me as I slip inside. A quick escape route if things go south. "

"Talon is switching positions. I can see you. The other heat signature is straight ahead of you. Off to the left a bit. It's not reading as hot as the other one."

Well, that can't be good.

The apartment is dim, illuminated only by the glow of a single lamp in the corner. The place reeks of stale cigarettes and something else—something iron tinged that makes my stomach clench.

That scent—there's no mistaking it— it's fresh blood.

I draw my gun as I scan the living room. Furniture overturned, drawers emptied onto the floor, pictures smashed. Someone tore this place apart looking for something. "I think I might know why the other signature wasn't as hot. I smell blood."

I edge left, gun raised, following the strengthening iron scent around a partial wall divider. My boot connects with something solid, and I glance down.

"Fuck."

Ricky lies sprawled on his back. His shirt is now crimson, soaked through with blood still seeping from multiple stab wounds across his chest and abdomen. The pool beneath him spreads across the cheap laminate flooring, dark and viscous.

"Alex, Ricky's down. Multiple stab wounds."

"Is he alive?"

I drop to my knees beside him, pressing my hand against the worst of the wounds, though I know it's clear he is hanging on by a thread. His blood is warm and slick between my fingers, but his skin is cooling and his chest barely rising.

"Ricky, who did this? Who was here?" I demand, leaning close to his face.

His lips move, bubbles of blood forming at the corners of his mouth. The gurgling sound from his throat sends ice through my veins. He's drowning in his own blood.

"Stay with me," I hiss, tapping his cheek with my free hand. "Focus. Who did this to you?"

His eyes drift, then lock onto mine with sudden clarity. His bloody hand shoots up, grabbing my wrist with surprising strength.

"C-Collector," he chokes out, the name clear despite the wetness in his voice.

"What about the Collector?" I stop myself before I shake the dying man before me. He has minutes, if that, left based on the blood pooling around him. I need fucking answers. "Come on, Ricky. Tell me what you know."

His lips part again, but this time only blood spills out. The grip on my wrist slackens as the light fades from his eyes, pupils dilating until they're almost black. One final, rattling breath escapes his lungs, and then...nothing.

"Fuck!" I slam my fist against the floor, blood spattering across my sleeve. "Goddammit!"

"Oz? What's happening?" Alex's voice cuts through my rage.

"Ricky's dead." I stand, blood dripping from my gloves, creating a macabre pattern on the floor. "Said something about the Collector before he died."

"Shit." Alex pauses. "I'm landing the drone now and coming to you. Don't touch anything else. Two minutes."

I scan the apartment again, careful not to disturb the scene more than I already have. The sound of footsteps in the hallway alerts me. I shift my position, drawing my gun from my ankle holster, until Alex's familiar silhouette appears in the doorway.

"Jesus Christ," he mutters, gloved hands pulling the door closed behind him. He scans the room before settling on Ricky's corpse.

Alex crouches beside the body, tilting his head as he examines the wounds. His latex-covered fingers hover over but don't touch the torn fabric of Ricky's shirt.

"Military-grade combat knife," he says, his voice clinical. "Serrated edge, probably six inches. Look at the entry wounds—clean initial puncture with jagged tearing on the exit." He points to a particularly nasty wound near Ricky's sternum. "Whoever did this knew exactly where to strike for maximum damage."

"He didn't stand a chance," I say, the sharp scent of blood growing more suffocating with each breath.

Alex's fingers ghost over Ricky's wrist. "Still warm. Blood hasn't fully congealed. We missed them by minutes, Oz. Maybe ten minutes, tops."

"I was outside for twenty minutes, Alex. I didn't see anyone come or go from the building."

"They knew another way out," Alex says, crossing to the kitchen. He pulls back a tattered curtain, revealing a metal escape ladder just beyond the window. "This building backs onto an alley."

I move closer, careful not to touch the broken glass as I peer down. The narrow structure glints faintly in the moonlight—an exit, if we're quick.

"There's a back way down," Alex confirms. "Leads straight to the alley. Talon?"

"Already scanning," comes the response through our comms. "Alley's clear. No movement."

"Shit," I growl.

"Talon is set up at the front of the building. He could have missed whoever did this when he was getting into position."

"And you didn't catch it with your drone?" I ask.

"Other people live here, Oz. It's not like the killer had a bright red X painted on them."

I pinch the bridge of my nose, forcing myself to think through the anger. The Collector would never reveal himself like this. An associate, on the other hand, is more likely.

"Where's his phone?" Alex asks before returning to Ricky's cooling body. "Help me check his pockets."

I kneel beside him, careful to avoid the pool of blood. I pat down Ricky's jacket pockets–empty. Front pants pockets yield nothing but a crumpled receipt and some loose change. Back pockets–also clear.

"Nothing. Not even a wallet."

Alex carefully turns the body, checking for anything we

might have missed. "Whoever killed him probably took his phone. They didn't want us finding whatever information he was going to share."

"Can you track it?" I ask, wiping blood from my gloves onto a clean section of Ricky's shirt. "With his number, I mean."

Alex shakes his head, lips pressed into a thin line. "Unlikely, but I can try. Ricky doesn't strike me as the type to pay for a proper phone. Probably uses a burner."

"Worth a shot," I say, standing up and surveying the apartment again.

Alex snaps his fingers suddenly. "Call his phone."

"What?"

"Call Ricky's phone. Maybe he stashed it somewhere before he got jumped."

I nod, seeing the logic. Removing my bloodied gloves, I carefully tuck them in my back pocket before retrieving my own phone. I scroll through my contacts, finding Ricky's number.

I hit dial, and we both freeze, listening intently.

Three seconds pass. Four. Five.

Then I hear it—a distinct vibration, muffled but unmistakable, coming from somewhere in the apartment.

"There," Alex declares, tilting his head toward the sound.

The vibration continues as we follow the noise to the kitchen. It's coming from inside a cabinet beneath the sink. Alex pulls it open, revealing a trash can with a false bottom. He reaches in, carefully extracting the phone.

"Clever bastard."

Alex passes me the device. The screen is locked, but the notification of my call is visible. I end the call and examine the phone—a cheap burner for sure.

"Can you crack it?"

"Yeah, but not here. I'll have to take it with us."

Alex pockets Ricky's phone into his back pocket and reaches into his jacket. I watch as he pulls out another pair of latex gloves. Always prepared, that's Alex. He snaps them on with practiced efficiency.

"I'm going to roll him onto his back. I need you to take a couple of pictures."

My eyebrow arches. "Why?" The last thing I need is a picture of a dead man's face and hands on my phone. "Please tell me you haven't gone down that serial killer path again and you want to add this to your collection."

"Facial and fingerprint recognition, asshole. You don't even know if Ricky is his real name."

"You think he was using an alias?" I ask, pocketing my phone.

"In our line of work, everyone's using something," Alex mutters, rising to his feet. "Talon, status?"

"Still clear," comes the immediate response through our earpieces.

"Fine," I pull out my phone again, opening the camera app.

"Wait," Alex says, holding up a hand. "Use my phone instead. Less chance of it being traced." He tosses me a sleek black device that looks military-grade.

As Alex carefully rolls Ricky back over, I snap several clear shots of the man's face, contorted in death.

"Hands, too," Alex reminds me.

I photograph each hand, noting the defensive wounds across his palms and fingers. He'd fought back, at least.

"This wasn't just a hit," I say, handing Alex back his phone. "This was a message."

"But who is the intended recipient?" Alex points out, pocketing his phone. "Either Ricky double crossed him, or he knows Ricky tipped us off about Vesper's auction. Either scenario isn't good."

"We should go through his place properly. There might be more—"

"No time," Alex cuts me off. "We need to be gone before someone calls this in. The neighbors might have heard something."

He's right. We already spent too long here.

My comm crackles to life. "Guys," Talon's voice is urgent in my ear. "We've got movement. Patrol car. You need to get the fuck out of there now."

"Once we're out, you rendezvous with Z and Vesper."

"Copy," Talon answers.

"Your jacket's a mess," Alex points out. "Take it off."

I shrug out of the black blazer, turning it inside out before folding it carefully. The shirt underneath has only a few drops of crimson, but in the dim light, it could pass for anything.

"Fire escape. Now."

I follow, tucking the folded jacket under my arm. The

window slides open with a soft groan of protest, letting in a rush of cold night air that momentarily clears the scent of death from my nostrils.

Alex slips through first, his movements fluid and silent despite his size. I follow, careful not to touch the frame with my bare hands. The metal grating beneath my feet feels precarious, rattling slightly.

"Patrol car is turning onto the street now."

We descend rapidly. Three floors down, my foot slips on a wet patch, sending a loud clang that echoes through the alley. We both freeze.

"Keep moving," Alex hisses after a moment.

When we reach the bottom, Alex drops silently to the ground. I follow, landing in a puddle that splashes muddied water onto my pants. At least it will cover any blood on them.

"Patrol car is passing the building," Talon relays. "Shit. They're turning towards the alley."

"Go, go, go!" I whisper-shout, grabbing Alex's arm as we sprint down the alley.

We stay tight against the brick wall. The beam of head-lights sweeps across the entrance to the alley. We quickly duck behind an open dumpster.

"Fuck," Alex breathes next to me.

"Get in," I tell him, climbing up the backside of the dumpster.

Alex gives me a look like I've lost my mind, but the patrol car's headlights grow closer with each passing second. We tumble into the dumpster, sinking into a nauseating soup God knows what. We duck lower into the disgusting muck.

"If we survive this, I'm going to kill you myself."

I suppress a gag as something slimy slides down my neck. "Noted."

Through our comms, I hear Talon's controlled breathing.

"They're getting out. Two officers, flashlights out."

Footsteps approach, crunching on broken glass and gravel. A beam of light sweeps over the dumpster, lingering just long enough to make my heart stutter. I feel Alex tense beside me, his hand moving slowly toward his weapon.

"Dispatch, this is Unit 47," a gruff voice calls from just outside our hiding place. "Nothing in the alley except garbage. It was probably just a stray cat."

The radio crackles with an unintelligible response.

"Roger that. Heading back to patrol."

The footsteps retreat. Car doors slam. The engine grows louder, then gradually fades as the cruiser pulls away from the alley.

"They're gone," Talon confirms through the comms. "Clear to move."

I exhale a breath, the stench of our hiding place hitting me full force again. Alex and I exchange a glance, his expression murderous.

We climb out, both of us reeking. A piece of something I don't want to identify clings to my sleeve. I flick it away with barely concealed disgust.

"We'll never live this down," I mutter, wiping futilely at the slime coating my arm.

"Next time, I'm choosing the hiding spot," Alex remarks. "Just let me shoot them."

"And then we'd have the entire Boston PD on our asses," I remind him as we move swiftly through the darkness towards my car at the front of the building.

"And?"

We return to the car without being noticed, though the stench lingers strongly around us. I get into the driver's seat, and Alex settles into the passenger seat. The odor is intense between us. I start the engine while we both crack the windows to let in some fresh air.

"You know this will never come out of the leather, right?"

"No shit," I snap back before peeling out of the parking spot and heading toward the apartment—where the longest, hottest shower of my life awaits...along with the mental list of cars I'll never let him touch again.

# Chapter 10

VESPER

"WHAT THE ACTUAL HELL?" I gasp, covering my nose with my sleeve as Z slams the apartment door behind us. "I thought you said they had to hide in a dumpster, Talon. It reeks like they dragged it home with them."

The apartment smells like something crawled into a dumpster, died, fermented for a week in the summer heat, and then was placed in the hallway. Talon's reaction is immediate and theatrical—he darts to the kitchen, grabs the tropical breeze air freshener from under the sink, and begins prancing around the living room, spraying in wide, graceful arcs.

"This isn't helping!" I choke out.

"I think I can taste it," Z chokes out next to me. "What

the fuck kind of dumpster was it? Hazardous waste? Dead bodies?"

"All of the fucking above," Alex's voice carries as he emerges from the hallway. My brain short-circuits momentarily when he comes into view. He's wearing nothing but black boxer briefs, his lean, muscular body on full display. Water rivulets drip from his still wet hair down his stomach, accentuating his defined abs. A tribal tattoo I've never noticed before snakes around his left bicep, disappearing over his shoulder.

If it weren't for the stench and the tied-up trash bag that he's keeping at arm's length, I'd happily keep staring.

"Don't just stand there," he grunts at us. "There's another bag outside Oz's room that needs to go down to the incinerator in the basement. Now."

"I am not touching that," Z protests.

"Don't look at me," I chime in.

Talon ceases his air freshener ballet, snatches the bag from Alex, and moves to collect the bag outside of Oz's door, gagging as he heads towards the basement door.

Alex gives us a withering look before stalking back towards his room. His door slams as he retreats back inside. I wander over to open a window, desperate for fresh air, when Talon emerges from the basement. His face is a horrible shade of green.

"I...am going to vomit, shower, and maybe do it all again," he declares before disappearing into his own room.

I shake my head as Z and I move toward the rest of the windows, throwing them all open despite the chill in the air.

Fresh oxygen becomes more important than warmth when biological warfare has been declared in your living space. Minutes pass by, and the apartment still reeks even with the window open.

The sound of another door opening draws my attention. Oscar emerges from his room wearing clean clothes—dark jeans and a simple gray t-shirt that clings to his body.

"Four showers. Four, and I can still smell it."

"We all can," Z groans.

A gust of wind finally sweeps through the apartment, carrying away some of the noxious fumes. I take my first full breath since walking in, mentally thanking whatever weather god decided to show us mercy.

"So," I venture, settling onto the arm of the sofa, "are we going to talk about what happened with Ricky?"

"There's really not much to say. He's dead, and all we have is his burner phone as long as it survived the dumpster." At the mention of the dumpster, Oz gags a little. "There wasn't any time to search the apartment, but I highly doubt we'd have found anything. The place was ransacked. If there was anything to be found, it's gone, and going back there isn't an option."

"So, we're back to square one again and no closer to finding my brother or The Collector?"

"Not entirely square one," Oscar says, his voice dropping to that calculated tone he uses when formulating a plan. "We know more than we did yesterday."

Z crosses to the kitchen, opening the refrigerator. "Like what? That Ricky was a dead end who is now just...dead?"

He pulls out a beer and pops the cap against the counter edge.

"We know someone wanted him silenced," Oscar continues, moving to sit on the couch near me. "That means he knew something important."

I pull my knees to my chest, trying to process everything. "But we don't know what that something was. It could have been anything."

"We just have to keep digging. The burner phone might give us something," Oscar says, leaning forward. "If it doesn't, we figure out our next steps. We're going to find Luca, Vesper."

"We better," I mutter. "I can't keep living like this, wondering if he's safe, if he's even still alive."

Oscar's hand finds my knee, his touch gentle but firm. "We will, solnishko. I promise you that."

The endearment makes something flutter in my chest despite the circumstances.

"We should rest. None of us has slept much the last few days." Oscar continues, his thumb making small circles on my knee. "We might see something we're missing with fresh eyes."

I want to argue, to insist we keep working, but exhaustion is seeping into my bones. The emotional rollercoaster I've been on has left me drained. "Maybe you're right," I concede.

"A few hours of sleep wouldn't hurt," Z says, setting his beer down on the coffee table. He stretches his arms above his head, his shirt riding up to reveal a sliver of tattooed skin.

"I'm going to see if Alex has made any progress with that phone before anything else."

He walks over to where I'm perched on the arm of the sofa and leans down. His lips brush against mine in a soft, almost hesitant kiss. The gesture catches me off guard, but I don't pull away. His mouth lingers for just a moment, warm and surprisingly gentle, before he straightens up.

"Get some rest." Z watches me before he turns and heads down the hallway toward Alex's room.

The apartment falls quiet except for the distant sound of traffic filtering through the open windows. Oscar's hand is still on my knee, his touch burning through the fabric of my jeans. "Is everything okay between you and my brother?" he finally asks, his voice carefully neutral.

I blink, caught off guard by the directness of the question. We hadn't really gotten around to talking about the mechanics of how things would work. The three of us kind of just happened.

Oscar's thumb continues its slow circles on my knee. "You don't have to tell me details. I just want to make sure you're okay."

"I am," I insist. "Z and I have some things to work through."

Oz nods, accepting my vague answer without pushing for more.

"Do you want to stay with me tonight?" I ask. "Considering your room might be classified as a toxic waste dump."

"Not funny."

"But also not wrong," I fire back.

A hint of a smile touches his lips as he stands, offering me his hand. "Fair point."

His palm is warm against mine as he pulls me to my feet. The simple contact sends a current through my tired body, a reminder that even with everything falling apart around us, our connection remain solid. We move down the hallway in comfortable silence, his presence steady behind me.

My bedroom is the furthest from the epicenter of the dumpster disaster, and I breathe a sigh of relief when we step inside the relatively clean space. I close the door behind us, shutting out the lingering stench.

"I should probably shower," I mutter, suddenly aware of how disheveled I must look.

Oscar nods, already moving to sit on the edge of my bed. "Take your time. I'm not going anywhere."

The bathroom offers a momentary sanctuary. Hot water cascades over my body, and I close my eyes, letting the steam loosen the knots in my shoulders. It's a brief reprieve. I scrub hard, trying to wash away the grime of the day.

When I emerge, wrapped in a towel, Oscar is still sitting on the edge of my bed, scrolling through his phone. He looks up, his gaze flicking briefly down my body before returning —respectfully—to my face.

"Feel better?" he asks.

"Marginally," I admit, grabbing a pair of sleep shorts and an oversized t-shirt from my drawer.

I don't bother retreating to the bathroom to change. There's no point in faking  modesty—not when Oscar has already explored every inch of me. I let the towel fall, cool air raising goosebumps across my damp skin.

Oscar goes still, his phone slipping from his hand onto the mattress. His attention sharpens. I take my time, stepping into the shorts slowly before sliding them up my legs.

"You're fucking beautiful, Vesper," he says, voice pitched low, rough at the edges. "Do you have any idea what you do to me?"

I grab the oversized t-shirt and pull it over my head, allowing myself a small smile when I catch his disappointed expression as the fabric falls to cover my bare torso.

"I might have some idea," I reply, gathering my wet hair to one side, wringing out excess moisture. "Though, I could say the same about you."

He extends a hand toward me, and I cross the small space to stand between his knees. His fingers find my hips, thumbs brushing exposed skin.

"We should sleep," he suggests, though his touch says otherwise. "Tomorrow's going to be another long day."

"Sleep," I agree, even as I lean down to brush my lips against his. "Just sleep."

Oscar pulls me closer, deepening the kiss as his touch glides up my back. The exhaustion that clung to me moments ago evaporates, replaced by a rising tension that spreads through me like a lit fuse—slow, consuming, impossible to ignore.

I push him back onto the bed, climbing over him until I'm straddling his hips. His grip tightens on my thighs, grounding me firmly over the growing hardness pressing between us.

"I thought you said we needed rest," I tease, leaning down to nip at his lower lip.

"I've changed my mind." His touch slips beneath my oversized shirt, tracing lazy patterns over bare skin. "This seems like a much better way to relieve stress."

"Sleep is overrated."

His fingers trail along my sides, drawing shivers that dance over my skin despite the warmth building between us. I grind against him, slow and deliberate, and he answers with a low groan that rumbles in his chest, the sound as dark and hungry as the way he's looking at me.

"Stress relief, huh?" I murmur, lips hovering just above his. "And here I thought you just couldn't resist me."

Oscar cups my face, thumbs brushing my cheekbones with a tenderness that steals my breath. "Both can be true, solnishko."

I lean into his touch, letting my guard down in a way I rarely allow myself. With Luca missing and danger pressing in from all sides, these moments of connection feel stolen—precious contraband.

His lips find mine again, more urgent this time. I respond in kind, pouring my frustration and fear into the kiss until it transforms into something else entirely, something hungry and alive.

Oscar sits up suddenly, keeping me in his lap as he flips our positions. My back hits the mattress, and he settles between my thighs, his comforting pressure pinning me to the bed.

"Let me take care of you." He places kisses along my neck, teeth grazing the sensitive spot below my ear.

"Please," I breathe, not caring how needy I sound. Right now, I need this—need him—more than I need sleep.

His touch slips beneath my shirt again, this time pushing it higher until I lift my arms, letting him peel it over my head. Cool air brushes my skin—but only for a heartbeat—before Oscar's mouth finds me, tracing a slow path from collarbone to breast.

His tongue circles my nipple before he draws it between his lips, coaxing a gasp from my throat.

"Oscar," I moan.

He hums against me, the vibration sparking through my nerves. "I love the way you say my name," he murmurs, shifting to lavish attention on the other breast. "Especially when I'm touching you like this."

His hand glides down my stomach, fingers teasing the waistband of my shorts before slipping lower. I arch into him, already aching, already soaked with need. When he finally finds me—skin against skin—we both groan, the sound raw and shared.

"You're so fucking beautiful like this" he breathes, eyes locked on mine as his fingers work my clit with devastating control. "Look at you—already shaking for me. So fucking needy. So mine."

I bite my lip, fighting to keep quiet even as pleasure builds inside me.

It's like he hears my thought form, leaning in to claim my mouth in a kiss that devours the moan rising in my throat as his finger slips inside me. I grind down against his hand, chasing every flicker of pleasure.

"Don't stop," I moan against his mouth, breathless and aching.

Oscar adds a second finger, curling them in a way that makes my vision blur at the edges. His thumb continues its relentless circles against my clit.

I'm teetering on the edge, my body coiling tight as Oscar's fingers work their magic inside me. The pressure is building, my breath coming in short gasps as his thumb fingers my clit with maddening precision. Just as I'm about to topple over that precipice, a sharp knock interrupts the haze of pleasure.

The door swings open without waiting for a response. Z stands in the doorway, his muscular frame silhouetted against the hallway light. I freeze, instinctively trying to cover myself, but Oscar doesn't stop. His fingers continue their relentless rhythm inside me.

"She's supposed to be sleeping," Z says.

Oscar doesn't even look up, his focus entirely on the way my body responds to his touch. "She will," he replies, moving his fingers in a way that makes me bite back a moan. "When we're done with her."

The invitation hangs in the air between them. Without hesitation, he steps inside and closes the door behind him.

"Is that right, moya koroleva?" Z asks as he approaches the bed. "Are you going to let us wear you out?"

I can barely form words with Oscar's fingers still pumping inside me, but I manage a breathless "Yes" that sounds more like a plea than permission.

Z's lips curl into a dangerous grin as he reaches the edge of the bed. He strips his shirt off in one fluid motion, revealing the intricate tattoos that ripple across his chest and arms. Unlike Oscar's controlled precision, there's something raw about Z—a wild, reckless energy that both terrifies and thrills me.

"Don't stop," Z commands his brother as he unbuckles his belt. "I want to see her come apart for you first."

Oscar's rhythm doesn't falter. If anything, his brother's presence seems to fuel his determination. His fingers curl deeper inside me, his thumb pressing more firmly against my clit.

"Look at her," Oscar drawls. "So fucking beautiful when she's wrecked like this—spread open and desperate for the two of us."

I'm exposed. Vulnerable. Caught between them in the most intimate way possible. Yet instead of feeling self-conscious, I feel powerful, wanted in a way that makes my entire body hum with anticipation.

Z kneels on the bed beside us, his hand coming to rest on my throat. His touch is gentle but possessive, thumb tracing my jawline as he leans down to capture my mouth in a kiss that's barely restrained hunger.

"Do you like feeling my brother's hand between your legs?"

I can't find words to answer Z's question as Oscar's

pushes me closer to the edge. My hips arch off the bed, chasing the pleasure building at my core.

"Answer me," Z demands against my lips, his hand tightening slightly around my throat.

"Yes," I gasp, the word barely audible as Oscar curls his fingers just right. "God, yes."

Z smiles against my mouth, satisfied with my response. His free hand moves to my breast, rolling my nipple between his fingers. The dual sensation—Oscar between my legs and Z at my breast—sends electricity coursing through my veins.

"That's it," Oscar grits out as I writhe beneath their touches. "Chase that high, solnishko—show us how fucking good you can come."

Z's mouth replaces his fingers, hot and wet around my nipple, teeth grazing the sensitive peak. The combination of sensations is too much. My orgasm crashes through me without warning, my back arching off the bed as I cry out, vision blurring at the edges.

Oscar works me through it, slowing his movements as the aftershocks ripple through my body. Z lifts his head to watch my face, his pupils blown wide with desire.

"Fucking stunning," he mutters. "But we're not even close to being done with you."

Z's eyes darken, and the look he gives me sends a fresh surge of need through my veins, even though I'm still quaking from the last orgasm. Beside him, Oscar slowly pulls his fingers from me, glistening and wet, then licks them clean with a slow, deliberate swipe of his tongue that makes my breath hitch all over again.

"My turn," Z demands, stripping off the rest of his clothes like he's seconds from tearing through them. The way he looks at me, like he's about to devour me, makes my breath stutter.

Oscar shifts to make room but doesn't leave. Instead, he moves beside me, propping himself on one elbow to watch as Z positions himself between my thighs. There's something intimate about the way they share this space—not competitive but complementary.

"Is this okay?"

I nod, unable to form words as his cock presses against my entrance, thick and hard. He pushes in slowly, giving me time to adjust to his size. My body, still sensitive from Oscar's attention, clenches around him, drawing a groan from deep in his chest.

"Fuck, you feel good," Z hisses through clenched teeth, his hips stilling once he's fully seated inside me. "So fucking tight."

Oscar's hand cups my cheek, turning my face toward him. His kiss is gentle compared to Z's intensity, but no less passionate. I moan into his mouth as Z begins to move, setting a rhythm that's just shy of punishing.

"You're taking my brother so well," Oscar continues, his voice a sensual caress against my ear. "Does it feel good, solnishko? Having him inside you while I watch?"

I can barely form words as Z's thrusts grow more insistent, each one sending shockwaves of pleasure through my already oversensitive body. "Yes," I manage to gasp, my fingers clutching at the sheets beneath me. "God, yes."

Z grips my hips with bruising intensity, shifting the angle to drive into me with even more force. Unlike Oscar's measured control, Z fucks like he does everything else—with raw, untamed passion.

"Look at me," he commands, one hand sliding up to grip my jaw. "I want to see your eyes when you come on my cock."

Oscar's lips trail down my neck, teeth grazing the pulse hammering beneath my skin as his hand closes over my breast. The difference between them is intoxicating—two men, one storm, both completely focused on my unraveling.

"She's close again," Oscar murmurs. "Aren't you, Vesper?"

I nod, frantic, the words lost to the need spiraling out of control inside me. Zaire drives into me with relentless precision, every thrust harder than the last, his thick cock stretching me with a pressure that borders on unbearable—until it's everything I need.

Oscar's fingers find my clit, his touch expert and relentless, circling just right—dragging me higher with every pass. The dual onslaught of pleasure is threatening to detonate all at once.

"Don't you dare hold back," Z snaps, voice rough with command. "You come when I say. I want to feel this sweet cunt tighten all over my cock while I own every fucking inch of you."

His pace shifts—no longer teasing, no longer patient. He fucks me like he means to break something open, every thrust deep and relentless, his hips slamming into mine with a force that steals the breath from my lungs. I'm already close, teetering on the edge, when his fingers find my clit.

He doesn't ease into it. He circles it with purpose, fast and firm, each stroke sending shocks of heat through me. The pressure builds sharp and immediate, a wildfire licking up my spine, burning me from the inside out.

My back arches, a strangled cry ripping from my throat as I claw at the sheets. "Z—please—"

"Don't beg," he growls, voice like gravel and flame. "Take it."

His cock drives into me again, harder this time—perfect, punishing—while his fingers never let up. The dual assault has me unraveling fast, hips rocking desperately to meet every ruthless thrust, every flick of his fingers.

"Now," he commands, low and brutal. "Come for me. Let me feel you break."

The orgasm hits like a freight train—sudden, violent, glorious. My vision whites out as my body clamps down around him, pulsing hard, pleasure crashing through me and stealing the air from my lungs. He groans, deep and guttural, as he feels me seize around him.

His rhythm falters—just enough for me to know he's close too—as he watches me come undone beneath them. Utterly wrecked. Still aching. Still begging for more.

Oscar's lips find mine again, swallowing my cries as the climax rips through me, fierce and consuming. My inner walls tighten around Z's cock, milking him with every pulse of aftershock. A guttural string of Russian curses spills from his lips as he thrusts harder, chasing the edge of his own release with savage, desperate urgency.

"Fuck, fuck, fuck," Z chants, his movements becoming erratic. With a final, powerful thrust, he stills, his body tensing as he empties himself inside me. His face drops to my shoulder, breath hot against my sweat-slicked skin as he rides out the aftershocks of his orgasm.

For a moment, the only sound in the room is our ragged breathing. Z presses me into the mattress, a comforting heaviness that grounds me as I float in post-orgasmic bliss. Oscar's hand strokes my hair, his touch gentle and soothing.

"What about you?" I manage to ask. His arousal is evident, straining against his jeans.

His lips quirk into a small smile. "This was for you, solnishko. I'm content watching for now." He presses a kiss to my temple, but I can see the strain in his jaw, the tautness of his muscles.

Z lifts his head, giving his brother a knowing look as he carefully withdraws from me. The loss of his warmth leaves me momentarily bereft, but he doesn't go far, collapsing onto the bed beside me.

"Bullshit," Zaire pants, still breathless. "There is no reason to be noble when we are in bed together..."

I shift toward Oscar, fingers dragging down the hard lines of his chest until I reach the thick bulge straining against his jeans. "He's right," I purr, the afterglow still making me bold. "I want you too."

A flicker, barely there, cracks across Oscar's composed face. Control slipping. Just for a second. "You don't have to."

"I know I don't," I cut him off, already popping his belt open, knuckles brushing him through denim. "But I *want* to. Or would you rather sit back and jerk off while I'm right here, on my knees, wanting you?"

Z chuckles low beside me, his hand trailing possessively over my hip. "Always the fucking martyr, my brother. Let her worship you."

Oscar shoots him a look that would wither most men, but Z merely grins, unaffected. The dynamic between them fascinates me—an unspoken understanding that seems to exist on a level I can't fully comprehend.

I succeed in unfastening Oscar's belt and unzipping his jeans, my fingers brushing against his rigid length through the thin fabric of his boxers. His breath catches, muscles tensing beneath my touch as I free him from the confines of his clothing. His cock springs up. He's thick and hard, a bead of moisture glistening at the tip.

"See?" Z mutters into my ear as he watches me wrap my hand around Oscar's cock. "He wants you just as badly."

Oscar's jaw clenches, his control visibly fraying as I stroke him slowly from base to tip. "Vesper," he warns.

"Shut up." I push him onto his back. "Let me take care of you now."

I straddle his thighs, still sensitive from Z's attention but eager to feel Oscar inside me. Z shifts beside us, propping himself up to watch with hooded eyes as I position myself above his twin.

"Fuck," Oscar grits out as I sink onto him, inch by thick inch, until he's buried deep inside me. His grasp tightens—

not to control, but to steady me, like he's holding himself together by a thread.

I start to move, rolling my hips in slow, deliberate circles that pull a low groan from his chest. The stretch, the fullness—it's different from Z. Not better. Not less. Just...Oscar. Where Z devours, Oscar worships. He watches me like I'm the only thing that's ever mattered, drinking in every gasp, every flutter of movement.

His grip tightens when I grind down just right. "My good girl," he groans. "Always so ready. Always so fucking sweet." One hand glides up to cup my breast, thumb flicking over my nipple until sparks ripple down my spine.

"That's it, Vesper. Soak my brother's cock with your come."

The words hit me like a match to gasoline. A fierce need floods my core, and I move faster, harder, chasing that sharp edge as my thighs start to tremble from the relentless pleasure. Oscar thrusts up to meet me, his composure fraying with every grind of my hips.

Z shifts beside us. "Look at you," he says, voice thick with hunger. "Still so fucking greedy even after coming undone on both our cocks."

Oscar notices the shift in my body instantly. His hand slips between us, thumb finding my clit with maddening precision. "That's it. One more, solnishko. Be a good girl and give it to me."

I didn't think I had anything left, but the way he continues to fuck up into me—his cock hitting just right, his thumb circling with relentless pressure—pulls a broken moan from my lips. The pleasure blinds me, curling through my muscles like smoke before igniting something deep and uncontrollable.

Z's mouth finds my shoulder, his teeth dragging over the sensitive skin before his tongue soothes the sting. His hand fists in my hair, tilting my head back to bare my throat, and then he's there—biting, sucking, claiming.

I'm caged between them. Oscar's cock filling me, Z's mouth marking me. Their hands, their heat, their hunger— every inch of me is owned, devoured, undone.

The orgasm slams into me, raw and violent. My body convulses, inner walls clenching hard around Oscar's cock. His hips jerk beneath me, and I hear him curse low, almost broken, as he fights to hold on while I fall apart in his lap.

"That's it," he hisses through clenched teeth, his grip on my hips tightening as he thrusts up to meet my weakening movements. "Fuck, Vesper—"

His control finally shatters. With a fluid motion that takes me by surprise, he flips our positions, pinning me beneath him. I barely take a breath before he's seated back inside of me. His thrusts become harder, more desperate, the measured restraint he's maintained all night giving way to raw need.

Z shifts to accommodate us as he watches his brother chase his release. There's something almost reverent in the way he observes, like he's witnessing something sacred rather than carnal.

"Give her everything," Z demands.

Oscar's rhythm falters, his movements becoming erratic

as he drives into me. With a final, deep thrust, he stills, his entire body tensing as he finds his release.

For several heartbeats, we remain frozen in that tableau—Oscar buried inside me, Z watching over us. Then Oscar collapses beside me, careful not to crush me.

The three of us lie there, a tangle of limbs and sweat-slicked skin, our breathing gradually slowing in the aftermath. Z's hand moves to trace lazy patterns across my stomach while Oscar's fingers replace his. Their tender touch feels all the more profound after the intensity of what came before.

"Still think sleep is overrated?"

A low chuckle rumbles in his chest. "In this case, absolutely." His lips brush my temple, surprisingly gentle. "Though you might actually get some rest now."

"Fucked into oblivion," Z adds with characteristic bluntness, though his hand remains gentle as it strokes my hip. "Best way to combat insomnia."

# Chapter 11

ALEX

I'VE STARED at this code so long my vision's starting to blur, but Ricky's secrets are worth the headache. The rest of the apartment is quiet. I check the time, 3:42 AM. Great. Another sleepless night to add to my collection.

I roll my shoulders and crack my neck, trying to loosen the tension.

My fingers hover above the keyboard, cramping slightly from hours of continuous typing. My desk is littered with empty energy drink cans and half-eaten protein bars. The blue light from my screens casts an eerie glow across my workspace.

Ricky's phone sits mockingly beside me, plugged into one of my computers. Locked. Secured. A goddamn fortress of digital protection that shouldn't be this difficult to crack. But whoever set up his security protocols knew what they were doing, and I'd like to meet them.

"Come on, you piece of shit," I mutter, typing in another algorithm.

*Access Denied* flashes mockingly on my screen. I slam my fist down next to my keyboard. If Ricky was still alive, I'd beat the password out of him. Slowly. With a pickaxe and a very tiny hammer. One fucking tink at a time. I've cracked secret government military installations with more ease than Ricky's phone. A cheap cell phone shouldn't be this hard. Hacking cell phones were what I cut my teeth on, which begs the question, why is this so fucking hard?

I take another swig of lukewarm coffee and try a different approach, my mind racing through possibilities. If I can get into this phone, it might lead us to The Collector, and then to Vesper's brother.

*Access Denied.*

"Fuck this," I mutter, standing up and stretching my legs. I need a new angle. Something personal.

I glance over at my third monitor, where photos of Ricky's corpse cycle through various recognition algorithms. Oz and I were thorough—fingerprints, facial structure, even the partial tattoo on his forearm. The programs have been churning for hours now, cross-referencing every criminal and federal database I've hacked into over the years.

Nothing. Absolutely fucking nothing.

"Who the hell are you?"

It doesn't make sense. Everyone leaves digital footprints

—especially criminals. Even the careful ones slip up somewhere. But according to every database I've run him through, Richard "Ricky" Novak doesn't exist. No criminal record. No parking tickets. No tax returns. Not even a fucking library card.

There are only two possibilities. Either Ricky was some kind of choir boy who somehow fell into information brokering without ever getting caught, or he's someone else entirely. The first is laughable, the second is more probably. Someone whose identity is protected at levels even my software struggles to penetrate.

Deep cover. Government maybe. Or worse. A plant by The Collector.

A notification pings on my third monitor—the scan has expanded to international databases. Still nothing. It's like Ricky was born yesterday and died today with nothing in between.

"God fucking dammit," I snarl. The last time my information pool was this dry, I was ten years old trying to hack into my sister's Barbie laptop. This isn't how I operate. I always find something.

I run a high-level encryption decoder, something I coded myself after a particularly nasty job in Singapore last year. If this doesn't work, I'm going to need to physically dismantle the phone's hardware and extract the data directly—messy, time-consuming, and risky.

"Come on, come on..." I mutter, watching the progress bar crawl forward.

*ERROR: SECURITY PROTOCOL ACTIVATED.*

The phone's screen flashes once, then goes completely dead. A failsafe. Whoever designed this security system just initiated a self-destruct sequence for the data.

"Son of a bitch!" I slam my palm against the desk so hard my monitors shake. I'm about to throw the useless phone across the room when I hear it—a soft click from somewhere in the apartment.

My body freezes, senses immediately on high alert. That wasn't the building settling. That was a door.

My hand moves instinctively to the Glock nestled under my desk, fingers wrapping around the familiar grip as I silently push back my chair. With my free hand, I tap three keys in quick succession, and my main monitor switches to a grid of security feeds I installed throughout the apartment.

I scan each camera view methodically, my breathing shallow and controlled. Front door alarms—still locked, no signs of tampering. Window monitors—still sealed after I went through the apartment and secured them after everyone went to bed. Fire escape—empty. The hallway outside shows nothing but silence.

No movement anywhere, which doesn't make sense. I heard something.

I flick through each room's cameras individually. Kitchen —clear, just the dim light from the refrigerator illuminating empty countertops. Living room—nothing but furniture. Hallway—empty.

I know I fucking heard a door. Could it be...?

My finger hovers over the last set—the bedroom cameras. The ones I installed after Vesper moved in with us, a precaution I never mentioned to her or the guys. A contingency plan. A safeguard I promised myself I'd only use if someone's life depended on it.

Privacy is sacred in our arrangement. I know that. But so is security.

I hesitate, guilt and necessity warring within me as I stare at the blacked-out icon. Fuck it. If someone is in the apartment, all bets are off.

I click the camera link, and Talon's bedroom pops up on the screen.

He's sprawled face-down across the mattress, one arm hanging off the edge, the other shoved under his pillow. The sheets are twisted around his waist, and he's snoring like he's trying to shake the walls. Classic Talon—man could sleep through the apocalypse.

I switch to Oz's room next, half expecting to catch him curled up with a book like the night owl he is.

Empty.

My pulse stutters as I toggle over to Zaire's camera. His room's just as vacant. Clothes everywhere, bed a mess—typical Z. But no sign of him either.

"Shit," I mutter, fingers tightening around the gun. That only leaves one place—Vesper's. If someone's after her...

I don't hesitate. I click into her room's camera.

The bed comes into view—and she's not alone. Z stands near the door, while Vesper and Oz are on the bed. His hand is...

Oh fuck.

I move to close the window, but my finger stalls above the button. I should look away. I *should*. But I don't.

Oz's hand disappears inside her sleep shorts, and her back arches off the mattress. Her beautiful tits on full fucking display. Oz leans down, sucking one into his mouth. My throat goes dry as I watch her bite her lower lip, clearly trying to stay quiet.

This is wrong. I'm violating something sacred between them. But my body betrays me, rooted to the spot.

"Fuck." I should be ashamed. I am ashamed. But I can't tear myself away from the screen. I notice the small speaker icon next to the video feed. My finger hovers over it, the rational part of my brain screaming to shut this down. But then Vesper's back arches higher, her lips parting, and before I can stop myself, I click.

Her moan fills my room, soft and desperate, the sound so fucking beautiful it makes my cock instantly hard in my sweatpants. My breathing turns shallow as I watch her come undone, her body trembling as Oz works his fingers against her.

"Shit," I hiss, adjusting myself painfully.

This could have been me tonight. Just hours ago, she was in my room, looking up at me with those green eyes, practically begging me to touch her. And what did I do? I sent her away. Told her she needed to be fully present, mind and body, before I fuck her.

Like a goddamn saint. Or an idiot. Definitely an idiot.

I watch as Oz pulls back. The unspoken communication between them sends a jolt straight to my groin. Z pushes off from the doorframe in one fluid motion, stalking toward the bed.

Oz slides away, helping Vesper shimmy out of those tiny sleep shorts. My breath catches as the soft glow of the bedroom light reveals every inch of her. Absolutely fucking breathtaking.

I shouldn't be watching this. I've never claimed to have morality, but fuck, I know this wrong.  My hand is already sliding beneath my waistband, wrapping around my painfully hard cock as Z pushes forward, entering her in one slow, deliberate thrust.

"Fuck," I hiss, matching my strokes to his rhythm, imagining how she must feel—tight, wet. The way her back arches off the bed, the way her fingers dig into Z's skin hard enough to leave marks—it's the most beautiful torture I've ever witnessed.

"Look at me," Z's voice commands Vesper through the speakers, one hand sliding up to grip her jaw. "I want to see your eyes when you come on my cock."

I bite my lip hard enough to taste blood, trying to ground myself as my hand moves faster. The shame burns hot in my chest, but the arousal burning in my veins is stronger.

Then I see it—Vesper looking directly at the camera hidden in the corner of her room. For one heart-stopping moment, I think she's caught me, that somehow she knows I'm watching. But her mind drifts away, lost again in the sensations Z is creating.

"She's close." I hear Oscar declare. Her and I both. My strokes quicken, pressure building at the base of my spine as

Z increases his pace, driving into her with a force that makes her gasp.

Vesper's body tenses as she comes undone. The sound that escapes her lips—half moan, half cry—pushes me over the edge. Release hits me like a freight train, my vision blurring as I bite down on my fist to stay silent.

As the haze clears, reality crashes back.

"What the fuck am I doing?"

"I could ask you the same thing," a voice says directly to my left.

I nearly jump out of my fucking skin, spinning around with my gun raised before my brain can process who spoke. Hand still on my hard cock.

Talon stands in my doorway, leaning against the frame with his arms crossed. His attention shifts from my face to the monitor and back again, his expression unreadable in the blue glow of my screens.

"Jesus fucking Christ," I hiss, lowering my weapon. "Make some noise next time before you give me a heart attack."

He doesn't move, doesn't flinch—just keeps watching me with that unnerving calm.

"Interesting surveillance angle you've got there," he says evenly.

My stomach drops. There's no way to explain this away, no excuse that wouldn't sound pathetic. "It's not what it looks like."

"Really?" Talon raises an eyebrow, stepping into my room and closing the door behind him. "Because it looks like you're watching our girlfriend get fucked while jerking off."

Girlfriend? I'd never spent more than a few nights with my previous partners, so this is all new territory for me. Girlfriend does sound nice, though. *Now is not the time to put a label on your relationship with Vesper, dumbass. Your hand is still on your softening cock.*

I quickly remove my hand from my pants, fumbling to close the screen. "I heard a noise. Thought someone broke in."

"And decided to watch the show instead of, I don't know, helping?" His voice remains even, which somehow makes it worse. Angry Talon, I can handle. This calm, measured Talon unnerves me.

"It wasn't like that," I snap, though we both know it's bullshit. "I was checking security cameras when I saw—"

"When you saw something private and decided to keep watching." Talon moves closer. "And turned on the audio."

I wipe my hand on my sweatpants, shame burning through me like acid. "Look, I fucked up, okay?"

"And couldn't help yourself." Talon finishes, his voice dropping lower. "You know, if you wanted to join them, you could have just knocked."

I blink, thrown off by his response. "What?"

Talon's lips curve into something that's not quite a smile. "You think they'd mind? Hell, you think I mind? We're all dancing around each other. It might be easier to just have a meeting and schedule our time with her."

My throat goes dry. "That's not—"

"Not what? Not what you want?" He steps closer, invading my space. "I've seen how you look at her. It's only a matter of time, Alex. It seems like anyone in her orbit can't help wanting her. What was it you called it? Love square? Guess it's a pentagon now."

"I don't—" I start, but the lie dies in my throat. There's no point. "Fuck."

Is Talon right? Yes. Does it annoy me that not only has he caught me with my hand literally down my pants, but also my spying? Fuck yes. Should I have checked the lock on my door? Also, yes. Is he wrong about the four of us and the unhealthy obsession we have with the same woman? No. But, despite all of that, it doesn't change what he just walked in on. Me, hands down my pants, getting off to Oz and Z fucking Vesper.

Talon moves closer, his footsteps silent on the hardwood floor. He glances at my desk—at the open feeds, the failed hacking attempts on Ricky's phone, the scattered evidence of my all-night obsession.

"How long have you had cameras in our rooms?" he asks quietly.

I swallow hard. "Since she moved in."

"Does she know?"

"No one knows. It was just a precaution."

Talon nods slowly, processing this information with that tactical mind of his. I brace for the explosion, the righteous anger, maybe even a fist to my face. I deserve it. But Talon just sighs. "You're a creep, you know that?"

"I'm aware," I mutter, reaching over to shut down the

camera's live view. The screens go blank, leaving only the glow of my coding programs running in the background. If there were fucked up boy scout badges, I'd have them all. I'd be the poster child for fucked in the head.

"So what happens now?" I ask, tension coiling in my muscles. "You going to tell them?"

Talon studies me for a long moment, his expression unreadable. "I should. It's the right thing to do."

I nod, accepting my fate. Maybe Vesper will insist on a nice place for my body. View of the water or the server room of The Federal Reserve. Either would be nice. "I know."

"But I'm not going to," he says finally. "Not yet, anyway."

My head snaps up. "Why the hell not?"

"Because we need you focused on finding The Collector and getting to Vesper's brother. This—" he gestures to my screens, "—would be a distraction we can't afford right now."

I exhale slowly. "That's...surprisingly pragmatic of you."

"Don't mistake practicality for forgiveness," Talon says, his voice hardening. "What you did crosses a line. But we've all crossed lines for her already, haven't we?"

The truth of his words hits me like a physical blow. We have. All of us. Since the moment Vesper Rossi walked into our lives, we've been redrawing boundaries.

"The bedroom cameras come down," Talon says. It's not a suggestion, but a demand.

"First thing in the morning," I agree.

Talon nods towards Ricky's phone, still connected to my computer. "Any luck with that?"

"Nothing," I admit, grateful for the subject change. "When I tried to force it, it activated some kind of kill switch."

"Someone went to a lot of trouble to protect him," Talon muses.

"Or to protect what he knew."

Talon shifts, and for the first time, I notice he's holding something. "That's actually why I came to find you. I woke up from a dead sleep. Guessing because I was being watched," he side eyes me. "An idea popped in my head as I was going back to sleep, and it panned out. I logged into the e-mail account you made for my alter ego for Vesper's auction and found this."

He tosses an iPad onto my desk, narrowly missing my keyboard. I grab it before it slides off the edge, noticing an email already pulled up on the screen. The subject line reads: *Exclusive Private Auction: Invitation Only.*

"Holy shit."

"Turns out we didn't need Ricky after all," Talon says with a grim smile. "He's coming to us. Or, well, my alter ego. They're having another auction. Online this time."

I look up sharply. "How'd you get this?"

"Apparently, once you're a customer, you stay on the mailing list."

I scroll through the email, taking in the details. The auction is scheduled for three days from now. A private, encrypted livestream event featuring 'rare and exclusive merchandise.' The euphemism makes my stomach turn.

"Keep reading," he orders.

My blood runs cold when I read the item descriptions like it's a menu at a Michelin Star restaurant.

"Prime acquisition. Male, 27, exceptional resilience, trained resistance. Warning, requires experienced handler. "

Too old to be Luca.

I scroll to the next listing. "Legacy package. Matched pair, superior genetics, limited availability." I try to swallow my disgust. "They're selling siblings, Talon. Actual human siblings."

"And this one," Talon taps the screen, indicating the third listing. "Rare male specimen, early twenties, untouched condition," I read aloud, bile rising in my throat. "Exceptional bloodline. Jesus fucking Christ."

"That's..." I can barely form the words. "That could be Luca."

"That's what I thought, too," Talon says grimly. "Age is right.

"Look at the starting bid."

"Five million? That's—"

"Three times higher than any other lot," Talon finishes. "Just like Vesper."

"This is our chance." I stare at the screen, possibilities racing through my mind. "If we can access this auction..."

"We can find Luca," Talon finishes, his expression hardening. "And maybe The Collector himself."

I'm already typing, fingers flying across the keyboard as I pull up multiple windows. "I'll need to create a secure pathway. These auctions are heavily monitored. One wrong move and they'll know we're not legitimate buyers."

"Can you get us in?" Talon asks, leaning closer to watch my screens.

"Give me three hours and enough caffeine, and I could hack into the Pentagon's most secure server," I mutter, already deep in code. "But this is trickier. The Collector's tech guy will be good."

"Better than you?" There's a hint of challenge in Talon's voice.

I shoot him a look. "Nobody's better than me."

"Good because we're counting on you."

Talon nods. "We'll need to tell the others."

"Not yet," I say, my fingers already building the architecture for our digital infiltration. "Let me confirm it's viable first. No point getting Vesper's hopes up if we hit a dead end."

"She deserves to know," Talon counters, but there's hesitation in his voice.

"And she will. Once I've verified we can actually access the auction without getting flagged." I glance at him, my expression hardening. "You want to explain to her why her brother slipped through our fingers because we rushed in unprepared?"

He exhales slowly, conceding the point. "Fine. How much time do you need?"

"I won't know until I get into it and see what they're working with. Hours, maybe half a day."

"Deal. Then we bring everyone in." Talon straightens, moving toward the door.

"Wait." I hesitate, guilt gnawing at me again. "About what you saw..."

Talon pauses. "We all have our demons, Alex. Just make sure yours don't fuck this up for all of us. Especially for her. Take the fucking cameras down."

"I will," I promise, and Talon gives me one last hard look before he slips out of my room, closing the door behind him.

The moment he's gone, I drop my head into my hands, shame burning through me like acid. What the fuck is wrong with me? I've done some questionable shit in my life, but this is a new low.

"Fucking idiot," I mutter, pushing away from my desk.

The code can wait fifteen minutes. I need to wash the shame off of me.

# Chapter 12

TALON

I STILL SEE it every time I close my eyes. Alex, hunched forward, one arm buried beneath the waistband of his sweatpants, eyes glued to the monitor as Z and Oz took their turns with Vesper. Fuck. Some things burn themselves into your brain. You don't come back from that.

The basement gym is pitch black when I flip the switch, fluorescent lights humming to life and revealing the sparse equipment we've managed to cram into the small space adjacent to Alex's medical setup. The smell of antiseptic from his little 'operating room' mingles with the scent of sweat and metal. It's 4:30 in the morning, and sleep is officially a lost cause.

I drop my water bottle and towel on the bench and jam

my earbuds in, scrolling through my playlist until I find something angry enough to match my mood. The haunted melody of 'Dangerous' by Sleep Token thunders through my skull as I approach the punching bag hanging in the corner.

My first hit lacks proper form—all frustration, no technique. Uncle Leo would've made me do fifty burpees for that sloppy shit. I reset my stance, remembering his endless drills. Feet shoulder-width apart. Protect the face. Rotate from the hips. The second punch lands with a satisfying thud that reverberates up my arm.

Better.

I fall into a rhythm, each impact harder than the last. Left jab. Right cross. Left hook. The bag swings wildly as I unleash combinations that would make my old boxing coach proud. Sweat begins to bead on my forehead as I lose myself in the movement, my knuckles beginning to sting despite the wraps. The music pounds in sync with my heartbeat, drowning out everything but the satisfying percussion of flesh against leather.

I'm not even sure what I'm angry about anymore. Alex's voyeurism? The Collector and what he's done to Vesper, and now is doing to Luca?

The Collector's twisted empire—the auctions, the way he treats people like commodities—feeds a fury in me that builds with every punch. If I ever get my hands on him, I'll make him suffer in ways that would make even Alex look away.

The punching bag becomes his face in my mind. I strike harder, faster, my technique unraveling into raw aggression.

The rage I've been holding back finally breaks free, uncoiling like something primal. Unrelenting. Uncontrolled. My inner demon, unleashed at last.

I picture him watching Vesper's medical rape. I imagine him holding Luca captive, preparing to sell his sperm to the highest bidder. The thought ignites a fresh surge of rage, and I unleash a flurry of punches that sends the bag swinging violently on its chain.

A tap on my shoulder sends primal instinct surging through me. I pivot hard, right fist already cocked back, ready to strike—

"Shit!" I barely pull the punch in time as Vesper jumps backward, her green eyes wide with surprise. My fist freezes inches from her face, trembling with the effort of stopping mid-swing.

"Jesus Christ, Vesper," I gasp, yanking out my earbuds. "I almost took your head off." My heart hammers against my ribs. "What are you doing down here at this hour?"

"I could ask you the same thing." She's wearing loose sleep shorts and one of Z's t-shirts. It's so big on her that the shorts are barely visible under the hem. The hint of bedhead that somehow makes her look even more beautiful. There's a slight flush to her cheeks, and I briefly wonder if it's from climbing down the stairs or from what she was doing earlier with the twins.

"Couldn't sleep," I manage, trying to regulate my breathing. My heart rate is still elevated, adrenaline coursing through my veins from both the workout and nearly punching her. "Sorry about the...you know." I gesture vaguely with my still-clenched fist.

"My fault for sneaking up on you." She moves past me to grab my water bottle, taking a sip before handing it to me. The casual intimacy of the gesture doesn't escape me.

"Why are you awake?"

"Nightmare," she freely admits.

A nightmare? Unlikely, considering Z would have been awake in half a second if she so much as whimpered in her sleep. I don't call her on the obvious lie. She clearly doesn't want to share the real reason that drove her down here in the middle of the night.

"Z or Oscar know you're down here?" I ask, taking the water and downing half of it in one go.

She shrugs, her gaze dropping to my knuckles. "Your wraps are coming loose."

I glance down at my knuckles, where the fabric has indeed started to unravel. "Hazard of trying to murder a punching bag."

"Here," she murmurs, reaching out. "Let me."

I hesitate before extending my arm, watching as she takes my hand in hers. Her fingers are cool against my slick skin as she gently unwraps the fabric, then begins winding it back into place with smooth, confident movements.

"You've done this before," I observe.

"My father had one of the enforcers teach Luca to fight. They let me observe sometimes. He always had trouble with his wraps."

Her fingers work methodically, the gentle pressure

against my skin sharp against the violence I just unleashed on the bag. There's something intimate about the way she tends to me—careful yet confident.

"Your brother boxed?" I ask, trying to distract myself from the electricity shooting up my arm at her touch.

"He was good, too. Quick on his feet."

"And what about you?"

She rolls her eyes at me. "My father would never allow that. My role was to get married and have babies. Luca was meant to rule the empire. To be ruthless, cruel, and vicious. All things that he isn't."

"Do you want to learn?" The question tumbles from my lips before I can think better of it.

Vesper's fingers pause on my wraps. "Learn what? Boxing?"

"No. Self-defense. How to throw a proper punch." The idea feels right as soon as I say it. "Everyone should know how to protect themselves."

A flicker of interest crosses her face, quickly replaced by hesitation. "I wouldn't even know where to start."

"I could teach you," I offer. "Now, if you want."

The way her father saw her—as nothing but a vessel for continuing the family line—makes my blood boil. It's too familiar, cuts too close to home. My own mother was just a convenient womb to Marcus St. James, discarded once she'd served her purpose. A mistress who gave him a bastard son, then disappeared from his life like she never mattered.

She deserved better. Vesper deserves better.

"You're more than what they've reduced you to," I say

quietly, watching as she finishes securing my wrap. "You're not just some prize mare to be bred."

Her head lifts slightly, something flickering across her face—surprise, maybe. Or recognition.

"My father would disagree."

"Your father is dead, princess. His opinions don't matter anymore." My voice hardens, steady with conviction. "Women aren't baby factories. My mother was treated as if she didn't matter after she gave birth to me. Like she'd served her only purpose. I won't let anyone treat you that way."

Vesper's features soften at my admission. She brushes her thumb gently over my wrapped knuckle, the tenderness of the gesture unraveling something inside me.

"You remind me of him sometimes," she says quietly. "Luca, I mean. He never saw women as objects either. My father hated that about him."

"Your brother sounds like a good man."

"The best," she says, her voice catching. "Which is why I'm terrified of what they're doing to him."

Before I can think better of it, I reach out, cupping her face with my free hand.

"We're going to find him, Vesper. I swear it." She leans into the touch for a breath, her eyes fluttering shut. When they open again, they shine with fresh resolve.

"Teach me," she says, firm. "Show me how to fight." I nod and slowly let my hand drop from her cheek.

"First things first—stance."

I step back, giving her space, and settle into position.

"Feet shoulder-width apart, dominant foot slightly behind. Guard your face." I raise my fists, demonstrating.

Vesper mimics me, her movements cautious but determined. I circle her, making small corrections—tilting her elbow, nudging her shoulder, adjusting the placement of her feet.

"Good," I say, tapping her shoulder lightly to shift her posture. "Now, the jab. It's not about power. It's speed and precision. Quick out, quick back."

I show her slowly, left fist darting forward, then snapping back to guard.

"Your turn," I encourage.

Her first attempt is hesitant—arm not fully extending, wrist slightly bent.

"Almost. Keep your wrist straight, and punch through your target." I step behind her, gently taking her arm. "May I?"

She nods, and I guide her through the motion, feeling the tension in her muscles. "Relax your shoulders, but keep your core tight. Power comes from here," I tap her midsection lightly, "not just your arm."

Vesper tries again, this time with more conviction. The movement is cleaner, her form improving already.

"Better. Again."

She throws another jab, and another, each one more confident than the last. There's a natural athleticism to her movements that suggests she could become proficient with proper training.

"Now add the cross—right hand straight from the chin,

rotating your hip as you extend." I demonstrate, then watch as she attempts to replicate the motion.

"I feel ridiculous," she admits after a particularly awkward attempt.

"Everyone does at first. Fighting isn't natural until you train it." I step closer, adjusting her position. "Think of it like dancing. There's a rhythm to it."

I move to stand behind her, close enough that she can feel my presence without us actually touching. "Let your body flow with the movement." I demonstrate the combination again, letting her watch my reflection in the mirrored wall. "Jab-cross. Jab-cross. See how my weight shifts?"

She nods, determination setting her jaw as she tries again. This time, her hips rotate with the punch, generating more power.

"There you go. Now faster."

Vesper falls into a rhythm, her movements becoming more fluid with each repetition. The hesitation melts away, replaced by a focused intensity that transforms her face. She's a quick study, adapting and improving with minimal instruction.

After several minutes, a sheen of sweat glistens on her forehead, her breathing slightly labored but controlled. There's a new energy radiating from her, something primal and fierce that wasn't there before.

"How does it feel?" I ask, watching her reflection in the mirror.

A smile curls at the corner of her mouth. "Good. Really good."

"Want to try hitting something besides air?"

I retrieve the focus mitts from a nearby shelf and slip them on. "Same combination, but this time with a target." I hold up the padded mitts. "Don't pull your punches. Hit them like you mean it."

Vesper's first hit lands with surprising force, the impact reverberating up my arm. Her second follows immediately, more powerful than the first. She intensifies with each strike, her technique improving in real time.

"That's it," I encourage, moving the targets to different positions. "Jab-cross, jab-cross. Now add a hook."

She pivots, throwing her weight into a left hook that lands with a satisfying smack against the mitt. A sound escapes her—part growl, part breathless triumph.

"Again," she says, bouncing lightly on the balls of her feet.

We settle into a rhythm, the steady beat of her fists echoing through the small space. With each combination, her movements sharpen, confidence building as her body finds its flow. I push the pace, calling out combos quicker, shifting the mitts unexpectedly to force her to adapt.

"Hook-cross-uppercut," I call.

She hits each mark, and the final uppercut nearly catches me off guard.

"Damn," I say, grinning. "You're a natural."

Vesper's smile is radiant, her cheeks flushed with exertion and something that looks like pride. "It feels..." she searches for the word, "empowering."

"That's the point," I tell her, lowering the mitts. "Knowledge is power. Knowing you can defend yourself can mean the difference between being a survivor or victim."

"I'm done being the victim."

"Good," I say, tossing the mitts aside. "Because that's exactly what I want to hear."

Her eyes gleam with newfound determination with a spark that wasn't there before. She pushes her damp hair away from her face, her breathing still slightly elevated from the workout.

"Show me more," she says, not a request but a demand.

I move closer, circling her like a boxing coach. "Let's work on your defense. Knowing how to throw a punch is important, but knowing how to avoid one is even more crucial."

I demonstrate a basic slip, moving my head to the side as if dodging an incoming jab. "The goal is to use minimal movement for maximum effect. Conserve energy. Make them miss by inches, not feet."

Vesper mirrors my movement. I can see her cataloging each move, storing it away like ammunition for future use.

"Now," I continue, "if someone grabs you from behind—"

Before I can finish explaining, the door to the gym swings open. Z stands in the doorway, sweatpants hanging low on his hips. The tribal tattoos covering his chest and arms seem to shift in the harsh lighting as he crosses his arms.

"So this is where you disappeared to," he says to Vesper.

"Talon's teaching me to fight," Vesper finishes. She

doesn't look guilty, just slightly defiant as she meets Z head on.

"I can see that," he says evenly, pushing off from the doorframe.

"Is that a problem?" I ask, watching Z carefully. His expression remains guarded, but there's something else there. A hint of approval, maybe.

"No," he answers after a moment. "It's actually a good idea." He approaches us, his bare feet silent on the padded floor. "But your form needs work."

Vesper rolls her eyes. "I've had exactly one lesson, Z."

"You showing her how to break holds yet?"

"We were just getting to that," I reply.

"Good. That's the most important thing for her to know. I'll leave you to it."

Z gives her one more appraising look before turning to leave. As the door closes behind him, I catch the briefest smile on his face. It's gone in an instant, but I saw it.

"He approves," I remark, turning back to Vesper.

"Since when do I need his approval?"

"You don't. But having him on board means you'll have two instructors instead of one." I position myself behind her. "I'm better with a gun."

"And Z is better with his hands?" Vesper challenges, a playful smirk tugging at her lips.

"I didn't say that. We all have our talents, princess. You just have to figure them out yourself. Now, when someone grabs you from behind, your instinct will be to freeze. We need to override that response."

We run through several scenarios and holds until she gets a good mastery of each one. By the time we're done, we're both sweating.

"I think that's enough for today," I say, grabbing my towel and wiping sweat from my face. "You'll be kicking all of our asses in no time."

She beams at the praise, still bouncing slightly on the balls of her feet, adrenaline clearly flowing through her system. There's a flush to her cheeks that makes her look vibrant, alive in a way I haven't seen before. Something about teaching her to defend herself has awakened something in both of us.

"When can we do this again?"

"Tomorrow, if you want. I usually work out before breakfast," I tell her, gathering the focus mitts and hanging them back on their hooks. "You hungry?"

She nods, but instead of heading straight for the door, she steps closer to me. Before I can process what's happening, she rises on her tiptoes and presses her lips to mine. The kiss is quick but deliberate, her mouth soft against my own for just a heartbeat before she pulls away.

"Thank you," she says simply. "For treating me like I'm capable." She starts to leave, but I grab her wrist, pulling her back to me with a gentle tug.

"Hold on. That wasn't a real kiss." Before she can respond, I cradle her face, my thumb sweeping over her cheek. I dip my head and capture her mouth with mine, tasting the salt of her sweat. Her lips part beneath mine, a soft gasp escaping as I deepen the kiss.

She melts against me, her body molding to mine. Her nails dig into my flesh. I lose myself in the taste of her, the soft sounds she makes as I explore her mouth with my tongue.

When we finally pull apart, her pupils are dilated.

"You are capable of anything, Vesper," I tell her, my thumb still tracing the line of her jaw. "Don't ever let anyone make you believe otherwise."

She nods, a shy smile playing at her lips as she steps back. "I'll see you upstairs."

I watch her leave, the sway of her hips in those tiny sleep shorts doing absolutely nothing to settle the tension pulsing through me. When the door clicks shut behind her, I exhale slowly.

"Fuck," I mutter to the empty room, shifting uncomfortably in my workout shorts. I need to cool off—in every possible way.

A cold shower. Preferably glacial.

The last thing I need is to be flipping pancakes with a damn kickstand.

# Chapter 13

VESPER

EVERY MUSCLE in my body protests as I shift on the couch, trying to find a position that doesn't make me wince. This morning's workout with Talon has left me feeling like I've been hit by a truck. A surprisingly satisfying kind of pain that reminds me that my body can take being trained. That with enough practice, I can protect myself.

The apartment has fallen into an odd rhythm today while we wait for updates on whether or not Alex can get anything off Ricky's phone. He hasn't emerged from his room since last night, which means he's still working through what he found, or he hasn't been able to crack it yet. Talon keeps glancing down the hallway toward Alex's sanctuary, his expression cycling between concern and annoyance. While Oscar has been buried in his laptop at the dining table, occasionally muttering to himself in Russian as he types, working on something he hasn't clued the rest of us in about yet. And Z has been doing what he does best, hovering. Leaving me sore, satisfied, and worried that Oscar's risky meeting with Ricky was for nothing, and that we are no closer to finding my brother than we were before the meeting.

I shift again, unable to suppress a small groan as my body protests the movement. Z's head snaps up immediately.

"I'm fine."

"Your groan says otherwise. You went too hard this morning for your first lesson."

"I'm fine," I insist, "My body isn't accustomed to being used in that way."

Z arches a knowing eyebrow.

"You know what I mean."

"Should have stretched first," Z smirks back at me.

"I did," I lie. I mean, considering a few hours before I was doing cardio with him and his brother, I'd put myself in the well-worn and stretched category, but clearly, good sex is not a great pre-workout routine. Lesson learned.

"You overworked her this morning. This is on you, Talon."

Talon's smile thins.

"Unless..." Z smiles with a shrug. "That's not the only reason you're sore this morning."

"Really?" Talon remarks, shaking his head.

I throw a decorative pillow at Z's smug face. He catches it without effort, his reflexes infuriatingly sharp—even while lounging like he owns the place.

"You're insufferable," I declare.

"Yet you suffer me anyway," he replies, tossing the pillow back with gentle precision. It lands softly in my lap.

Oscar glances up from his laptop, the corner of his mouth quirking upward before he returns to whatever has him so engrossed. The quiet tapping of his keyboard fills the comfortable silence.

Talon shifts from his spot, heading towards the kitchen, and emerges a few minutes later with a steaming mug in each hand. "Chamomile with honey," he says, offering one to me. "Should help with the muscle soreness."

"Thanks," I say, gratefully accepting the warm mug. Our fingers brush during the exchange. The memory of his lips on mine in the gym this morning sends a rosy flush to my cheeks.

"Show off," Z remarks.

"I prefer to say that I am attentive. It's better than being an asshole all the time."

"I'm not an asshole all the time," Z counters, stretching his arms above his head. The motion lifts his shirt, revealing a sliver of tattooed skin and defined muscle. "Just when it's warranted."

I hide my smile behind the rim of my mug, the steam warming my face as I take a careful sip. The chamomile is just right—sweetened with honey but not cloying, the floral notes calming the frayed edges of my nerves.

"Warranted is subjective," Oscar comments. "Especially in your case, brother."

"Wow, turning against your own blood? Rude."

"Truth hurts, Z. Learn to live with it."

"Alex still locked in his cave?" Oscar redirects the conversation away from the pissing match brewing between Z and Talon.

"Yup," Talon confirms, settling back into the armchair across from me. "He was awake all last night, too."

"How would you know that?" Oscar remarks.

"Hunch," Talon shrugs indifferently.

I sip my tea, savoring the soothing warmth as it slides down my throat. "Should someone check on him? Make sure he's okay?"

"I wouldn't," Talon says quickly, something flickering across his face too fast for me to interpret. "He's in the zone. Interrupting him now would just piss him off."

"Even if I interrupted him?"

"Yes," they all answer in unison.

Their unanimous answer startles me. I set my mug down on the coffee table with a soft clink, suddenly feeling the need to check on Alex myself. Whatever he's working on has kept him locked away for hours. What if he needs something? Food? Water? A reminder that other humans exist?

I push myself up from the couch, wincing slightly as my sore muscles protest.

"Where are you going?" Z asks, already half-rising from his seat.

"To check on Alex," I answer, taking a step toward the hallway.

Talon clears his throat. "Before you do that, I was wondering what you were thinking for dinner tonight?"

I pause, turning to face him. "Dinner?"

"Yeah," he says casually, though something in his expression seems almost too deliberate. "Your choice. Anything you want."

I narrow my eyes, suspicious of the sudden change of subject. "Are you trying to distract me?"

"No," Talon says, looking offended. "I'm trying to plan ahead. In case I need to hit up the grocery store."

"I'm thinking..." I draw out the word as I study Talon's face. "That you're a terrible liar."

Z snorts from his position on the couch. "He really is."

"I'm not lying," Talon protests, but there's a slight flush creeping up his neck that betrays him. Talon is many things. A great cook, someone who always seems to be able to make me laugh, but a liar, he is not. "I'm genuinely curious about dinner."

"At two in the afternoon?" I cross my arms. "What's going on with Alex that you don't want me to see?"

"Vesper," Oscar begins carefully, closing his laptop. "Alex gets...intense when he's working. He doesn't like interruptions."

"That's putting it mildly," Talon mutters. "Last time I walked in on him mid-hack, he nearly threw a keyboard at my head."

"So you're saying I should just let him starve in there?"

"He's got protein bars and energy drinks stashed every-where," Z offers. "Like a squirrel preparing for nuclear winter."

"That's not healthy," I argue.

"Neither is disturbing him right now," Oscar counters, his voice gentle but firm. "Trust me, solnishko. When he's ready, he'll emerge."

Something in their collective reluctance makes me more determined. Perhaps it's the lingering spark from this morn-ing's training session with Talon, or maybe it's just my natural stubbornness, but I find myself stepping toward the hallway with renewed purpose.

"I'm just going to knock," I insist. "If he tells me to go away, I will." I pause, giving them all a pointed look.

The three men exchange glances, some silent communi-cation passing between them that I can't quite decipher. Finally, Oscar sighs. "Fine, but don't say we didn't warn you."

"I can check on him," Talon offers.

"No, I will," I demand, not dismissing Talon's odd behavior when it comes to Alex. What the hell is going on between the two of them?

I make my way down the hallway, ignoring Z's muttered, "This'll be good," behind me. The door to Alex's room is closed, a thin strip of light visible underneath. I hesitate for just a moment before I knock.

Three gentle taps. No response.

I try again, a little louder this time. "Alex? It's Vesper."

Silence stretches for so long I begin to wonder if he's

wearing headphones. Just as I'm about to knock a third time, I hear movement from within—the creak of a chair, footsteps approaching the door.

The door swings open suddenly, revealing Alex in a disheveled state I've never seen before. He's wearing a different pair of sweatpants than he was last night, with his bare, chiseled chest on full display again.

"Vesper," he says, his voice rougher than usual. "Did you need something?"

I take in the chaos visible behind him—multiple monitors displaying scrolling code, empty energy drink cans scattered across his desk, crumpled papers littering the floor.

"I was worried about you," I admit, crossing my arms over my chest. "You've been in here since last night."

"I'm fine. Just working."

"On Ricky's phone?"

"Among other things."

"Any progress?"

"Nothing worth sharing yet." His fingers tap an impatient rhythm against the doorframe. "Is that all?"

His dismissive tone stings more than it should. "Have you eaten anything? Or slept?"

"I don't need a babysitter, Vesper." The edge in his voice is sharper than I expected.

"I never said you did," I counter, refusing to be intimidated. "But humans generally require food and rest to function. Even brilliant ones." I duck under his arm, pushing myself into his room.

"What do you think you're doing?" He hisses as he whirls, hot on my heels.

"Tell me what you've found," I say, turning to face him. "Or what you haven't found. Either way, I deserve to know."

Alex's jaw clenches as he shuts the door behind me. He glances at one of his monitors and quickly taps a key, blanking the screen before I can see what's on it.

"I told you. I don't have anything to share yet," he repeats.

I study his face—the twitching muscle in his jaw, the way his eyes flick between me and the now-blank monitor. There's something he's hiding, something important enough that he's willing to snap at me to protect it.

"I don't believe you," I say, stepping closer to him. My frustration transforms into something else—a strategy forming in my mind. If direct questioning won't work, perhaps another approach will.

I move deliberately into his personal space, close enough that I can feel the heat radiating from his bare skin. His breath hitches almost imperceptibly as I place my palms flat against his chest, feeling his heart thundering beneath my fingertips.

"What are you doing?

My hands slide slowly upward, tracing the contours of his muscles, feeling him tense beneath my touch. His skin is warm, smooth, except for the light dusting of hair that narrows down his abdomen.

"Are you lying to me like Talon is?" I ask softly as my fingers continue their exploration.

Alex's carefully constructed facade cracks instantly. His eyes widen.

"What did Talon tell you?" he demands, his voice tight with an emotion I can't quite place.

I maintain my gentle caress, feeling a surge of power as his breathing grows more uneven. "Nothing," I reply, letting my nails scrape lightly down his torso. "But your reaction just now tells me there's something you're both hiding."

Alex catches my wrists, stilling my movements. His grip is firm but gentle, his thumbs unconsciously tracing circles on my pulse points. "It's not what you think."

"Then what is it?" I press, not pulling away from his hold. "If it's about Luca, I deserve to know. He's my brother."

Something shifts in Alex's expression—a flash of guilt quickly replaced by resolution. He releases my wrists with a sigh.

"You're right," he admits finally. "We found something, but I didn't want to tell you until I was sure it was viable."

My heart leaps into my throat. "What? What did you find?"

Alex hesitates, then moves to his desk and taps a key. One of his monitors flickers to life, displaying what looks like an email. He gestures for me to come closer.

"Talon found this last night. It came to the email account I created for him for the auction."

The subject line makes my blood run cold: *"Exclusive Private Auction: Invitation Only."* As I read further, my legs nearly give out beneath me.

"Oh my God. This could be Luca."

"It could be," Alex remarks. "But, if we join that auction without any protections in place, the connection could lead The Collector right to us. To you."

"And that's why you've been locked in here," I breathe, the pieces finally clicking into place. "You're trying to make sure we can safely join the auction without exposing ourselves."

Alex nods, relief washing over his face now that the truth is out. "I didn't want to get your hopes up until I knew for sure we could do this safely. These people, they're sophisticated. Their digital security is unlike anything I've seen before."

"Do Oz or Z know about this?"

"No," he answers plainly. "Talon brought it to me in the middle of the night." His cheeks flush at the statement. "Everyone else was occupied, and I needed to verify that this is real."

"And it is?"

Alex nods his head. "From everything I can tell, it's legitimate. The email address they used was only used for your auction details, and the auction previews...are, well, pretty straightforward."

My fingers trace the screen, as if somehow, I could reach through it and pull my brother to safety. "When is this happening?"

"In three days. Well, less than that now."

Less than three days. The timeline makes my chest tighten with anxiety. "Can you hack their security by then?"

Alex's expression hardens with determination. "I'm

close. Very close. Just need to finish building a few more layers of protection." He gestures to the code scrolling across another monitor. "I've been working on a digital tunnel that will conceal our real IP address and location, bouncing our signal through dozens of servers around the world. They'll never be able to trace it back to us."

I study the complex lines of code, understanding none of it but trusting completely in Alex's expertise. "And once we're in the auction, what's the plan? We can't exactly outbid everyone."

"That's where it gets complicated," Alex admits, dropping into his desk chair. He rubs his face, exhaustion evident in every line of his body. "We need to identify who's running the auction, track their payment processing system, and if possible, pinpoint where they're holding the 'merchandise.'" The word drips with disgust as it leaves his lips.

"And you think you can do all that while the auction is happening?"

"In theory, yes."

I pace the small space between his bed and desk, mind racing. "So what's the holdup? Why not tell everyone now and start planning?"

Alex hesitates, his fingers drumming on the desk. "There's a chance that this is a trap. That auction listing could be bait."

"For me? For all The Collector knows, I am enslaved to my new owner. What evidence have we given him to think otherwise?" I retort.

"Natasha," Alex sighs. Hearing her name brings back a

flash of memories from her brief stint in Alex's medical playroom in the basement. How I watched him work to extract information from her by any means necessary to protect me. To find information on my son. "If she communicated to anyone that she was meeting Talon to talk about your reproductive rights, it could be a trap. It's a risk I am not taking."

My stomach clenches at the mention of Natasha. Alex is right. There are too many variables, too many ways this could go wrong. But it's Luca. My brother. I can't ignore even the smallest chance of finding him.

"I understand the risk," I say softly. "But we have to try."

Alex's shoulders slump slightly, whether from relief or exhaustion, I can't tell. "I know. That's why I haven't stopped working."

I study him more carefully now, the slight tremor in his hands as he reaches for an energy drink. He looks like he's running on fumes, pushing himself beyond normal human limits. I make a decision then. Alex needs to stay focused, but he also needs to stay awake. And I know just how to help with both.

"Move back," I command, rolling his chair away from the desk.

"What are you—"

I don't let him finish. I sink to my knees between his legs, looking up at him through my lashes as my hands come to rest on his thighs.

"What are you doing?" His voice cracks slightly.

"Helping you stay awake."

"Vesper." Alex grips the armrests. "You don't have to—"

"I know I don't have to," I say, my fingers tracing patterns along his inner thighs. "I want to." I lean closer. "Consider it motivation to work faster."

His breathing quickens as my hands glide higher, fingers flirting with the edge of his waistband. I see it in his eyes—the flicker of conflict. Desire burning hot, tangled with something heavier. Guilt, maybe.

"This isn't..." he starts, but his words dissolve into a sharp intake of breath as my palm presses against the hardening length beneath the fabric.

"Isn't what?" I challenge, looking up at him. "Isn't something you want? You told me it was my choice." I hook my fingers into his waistband, tugging slightly. "Well, I'm making it."

Instead of answering, Alex catches my wrists, stilling my movements. The touch is gentle but firm, his thumbs pressing against my pulse points. "You don't know what you're asking for."

"I'm pretty sure I do," I counter, not backing down. "Unless you're hiding something else from me?"

Alex's jaw clenches, the muscle ticking beneath his skin. For a heartbeat, we're caught in a silent stand-off. His grip is firm around my wrists, my body lingering between his legs —close enough to feel the tension rolling off him, thick and electric.

"Vesper..." His voice holds a warning, but there's something else beneath it—a hunger he's fighting to control. "This isn't just about sex for me."

The admission hangs between us, heavy with implications I'm not sure I'm ready to face. I swallow hard, suddenly feeling vulnerable despite being the one who initiated this.

"Then what is it about?"

His thumbs trace slow circles on my pulse points. "There are things you don't know about me. Things we need to talk about."

Before I can process his words, someone knocks at his door. Alex releases my wrists instantly, his expression shuttering close as he rolls his chair back toward his desk.

"Alex?" Talon's voice filters through the door. "We need to talk. Now."

Alex and I exchange a look. The moment is gone, shattered by Talon's impeccable timing.

"Give me a minute," Alex calls back.

I rise to my feet, smoothing my clothes as Alex stands. He towers over me. More than the rest of them.

"We're not done with this conversation," I tell him quietly.

A ghost of a smile touches his lips. "No, we're not. Not in the slightest."

Talon's expression when I open the door is a mixture of surprise and something that looks suspiciously like relief. His eyes dart between Alex and me.

"Everything okay?" he asks, his tone deliberately casual.

"Peachy," I reply, brushing past him. "He's all yours."

# Chapter 14

VESPER

THE SCENT of freshly baked garlic bread fills the apartment, but the only thing I can taste is anticipation. If Alex doesn't emerge soon, I might just kick his door down myself. He had said it would only take a few hours. It's been almost a full day since I last laid eyes on him. Even the plate of food from dinner I'd left outside his door for him remained untouched.

"Seriously, where the hell is he?" Z mutters, piling pasta onto plates with more force than necessary.

My muscles ache pleasantly, from my workout with Talon this morning. "He said he was almost done yesterday."

Oscar glances up from his phone. "Almost done with

what, exactly? Since neither of you thought it necessary to fill us in."

The tension in the room has been building since Talon let slip at breakfast that Alex was working on something important. That unleashed a barrage of questions from the twins, which Talon and I had deflected with vague promises that Alex would explain everything soon.

"You'll know when we all know," Talon replies calmly, setting glasses of water around the table. His casual tone only seems to irritate the twins further.

Z slams a serving spoon onto the counter. "This is bullshit. We're supposed to be a team. I expect secretive bullshit out of Alex, but you two?"

"We are a team," I say, moving to help him with the plates. "Which is why Alex wants to be sure before getting everyone's hopes up. This isn't just some random lead. This could be it."

"You found Luca?"

"Maybe," I admit, glancing toward the hallway. "Alex is trying to make sure it's safe to pursue."

Oscar appears at my side. "And you didn't think we deserved to know this immediately?"

"We were going to tell you," Talon interjects, leaning against the counter. "As soon as Alex confirms it's possible."

The sound of a door opening down the hallway silences us all. We turn collectively as Alex emerges, looking like he's been through hell and back.

"I did it," he announces without preamble. "We've got a secure way into the auction."

The room freezes for a heartbeat before chaos erupts.

"What auction?" Oz demands, his voice cutting through the sudden tension. "Start talking. Now."

Alex holds up his hands, fatigue etched into every line of his face. "The Collector is hosting another auction, online this time, in two days. High-end 'merchandise,'" he spits the word like poison "Including a male in his early twenties with an 'exceptional bloodline.' The description matches Luca."

Oz sucks in a sharp breath beside me. "How did you find this?"

"I didn't," Alex admits. "Talon did."

"They emailed me," he shrugs nonchalantly.

"And you didn't think to tell us?" Z's voice is razor-sharp, quiet in a way that makes the air feel heavier. "Why is it everyone knew—except Oz and me?"

"I wanted to be sure," Alex counters, crossing to the kitchen island. He grabs a slice of garlic bread, tearing into it.

"Technically...I kind of forced it out of him yesterday when you all were too scared to interrupt him."

"Forced it out of him? What the hell does that mean?"

"It means I'm persuasive," I reply, raising my chin slightly. "And that Alex isn't as impenetrable as he likes to pretend."

Oscar's thumb traces circles on my palm, the gesture at odds with the tension radiating from his body. "So let me get this straight. The Collector is hosting another auction, and you think Luca might be one of the...items for sale."

"Well, not Luca physically. From the description, it looks

like they're auctioning off his samples," Alex says, reaching for another piece of garlic bread.

"And when is this auction?"

"Day after tomorrow," Talon answers. "Thus, the urgency to see if this is even possible for us. If we can secure one of his samples," he swallows hard at the word, "We may be able to track down their new clinic."

"And if we can find the clinic, it can lead us to Luca," Oz remarks.

"Exactly."

Z slams his palm on the counter, making the plates rattle. "So, while we've been sitting around twiddling our thumbs, you three have been planning a mission without us?"

"No one's been twiddling anything," I snap, my patience finally fraying. "Alex has been working nonstop to make sure we can even access this auction without getting caught. Without putting all of us, especially me, at risk."

"She's right, Z. While I don't agree with the secrecy, I understand the motive behind it. If The Collector realizes Vesper isn't the captive he sold her off to be, and that she's coming for her brother, Vesper will be his first target."

"And you think I don't understand that?" Z's voice rises, his tattoos seeming to ripple as his muscles tense. "That's exactly why we should have been told immediately. More minds working on protection, the better."

Alex sets down his half-eaten bread. "The security protocols I've put in place are complex. I needed total concentration, not a committee debate slowing me down."

"So now we're a hindrance?" Z challenges, taking a step toward Alex.

Talon smoothly slides between them. "That's not what he meant. We were going to brief everyone as soon as Alex confirmed we could safely access the auction."

"Which is now," I interject, moving to stand beside Talon. "Can we please focus on what matters? This might be our only chance to find Luca."

"Fine," he concedes, crossing his arms across his chest. "Let's hear it then. What's the plan?"

"The auction is being hosted on a private server with military-grade encryption."

"You're sure it can't be traced back to us?" Oscar asks, his tactical mind already assessing risks.

"As sure as I can be," Alex replies, accepting the plate of pasta Talon slides in front of him. "I've routed our connection through seventeen different servers across twelve countries. Even if they detect something unusual, they'll chase ghosts."

I take a seat across from him, my appetite forgotten as hope swells in my chest. "And once we're in the auction, what then?"

"We buy one of his samples."

Z starts to interject, but Alex cuts him off with a sharp look. "The funds are secured."

"Ok, we buy one of his samples, and then what?"

"I have created a nasty little virus that I am going to tack onto the funds transfer. With a single click, they get paid and I get access to their servers."

"And if that doesn't work?" Oz interjects. "What's plan B?"

"The sample itself. Something that expensive isn't going to be dropped into the mail. They'll want it picked up. They'll be expecting Talon or a courier."

"Which means we'll need to track the pickup location," Oscar says, his mind already racing through the logistics. "That could lead us directly to their operations."

"Exactly," Alex nods, shoveling a forkful of pasta into his mouth. "The beauty of this plan is that it gives us multiple points of entry. Digital through the virus, physical through the pickup."

Alex swallows, his attention shifting between us. I can see the gears turning. "It all depends on timing," he says finally. "Once we're in the auction, things will move quickly. We'll have to be ready to adapt."

"The one thing you're good at," Talon says, the hint of a smile on his lips. "Oz and Z aren't big on changing plans."

Z glares. "As long as she's safe, I'll adapt to whatever the hell is necessary."

Oscar nods. "And you?"

"I'm the safest I've been in months with all of you. I trust Alex's plan, and I trust all of you." I take a deep breath, my voice steady with conviction. "We're going after Luca."

Silence falls as my words settle over us. I can see the shift in the group, the way skepticism gives way to determination. This is happening. We're doing this. We're getting my brother back.

# Chapter 15

## VESPER

ANTICIPATION HANGS SO thick in the air, I could slice it with a knife—and maybe shoot it for good measure. It's the night before the auction, and the last thirty-six hours have dragged by like molasses. Not even Z's brutal gym sessions, Oscar's shooting drills, or the very enthusiastic, thoroughly naked efforts they've both made to keep me distracted have done a damn thing to make time move faster.

After our heart-to-heart and a few strategically placed kisses yesterday, Alex locked himself away again, fine-tuning his plan. Despite the urgency, despite the minute-by-minute countdown to this pivotal moment, it's the waiting that kills me. Not the planning or the risks. Just the fucking waiting.

I wake up alone, the sheets cold beside me. I sit up as I try to orient myself. The clock on my nightstand reads 2:57 AM. Oscar and Z must have slipped out sometime after I fell asleep, probably to meet up with Alex and Talon for one last rundown of the plan.

Anxiety coils beneath my skin, a constant, low-level hum that won't let me settle. I swing my legs over the side of the bed, feeling the chill of the hardwood against my bare feet. The oversized t-shirt I'm wearing offers little protection against the cool air. I pull it down over my thighs and pad down the hallway, the apartment silent around me.

I bypass the living room and head straight for the kitchen. I pull open the freezer and grab a pint of lavender honey ice cream that Talon keeps stocked for me. The first few bites melt quickly on my tongue. My mind is racing, a chaotic whirl as I lean against the counter, the spoon poised between my lips.

Ice cream has always made me feel better, a temporary balm for the unease knotting my stomach. But tonight, even its soothing sweetness can't distract me from the enormity of what's coming. The auction. Luca. The Collector. It's all so close and the stakes are high.

Worry gnaws at the edges of my thoughts. What if something goes wrong? What if Alex's carefully constructed plans crumble? What if we spend all that money and don't find Luca? Or if we do, the brother I knew is gone. Changed by whatever horrors The Collector has inflicted on him?

Strong arms slip around my waist, drawing me toward them.

"Couldn't sleep?" Talon asks, resting his chin on my shoulder.

"Drowning my worries in ice cream," I admit, feeling the tension in my muscles start to unwind under his touch. "It's not working."

"Mind some company?"

I pass him the spoon, relaxing against the solid warmth of his chest. His presence is calming, like tomorrow won't crush us after all.

"Are the others still up?" I ask, watching as he takes a bite.

"They're making sure everything is in place. Putting plans C and D together in case things go sideways."

"And you?"

"Making sure you're okay," he says, a teasing edge to his voice. "And stealing your ice cream."

I try to smile, but it's forced, brittle. Talon reads me too well for it to go unnoticed.

"It'll be okay, princess" he tells me. "We have a plan, and we have you. Those two things pretty much guarantee success." He sets the ice cream down and spins me to face him, his expression shifting from lighthearted to serious. "We're going to get him back. You know that, right?"

I nod, but the fear hasn't left me. "I just...I don't know what I'd do if we lost him again. If after all of this, he's still not safe."

Talon cups my face. "We'll figure it out. Together. We've been through worse than this."

His certainty is a buoy, and I cling to it. "But what if—"

Talon's lips brush against mine, silencing my doubt. The kiss is tender, reassuring, the promise that whatever happens tomorrow, I won't be facing it alone. When he finally pulls back, my head is swimming for reasons that have nothing to do with fear.

"But what if it isn't?" I finish weakly.

"It will be," he insists, his grin returning. "When have you known me to lie?"

"I mean, you did lie about the auction."

"That was necessary, princess."

"Still a lie. A pretty shitty one. You don't have a poker face when it comes to lying."

His chuckle vibrates through me. As we stand there, tangled together in the kitchen, I begin to believe him.

"You should get some sleep. We don't know what tomorrow will bring once the auction is over."

"I'm not tired," I insist, though we both know it's not entirely true.

"Want to be?" Talon sets the ice cream aside and scoops me into his arms.

A surprised laugh escapes as he lifts me onto the counter, my bare leg exposed between the hem of my t-shirt. He steps closer, the heat of him chasing away the chill from the kitchen.

"Do you ever not flirt?" I ask, feigning exasperation.

"Not with you." He reaches around me, grabbing the ice cream again. "Why? Is it working?"

"Maybe a little."

His lips find mine, soft and teasing as he crowds closer.

My legs hook around his waist instinctively, pulling him to me until there's no space left between our bodies.

"More than a little, I think."

My uncertainty about tomorrow dissipates, replaced by the immediacy of Talon's touch, the grounding reality of his presence.

"It's late. You should sleep."

"I told you, I'm not tired," I insist, tightening my legs around his waist.

A slow smile spreads across his face as he reaches for the ice cream container between us. He dips the spoon in, gathering a scoop of lavender honey sweetness. He brings it to my mouth, and I part my lips, letting him slide the cold treat between them. The flavor blooms on my tongue—floral, sweet, with just a hint of something wild underneath.

"Good?" he asks, his voice dropping lower.

I nod, watching as he digs the spoon back into the container. This time, when he withdraws it, he doesn't bring it to my mouth. Instead, his free hand slides up my thigh, pushing my t-shirt higher until I'm exposed from the waist down. The cool air makes me shiver.

With deliberate slowness, Talon presses the cold spoon against my inner thigh. The shock makes me gasp, hips jerking, fingers digging into his shoulders for balance.

"Talon..." His name leaves my lips like a plea as he drags the spoon upward, leaving a slick trail of melting ice cream that clings to my warm skin.

"I've been thinking about this since the first time you

said my name like that," he mutters, dropping to his knees between my legs. "Sweet. Breathless. Needing more."

His breath ghosts over the sticky line he's drawn, warm and sinful against the cold. I shudder, caught between the chill of the ice cream and the burn of anticipation. My fingers curl against the counter behind me as he leans in, tongue teasing the path he's made with slow, deliberate licks.

It's maddening. Intimate. Raw.

My head falls back as a moan escapes me, hips rocking forward. He groans against my skin like he's starving for it, licking up every trace of sugar.

"You taste fucking divine," he breathes into my thigh, his grip on my hips possessive, holding me right where he wants me. "And I haven't even started."

When his mouth finally reaches the apex of my thighs, I nearly come undone at the first touch of his tongue. The contrast between the cool residue of ice cream and the heat of his mouth sends electricity coursing through my veins. My fingers tangle in his hair, holding him against me as pleasure builds, threatening to shatter me completely.

"Someone might come in," I gasp, even as my body arches toward him.

Talon looks up at me. "Let them," he says before returning his attention to my center, his tongue circling my clit with devastating precision.

My thighs begin to tremble as tension coils tighter in my core. Talon slides one hand beneath me, lifting my hips just enough to deepen his reach. The new angle sends sparks across my vision as he slides a finger inside, curling it forward until he finds the spot that makes me shatter.

He devours me like a starving man at a feast, each deliberate stroke of his tongue designed to build my pleasure without letting me fall over the edge. Sweet, maddening torture that has me writhing against the cold counter as I fight the urge to beg. He tightens his hold on my thighs. I instinctively try to close them around him, drawing out the exquisite torment.

"Talon, please," I gasp, my head thrown back as he sucks my clit into his mouth, gentle at first, then maddeningly slow as he pulls away again. If anything, he gets more focused. More ruthless.

"Not yet," he breathes against me, his lips brushing slick skin. "I want to remember every fucking sound you make when I ruin you."

The words vibrate straight to my core. The counter digs into the backs of my thighs, grounding me to make every stroke of his tongue feel sharper, every pulse more unbearable.

Just when I think he's going to tease me until I explode, he thrusts two fingers deep, curling them inside me. His mouth finds me again—tongue and fingers moving in tandem, building me fast, hard, and with no escape.

It's too much. Too good.

My body arches off the counter as the orgasm hits, tearing through me in relentless pulses until I'm trembling, boneless, wrecked.

But Talon isn't finished.

As my breath catches in my throat, he rises slowly. He drags the hem of my shirt up and over my head, leaving me bare and sprawled across the counter, marked by his mouth, his hunger.

"You're not going anywhere," he commands, stepping between my thighs again. "We're just getting started." He reaches for the ice cream container again. The cool air pebbles my exposed skin, but it's nothing compared to the shock of cold when he spoons a dollop of lavender honey ice cream onto each of my nipples.

I gasp, arching into the sensation as he leans forward, his mouth closing over one ice cream-covered peak.

"You're spread out for me like a fucking feast," Talon's mouth hot against my skin as he moves to my other breast. His tongue licks up the last of the melting sweetness, slow and methodical, like he's savoring every second. "And I'm going to devour every inch of you."

I'm still trembling from his mouth between my thighs, every nerve raw and begging. I want his body pressing me into the counter, his cock stretching me open, his body claiming mine completely.

"Talon," I pant, tugging at his shirt, desperate to feel him, all of him. "I need you."

His lips curl against my skin. "Your wish is my command, princess."

His hands grip my thighs, spreading me wider, locking me in place. My pulse pounds, anticipation crashing through me as he straightens. He strips his shirt off in one fluid motion.

The light catches the sharp lines of his torso, the tattoo winding across his left shoulder now fully visible—inked curves and shadows that beg to be traced. I reach out, my fingertips gliding down the path of black and gray, following it to the waistband of his sweats.

"These need to go," I tell him, voice low but commanding, hooking my fingers under the band and tugging.

Talon smirks, already working them down his hips. "Then take them off, baby. But just know, once I'm inside you, I'm not stopping until your legs are shaking and you can't remember your own name."

Talon's smile is feral as he steps back just enough to shove his sweatpants down, kicking them aside. He's gloriously naked now, his arousal evident and impressive. My mouth goes dry at the sight of him, all coiled strength and barely restrained hunger.

"See something you like, princess?" Talon asks, his voice rough.

"Everything," I answer without hesitation, reaching for him again. "Now get over here."

He steps between my thighs, dragging me to the very edge of the counter. The position leaves me completely exposed, utterly at his mercy, and the power in that vulnerability makes my pulse race. His cock presses against my entrance, hot, thick, teasing, and my breath catches at the promise of him.

"Tell me what you want," he orders, his palm sliding up to cup my breast, thumb circling the still-sensitive peak until I squirm.

"You," I gasp, body already trembling with need.

Talon tightens his grip, eyes dark. "Not good enough. Use your words, sweetheart. Tell me exactly what you want me to do to you."

"I want you to fuck me."

He arches a brow, still holding back. "Say it again. Beg for it."

"I want you, Talon. I want your cock inside me. Now."

That's all it takes. He drives into me in one brutal, breathtaking thrust, burying himself to the hilt. I cry out, the stretch toe-curling and obscene, every inch of him thick and pulsing inside me. My walls clamp down, greedy and aching for more.

He stills, forehead pressed to mine as our breaths mingle —hot, ragged, trembling.

"Fuck, princess," he groans, hips twitching as he fights for control. "This...this is better than every dream I've ever had of you. No fantasy ever came close to how tight your cunt feels around my cock—how real this is, how fucking perfect you feel. I used to imagine this, over and over, thinking it would never happen. But nothing in my head— not the sounds you'd make, not the way you'd look when I plunged inside of you—*nothing* could ever prepare me for this. For you. For how fucking wrecked I feel just being inside you."

Before I can answer, he starts to move, building a rhythm. Each thrust hits with force, deliberate, and unrelenting.

My legs wrap around his waist, heels digging into the

small of his back. He tugs me just enough to expose my throat to his mouth. His lips and teeth work the sensitive skin there, surely leaving marks. Marks I will wear proudly.

"Mine," he rasps against my pulse point, the possessive edge in his voice igniting something molten inside me. His pace picks up, driving harder, like he's trying to brand himself into my very core.

I'm dimly aware we're being reckless. Anyone could walk in at any moment, but it only heightens the intensity, makes each sensation sharper, more immediate.

"Talon," I gasp as he shifts, changing angles. "Right there —don't stop—"

His rhythm falters for just a moment as he looks at me, pupils blown wide with desire. "Never," he promises, his voice rough. "I'll never stop giving you what you need."

The counter edge digs into my thighs, but the discomfort is distant, overwhelmed by the building pressure. Talon's movements grow more urgent, more demanding, driving me toward another peak.

"Scream my fucking name, princess. I need to hear it on those sweet lips of yours," he commands, his thumb finding my clit, circling it in time with his thrusts. "Wake up the entire fucking apartment, princess."

My body obeys like it was made to respond to his command. Pleasure crashes over me, intense and unrelenting, my inner walls clenching around him as I cry out his name. The sound echoes through the quiet kitchen, probably loud enough to wake the others, but I'm beyond caring.

Talon's rhythm falters as my release triggers his own.

With a final, powerful thrust, he buries himself deep inside me, his body tensing as he finds his release. His groan mingles with my gasps, our bodies locked together in shared ecstasy.

We stay like that for a while. Me still trembling on the counter, legs draped around his waist, Talon pressed between them, his chest heaving against mine. Sweat clings to our skin, the air thick with sex and something heavier neither of us is ready to name.

I drag my fingers slowly over his shoulders, tracing the curve of muscle and ink, grounding myself in the steady thump of his pulse beneath my touch.

"That was..." I start, but the words vanish—too small for what just happened.

Talon exhales, the sound rough, almost a laugh. "Yeah." He presses a kiss to my temple, softer than I expect, lingering just long enough to make my chest ache. "It fucking was."

A soft chuckle escapes him as he carefully withdraws from me, the loss of connection making me whimper slightly. He reaches for a dish towel hanging nearby, dampening it with warm water from the sink before tenderly cleaning between my thighs. The gesture is unexpectedly intimate, his touch gentle as he takes care of me.

"The ice cream's melted," I observe, glancing at the forgotten container on the counter beside us.

Talon grins. "I'll buy you more."

He helps me down from the counter, my legs wobbling slightly. The cool air of the kitchen raises goosebumps across my naked skin, and Talon quickly retrieves my discarded t-shirt, pulling it over my head with surprising tenderness.

We hear someone clear their throat and turn to see Alex standing in the shadows. His expression is unreadable, but his rigid posture speaks volumes.

"Fuck," Talon hisses under his breath, positioning himself slightly in front of me despite the fact I'm now covered by my shirt. "We need to put a fucking bell on you, man."

"Sorry to interrupt," Alex says deceptively casual. "The ice cream was a nice touch."

Heat floods my cheeks as I realize what his words imply. "How long have you been standing there?"

"Long enough." His glances from my face down to my bare legs and back up again with deliberate slowness. "Don't stop on my account. The kitchen counter is an....inspired choice."

Talon reaches for his sweatpants, pulling them on with quick efficiency. "Did you need something, or are you just enjoying the show?"

"I came to get some coffee," he explains, though his tone suggests coffee is the furthest thing from his mind. "I didn't expect anyone else to be up, or fucking on the kitchen counter."

"We were just heading back to bed."

"Were you?" Alex's attention flicks to the melted ice cream container, then back to my flushed face. "Looks to me like you were just getting started."

I should feel embarrassed, being caught like this, but

Alex's face stirs a different emotion entirely. He's shut me down twice now. His blue balls are his own fault.

"Do you often lurk in the shadows watching people?" I ask him.

A hint of a smile touches Alex's lips. "Only when the show is worth watching."

"Alex," Talon warns, but there's a strange undercurrent to his voice that I can't quite decipher. "Enough."

"What?" Alex shrugs before heading towards us. "Don't fuck in the common spaces if you don't want spectators." He stops, reaching over finger and grazes against my cheek. On the pad of his finger is a smear of melted ice cream. He smiles as he draws his finger to his mouth, sucking it between his lips. "Chocolate is better," he comments.

My thighs press together involuntarily. "Chocolate with caramel," I reply, my voice steadier than I feel. "Sweet and salty."

"I'll remember that."

Talon clears his throat, his hand finding the small of my back. "We should get some sleep."

The word choice isn't lost on any of us. Alex's lips quirk up at one corner as he turns away, busying himself with the coffee maker.

"You should," he agrees without looking back at us. "I still have some final checks to run before the auction."

"Don't stay up too late," I tell Alex. "We need you sharp tomorrow."

Talon guides me from the kitchen, his arm wrapped protectively around my waist.

"Your place or mine?" Talon asks as we reach his door, his knuckles brushing mine.

"Can we stay here?" I ask.

"Yeah," he says, stepping aside to open the door. "This is your space now, too."

He closes the door behind us, shutting out everything else.

I slide onto the bed, still bare beneath his shirt, and he joins me, an arm curling around my waist like it belongs there.

"Get some rest," he says as he pulls me close, his breath warm against my neck.

I press against his chest, letting the silence settle. His fingers trace lazy circles against my hip, grounding me.

And for the first time in what feels like forever, my body stops bracing for the next hit.

# Chapter 16

VESPER

THE TIMER on Alex's laptop counts down ruthlessly, each second tightening the coil of tension in my chest. Auction begins in four minutes and thirty-seven seconds. We're gathered in his room, the glow of multiple screens casting an eerie light across our faces. Alex sits at the helm, fingers flying over keys as he patches the final layers of security into place. The rest of us crowd around him.

"Your room is so...boring," Talon remarks.

"And that's why I don't let any of you in here," Alex mutters under his breath.

"Except for Vesper," Talon fires back at him. A rosy flush blooms on my cheeks at his observation. If the others only knew where I was a few days ago, perched on my knees under this very desk.

"Four minutes," Z mutters, pacing the limited space like a caged animal. His agitation is palpable. "Our connection better hold."

"It will," Alex says tersely, his focus absolute. "This should be the easy part."

"Should be," Oscar echoes, resting against the edge of the desk. He crosses his arms, his attention fixed intently on Alex's screens. "We can't afford any surprises."

"One way or another, we're getting your brother back." Alex promises, glancing at me briefly before returning to the screens.

"Three minutes," Talon announces, pushing off from the wall to move closer. "Run me through it one more time."

Alex sighs but complies. "We enter through the secure tunnel I've created. Our identity will show as Charles Blackwood—Talon's auction alias. We'll be bidding on Lot 27, the 'rare male specimen.' Once we secure the winning bid, I'll initiate the payment protocol with the embedded virus."

"And if the virus doesn't take?" Oscar asks, his voice carefully neutral.

"Then we track the sample pickup," Z finishes, stopping his pacing to stand beside me. His presence is warm, solid. "We follow the trail physically."

"Exactly," Alex nods, typing a final string of code before leaning back. "Both approaches should lead us to the location.'"

The clinical way he says it makes my stomach turn, but I understand the necessity. We have to think of this as a mission, not let our emotions overwhelm us. Not yet.

"Two minutes."

Oscar's fingers interlace with mine in silent support. His thumb traces small circles on my palm, a gesture so subtle yet so comforting that I find myself leaning into his touch.

"One minute," Talon announces.

The air in the room feels electric, charged with anticipation. I struggle to control my breathing. This could be it—the moment that changes everything, that leads us to Luca. Or it could be another dead end, another cruel joke from The Collector.

"Thirty seconds," Alex mutters, his fingers poised over the keyboard. "Everyone stays quiet once we're in. No sudden movements, no distractions."

I'm surrounded by them now. Oscar holding my hand, Z at my shoulder, Talon hovering nearby, Alex leading us into the digital battle. Four men who have become my lifeline, my protection, my...everything.

"Ten seconds."

My heart pounds so loudly I'm certain everyone can hear it. The countdown reaches zero, and Alex hits enter with a deafening click.

The screen flickers, then resolves into an elegant black interface with gold trim. A stylized logo pulses at the center —two intertwined serpents forming an infinity symbol. The Collector's mark.

"We're in," Alex breathes.

A welcome message scrolls across the top: "Mr. Black-wood, we're pleased to have you join us again."

"They recognize the alias," Talon comments.

Alex nods. "That's good. Means we're properly authenticated."

A list of available lots appears on the left side of the screen, each with a brief description and starting bid. I scan frantically until I find Lot 27.

"There," I declare.

The starting bid makes my stomach drop. Five million dollars for my brother's...I can't even finish the thought without feeling ill.

"Focus," Alex commands, clicking on the lot to bring up more details. A timer appears, showing the auction for this specific item begins in three minutes. "We need to be strategic here. Bid too aggressively, we'll attract attention. Too conservative, we lose him."

"Can we afford it?"

Oscar's thumb continues its soothing circles on my palm. "Yes," he says simply. "Whatever it takes."

A chat window pops up in the corner of the screen, a message appearing in elegant script.

*Welcome, valued patrons. Today's offerings are particularly exceptional. We hope you find what you're seeking.*

The clinical politeness makes bile rise in my throat. These people are selling my brother. I swallow hard, fighting to maintain my composure.

"How many other bidders?" Z asks, his voice tight with controlled rage.

Alex navigates through the interface, pulling up a participant list. "Twenty-three active connections, including us."

"Twenty-three people willing to pay millions for..." Oscar doesn't finish, his jaw clenching.

"Considering what you paid for me..." I trail off.

"One minute until our lot opens," Talon announces.

My heart hammers against my ribs as Alex positions the cursor over the bidding field, ready to submit our first offer. The screen refreshes, and Lot 27 is active, the description expanded to include more details.

*Male specimen, 23 years old, exceptional bloodline, untouched condition. Genetic testing confirms superior traits. Sample viability guaranteed for 24 months under proper storage conditions.*

A small icon pulsates next to the description—a video preview. Alex hovers over it, looking to me for permission.

"Do it."

He clicks, and a brief clip begins to play—clinical footage of a lab technician holding up a vial to the light, examining its contents. The camera pans to show a small label on the container, bearing a barcode and an identification number: LR-0723.

LR. Luca Rossi.

My knees nearly buckle. Z's grip on my shoulders tightens, keeping me upright as a strangled sound escapes my throat.

"It's him," I breathe, staring at the screen. "It's really him."

The bidding begins immediately, numbers climbing rapidly as invisible competitors stake their claims. Five million quickly becomes six, then seven. Alex enters our first bid, eight million, his expression impassive as he watches the counter tick upward.

"They're going higher than anticipated," Oscar observes.

The numbers continue to climb, nine million, ten, eleven. Each increase feels like a physical blow. Not because of the money. I know the men surrounding me have access to funds I can barely comprehend, but because of what it represents. My brother's life, his future, reduced to a digital auction block.

"Twelve million," Alex announces as he enters our next bid, his voice eerily calm despite the tension radiating from his body.

A notification pops up on screen. *Three active bidders remain.*

"We're getting close," Talon says. I'm surrounded by them now, their presence forming a protective barrier between me and the horror unfolding on screen.

The counter jumps to thirteen million, then fourteen. Alex responds with fifteen.

A message appears in the chat. *Final call for bids on Lot 27.*

Alex's fingers hover over the keyboard. *Sixteen million*, he types, the number appearing instantly.

The interface falls silent for three agonizing seconds

before a notification flashes. *Lot 27 secured. Congratulations, Mr. Blackwood.*

"We got it," I breathe, relief washing through me like a physical blow. My legs tremble as the tension that's been holding me upright suddenly releases.

"Now for phase two," Alex mutters, his focus unwavering as he navigates to the payment portal. His fingers fly across the keyboard, initiating the transfer while simultaneously activating the virus embedded within the code.

"Is it working?" Talon asks, leaning closer to the screen.

Alex doesn't answer immediately. "Payment processing...virus deploying...come on, you bastard, take the bait..."

The screen flickers, numbers and symbols racing across it faster than I can follow. Alex's expression shifts from concentration to triumph as a small notification appears in the corner. *Access granted.*

"I'm in," he announces.

"What are you seeing?"

"Everything," Alex breathes, opening multiple windows on his secondary monitors. "Server architecture, transactions for all of the lots in this auction—"

The screens suddenly go black. All of them.

"What the fuck?" Alex slams his palm against the desk. "No, no, no!"

The monitors flicker back to life, but the data is gone. Empty windows stare back at us, the server connection severed. Where moments ago there had been a wealth of information, our key to finding Luca, now there's nothing but a blank screen.

"What happened?" I demand, panic clawing up my throat.

Alex's fingers fly across the keyboard, his expression morphing from triumph to horror. "It's some kind of automated purge protocol." He pulls up command lines, typing furiously. "As soon as the payment cleared, everything wiped itself from their servers."

"Can you recover it?" Oscar asks, his voice tight.

"I'm trying," Alex snaps, hunched over his keyboard like a man possessed. "But it's not just hidden or encrypted. It's gone. Completely scrubbed."

Z's grip on my shoulder tightens to the point of pain. "You said this wouldn't happen."

"It shouldn't have," Alex snaps back, not looking up from his desperate attempt to salvage something—anything— from the digital ashes. "This level of security is...fuck, it's better than military grade."

My stomach plummets as the reality sinks in. We've spent sixteen million dollars and have nothing to show for it. Alex's virus was our way into their systems. The safest way to find Luca, and it's gone in a matter of seconds.

"We still have the sample," Talon says firmly, breaking the heavy silence. "Plan B is still in play."

I nod mechanically, trying to cling to even the smallest thread of hope. "When do we get instructions for pickup?"

As if responding to my question, a notification pings on Alex's screen. A new message in the auction interface.

*Congratulations on your acquisition. Your purchase will be available for collection in 48 hours. Detailed instructions will be provided 12 hours prior to pick up time. Thank you for your patronage.*

"Two days." Oscar's thumb resuming its soothing circles on my palm. "That gives us time to prepare."

Z finally releases my shoulder, resuming his agitated pacing. "Or time for them to realize they've been compromised and change the location."

"They won't," Alex says, his voice hardening with renewed determination as he swivels in his chair. "The virus deployed exactly as designed. It was their security system that was better than anticipated. They have no way of knowing we attempted to access their systems."

"So we wait for the pickup instructions and follow the trail physically."

Alex nods. "We track the sample, find the facility, locate Luca."

I want to believe them. Need to believe them, but the crushing fear of another setback presses down on my chest, making it hard to breathe.

"I can't wait two more days. He's been captive for years. Every minute..."

Oscar pulls me against his chest, his arms encircling me in a protective embrace. "We're closer than we've ever been, solnishko. Two days and we'll have a direct line to their operation."

"What if they change the pickup location?" The words tumble out before I can stop them. "What if they realize something's wrong? What if—"

"They won't," Alex cuts in. "The virus was designed to

self-destruct after deployment. As far as they're concerned, the transaction was clean."

Z stops pacing, turning to face us with determination etched into his features. "We'll be ready. All of us."

Talon nods, his expression hardens. "We've been planning for this. Surveillance equipment, weapons, vehicles. We're ready to move at a moment's notice."

"And if they're expecting that?" I can't help the doubt creeping into my voice. "The Collector has stayed hidden for years. He has to be prepared for someone trying to track him."

"Then we'll be more prepared," Oscar says, his voice steady and reassuring against my ear.

"What do we do now?" I ask, pulling away from Oscar's embrace to look at each of them in turn.

Alex swivels back to his computer, fingers already typing again. "Now I monitor the network for any unusual activity. Any hint they might have detected us. If they do, we burn this location and head to the next one."

"We prepare, and Vesper trains."

Z nods in agreement. "If we're going in physically to extract Luca, she needs to be ready."

"I am ready," I insist, though the tremble in my voice betrays me.

"You're getting there," Talon offers. "But if we're potentially walking into The Collector's territory, you need more than basic self-defense."

"I need some air," I announce suddenly, pushing past

Talon toward the door. The walls of Alex's room feel like they're closing in.

No one tries to stop me as I hurry down the hallway and out onto the apartment's small balcony. The cool night air hits my face, a stark relief from the suffocating tension inside. I clutch the railing, fingers digging into the metal as I stare out at the city lights blurring through unshed tears.

Two more days of waiting. Two more days of not knowing if Luca is okay. Two more days for something to go wrong.

The sliding door opens behind me, but I don't turn. I know who it is without looking. Oscar's presence is unmistakable.

"I'm fine," I say before he can speak, the lie bitter on my tongue.

He doesn't respond immediately, just comes to stand beside me, his shoulder barely brushing mine as he leans against the railing. The silence stretches between us, not uncomfortable but heavy with everything unsaid.

"You don't have to be fine. Not with me."

Something in his tone breaks the dam I've been desperately trying to hold together. A sob escapes me, raw and painful. Oscar turns me toward him, gathering me against his chest as I finally let go.

"I thought we had him," I choke out between sobs, my fingers clutching the fabric of his shirt. "I thought it was over."

"I know, solnishko." His arms tighten around me. "But

this isn't a setback. It's progress. We're closer than we were yesterday."

I want to believe him. Need to believe him. But the disappointment of watching our digital lifeline disappear has left me hollow.

"What if he's suffering?" The words escape before I can stop them. My greatest fear finally given voice. I know what I endured in that place, but Luca...he may not have been afforded anesthesia like I had been during my procedures. "What if by the time we find him, he's..."

"Don't," Oscar says firmly. "Luca is alive. The sample proves that."

The certainty in his voice anchors me, even as tears continue to stream down my face. Oscar's thumb gently wipes them away, his touch so tender it makes my heart ache.

"Two days," I mutter, trying to convince myself. "We can do this."

"We can," he agrees. "And we will."

The sliding door opens again, and Z steps onto the balcony. His expression softening when he sees my tear-streaked face. Without a word, he moves to my other side, his hand settling on the small of my back.

"We got this far," he says quietly. "We're not stopping now."

His presence, combined with Oscar's, creates a cocoon of safety I hadn't realized I needed. The night air wraps around us, the distant sounds fade away as my sobs finally slow.

"What do you need, moya koroleva?"

"I need it to be over," I sob, the words raw and painful as they scrape past my throat. "I need to stop failing him."

Another sob wracks my body, but this time it transforms into something else—a sound closer to a growl than a cry. My fingers curl into fists at my sides as I pull away from Oscar's embrace.

"We were so close," I hiss, slamming my palm against the metal railing. The sting shoots up my arm, but I welcome the pain. It's cleaner than the ache in my chest. "So fucking close!"

"We still are close," Oscar tries, his voice placating.

"Don't!" I scream, spinning around to face him, my whole-body trembling with emotion that won't be contained. "Don't tell me to calm down! I don't want calm—I want my brother back! I want The Collector's head on a pike! I want—"

My voice cracks, the scream tearing out of me before it collapses into silence, strangled by the grief and fury clawing up my throat like barbed wire I can't choke down.

"You're right," Z agrees, "Being calm won't help."

Oscar shoots him a warning look, but Z ignores it, stepping closer to me.

"Come on," he says, taking my wrist. His grip is firm, but not painful, as he tugs me toward the door. "I have a better idea."

"Where are we going?" I demand.

"To the gym."

"The gym?" I stare at him incredulously. "You want me to work out right now?"

"I want you to hit something," he clarifies. "When every-thing is falling apart and you can't control it, at least you can control how hard your fist connects with something. And right now, you need to hit something before you explode."

I consider arguing, but there's a certain logic to his suggestion. He's right.

"Fine."

Z's grip on my wrist loosens as I follow him willingly toward the door. Oscar trails behind us, his presence a silent support as we make our way down to the basement gym.

The lights flicker to life, revealing the modest space where Talon has been training me.

Z crosses to the punching bag, giving it a testing push before turning to me. "No gloves. No wraps."

"That's not safe," Oscar objects from the doorway.

"It's not meant to be," Z counters. "Sometimes pain clarifies."

I step forward without hesitation, the rational part of my brain acknowledging that this is reckless, but the storm inside me doesn't care. My knuckles are already tingling in anticipation. Z positions himself behind the bag, bracing it with his body. "Hit it like you mean it. Like it's The Collector."

The name ignites something in me. I pull back my arm and drive my fist into the leather surface with a force that is laced with rage. Pain blossoms across my knuckles, sharp and immediate, but Z is right, it's cleansing.

"Again," Z commands.

I strike the bag again and again, each hit harder than the

last. The pain in my knuckles becomes a dull throb, then a sharp sting, morphing into something beyond pain—a fever beneath my skin that refuses to break.

"That's it," Z encourages, his voice rough with approval. "Let it out."

My fists connect in a rhythm that grows more frantic with each impact. Left, right, left, left, right. I pour everything into each punch—my fear for Luca, my rage at The Collector, my frustration at another dead end, my guilt for not finding him sooner. Blood smears across the leather, but I barely notice.

"He took everything from me," I snarl between blows. "My brother—" Punch. "My son—" Punch. "My choice  " Punch.

Oscar says something from behind me, concern lacing his voice, but Z silences him with a look. He understands that what I need right now isn't gentleness.

The world narrows to the sound of my fists hitting leather, the burn in my muscles, the copper taste of tears and sweat on my lips. I lose track of time, of how many blows I've landed. My vision blurs, not from tears now but from pure exhaustion.

With one final devastating punch, I throw everything I have left into the bag. My legs give out beneath me, and I collapse forward, suddenly boneless. Strong arms wrap around me, lowering me gently to the mat. I'm vaguely aware of Z's voice as he cradles me against his chest. A dull, persistent throb pulses through my fists, the skin across my knuckles split and bleeding.

"That's enough," Oscar says, kneeling beside us. His fingers gently take my wrists, turning my hands palm-up to examine the damage. His expression is tight with concern, but not reproachful. "You need ice."

I should feel something, pain, exhaustion, maybe even regret. There's only a strange, hollow calm. The storm that was raging inside me has burned itself out, leaving behind an eerie stillness that feels almost like peace.

# Chapter 17

ALEX

I'M STILL STARING at the blank screen like somehow, it'll change if I glare hard enough. Sixteen million dollars and all I have to show for it is a black void. Fucking amateur hour.

The others left my room hours ago, but the sting of failure hasn't dulled. I slam my fist against the desk, sending an empty energy drink clattering to the floor. The sound echoes in the silence of my room.

How did I miss this? A self-destruct protocol should have been the first thing I anticipated. It's Security 101 for criminal enterprises operating at this level. I've spent years hacking into systems more complex than Fort Knox, yet I walked right into this like some script kiddie on his first hack.

"Fucking idiot," I mutter.

The worst part isn't the money. It's the look on Vesper's face when those screens went black. The hope draining from her face, replaced by that hollow resignation I've come to recognize too well. She trusted me to find a digital path to her brother, and I failed her.

I pull up the transaction record again, the only evidence we have that the auction even happened. Sixteen million dollars transferred to a ghost account that's probably already been emptied and erased from existence. The pickup instructions are our only remaining lead, and even that feels tenuous now.

What if they don't send them? What if this was all an elaborate trap?

My door creaks open, and I don't have to look up to know who it is. Only one person in this apartment moves that silently.

"If you're here to tell me I fucked up, save it," I growl, still staring at my screens. "I'm well aware."

"Not why I'm here," Talon replies, shutting the door behind him. He crosses to my desk and sets down a steaming mug of coffee. Black, no sugar.

I grunt in acknowledgment, curling my fingers around the mug. "She okay?"

"Define okay." Talon leans against the wall, arms crossed. "Z took her to the gym. Let her beat the shit out of a punching bag until her knuckles bled. Oscar's patching her up now."

"Fuck." I take a scalding sip, welcoming the burn. "She shouldn't have to deal with this."

"None of us should." He studies me. "If we had been born into normal families, it would be different. But we weren't, so here we are." He pushes off from the wall and drags my spare chair over, straddling it backward. "So what's our next move?"

I set the mug down, the coffee turning bitter in my stomach. "I'm tracking the payment. Following every digital breadcrumb, setting up alerts for any system that might process those pickup instructions. When they send them, I'll know instantly."

"And if they don't send them?"

The question hangs between us, the possibility I've been avoiding since the screens went black.

"Then we're fucked." There's no sugarcoating that. We're out of the money, and Luca. The latter is a more devastating blow than the former. We can always make more money. We can't do the same for Luca.

Talon doesn't flinch at my bluntness. "We'd find another way. We always do."

"This was our best shot," I admit, the words tasting like ash. "The most direct line to The Collector's operation. If they ghost us after taking the money..."

"They won't."

"You don't know that."

"I do," Talon insists. "Think about it. The Collector's entire business model depends on reputation. If word gets out that he takes the money and doesn't deliver, his whole operation collapses."

It's logical, but logic feels tenuous right now. "Unless this was never about business. What if it's personal? What if they know who we are—where she is?"

"Then they'd have made their move already," Talon says, his voice steady with a confidence I wish I felt. "They wouldn't play games with sixteen million dollars just to mess with us."

He's right. I turn back to my screens. Talon watches me work in silence for a few minutes, his expression unreadable in the blue glow from my monitors. "You should get some sleep."

"Not an option."

"Alex—"

"I said no." My voice comes out harsher than intended. I exhale slowly. "I can't, okay? Not until I know we haven't completely fucked this up."

Talon studies me. "This isn't just about the auction, is it?"

I keep typing, ignoring his question.

"You're punishing yourself. For what happened with Vesper," Talon finishes. "For watching her through the cameras."

My fingers freeze over the keyboard.

"You weren't going to bring that up. Not until all of this is done. Have you changed your mind?"

"That was before you decided to spiral into self-destruction." He leans closer. "You think drowning in guilt is going to help her? Help us find Luca?"

I slam my laptop closed, the sound sharp in the quiet room. "What do you want from me, Talon? A fucking apology? Fine. I'm sorry I watched. I'm sorry I'm a goddamn creep who couldn't look away. Happy now?"

"This isn't about me being happy." His voice remains infuriatingly calm. "It's about you being functional. We need you at your best, not wallowing in self-loathing because you made a mistake."

"A mistake?" I laugh, the sound hollow and bitter. "Is that what we're calling it? I violated her privacy in the worst possible way, then lied to her face about it."

"And you took down the cameras like you promised."

"Only after getting caught," I snap. "Let's not pretend I'm some noble bastard who did the right thing. I was jerking off to her getting fucked. There's no coming back from that."

"Do you honestly think I would have outed you? Get a fucking grip, Alex. I would have lorded it over you in private, but I would have never say anything to her, Z, or Oz. I don't have a death wish for you." Talon says, leaning back. "We need you here. Fighting for her. Trying to find her brother. This fucking rescue mission doesn't happen without you."

I shake my head, unable to accept the absolution he's offering. "It doesn't erase what I did."

"No, it doesn't." Talon's frankness catches me off guard. "But beating yourself up isn't going to help her."

The truth in his words stings worse than any accusation. I reopen my laptop, illuminating the screen.

"You really care about her, don't you? It's not just guilt."

The question hangs between us, demanding honesty I'm not sure I'm capable of. I've spent years building walls, keeping everyone at a safe distance. Even these men—the closest thing I have to a family. Other than my sister, who is an ocean away from me at the fancy boarding school until our father can marry her off.

I stare at the keyboard, suddenly fascinated by the worn letters, anything to avoid the smirk I know is on his face.

"What difference does it make?"

"All the difference in the world," he responds. "Because if it's just guilt, you'll keep punishing yourself until you're useless to everyone. But if it's more…"

"Then what?" I snap. "What magical solution does that provide? She's already got three men falling over themselves for her. You think she needs another fucked-up asshole in the mix?"

Talon's expression doesn't change. "Dude, you're so fucking blind. She needs all of us. Every single one of us. Even you."

"You didn't see her face when those screens went black," I say, deflecting. "The way she looked at me like I personally failed her."

"I saw her face just fine," Talon counters. "What I didn't see was blame. That's all in your head."

I let out a bitter sound that barely qualifies as a laugh, rough and raw in my throat. "Add it to the fucking list."

I turn back to my work, hoping he'll take the hint and leave. But Talon remains stubbornly in place.

"The twins are crowding her," he says after a moment of silence. "Z, especially. She needs space to breathe sometimes."

"And I'm supposed to be that space?" I scoff. "The creep who watches her from security feeds? Yeah, I'm sure that's just what she needs."

"You're not giving her enough credit," Talon says. "Or yourself."

I snort, fingers returning to the keyboard. The code flows almost automatically, my brain operating on muscle memory while my thoughts scatter in a dozen different directions. "You've got a real talent for bullshit, you know that?"

"It's called perspective," Talon counters. "Something you could use right now."

A notification pings on my second monitor—one of my dark web crawlers has picked up something. I switch screens immediately, scanning the alert.

"What is it?" Talon asks, leaning forward.

"Chatter about the auction," I mutter, already diving into the encrypted message board. "Someone's complaining about losing the bid on Lot 27."

"Our lot," Talon confirms, moving to stand behind me.

I nod, translating the coded language on the fly. "They're pissed they lost to a newcomer—that would be us. They are asking around about 'Charles Blackwood.'"

"Is that a problem?"

"Not necessarily," I say, quickly setting up a monitoring

protocol for the username. ". As long as they're just bitching and not actively investigating..."

Another ping, this one from a different alert system. My heart rate accelerates as I click through to the source. A different forum, a different user, but the same topic, the mysterious Charles Blackwood, who outbid everyone on Lot 27.

"Shit," I mutter, opening three more windows to track the spread of interest. "It's picking up traction."

"Can they trace it back to us?" Talon's voice remains steady, but I can hear the undercurrent of tension.

"Not through my security measures," I say, fingers flying across the keyboard. "But if enough people start digging into Charles Blackwood's background, they might realize the identity doesn't hold up to scrutiny."

I deploy another layer of digital misinformation, seeding false details about Charles Blackwood across several hidden web forums and his wealthy, reclusive family based in Geneva. Enough to seem credible but impossible to verify.

"Do you think that will work?"

"It has to," I mutter, launching one final algorithm to obscure our digital footprint. "If they link Charles Blackwood to us, we're exposed."

"You've covered our tracks. We're secure."

"For now," I admit, scanning the alerts with growing unease. "But if The Collector decides to investigate personally..."

The thought lingers, heavy with consequences. If The

Collector uncovers the truth behind Charles Blackwood, Vesper becomes a target again. Worse, they could move Luca before we have a chance to find him. Sixteen million dollars lost—and the one person we're desperate to save slipping through our fingers.

"I need to monitor this."

"You need to sleep," Talon counters. "Even for a few hours."

"Not happening."

"Alex—"

"I said no." My voice is flat, final.

"Two hours. Then I'm taking over."

"Always the mother hen," I mutter. "Does it get exhausting being the good guy all the time?"

"No," he admits. "Maybe you should try it sometime. You might actually allow yourself to be happy."

"Fuck off," I growl. Talon just quirks his lips, immune to my prickly bullshit after all these years.

"Two hours," he repeats, rising from the chair. "Then I'm back, whether you like it or not."

The door clicks shut behind him, and I'm alone again. I dive back into the code, setting up more sophisticated monitoring systems, creating digital tripwires that will alert me to any unusual activity.

Time blurs as I work, the minutes bleeding into each other. My eyes burn. Sleep is a luxury I can't afford.

The soft ping of an incoming message pulls me from my coding trance. A web forum I've been monitoring—someone else asking about Charles Blackwood. I deploy another false trail, seeding information about the reclusive billionaire with exotic tastes.

My phone buzzes with a timer alert. Talon's two hours are up. I ignore it, continuing to fortify our digital defenses. Let him come and try to drag me away from this desk. I'll chain myself to it if I have to.

Minutes tick by, but Talon doesn't return. Maybe he's finally learned to take a hint.

There's a soft rap at my door. I grunt, pushing back from my desk with a wince. My muscles scream in protest as I stand, stiff from hours hunched over my keyboard. Every joint pops as I stretch, the physical reminder of how long I've been sitting in the same position.

"Coming," I mutter, assuming it's Talon back to nag me about sleep. He's nothing if not persistent.

I drag myself to the door, already preparing my 'fuck off, I'm working' speech. But when I swing it open, the words die in my throat.

Vesper stands in the hallway, her blonde hair catching the first rays of sunlight streaming through the apartment windows. She's wearing a loose tank top and yoga pants, like she's just come from a workout. Her knuckles are freshly bandaged, white gauze stark against her skin.

"Hey," she says, her voice soft but steady. "Can I come in?"

I blink stupidly, my sleep-deprived brain struggling to process her presence. Vesper. At my door. Voluntarily. After I failed to find her brother.

"Alex?" she prompts when I don't immediately respond.

"Yeah, sorry." I step aside, suddenly self-conscious about my disheveled appearance.

"Did Talon send you?" I ask, already knowing the answer. My voice sounds rough even to my own ears.

She hesitates for just a moment before nodding. "He did, but I would have come anyway. I'm worried about you, too."

Of course she is. Even after I fucked everything up, she's still here, checking on me like I deserve her compassion.

"Vesper, I'm so sorry about the auction," I start, the words rushing out. "I should have anticipated their security protocols, should have had better contingencies in place. Sixteen million dollars and all we got was—"

Her fingers press against my lips, silencing me mid-sentence. The unexpected touch sends a jolt through my system, my body suddenly hyper aware of her proximity. Her skin is warm against mine, the faint scent of her shampoo—something floral and clean—cutting through the stale air of my room.

"Don't," she says firmly. "This isn't your fault."

I gently remove her hand, though every cell in my body protests. "It is, though. Security systems are my specialty. I should have seen this coming."

"Even you can't predict everything," she counters, stepping further into my room and closing the door behind her.

"I should have seen it coming," I insist, pacing now. "Anyone with half a brain would have anticipated a data wipe protocol. It's standard procedure for high-level criminal enterprises. I got cocky and—"

"Alex, stop." Vesper moves directly into my path, forcing

me to halt or collide with her. "Look at yourself. When's the last time you slept?"

I wave dismissively. "Sleep is irrelevant. We have forty-eight hours until pickup, and I need to monitor these forums. Someone's asking questions about Charles Blackwood. If they connect him to us..."

"You're dead on your feet," she interrupts, reaching up to touch my face. "You can't help anyone like this."

"I'm fine," I mutter, though my body betrays me with a massive yawn. "Just need more coffee."

"What you need is sleep." Vesper's tone leaves no room for argument as she steers me toward my bed. "Six hours, minimum."

I resist, planting my feet. "I can't. Not with everything that's happening. Those forums—"

"Will still be there after you've rested." She pushes against my chest, surprisingly strong as she forces me to sit on the edge of my bed. "Your algorithms will alert you if anything critical happens."

"Vesper, I appreciate the concern, but I don't have time for this."

"Yes, you do."

"No, I don't," I insist, trying to stand back up. "There's too much at stake."

Vesper shoves me back down. "You do have time because I'm making time for you. I'm not leaving until you get some rest, even if that means that I stay right here with you."

"That's ridiculous," I scoff, though my traitorous body

sways slightly under her touch. "You don't need to babysit me."

"Clearly I do," she counters. "Since you refuse to take care of yourself."

I open my mouth to argue further, but she presses one finger against my lips.

"Enough, Alex. Bed. Now."

Something about her tone makes my protest die in my throat. Her voice carries an authority I've never heard from her before. And to my complete confusion, I find myself responding to it, my resistance crumbling.

"I need to check—"

"The only thing you need to check is the inside of your eyelids," she interrupts, stepping closer until her knees brush against mine. "Don't make me force you."

"You're going to force me? How exactly?"

A mischievous smile crosses her face. "Try me and find out."

She places her palms on my chest and gives a gentle but firm push. Caught off guard, I topple backward onto the mattress. Before I can react, Vesper swings her leg over me, sitting on my hips, one hand pressing against my sternum to keep me in place.

Fuck, she feels good. Her cunt so close to my cock. All that separates us is the thin material of her leggings. Material that would take no effort at all to rip away. To take what I want. What she has freely offered me twice already.

*Not the time, asshole.*

"See? Not so hard," she says, her voice softening as she looks down at me.

I should protest. Should push her away and get back to my monitors, but my body isn't as willing as my mind.

"Six hours," I negotiate, already feeling my body surrendering to the pull of exhaustion.

"Eight," she counters.

"Seven," I offer, "and I get to set an alarm."

Vesper considers this, then nods. "Deal. But I'm staying to make sure you actually sleep."

"That's not necessary," I mumble, though the thought of her keeping watch over me sends an unexpected warmth through my chest.

"It absolutely is," she insists, shifting off me to sit more comfortably beside me. "I don't trust you not to sneak back to your computer."

She's not wrong. I exhale slowly, the fight draining out of me. My eyelids feel impossibly heavy, my limbs leaden.

"Fine," I concede, "but this is completely ridiculous."

"So you've said. Now close your eyes."

The irony isn't lost on me. She is comforting me when I'm the one who failed her. But I'm too exhausted to fight it, too selfish to push her away.

With one quick motion, I tug her beside me, wrapping my arm around her waist before she can protest. Her body tenses in surprise, but I hold firm, pulling her closer until her back is flush against my chest.

"Alex," she gasps. "What are you doing?"

"Compromising," I mumble against her head, inhaling the scent of her shampoo. "If I'm sleeping, so are you."

"This wasn't part of the deal."

"I'm renegotiating," I reply, my words already slurring as exhaustion pulls me under. "Fair's fair."

We fall silent, our breathing gradually synchronizing in the quiet room. Her presence in my arms feels right in a way I can't articulate, like a missing piece slotting into place. My thumb traces idle circles on her hip, a soothing gesture as much for me as for her.

The steady rise and fall of her chest slows, becoming more rhythmic. I fight against my own exhaustion just to savor this moment a little longer.

"Sleep, Alex," she orders. "I'll be here when you wake up."

Those words settle something within me. My eyes grow impossibly heavy, and I finally surrender to the exhaustion that's been clawing at me for days. As consciousness begins to slip away, I feel her fingers intertwine with mine against her stomach. The last thing I register is the soft, even cadence of her breathing, a lullaby drawing me into oblivion.

# Chapter 18

ZAIRE

MY KNEE WON'T STOP BOUNCING. Six hours. She's been in there with him for six fucking hours. I check my watch again, though the time hasn't changed since I looked thirty seconds ago.

"If you keep that up, you're going to wear a hole in the floor," Oscar says, not looking up from his phone. My twin's calm exterior would fool anyone else, but I know better. The slight tension in his jaw, the fact that his phone doesn't have a single app open, he's just as concerned as I am. He's just better at hiding it.

"It's been six hours," I mutter, standing to pace the length of our living room. "What the hell are they doing in there?"

"Sleeping," Talon answers from his spot on the armchair, scrolling through his phone. "Like normal humans do after being awake for forty-eight hours straight."

"Together," I point out, the word coming out sharper than intended. *Shit. Get a hold of yourself.*

Talon raises an eyebrow. "Jealous?"

"Concerned," I correct, though the burning sensation in my gut suggests otherwise. "Alex isn't exactly the warm and fuzzy type."

"She went in to make sure he actually slept instead of working himself to death," Oscar reminds me. "Which is what we all agreed needed to happen. Out of all of us, she is the only person he'll listen to."

"We agreed someone should check on him," I counter. "Not crawl into bed with him."

Talon snorts. "You don't know that's what happened. She could have him tied down to the bed for all we know."

"Really?" I mutter, though Oscar's poorly concealed smirk tells me he disagrees.

"What? Desperate times call for desperate measures."

"You're overthinking this," Oscar says, finally setting his phone down. "They're sleeping. That's it."

"You don't know that," I counter.

"'And you don't know otherwise," he replies evenly. "Getting worked up over hypotheticals is pointless."

I hate when he's reasonable. It's infuriating how he can remain so composed while I feel like I'm about to crawl out of my skin. The rational part of my brain knows he's right. We all agreed Vesper would check on Alex, make sure he got some rest before he collapsed. But rationality is in short supply when it comes to her. Alex is and always has been our wildcard. A genius with a kill count. While I know he won't purposely hurt Vesper, a part of me can't be certain that he won't.

"Still, I don't like it," I mutter, resuming my pacing.

"What exactly don't you like?" Oscar sets his phone down, finally giving up the pretense of distraction. "That she might be connecting with someone besides us? Or that it's Alex specifically?"

"Both. Neither. He's not...he doesn't know how to be gentle with her."

"Have you seen our girl's knuckles lately? After you let her beat a punching bag until she bled? Glass houses, Z."

"That was different," I snap. "She needed that."

"And maybe she needs this too," Oscar says quietly. "She's not just ours, Z. She never was.""

The truth of his words lands like a blow. We've been so focused on protecting her, on keeping her safe within the boundaries we've established, that we've forgotten she isn't something to be possessed.

"I know that," I mutter, though the admission costs me.

"Do you?" Talon challenges. "Because from where I'm sitting, you're about two seconds away from kicking down his door and throwing her over your shoulder. You know, this jealousy issue of yours would be more in control if you accept that at some point, now, or later, Vesper and Alex will happen. It happened with you, Oz, and me. It's inevitable, and her choice."

I am well aware it is her choice. I just don't have to like it.

"The four of us need to sit down. Hash it out, preferably without bloodshed, make decisions, set boundaries, and move on. We could call it the LPM."

Oz stares at Talon. Eyebrow arched. "And that means?"

"Love Pentagon Meeting. Get it?"

"No," Oz and I answer at the same time.

"Oh, come on, it would solve all of our problems. We can meet monthly, discuss schedules, and figure out the room sharing situation. Think about it. No more stepping on toes or awkward interruptions. I mean, I love you guys, but I want time alone with her, too."

"The answer is still no."

"Aw, come on, it could be a great bonding experience for all of us. We could each come up with our couple names. Dibs on Tesper," Talon smiles at me. "Oh! Yours could be Vere. No, we can do better than that..." he trails off.

"I hate you, Talon."

"That's not true," Talon grins with an infuriatingly smug look. "You adore me."

"Can't say I see it that way," I retort, attempting to keep my frustration from spilling over.

"Oh, I think you do," Talon shoots back, an insufferable teasing edge to his voice. "I could act offended, but I know you don't really mean it."

"But I really do." I glare at him, however, my irritation only seems to fuel his amusement.

"I have to admit I kind of like seeing you so on edge. So... what's the word I am looking for, Oz?"

"Unstable? Capricious?" Oscar offers without hesitation, clearly enjoying my unraveling.

"Okay, Merriam Webster," I snap, the defensiveness raw in my tone. "Still not funny."

Unable to suppress his smile Talon adds, "It's amusing to watch you uncomfortable."

Oscar chuckles. "Vesper's got you just where you deserve."

"Strung out?" Talon suggests. "A nervous wreck?"

"Shut up. Both of you," I mutter, though their relentless banter starts to chip away at my resolve.

"We should document this," Oscar continues, sounding far too pleased.

"Don't you dare," I warn them both.

"Z is growing a sense of humor. Next thing you know, he'll start having fun. Speaking of fun," Talon chimes in, his grin widening. "I've been thinking about something. When's the last time you saw Alex with anyone? Like, actually with someone. Dating, hooking up, whatever."

The question catches me off guard. I pause my pacing, trying to recall a single instance of Alex bringing someone home or mentioning a date.

"I can't remember," I admit reluctantly. "But that doesn't mean—"

"Exactly," Talon cuts in. "In the three years I've known him, not once. Not a single person. I was starting to think he was in a committed relationship with his computer."

Oscar lets out a low chuckle. "He does spend more time with it than any human."

"He doesn't broadcast his hook-ups."

"Hook-ups require leaving your room occasionally," Talon points out. "When does he ever go out unless it's for a job?"

I frown, trying to counter his logic and coming up empty. I hate that Talon's right. But as much as I'd like to deny it, the signs have been there all along. Alex tracks her across rooms. The way he softens, just barely, when she speaks. How he lets her into spaces he keeps locked away to the rest of us. It's the same gravitational pull we've all felt, drawing us into her orbit one by one.

"Look, I'm not saying you need to throw a parade for him," Talon continues, his voice gentler now. "But maybe cut the guy some slack. This thing with Vesper...it's different for him."

"Different how?" I challenge, though part of me already knows the answer.

"She makes him human, Z. Just like she does for you. For all of us."

The truth in his words cuts deeper than I want to admit. Before Vesper crashed into our lives, we were functional at best—damaged men working together out of necessity, not choice. But now, there's something different holding us together. Vesper.

When we got her back, something shifted in all of us. She became the center of everything. The constant. The one pulling us home like four lost ships in a storm.

She's the gravity that keeps us from drifting too far. The reason we fight. The reason we stay.

"I still don't like it," I mutter, but the heat has drained from my words.

"You don't have to like it," Oscar says. "You just have to respect it. Her choice."

The sound of a door opening down the hall silences us all. We turn collectively, watching as Vesper emerges from Alex's room. She pauses when she notices us all staring, a faint blush coloring her cheeks.

"Hi," she yawns, padding barefoot into the living room. "Alex is still out. I didn't want to wake him."

"And you?" I ask, unable to keep the edge from my voice. "How did you sleep?"

"Better than I have in days, actually."

Something in her expression dares me to make an issue of it. I swallow the jealousy rising in my throat, forcing myself to nod. "Good."

"You know this place echoes, right?" she mentions as she shuffles by me and settles onto the couch next to Oz, curling her body against his.

"Which means?" Talon asks, his smug expression faltering slightly.

"Which means I heard your entire conversation," she replies, her voice still husky with sleep. "Every word of it."

My stomach drops. Fuck. I shoot a glance at Oscar, whose impassive expression betrays nothing, though I catch the slight tensing of his jaw.

"Mmmhmm," Vesper confirms, stretching her arms above her head. The movement causes her shirt to ride up, revealing a sliver of skin at her waist. "The Love Pentagon Meeting, Talon? Really?"

"Just throwing ideas out there. Creative problem-solving."

She rolls her eyes but can't suppress a small smile. "And you," she turns to me. "We've talked about this. Do we really need to talk about your possessiveness again?" I open my mouth, then close it, unable to find a response that doesn't make me sound like an asshole.

"That's what I thought. For the record, we did just sleep, despite my best efforts."

I don't miss the comment, but I let it go.

"He turned you down?" Talon interjects before he stops himself. "You know what. That's not my business."

"You're right, it's not. What I have with each of you, is just that, ours."

Her direct challenge leaves me no room to maneuver, no space to hide behind excuses or deflection. The truth is, I hate the thought of her with Alex, but I hate disappointing her more.

Oscar's arm slides around her. "We won't. Z is just worried about you."

"I appreciate the concern, but I don't need three body-guards monitoring my every move."

"Four," comes a rough voice from the hallway.

We all turn to see Alex leaning against the wall. He looks almost human without his usual sharp alertness, softer somehow. Vulnerable in a way I've never seen him.

"I thought you were asleep," Vesper says, surprise evident in her voice.

"I was until I heard voices."

"Sorry," Talon offers, not sounding particularly apologetic. "We were just discussing our...arrangement."

"So I gathered." He pushes off from the wall and makes his way toward the kitchen, his movements still slow with lingering fatigue. "Coffee. I need coffee before whatever this is."

I watch him carefully, searching for any sign of what transpired between him and Vesper. There's something different about him. Something I can't quite place that sets my teeth on edge.

"How long was I out?" he asks, measuring coffee grounds with meticulous precision.

"About six hours," Vesper answers. "Not nearly enough, but it's a start."

Alex grunts in acknowledgment, his focus on the brewing coffee. The domesticity of the scene feels jarringly out of place. Alex in his rumpled clothes making coffee while Vesper watches him with something that looks like fondness. The coffee machine hisses and sputters, filling the awkward silence that's fallen between us. I can feel Oscar's stare on me, a silent warning to keep my emotions in check. He's right. This isn't the time for jealousy or territorial bullshit. Not when we're all off balance waiting for the pickup instructions that will lead us to Luca.

He stalks back to the living room, coffee in hand, and

plops on the couch on the other side of Vesper, who shifts away from my brother, settling between them both.

"Let's get this over with." Alex stares at me over the rim of his coffee mug as he takes another sip. "The sooner we get through this territorial alpha male showdown you're all dancing around, the better."

His directness catches me off guard. The Alex I know avoids emotional confrontations like they're contagious diseases. "There's nothing to address," I lie, crossing my arms. "We're good."

Vesper snorts. "Sure you are. That's why I could feel the tension from down the hallway."

Alex sets his mug down, his expression surprisingly open. "Look, I get it. I'm the outlier here. You three have your...arrangement with Vesper. I'm not trying to disrupt that. It's simple. I care about Vesper. You three care about Vesper. We all want to find her brother. Everything else is secondary."

"Everything else, meaning what exactly?" I press, needing him to spell it out.

"Meaning whatever happens between any of us and Vesper is her choice," Alex calmly offers. "Not yours, Z. Not Oscar's. Not Talon's. And not mine either."

"Well," Talon chuckles, clapping his hands together. "That was refreshingly direct."

Vesper leans forward. "Each of you gives me something different, something I need," she continues, her fingers squeezing mine gently. "With Oz, it's understanding. With

Talon, it's laughter. With Alex, it's...space to breathe. And with you, Z, it's safety. Protection. I need all of that. All of you."

I swallow hard, fighting against the possessive instinct that's been my default for so long. "And that's enough for you? This...arrangement?"

She shakes her head. "It's about what makes me happy. And right now, having all of you in my life, in different ways, is what I want. The only thing I want, besides finding Luca."

Something shifts inside me as I look at her—this fierce, beautiful woman who's somehow become the center of our fractured world. She's not asking for my permission or my blessing.

"Okay," I say finally, the word feeling insufficient, but it's all I can manage. "Okay."

Vesper's smile is like watching the sun erupt through clouds after a storm.

Oscar shifts beside her. I see the same understanding on his face that I've always counted on—my twin, my other half, knowing exactly what this costs me without a word being spoken.

"So, now that we've established this very modern arrangement, can we get back on track and focus on finding Luca?"

Alex drains the rest of his coffee and sets the mug down with a decisive click. "Sounds good to me. Let me grab my laptop." Alex pushes himself off the couch and heads toward his room, his movements still showing traces of the exhaustion he's fighting.

I watch him go. This new understanding we've reached feels fragile, like a freshly formed truce that could shatter with one wrong move. She settles into Oz's side, her head resting against his shoulder as we wait.

Talon gives me a small nod of approval. Maybe he's right. Maybe this arrangement isn't as impossible as it seems.

The floorboards creak as Alex returns, but the moment I see his face, everything else fades. He's clutching his laptop like a lifeline, fingers locked so tightly around the metal it looks as if he might crush it.

"They sent them," he says. "The pickup instructions. They just came through."

Vesper bolts upright, suddenly rigid with tension. "When? Where?"

"Tomorrow. 8 PM. Martha's Vineyard. They've sent coordinates for a dock on the north side of the island."

"That's not good," Oscar mutters, already on his feet. "The island is only accessible by boat or plane."

"It's not, but that's not the biggest issue we have right now."

Vesper stands, her body vibrating with a barely contained energy that mirrors my own. "Show me," she demands, moving to Alex's side to peer at his screen. Alex turns the laptop toward her, the screen illuminating her face in a harsh blue glow.

*Congratulations on your acquisition. Sample LR-0723 will be available for pickup tomorrow at 20:00 EST. Coordinates attached. Buyer must be present to complete the transaction. Authentication protocols will be in place. Any deviation will result in immediate termination of the agreement. Storage container will be provided. Payment has been processed. This concludes our business.*

"Buyer must be present," Talon repeats slowly. "Meaning Charles Blackwood. Me."

"This feels like a trap," I say, moving closer to examine the details.

"We don't know that," Alex counters, setting his laptop on the coffee table so we can all see the message. "Think about it. At Vesper's auction, all potential buyers appeared in person. It may just be their business model. You can't dispute a transaction if the buyer picks it up personally instead of by courier."

"But it's not just verification they're after," Oscar says, leaning forward to study the message more closely. "They're adding authentication protocols. They want to make sure Charles Blackwood is who he claims to be."

"Which he's not," I point out, the reality of our situation becoming clearer by the second. "He's a digital ghost we created."

Vesper's fingers curl around the edge of the laptop. "Can we fake it? Create some kind of physical documentation for Talon to present?"

"Possibly. But we'd need to know what kind of authentication they're planning to use. If it's just basic ID verification, we can handle that. If they're cross-referencing with other databases or contacts..."

"Then we're screwed," Talon finishes bluntly.

"Not necessarily. Remember, Charles Blackwood has

already shown up in person for a high-value purchase. This may just be a formality," Alex continues, fingers already flying across the keyboard. "Sixteen million is a drop in the bucket compared to what they think we spent on Vesper. They'll be expecting the same face."

"But even if that's the case," I interject, already seeing the next problem, "how the hell do we get there? Martha's Vineyard is an island. We don't own a boat or a plane.".

"We could charter something," Talon suggests.

"Too much of a paper trail," Oz argues back.

Alex looks up from his laptop. "I have that covered. I can get us a plane."

"And the pilot?"

"You're looking at him."

"You can fly a plane?" I stare at Alex in disbelief. The tech genius keeps revealing new layers like some kind of Russian nesting doll.

"Got my license when I was sixteen," he shrugs as if it's the most natural thing in the world. "My father insisted. Said every man of means should know how to pilot his own aircraft."

"And when was the last time you actually flew?" Oscar asks, ever the practical one.

Alex hesitates just long enough to make me nervous. "It's been a while, but it's like riding a bike. Once you learn, you don't forget."

"A bike doesn't plummet thirty thousand feet if you wobble," I point out.

"We won't be at thirty thousand feet," Alex counters

with a smirk. "Small aircraft, low altitude. Besides, I've logged the over two hundred hours necessary. Trust me, I can get us there."

"What about the rest of us?" Vesper asks.

"The rest of you aren't coming," Talon states. "Just me and Alex."

"The instructions were clear. Talon is the only one who can do the pickup. I have to go to get him there. The rest of you need to hang back," Alex demands.

Vesper crosses her arms, her stance widening as she plants herself firmly in the center of our group. "I'm going." Her voice catches slightly on the word, but she powers through. "I'm not sitting this out."

"It's not up for debate," Talon says, his tone gentler than mine but no less firm. "You're the one person who absolutely cannot be there. Alex and I will go and get the sample. It's the safest option."

I hate that we're doing this to her, forcing her to stay behind while we chase the one lead that might bring Luca home. But I hate the alternative more—her in the clutches of The Collector again, or worse.

"We leave at noon," Alex announces, pushing away from the coffee table. I watch as he disappears down the hallway, his footsteps fading as he descends the stairs towards the basement. Talon nods to Oscar before heading to his room, presumably to pack.

"I want to go," she insists. "Please."

"There's very little I would deny you, solnishko, but

please understand, you need to stay back with Zaire and me. It's for the best."

For a moment, I think she's going to argue further, but instead, she just shakes her head and turns away. I expect her to retreat to her room, but instead, she heads for the basement stairs.

After Alex.

# Chapter 19



THE BASEMENT STAIRS CREAK, betraying my presence with every step. I don't care. Let Alex hear me coming. Let him prepare whatever bullshit arguments he thinks will keep me on the sidelines while they chase down the only lead to my brother.

The air grows cooler as I descend to Alex's sanctuary—the place where he keeps his most secretive tools and sharpest skills hidden from casual eyes. I find him exactly where I expected, hunched over the weapons cabinet, methodically checking a matte black handgun before sliding it into a shoulder holster.

"I'm going with you," I announce it like a fact, not a request.

Alex doesn't even look up. "No, you're not."

"It wasn't a question." I move closer, positioning myself between him and the cabinet. "It's my brother."

"Which is exactly why you can't come." His voice is maddeningly calm. "You're too close to this, Vesper. Too recognizable. Too valuable."

"Too valuable?" I repeat, anger flaring hot in my chest. "I'm not some priceless vase you need to keep on a high shelf. I *am* going with you and Talon."

"No, you're not," Alex says, sliding past me to access another drawer in the cabinet. "And you know why."

I grab his arm, forcing him to face me. "We're this close," I hold my thumb and forefinger a hair's width apart, "and you're telling me to sit at home like some helpless princess waiting for her knights to return? Not happening."

Alex studies me for a long moment, his expression unreadable. Then he sighs, setting down the magazine he was holding.

"You think I don't understand?" His voice drops lower, more intimate somehow. "Vesper, if they see you, if they even suspect you're there, everything falls apart. This isn't about keeping you safe, though that's part of it. This is about getting Luca back."

"I'll stay hidden," I argue. "They'll never know I'm there."

"You can't promise that." He steps closer, close enough that I can smell the coffee on his breath. "These people took everything from you once already. Don't give them the chance to do it again."

"So I'm just supposed to what? Sit here and wait? While you and Talon risk your lives?"

"Yes." His bluntness is infuriating. "That's exactly what you're supposed to do."

I turn away, pacing the length of the basement, frustration building with each step. I hate that Alex is right.

I hate even more that I can't argue with his logic.

"I can't just do nothing," I finally say, my voice softer but no less determined.

Alex returns to his preparations, methodically checking each weapon before placing it in a black duffel bag. "You won't be doing nothing. You'll be coordinating with us from here. Oscar's

setting up a command center in the living room."

"That's not the same, and you know it." I lean against the workbench, eyes tracking the movements of his fingers. The same ones that held me as I slept just hours ago. "What if something goes wrong?"

"Something always goes wrong," he replies without looking up. "That's why we plan for contingencies."

I push off from the bench and move closer, deliberately invading his space. "And what's the contingency if they recognize Talon? What then?"

Alex finally stops what he's doing, setting down the knife he was inspecting. "Then we adapt," he says simply. "Like we always do."

"Not good enough."

"It has to be." His voice softens. "Vesper, I get it. I do. But this is the play we have to make."

I shake my head, frustrated tears threatening to fall. I blink them back, refusing to show weakness.

"You need backup. Not just Talon, "I insist. "Z and Oscar—"

"Are staying here with you," Alex finishes firmly. "If this goes sideways, you'll need protection. The last thing we want is to leave you vulnerable."

The truth of his words hits me like a physical blow. They're not just worried about me being recognized. They're worried about The Collector making a move against me while they're away. Using me as leverage if they discover who Charles Blackwood really is.

"I hate this," I admit.

"I know you do," he says. "But Luca needs you to be smart right now, not brave. There will be plenty of time for that after we get him home. He's going to need you. You're the only person who knows what he's gone through."

His words strike a chord deep within me. I've been so focused on doing something, anything, that I haven't considered what Luca would actually want. He wouldn't want me risking my safety, putting myself back in The Collector's crosshairs.

"Fine," I concede, though the word tastes bitter. "Promise me something? Promise me you'll bring Talon back. If something goes wrong, he'll be the first one to volunteer to try to fix it."

"I will," he answers flatly.

"The same goes for you. You seem to be more sensible than the rest of them, but I can't lose you either. As much as I want my brother back, I refuse to sacrifice you or Talon in the process."

I don't plan what happens next. One moment I'm standing there, begging Alex to come back to me, and the next, I'm pressing my lips against his. I deepen the kiss, drawing him closer. For once, I want to infiltrate that meticulous self-control he wears like armor. I want to see what lies beneath.

Alex responds by backing me against the weapons cabinet, the metal cool against my shoulder blades as his body presses against mine. One hand slides up to cradle my face, his thumb tracing my cheekbone with surprising gentleness, even as his kiss grows more demanding until he pulls away from me

"That wasn't fair."

"I don't play fair. Not when it matters."

"Vesper…" He takes a deliberate step back, putting space between us. "This isn't the time. You're looking for a distraction, and I told you. I will not be that for you."

"If we keep waiting for the right moment, Alex, it will never arrive. We keep hoping for a time without distractions, but we both know there will always be something. Even if we manage to bring my brother back, we'll just be bracing for the next crisis," I declare, rallying the courage to finish. "You told me to make the decision. Well, I'm making it."

His jaw clenches, a muscle ticking beneath the surface as he studies me. The basement feels suddenly smaller, charged with an electricity that makes the air heavy between us.

"You don't know what you're asking for. Not with me."

"I'm not asking for anything," I counter, stepping forward to close the distance he created. "I'm telling you what I want. There's a difference."

Something shifts in his expression, as if he's physically restraining himself from reaching for me.

"You deserve better than what I can give you. Better than what I am."

"That's not for you to decide." I place my palm against his chest, feeling his heart pounding beneath my touch. "I know exactly who you are, Alex. I've seen your shadows. I've witnessed what you're capable of, and I'm still here."

"No, you haven't. Not all of it."

"Then show me," I challenge, tilting my chin up. "Stop hiding from me."

Alex's expression hardens, his eyes turning cold in a way I've never seen before. He moves with startling speed, gripping my wrists and pinning them above my head against the weapons cabinet.

The metal digs into my back as he leans in, his breath hot against my ear.

"You think you want this? I'm not like them, Vesper. Not like Oscar, Z, or Talon. They want to please you, worship you, give you whatever you need." His grip tightens, not enough to hurt but enough to make his point. "I want to break you until there's nothing left. Until you're shattered and remade in the image I choose."

His words should repel me, but instead, they draw me closer, like a moth to a flame.

"I can't love you the way they do," he continues. "I don't have that softness in me. It was carved out long ago."

I stare back. "I never asked for softness."

His laugh is low and empty. "You say that now. But when you see what I really am—what I'm capable of—you'll run. They always do."

"I'm not them," I fire back. "I'm already broken, Alex. The Collector made sure of that. He took pieces of me I'll never get back. There's nothing left for you to shatter that hasn't already been destroyed."

His grip on my wrists loosens, just slightly. A flicker of something—surprise, maybe—crosses his face.

"You think I'm afraid of what you carry?" I press closer, our lips nearly touching. "I've lived in shadows for years. I've survived things that should have killed me. Whatever demons you're hiding...they don't scare me."

Alex steps back, releasing my wrists. For a breath, the mask he always wears slips, and I see it—raw, unguarded vulnerability.

"You don't understand," he says quietly. "I've broken people, Vesper. Men. Women. People who thought they could love me...fix me...survive me." He shakes his head, a bitter edge cutting through every word. "They all believed they could handle what I am. What I need. They were all wrong."

"And what is it you need?" I ask, rubbing my wrists where his fingers had been.

"I need to possess, to dominate, to own every part of someone until there's nothing left that isn't mine. You can't give me that when Oz, Z, and Talon have pieces of you, too."

"That's not how it works," I say, stepping forward to close the distance between us again. "They don't have pieces of me like I'm some puzzle being divided up. What I share with each of them, with you, is whole and complete in its own way."

Alex's jaw tightens as he scans my face as if searching for something. Whatever he sees there makes him shake his head slightly. "You think I'm incapable of giving each of you what you need?"

"I think," he says deliberately, "that what I need would terrify you."

"You clearly don't know me very well."

"This isn't a game, Vesper."

"I never said it was." I move closer until we're almost touching. "But you're making assumptions about what I can and can't handle based on nothing but your own fears. I decide what I am

capable of. Not you. Not the rest of them." I move again until we're chest to chest. "I want this. I want you."

He lunges forward, one hand tangling painfully in my hair while the other grips my throat. His mouth crashes against mine with bruising force, nothing like the controlled kiss we shared moments ago. This is hunger unleashed, primal and dominating. I taste blood. Mine or his, I'm not sure, as his teeth catch my lower lip.

The weapons cabinet rattles behind me as he slams me against it, his body pinning mine, which leaves no room for escape. His fingers tighten around my throat, not enough to cut off air but enough to make my pulse thunder in my ears.

I should be afraid. I should push him away. Instead, I find myself responding with equal ferocity, dragging my nails down his back hard enough to leave marks even through his shirt.

"Is this what you want?" he demands. "To be at my mercy? To surrender everything to me?"

"Yes," I breathe. The word hangs between us.

"I don't believe you," he challenges me. "Words are easy. Prove it."

His hands leave my hair and throat, moving to my hips as he spins me to face him again.

"On your knees," he commands, his voice leaving no room for negotiation.

I hold his gaze for a heartbeat, making sure he knows this is my choice before I slowly sink to my knees on the cold concrete floor. The basement air prickles against my skin, but it's nothing compared to the heat building inside me.

Alex looks down at me, something shifting in his expression. "Good girl," he says, the praise sending an unexpected shiver through me. His hand cups my cheek, thumb tracing my lower lip with surprising gentleness. "But, as I said, this isn't the time."

Confusion washes over me as he steps back. "What?"

"Stand up," he says, offering his hand to help me up.

"No," I answer, swatting it away before I shove myself off the floor on my own. "You can't keep edging me like this, Alex. You can't keep pulling me in and pushing me away.

Either you want this, want me, or you don't. I'm done with the mixed signals," I continue, my chest heaving with anger. "One minute you're pinning me against walls, the next you're acting like touching me would burn you. It's exhausting."

"You think I'm playing games? That this is fun for me?"

"I don't know what this is for you! The second I show you that I might actually want it too, you shut me down. You're giving me blue ovaries, Alex."

"I am not a good man." His voice scrapes like shattered glass. "I've spent my entire life learning how to destroy people from the inside out. Not just enemies—lovers, partners, anyone who dares to get too close."

He stalks toward me with wicked grace, backing me against the cabinet once more. This time, there's no desire on his face, only a cold, brutal honesty that makes my breath catch.

"You think I'm holding back because I don't want you? I'm holding back because I've watched what happens when I don't. The last woman couldn't even form complete sentences by the time I was done with her. The man before that killed himself."

I swallow hard but hold my ground. "I'm not them."

"No, you're not. You're stronger, which makes it worse." His fingers trace my jawline. "Because I could go further with you. Push harder. Take more."

"Maybe I want that," I challenge.

"No, you don't. You want the fantasy of it, the edge, the thrill. But what I need..." He shakes his head. "I don't just dominate in the bedroom, Vesper. I consume. I own. I remake people until they don't recognize themselves anymore."

"You're trying to scare me away."

"I'm trying to save you." His palm flattens against my chest over my heart. "I've destroyed every person who's ever tried to love me. Turned them into fragments of who they once were."

This is his truth—raw, jagged, and real. I realize now what he's been hiding behind those walls. Not just shadows, but devastation.

"You think you're the only one with a destructive streak?" I seethe, refusing to back down. "I've got demons too, Alex."

"Not like mine. The things I need...the things I've done...I've broken people, Vesper. Men and women who thought they could handle what I am." The confession falls between us like shattered glass. "I've left them empty shells, hollow versions of themselves. And I refuse—" His voice catches, revealing a crack of vulnerability. "—I refuse to do that to you until I have better control of myself."

The revelation hangs between us. This isn't just about desire or compatibility. This is about Alex believing he's fundamentally toxic to anyone who gets too close.

"You think you'll destroy me," I say, not a question but an understanding.

"I know I will." There's no arrogance in his voice, only certainty. "Shattering you will strip away that last piece of humanity inside of me. I can't let that happen."

I search his face, seeing beyond the cold exterior to the pain beneath. The fear.

"I don't think you give me enough credit," I say quietly. "Or yourself."

"This isn't about credit. It's about protection. Your protection."

"From you? The man who's risking his life tomorrow to save my brother?"

His jaw tightens. "Those things don't erase what I am."

"And what exactly are you, Alex? Because from where I'm standing, you're a man terrified of his own desires. A man who's convinced himself he's some kind of monster because that's easier than facing the possibility you might actually be worthy of a connection."

"You don't know what you're talking about."

"Don't I? You think you're the only one who's afraid of what they're capable of?" I step closer, refusing to let him retreat. "I've fantasized about killing The Collector. Not just killing him, making him suffer. Making him experience every moment of pain he's inflicted on others. Does that make me a monster?"

"I'm worse than a monster. I've tried to bury it. Starve it out. For years, Vesper. I did everything I could to lock this part of me away. The part *she* created." His mother. His first kill. The decaying root of the darkness inside of him. "That part of me? It never left. It's always there. Right under the surface. Just one thread away from snapping loose. And if it does..." His voice drops. "There's no putting it back."

"I've seen that side of you, Alex. It doesn't scare me. Do

you think I'd love you any less for embracing that side of you?"

"You should be. I've let myself get close to someone, thinking that maybe this time things would be different, but voices are still there. That night you shared my bed? The voices begged me to mark your skin."

My chest tightens, but I stand my ground. Alex thinks he's so unredeemable because of what his mother trained him to be, but my own father did the same to my brother. The same for Oscar, Zaire, and even Talon. This world we live in doesn't allow for weakness. The families breed ruthlessness. It's the only way we can survive.

"If you knew the kind of thoughts I have," he goes quieter now, like it's a confession meant for no one. "The kind of things I fight every goddamn day just to keep from drowning in it. If you knew what I did to your uncle after you put that bullet in him...You'd run because it wasn't justice, Vesper. It was feeding the monster that I am, on your behalf. That's who I really am when no one is watching."

His words hit me like a physical blow, stopping me in my tracks. "What did you do to his corpse?"

Alex's expression hardens, any trace of emotion slipping away behind a wall of detachment. "That's not something I'll ever tell you. Not now. Not ever."

"You can't just drop something like that and then refuse to explain," I argue, frustration building in my chest. "You're using these vague confessions as another wall to keep me at a distance."

"It's not a wall. It's a boundary. One I won't cross. No matter how much I want to."

"For your sake or mine?"

"Both." His eyes are cold again, distant. "Some things are better left buried, Vesper. What I did...that's why I can't let myself get close to you. It's for your own good."

Anger flares hot and bright within me. Always the same excuse. Always deciding what's best for me without giving me any say in the matter.

"My own good?" I spit the words back at him. "You don't get to decide that. You don't get to use whatever this is between us like bait and then yank them away when I bite."

"I'm not trying to—"

"Save it," I cut him off, already turning toward the stairs. "I'm done with this conversation. Done with your cryptic half-truths and self-imposed martyr complex. If you want to push me away, just say so. Stop playing games, Alex."

I turn and storm toward the basement stairs, frustration and hurt burning like acid in my chest.

"Do you know why I am going tomorrow instead of Oscar or Zaire? Because I'm the one you can live without. If it comes down to a choice tomorrow," Alex's voice cuts through the basement, stopping me at the foot of the stairs, "if it's between Talon coming back or me, I'll make sure it's him."

I freeze. The words hit me like a physical blow, knocking the air from my lungs.

"I'll make sure Talon comes back to you," Alex repeats, his voice flat and certain.

"No!" I lunge back down the stairs, crossing the distance between us in seconds. "You don't get to make that call. That's not your choice to make."

Alex's face remains impassive, as if he's already resigned himself to this fate. "It is my choice. The only one that makes sense."

"The hell it is!" I grab his shirt, bunching the fabric in my fists. "You don't get to decide who's worth saving and who isn't."

"I'm being practical." His voice is maddeningly calm. "You need Talon. You need the twins. They ground you, protect you, give you what you need."

"And you don't?"

"I'm the expendable one, Vesper." He gently pries my fingers from his shirt. "The one who doesn't fit. The one who's already broken beyond repair."

"Stop it. Just stop."

"It's the truth. I've made my peace with it. If something goes wrong tomorrow, I need to know you'll be okay. And for that, you need them."

"I need all of you. Especially you."

He shakes his head. "Vesper—"

"Promise me, Alex. I need to hear you say it." He studies me for a long moment, something shifting in his expression.

"I'm sorry." His thumb brushes away a tear. "I can't make that promise."

"Then I'm coming with you," I declare, my voice steadier than I feel. "If you won't promise to come back, I'll make sure of it myself."

Alex's jaw clenches. "We've already been through this."

"And we'll keep going through it until you understand. I refuse to send you off like some sacrificial lamb."

"It's not a sacrifice if it's a choice."

"It's not just your choice to make!" The words burst from me, echoing off the concrete walls. "You think your life belongs only to you? That what happens to you doesn't affect the rest of us? Affect me?"

"I don't understand why you're fighting so hard for this," he says quietly. "For me."

The vulnerability in his voice cuts deeper than any of his earlier confessions. This is the real Alex, I realize—not the calculating mastermind or ruthless hacker, but the man beneath it all who truly can't understand why anyone would fight for him.

"Because you matter to me," I say simply.

Alex stares at me, something shifting in his expression—disbelief warring with a desperate need to believe.

"You don't mean that."

"I do. I've lost too much already. I won't lose you, too."

He closes his eyes, breath shuddering between us. For a moment, we stay like that, heartbeats syncing in the quiet of the basement.

"I'll try," he finally says. "That's all I can promise. I'll try to come back."

It's not the absolute guarantee I wanted, but it's honest. More honest than he's been about anything else.

# Chapter 20

TALON

I'M NOT A PRAYING MAN, but if there was ever a time to start, it would be right now, watching Alex drive like he's auditioning for Fast and Furious while explaining how easy it is to "borrow" a plane.

"You're telling me," I say, gripping the door handle as he takes another curve too fast, "that some random dude on the dark web is just lending you an aircraft? No questions asked?"

"Not random. And not lending. It's a business transaction."

"Right. Because that makes it so much better." My stomach knots with each passing mile.

"You want details or you want plausible deniability?" Alex asks, weaving between cars on the highway.

"I want to know we're not about to steal a plane that will get us shot down by the Air Force." The trees along the road-side blur into a green smear as we accelerate.

Alex snorts. "Please. Give me some credit. The plane belongs to a gentleman who owes me a favor."

"What kind of favor involves lending out a plane?

"The kind where I kept him out of a federal supermax." Alex glances at me, his expression unreadable. "He runs a legitimate charter business now."

"That sounds..." I trail off, searching for the right word. "Illegal."

"Extremely." Alex's tone is matter-of-fact. "But it's our only play if we want to get to Martha's Vineyard undetected."

I stare out the window, watching the landscape rush by. Two hours until we're supposed to meet The Collector's people. Two hours until we're either one step closer to Luca or finding out we are walking into a trap. Possibly both.

"You think Vesper's okay?" I ask, changing the subject. Leaving her behind felt wrong, like amputating a limb, but we all knew it was necessary.

"Z and Oscar won't let anything happen to her."

"That's not what I asked."

A muscle ticks in his jaw. "No, she's not okay. She's furi-ous, terrified, and feeling helpless. But she's safer there than with us."

The bluntness of his assessment hits like a physical blow. "You two seem...closer now."

Alex's eyes flick to me briefly before returning to the road. "Looks can be deceiving, Talon. She's not my biggest fan right now."

The private airfield appears ahead, a small cluster of hangars and a single runway carved into the countryside. Alex slows as we approach the security gate, rolling down his window.

"Blackwood," he tells the guard, who checks a clipboard before nodding us through with barely a glance.

"That was easy," I mutter as the gate slides open.

"Like I said, legitimate business on paper." Alex navigates toward the furthest hangar, where a sleek Cessna Citation waits on the tarmac, its door already open. A stocky man in coveralls stands beside it, arms crossed.

"That's our ride?" I ask, eyeing the jet skeptically. "Looks small."

"It'll get us there in forty minutes," Alex says, pulling up beside the hangar.

We exit the car, and I grab our duffel from the backseat, containing the weapons we definitely couldn't get through airport security. The stocky man approaches, grinning like a fucking fool.

"Thanks for working with us on such short notice, Maddox." Alex shakes his hand. "Clean like we discussed?"

"Of course." Maddox tosses him a set of keys. "She's fueled up and ready to go. Return whenever, just let me know when you're inbound."

"Appreciate it." Alex pockets the keys, then tosses Maddox an envelope that I suspect contains more cash than most people make in a month. Maddox thumbs through the envelope, his expression unchanging as he counts the bills. He gestures toward the plane. "She's all yours."

"You sure you know how to fly this thing?"

Alex shoots me a look that could curdle milk. "Stop asking me that."

"Just making sure," I mutter, ducking through the cabin door. The interior is luxurious but compact with cream leather seats, polished wood accents, and a small bar area that's been stocked with top-shelf liquor. "Nice. Your friend Maddox has good taste." I finger through the bottles, selecting a particularly expensive Brandy. If we make it through this alive, this will be the first one I open.

"He caters to clients with expensive needs and deep pockets," Alex replies, stowing our bag in a compartment before sliding into the pilot's seat. "Buckle up. Pre-flight checks take about ten minutes."

I settle into the co-pilot's seat, watching Alex move through the pre-flight checks with calm precision. Each switch flipped, each gauge scanned, carries the same quiet control he shows when hacking or handling a weapon. He is methodical, focused, and leaving no room for error.

"You really do know what you're doing," I admit, impressed despite myself.

"Told you." He doesn't look up from the instrument panel. "My father believed a man should be able to escape at a moment's notice. Piloting was non-negotiable in my education."

"Your father sounds paranoid."

"My father was a bastard who made enemies in high places," Alex corrects, his voice flat. "But he wasn't wrong about the benefits of a quick exit strategy."

I've known Alex for years, but he rarely mentions his family. The few details I've gathered paint a picture of wealth, power, and dysfunction. The kind that breeds men like him, brilliant and broken in equal measure.

The engines whir to life, the vibration humming through the cabin as Alex communicates with the tower. His voice shifts when he speaks to air traffic control—smoother, more refined, the rough edges carefully tucked away. Another role he steps into effortlessly, like changing coats.

"Tower, this is Citation November-Six-Five-Charlie-Delta requesting clearance for takeoff to Martha's Vineyard. VFR flight, altitude four thousand."

The radio crackles with a quick response, granting us clearance. Alex guides the plane to the runway. For a guy who spends ninety percent of his time hunched over keyboards, he pilots the aircraft like it's an extension of himself.

"Ready?" he asks, not looking at me as he lines up for takeoff.

"Do I have a choice?"

His lips quirk. "Not really."

The engines roar as we accelerate down the runway, pressing me back into the leather seat. My stomach drops as the wheels leave the ground, the small plane climbing steeply into the clear blue sky. The airfield shrinks beneath us, becoming a miniature model before disappearing behind us completely.

"See? Piece of cake," Alex says, adjusting our course once we reach cruising altitude.

"Don't get cocky. We still have to land this thing," I mutter, trying to ignore the uncomfortable knowledge that we're suspended thousands of feet in the air in what amounts to a flying soda can.

"Landing's the easy part. You aim down until the plane hits the ground, right?" Alex replies.

"Not funny, asshole."

"It's what happens after we touch down that worries me."

"Let's go over the plan again," I say, needing to hear it spoken aloud, to find any holes before we're in too deep.

Alex nods. "We land at a private airstrip on the south side of the island. A car will be waiting for us. We drive to the northern dock, arriving a half an hour early to scout the location."

"And if it's a trap?"

"Then we don't approach. We observe from a distance, identify potential hostiles, and adjust accordingly."

"And if Charles Blackwood doesn't pass their authentication?"

Alex's jaw tightens. "We have three layers of documentation—physical ID, digital footprint, and financial trail. If that's not enough, we improvise."

"Improvise," I repeat flatly. "That's your backup plan?"

"Would you prefer I lie and say I've thought of every possible contingency?" He glances at me, one eyebrow raised. "We're flying into unknown territory with minimal intel. Some variables can't be controlled."

He's right, but that doesn't make it any easier to swallow. We're risking everything on this mission, not just our lives, but our only lead to Luca. If we fail, Vesper loses her brother forever. And the thought of her face if we return empty-handed is almost worse than not returning at all.

The ocean stretches beneath us, the late afternoon sun glinting off the waves like scattered diamonds. In another life, this might be a pleasure trip—two friends flying to a luxury island getaway. Instead, we're armed to the teeth, chasing ghosts and genetic samples.

I lean back in my seat, watching clouds drift past the windows. "Does it scare you?" I ask, genuinely curious. "Being responsible for someone else's happiness?"

"Terrifies me," he admits quietly. "I'm not built for it."

"None of us are," I counter, watching the clouds drift past. "But we're doing it anyway."

A rare half-smile crosses his face. "When did you get so philosophical?"

"Probably around the time we started sharing a woman instead of fighting over her." I adjust my seat, stretching my legs as much as the confined space allows. "Life's weird like that."

The plane hits a pocket of turbulence, dipping slightly

before Alex compensates. My stomach lurches uncomfortably.

"Martha's Vineyard, twelve o'clock," Alex announces, nodding toward the windshield.

The island materializes on the horizon, a smudge against the vast blue of the Atlantic. From this distance, it looks peaceful—rolling hills, pristine beaches, and dense forests. An ideal place to bury secrets in plain sight, cloaked in wealth and privilege.

"You might want to go ahead and change. Suit's hanging in the back."

"Did you steal that too?"

"Borrowed," he reminds me again. "Just think, if we crash land, you'll already be dressed for your funeral."

"How convenient," I mutter, unbuckling my seatbelt.

I make my way to the back of the cabin, unzipping the garment bag hanging against the wall. The bespoke navy suit inside costs more than most people's monthly rent, simply another piece of the Charles Blackwood illusion. I strip off my casual clothes and begin the transformation, each layer adding to the character I need to become.

"You think they'll buy it?" I call up to Alex as I button the crisp shirt.

"Just channel your inner entitled prick. Shouldn't be a stretch."

The plane banks slightly as Alex begins our descent. I brace against the wall, watching the island grow larger through the small window. Sprawling estates peek through the trees, private beaches curve along the shoreline, all screaming old money and exclusivity.

"You ready?"

"Almost done," I call back, adjusting my cufflinks—platinum with tiny sapphire inlays. The mirror mounted on the cabin wall reflects a stranger, perfect. I return to the cockpit just as we begin our final approach, the small airstrip appearing below us. It's barely more than a cleared stretch of land with a modest hangar at one end—discreet, private, exactly what we need.

"Prepare for landing," Alex mutters, his focus absolute as he guides the plane lower. The trees on either side of the runway seem too close, the strip itself too short. "Buckle up in the back. You're a rich asshole now, and I am merely just your pilot and driver."

"Harry Ballsack," I remind him. "That's your undercover name."

"I still have time to crash the plane, Talon."

"Fine," he scoffs. "You're not Harry Ballsack. I'll call you Jack. Jack Meoff."

"Not better," he groans.

The wheels touch down with a surprisingly gentle bump, the plane rolling to a smooth stop before Alex taxis toward the small hangar where a black Range Rover waits. He powers down the engines with steady efficiency, the sudden silence almost deafening.

"I'm going to change. Stay here. From this point on, you're the boss."

Alex disappears into the back of the plane, and I hear the

rustle of fabric as he changes. I take the opportunity to slip into character, adopting the slightly bored expression of a man who has never heard the word 'no' in his life.

When Alex emerges, the transformation is startling. Gone is the tech genius in casual clothes, replaced by a professional in a crisp black suit, white shirt, and narrow black tie with an added touch of non-prescription glasses with thin metal frames. Somehow managing to make himself look both forgettable and intimidating.

"Very chauffeur chic."

Alex's only response is a withering glare as he grabs our equipment bag. "Stay here until I get the car."

"Aye aye, captain," I mutter, watching as Alex descends the aircraft stairs.

Through the window, I observe him approaching the Range Rover, checking beneath it with a small mirror before circling the vehicle completely. Always thorough, always paranoid—and usually right. He pops the trunk, stows our bag, then slides behind the wheel to bring it closer to the plane.

I adjust my tie one last time, school my features into the calm, controlled expression of Charles Blackwood, and exit the aircraft. The island air hits me immediately.

Alex walks around to the driver's side, "Sir," he says, his voice pitched lower than usual, accent crisper around the edges as he opens the door.

I slide into the leather interior without acknowledging him, pulling out my phone as if checking important messages. The door closes with a solid thunk, and seconds later Alex is behind the wheel, adjusting the mirror to catch my eye.

"We've got about an hour until pickup," he says. "GPS shows the location is thirty-five minutes from here."

"We should check in." He reaches into the duffel bag sitting in the passenger seat and tosses a burner phone over his shoulder. I catch it one-handed.

"Good idea." I dial Oz's number from memory, listening to it ring three times before he picks up.

"Status?" Oz's voice is tense, clipped.

"En route to the pickup location," I reply, watching the scenery blur past my window. "How's everything on your end?"

"She's not fighting us anymore." A pause. "Z thinks she's planning something."

I pinch the bridge of my nose, trying to ward off the headache brewing. "Put her on."

There's a muffled conversation, then Vesper's voice fills the line, deceptively calm. "Talon."

"Princess," I keep my tone light despite the worry gnawing at my gut. "I hear you're behaving suspiciously well."

"Just accepting reality," she says, too smoothly.

Alex catches my eye in the rearview mirror, one eyebrow raised in disbelief.

"That's...surprisingly mature of you," I say carefully.

"I've been known to be reasonable occasionally." Her laugh sounds almost natural. *Almost.* The line goes quiet for a few seconds. "Vesper, you still there?"

"I am." Her voice softens. "Come home to me."

The simple request hits harder than I expected. "I will, princess. We both will. The next time you hear from us, we'll be on our way back. Behave, please?"

"No promises," she says, and I can practically hear her smile. "But I'll try."

The line goes dead before I can respond. I stare at the phone for a moment, unsettled by the conversation. Vesper giving in this easily feels wrong.

"Don't focus on what you can't control. She's Z and Oscar's problem."

"How far out are we from the pickup location?"

"About twenty minutes." Alex checks his watch. "Which gives us around fifteen to twenty to recon the area before the scheduled meeting."

The Range Rover hugs the curves of the coastal road. The wind has picked up, bending the trees along the roadside. I can't help but think this weather is a bad omen—nature itself warning us to turn back.

"There," Alex says, nodding toward a wooden sign half-hidden by overgrowth. "North Point Harbor."

He slows the vehicle, turning onto a narrow gravel road that disappears into a thick stand of pines. The suspension groans as we navigate the uneven terrain, branches scraping against the windows like skeletal fingers.

"Isolated," I observe. "Ideal for an exchange no one's meant to see."

"Or an ambush," Alex mutters, voice grim.

The trees suddenly give way to a small clearing overlooking a dilapidated dock. Three weathered boathouses line one side, their paint peeling from years of salt exposure. The harbor itself is small, sheltered by a natural breakwater of jagged rocks. A single wooden dock extends into the choppy water, creaking and swaying with each wave.

"Charming," I mutter, as Alex parks the Range Rover behind the largest boathouse, concealing it from immediate view. "Nothing says 'legitimate business transaction' like an abandoned harbor."

Alex kills the engine and turns to face me. "I'll sweep the perimeter. You stay with the car until I confirm it's clear."

Alex exits the vehicle silently, easing the door shut with barely a click. I watch through the tinted windows as he disappears into the shadows between the boathouses. For all his tech genius and dry sarcasm, it's moments like these that remind me—Alex is a weapon first, hacker second. Precision in combat, silence in the hunt. It's in his blood.

Ten minutes drag by like a slow bleed. I keep my eyes on the time, checking my watch again and again until I've lost count. Every second stretches tighter, each tick of the clock a reminder that we're too close—too damn close—to unraveling The Collector's trail. He has her brother. And if Alex screws this up now...

No. He won't. He can't. Failure isn't just a setback anymore—it's unforgivable.

Just as the tension curdles in my gut and I reach for the handle to go after him, the driver's door clicks open. Alex slides back into the seat without a word, jaw tight, eyes sharp. Something's changed.

"Clear," he says, his face grim. "Too clear."

"What do you mean?"

"No cameras, no security measures, not even basic surveillance." He starts the engine. "It's either incredibly sloppy or..."

"Or it's not the real meeting point," I finish. "They're watching to see if we follow protocol."

Alex nods, putting the Range Rover in drive. "Time to find out."

We cruise slowly down to the weathered dock, gravel crunching beneath the tires. The wind has picked up, sending whitecaps across the water. Alex parks facing the water, positioning us for a quick escape if needed.

Alex exits first, circling around to open my door with quiet deference. I step out into the biting wind, my suit jacket flapping against my sides. Salt air fills my lungs as I straighten my tie, settling into the impatient stance of a man who doesn't wait for anyone.

"Eight minutes," Alex reminds, standing a respectful distance behind me.

We wait in silence, the only sounds are the creaking of the dock and the crashing of waves against the rocky shore. The wind carries a hint of coming rain, and I scan the horizon, squinting against the fading daylight.

That's when I see it, a sleek object cutting through the choppy waters, heading directly toward us. A boat, its matte black hull absorbing what little light remains, making it seem like a hole moving across the ocean's surface.

"Contact," I mutter, not turning my head.

Alex shifts slightly behind me. "I see it. Thirty seconds out."

I straighten my posture, adopting the bored, slightly irritated expression of a wealthy man whose time is being wasted. Charles Blackwood wouldn't show anxiety. He'd show impatience.

The vessel glides toward the dock—a luxury speedboat designed for stealth rather than show. No identifying markers, no registration numbers visible. As it draws closer, I can make out two figures on board, one at the controls, another standing near the bow.

"Armed?" I ask under my breath.

"Definitely," Alex confirms. "Both of them. The one standing has a shoulder holster. Driver likely has something at his waist."

The boat slows as it approaches the dock, engine purring almost silently as it maneuvers alongside the weathered planks. Neither man makes a move to exit or secure the vessel. They're waiting for us to approach—a power play, forcing us to come to them.

"Sir?" Alex prompts, playing his role. "Shall we proceed?"

"Obviously," I drawl, letting annoyance color my tone as I step forward. Alex follows a half-pace behind, his presence solid and reassuring at my back.

As we near the boat, the standing figure steps onto the dock. He's tall, broad-shouldered, with a face carved from granite. His suit is expensive but practical, designed for movement rather than show.

"Mr. Blackwood?" His voice carries a faint Eastern European accent.

"You're late," I reply coldly, checking my watch for effect.

His expression doesn't change. "Check them."

The other guard at his side shifts towards us, patting down Alex first. He removes the gun from inside his coat, tossing it to the side. Satisfied he's unarmed Alex, he shifts to me, finding nothing.

"They're clean," he reports to his partner.

"Identification and proof of purchase."

I don't move, merely flicking my fingers toward Alex without looking back. "Jack, the documents."

Alex steps forward smoothly, producing an envelope from his inner jacket pocket. The folder contains everything we've prepared—the false ID, banking information, transaction receipts, all bearing the Blackwood name and details. The forgeries are flawless, indistinguishable from legitimate documents even under close scrutiny.

The man takes the envelope, nodding toward his colleague, who remains on the boat. He doesn't examine the documents himself, instead passing them to the other man, who begins scrutinizing them with unsettling thoroughness. My heart pounds against my ribs, but I keep my expression neutral.

"Authentication protocol requires verification," the man says, his accent thickening slightly. "You will place your hand on this."

He produces a small, black device from his pocket—flat, rectangular, with a glowing blue screen on one side.

"What is that?" I ask, injecting just the right amount of suspicious disdain into my voice.

"Biometric verification," he replies evenly. "Standard procedure for transactions of this magnitude."

Shit. We didn't anticipate biometric scanning. I can feel Alex tensing behind me, though his face remains impassive.

"I don't recall agreeing to biometric verification when I made my purchase," I say coldly. "My documentation should be sufficient considering my previous investment."

The man's expression doesn't change. "No scan, no sample. Those are the terms."

A standoff. I can almost hear Alex calculating our odds if this goes sideways—two against two, but they have the advantage of the boat for a quick escape. Plus, we don't know what's in the water around us.

"What exactly does this device scan for?" I demand, buying time.

"Pulse, body temperature, standard identification markers. It ensures you are who you claim to be, Mr. Blackwood."

A knot forms in my stomach as I weigh our options. If I refuse, we lose our only lead to Luca. If I comply and the scanner detects any anomaly, we're dead men.

"Fine," I snap, extending my hand with an impatient scowl. "But make it quick. I have dinner reservations at eight."

The device feels cool against my palm, a blue light scanning from my wrist to fingertips. I maintain my bored expression, though my pulse hammers so hard that I'm certain the machine can detect it. The man studies the read-out, his face betraying nothing.

After what feels like an eternity, he nods once and returns our documents.

"On the boat," he orders, gesturing toward the sleek vessel.

I freeze. "Excuse me?"

"Your purchase is not here. You come with us to complete the transaction."

"That wasn't the arrangement," I reply coldly. "The pickup location was specified as this dock."

"This is the pickup location. For you. Sample is elsewhere."

"Unacceptable," I declare, channeling every entitled billionaire I've ever met. "I was promised delivery at this location. I don't have time for nautical excursions."

"Then you don't get what you paid for." His hand shifts subtly toward his jacket.

Alex steps forward, voice low and deferential but with steel underneath. "Sir, perhaps we should consider their terms."

I hesitate, but the hard gleam in the man's eyes tells me this isn't negotiable. My mind races through the options, none of them good. Refuse and lose our only lead to Luca. Agree, and potentially walk into a trap. But what choice do we really have?

"Fine," I snap. "But I expect compensation for this incon-venience."

I catch the guard rolling his eyes. He believes I'm just another entitled, rich asshole. Good.

"Your man stays here," he says, nodding toward Alex.

"Absolutely not," I counter immediately. "My driver comes with me. I don't travel without security."

The two men exchange glances, a silent communication passing between them before the one on the boat gives a barely perceptible nod.

"Both of you then," the guard concedes, stepping aside to allow us passage onto the boat.

I step forward with feigned reluctance, making a show of checking my watch and sighing dramatically. Alex follows, his presence at my back the only thing keeping my nerves steady. The boat rocks gently beneath our feet as we board, the sleek vessel lower in the water than it appeared from shore.

"How far are we going?" I demand as the guard gestures for us to sit on the leather bench that runs along one side of the boat.

"Not far," is all he says before nodding to his partner.

The engine roars to life, and we surge away from the dock. I grip the leather bench, while mentally mapping our position relative to shore. The dock shrinks rapidly behind us, and within minutes, the coastline disappears.

"Where exactly are we headed?" I demand, letting impatience edge into my voice.

"Just a little further," the driver calls over his shoulder.

Alex catches my eye, a microscopic head tilt directing my attention to the starboard side. A black speck appears on the horizon, growing larger by the second. Then another appears portside.

Fuck.

"I believe we've gone far enough," I announce, rising to my feet with all the entitlement Charles Blackwood can muster. "I insist we complete this transaction immediately or return to shore."

"Sit down, Mr. Blackwood."

"I will not," I snap, channeling righteous indignation while subtly adjusting my stance for balance. "This is completely unprofessional. I demand to speak with your superior."

The approaching vessels are close enough now to make out their shapes. Fuck. They're twins to this boat and each likely carrying additional personnel. This was never about authentication. It was about isolation.

I look over at Alex, who gives me an almost imperceptible nod. Alex moves like lightning. One second he's next to me, the next he's on the move. The guard registers the movement a split second too late, already drawing his own weapon as Alex collides into him. His momentum throws him backwards while Alex disarms him.

"Down!" Alex shouts, and I drop instinctively as the first shot cracks through the air.

The guard jerks backward, red blooming across his pristine white shirt. The driver whirls, gun already drawn, but Alex is faster—two shots in rapid succession, and the man crumples over the controls. His gun falling to the deck.

The boat lurches violently as the throttle engages,

sending us careening across the choppy water. I scramble for purchase on the slick deck, my expensive shoes sliding uselessly as I lunge for the controls.

"Company!" I yell over the roaring engine, nodding toward the approaching vessels now closing in fast.

"Can you drive this thing?" he shouts, tossing me the weapon from the deck.

I shove the dead driver aside, taking the wheel with one hand while checking the magazine with the other. "I've driven worse!"

The sleek vessel responds to my touch, slicing through the water as I open the throttle fully. We surge forward, putting distance between us and the two boats chasing hard behind. The throttle jerks under my palm as gunfire erupts, bullets slicing past my ear and tearing into the control panel. Sparks fly as the dashboard explodes in a shower of plastic and metal, the GPS screen shattering inches from my fingers.

"Shit!" I duck lower, still gripping the wheel as the speedboat bucks violently across the chop. "Alex!"

He's already returning fire, body twisted toward the stern, weapon steady despite the boat's wild motion. The sharp crack of his gun cuts through the roar of the engine and the relentless slap of water against the hull.

"Keep driving!" he shouts, squeezing off three more rounds. I hear a distant cry and glance back to see one of the pursuing boats swerve sharply, its pilot clutching his shoulder.

Another volley of bullets rips through the air around us. One pings off the metal railing by my head, another tears through the leather seat where I'd been sitting just moments before. The control panel takes another hit, and suddenly the engine sputters, the RPMs dropping fast.

"We're losing power!" I yell, frantically trying to adjust the controls that are no longer responding. The speedometer begins to fall, our lead evaporating with every passing second. "They hit something vital."

Alex slides down beside me, ejecting his spent magazine and slamming a fresh one home. "How long can you keep us moving?"

"Minutes, maybe."

"Fuck!" he roars, he checks the magazine. "Running low on ammo."

Another shot cracks through the air just as a bullet tears into my shoulder—white-hot agony detonating like a flash-bang inside me. I bite back a scream, staggering as blood pours down my arm, soaking through my suit. The boat jerks and slows, the engine whining as water churns violently around us. Spray lashes my face, and the roar of our pursuers grows louder, closing in fast.

"They're on us!" I shout over the dying engine's protest. My vision blurs at the edges, the steering wheel slick with my blood. "Any bright ideas?"

Alex's face changes, something resolute and terrifying settling over his features. He glances at the shoreline— maybe half a mile away—then back at the approaching boats.

"You need to go." He pries my fingers from the wheel. "The water is your best chance."

"What are you talking about?"

He yanks me away from the controls, his grip surprisingly strong. "You get to shore, call for extraction. Get back to Vesper."

"We both go," I argue, but he's already shoving me toward the side of the boat.

"Not an option." His eyes meet mine, something like acceptance in them. "This boat's dead in the water. We both know it. But I can buy you time."

The realization of what he plans hits me like another bullet. "No. Alex, don't—"

"Tell her I kept my promise," he demands, and then his hands are on my chest, shoving me hard. My body tips backward, suspended in air for one sickening moment before I hit the water with a painful slap.

The cold shock steals my breath, saltwater filling my mouth as I plunge beneath the surface. My wounded shoulder screams in protest as I kick desperately upward, lungs burning. When I crest the surface, gasping and sputtering, I see Alex swinging the boat around, heading straight for our pursuers.

"Alex!" I scream, but my voice is swallowed by the roar of engines and the crash of water.

He's on a collision course with the nearest vessel, our dying speedboat lunging forward in one last desperate burst of power. The men on the other boat react too late. I catch the shouts, the flicker of gunfire—and then, the explosion.

The blast hits like a punch to the chest, the shockwave slamming into me even from this distance. A wall of water surges outward, lifting me briefly before dropping me back into the churning sea. Burning debris rains down around me, hissing as it hits the surface.

"ALEX!" I scream again, panic cracking my voice as I search for any trace of him in the wreckage. Flames lick across twisted metal. Nothing moves.

The second boat has pulled back, hovering at a safer distance, its spotlight sweeping methodically across the water—looking for survivors or confirming kills.

Pain pulses through my shoulder again, sharp and radiating. I bite back a groan. Salt burns the wound, but the cold numbs it slightly. My suit clings to me like dead weight, dragging me down with every stroke, every breath.

I need to move. The shore seems impossibly far away. But staying here means capture or death. With one last desperate look at the burning wreckage, I turn and begin swimming toward land, using my good arm to pull myself through the water.

"I'm sorry."

Though there's no one left to hear it.

# Chapter 21

VESPER

THE CLOCK on the wall is a traitorous bastard, each tick hammering another nail into my fraying composure. Almost two hours since their last check-in. Two hours of silence stretching between us like a chasm that grows wider with each passing minute.

"They should have called by now." My voice sounds strange to my own ears, too high and tight. I pace the length of our living room for the hundredth time, my bare feet wearing an invisible path in the hardwood. "Something's wrong. I can feel it."

"Vesper, please sit down." Oz's voice is steady, measured, the voice of reason I usually find comforting. Right now, it makes me want to scream. "There could be a dozen explanations for the delay."

"Name one," I challenge, whirling to face him. "One explanation that doesn't end with them dead or captured."

Z approaches slowly, palms raised like he's trying to calm a wild animal. In some ways, he's not wrong. "Poor reception. Equipment malfunction. They could be maintaining radio silence for security reasons."

"For two hours?" I rake my fingers through my hair, tugging at the roots until the pain gives me something to focus on besides the panic clawing at my chest. "No. They would have found a way to contact us by now. Alex always has contingencies for his contingencies."

Oz rises from the couch, crossing to the bank of monitors Alex set up before they left. His reflection in the screens reveals the tension he's trying to hide from me. He's worried too.

"Z, try the secondary protocol again," Oz orders, fingers flying across the keyboard. "Vesper's right, they should have checked in by now."

Z nods, already pulling out another burner phone. His usual cocky demeanor has evaporated, replaced by a precision that somehow scares me more than any outburst would. These men don't panic, but they're concerned, and that knowledge sits like ice in my veins.

"Nothing," he reports after a moment, tossing the phone onto the coffee table. "Straight to voicemail, just like the last three times."

I wrap my arms around myself, trying to contain the

trembling that's taken hold of my body. "We need to go after them."

"Not an option," Oz responds immediately, not looking up from the monitors. "We have no idea what's happening on that island. Rushing in blind would only endanger them further if they're in trouble."

"So, we just sit here?" My voice cracks on the last word.

"Yes," Z confirms. "We give them time to complete the mission. It's what they'd want us to do."

I'm about to argue when Oscar's phone rings, not his burner, but his personal cell. The unexpectedness of it freezes us all in place for a fraction of a second before he lunges for it on the coffee table.

"Unknown number," he mutters, brow furrowed as he answers. "Hello?"

His expression shifts so quickly it steals my breath. Without a word, he puts the call on speaker and places the phone on the coffee table between us.

"—Lieutenant Commander Wilson with the United States Coast Guard," a crisp female voice fills our living room. "We recovered a man from the water near Martha's Vineyard approximately forty minutes ago. He was suffering from hypothermia and a shoulder wound. Before losing consciousness, he asked us to contact this number as his next of kin."

My knees buckle. Z catches me before I hit the floor, his strong arms the only thing keeping me upright as the room spins around me.

"Can you confirm who you found?" Oz responds, his voice impossibly calm while my world implodes.

"The individual identified himself as Talon St. James. He's currently being transported to Newport Hospital."

"Is he alive?" I cry out.

"We're stabilizing him."

"Stabilizing?" My voice cracks. "What does that mean?"

Oz leans closer to the phone, his fingers pressing hard against the coffee table. "Was there anyone else with him?"

A brief pause stretches across the line.

"I'm sorry, sir," Lieutenant Commander Wilson responds with clinical detachment. "The individual we recovered was the only survivor located at the scene."

Survivor. The word echoes in my head like a gunshot, implying something too terrible to comprehend.

"What scene?" I already know the answer waiting to destroy me, but the question slips out before I stop it.

"There was a boat collision reported approximately three miles offshore from Martha's Vineyard," she explains. "One of our helicopter pilots spotted the burning wreckage during a routine patrol and observed an individual in the water. When our rescue team arrived, they found significant debris consistent with an explosion, and your friend floating nearby."

The room tilts sideways. Z's grip on me tightens as my legs give out completely. I hear myself making a sound I don't recognize—something between a gasp and a whimper.

"Alex," I breathe. "No, no, no..."

"We're continuing search operations in the area," the

Lieutenant Commander adds. "But given the water temperature and time elapsed since the incident, I must advise you that survival chances beyond the first hour are extremely low."

The words pierce my soul. Z's arms around me are the only thing keeping me tethered to reality as the room spins sickeningly.

"Thank you, Lieutenant Commander," Oz responds, his voice steady despite the pallor creeping across his face. "We'll be there as soon as possible."

"I'll have someone meet you at the hospital," she replies before the line goes dead, leaving us in a silence so profound I can hear my own heartbeat thundering in my ears.

No one moves. No one speaks. The enormity of what we've just learned hangs in the air like poison gas, slowly suffocating us all.

"He can't be gone. He promised he'd come back."

Z guides me to the couch, lowering me gently before kneeling in front of me. "Vesper, listen to me. We don't know anything for certain yet. The Coast Guard can recover people days after accidents sometimes."

"She said—"

"I know what she said," he cuts me off, his thumbs brushing away tears I hadn't realized were falling. "But Alex is too stubborn to die that easily. We need to focus on Talon right now. He's alive, and he needs us."

Oz is already moving, grabbing the keys and his phone. "I'll get the car. Z, pack a bag for her and yourself. Essentials only. We leave in five minutes."

The world around me feels distant, like I'm watching a movie of my life rather than living it. I should be moving, helping, doing something—anything—but my body refuses to respond. Alex can't be gone. Not after everything. Not after what we shared.

"Vesper." Z's voice cuts through the fog. "Look at me. I need you to focus. Can you do that?"

I nod mechanically, though focusing feels impossible with my thoughts splintering in a thousand directions.

"Good. I'm going to pack your things. You stay here, breathe, and be ready to move when I get back."

He disappears down the hallway, leaving me alone with the terrible silence and the echo of the Coast Guard officer's words. The only survivor located at the scene. My fingers curl into fists, nails biting crescents into my palms, the pain a welcome distraction from the hollow ache spreading through my chest.

This is my fault. I should have been there. I should have found a way to go with them. Maybe if I had been there, Alex would still be alive.

"Don't." Oz startles me. He's standing in the doorway, car keys dangling from his fingers. "Don't go there. This isn't your fault."

I want to argue, to scream that it is absolutely my fault, that my obsessive need to find Luca has now potentially cost Alex his life, but the words stick in my throat.

Z returns with a small duffel bag slung over his shoulder. "Let's go."

They lead me down to the car, Z guides me forward when

my feet seem to forget how to walk. The night air hits my face, cold and sharp, momentarily clearing the fog from my mind. Reality crashes back with brutal force.

Oz slides behind the wheel while Z helps me into the backseat, climbing in beside me rather than taking the passenger seat. The door closes with a soft thud that feels too final, too much like the closing of a coffin.

"Newport's about an hour away. Traffic should be light this time of night."

I nod mechanically, though neither of them is looking at me now. Z pulls me against his side. I should find comfort in his warmth, in the steady rhythm of his heartbeat beneath my ear, but I feel nothing except a vast, yawning emptiness spreading through my chest.

The city lights blur past my window, smearing into streaks of color as my tears blur everything together. The car is eerily quiet.

I can't breathe properly. Each inhale feels like glass in my lungs, each exhale a struggle not to dissolve into sobs. Z's fingers trace gentle patterns on my arm, but I barely register the sensation. All I can think about is Talon lying in a hospital bed, wounded and alone, and Alex...

Alex, in the cold water. Alex, sinking beneath waves. The ocean doesn't care about promises made in basements.

"He can't be gone," I mutter more to myself than to the twins. "He promised me."

Neither responds. What could they possibly say that wouldn't shatter the fragile thread of hope I'm desperately clinging to?

My mind drifts to Talon, his shoulder wound, and the hypothermia. What if we're racing toward another goodbye? What if he's already slipped away while we drive through the night? My quest for Luca might have cost me both of them.

"He's strong," Z offers. "Talon will pull through."

I nod mechanically, but the reassurance barely penetrates the fog of despair enveloping me. This is the price of loving these men, this constant, gnawing fear of loss. I thought I'd prepared myself for the worst when I agreed to this life. I was wrong. Nothing could have prepared me for this sense of being torn apart from the inside.

"We're almost there," Oz announces. His knuckles are white against the steering wheel, the only visible sign of his distress. "Ten minutes."

I straighten in my seat, trying to pull myself together. Talon needs me strong, not broken. I can fall apart later, when I'm alone.

The hospital looms ahead. Oz pulls into the emergency entrance.

"I'll find somewhere to park," Oz orders as Z helps me from the car. "You two go ahead."

The automatic doors slide open with a pneumatic hiss, blasting us with sterile air and fluorescent light that makes my skin look even more ghostly than I feel. My legs are moving automatically, Z's arm around my waist, the only thing keeping me from collapsing.

"Coast Guard patient," Z tells the intake nurse, his voice shifting into that authoritative tone that makes people snap to attention. "Talon St. James. Just brought in."

The nurse's fingers fly across her keyboard. "Are you family?"

"Yes," I say before Z can respond.

"He's in trauma bay four. They're prepping him for surgery." She gestures toward heavy double doors. "Through there, but you'll need to wait in the surgical lounge."

The corridor beyond feels endless, the beeping of machines and hushed tones of medical staff.

The surgical lounge appears at the end of the hallway—a small, sterile room with uncomfortable looking couches and outdated magazines scattered across coffee tables. My body moves on autopilot as Z guides me to a worn-out couch.

"Sit," he says gently, lowering me down before pulling out his phone. His fingers move quickly across the screen as he texts Oz our location.

Z settles beside me. He doesn't speak, doesn't offer empty reassurances. Instead, he simply takes my hand in his, thumb tracing slow, steady circles against my palm. The rhythm steadies me, drawing me back into myself one heart-beat at a time.

The door slides open, and Oz appears, his expression carefully composed. Our eyes lock, and something unspoken passes between us—a shared pain we're both struggling to contain.

"Any news?" he asks, crossing to sit on my other side.

I shake my head, unable to form words around the lump in my throat.

The door opens again before Oz can respond. A woman in scrubs steps inside. "St. James Family?"

"That's us," Z instantly answers.

"Your relationship to the patient?"

"Girlfriend," Oz answers for me, pointing in my direction. "We're his brothers."

"Mr. St. James has a fairly serious bullet wound. It was a through-and-through to his left shoulder, but he lost a significant amount of blood. Hypothermia has complicated the matters." Her clinical assessment does nothing to soften the blow. "The surgical team is removing bullet fragments and repairing tissue damage now."

"When can we see him?" Z's voice remains steady, though I feel the tension vibrating through his body where our sides touch.

"Once he's out of surgery and stabilized in recovery. It could be several hours." Her expression softens slightly as she takes in my shattered appearance. "There's a private waiting area for the families of emergency procedures. I can show—"

"No," I cut her off, the word sharp and sudden even to my own ears. "We'll stay right here. Thank you."

The nurse gives a tight nod, clearly accustomed to family members in crisis. As she turns to leave, a woman in a crisp Coast Guard uniform appears in the doorway behind her. Lieutenant Commander Wilson.

The nurse excuses herself as the officer steps into the room. My heart hammers against my ribs as I push myself to my feet, swaying slightly until Z's steadies me.

"Did you find him?" The question bursts from me before she can speak. "Alex, tall, blond hair, blue eyes, probably wearing a suit. Did you—"

"We have three vessels in the search area, but visibility is extremely low at this time of night. We are suspending our search shortly," she confirms, her professional demeanor softening slightly. "The recovery operation will resume in the morning at first light."

Recovery. Not rescue. The clinical term slices through me like a blade.

"What happened out there?"

Lieutenant Commander Wilson gestures for me to sit back down, her expression grave but not unkind. "We're still piecing that together. Your friend, Talon, was conscious only briefly when we pulled him from the water. He mentioned his name and the number that I called before he passed out."

I sink back onto the couch.

"What about the wreckage?" Oz inquiries.

The officer's hesitation tells me everything before she speaks. "We observed debris consistent with a high-velocity impact and subsequent explosion. Multiple vessels were involved. At this time, that is the extent of what I can share with you."

"What about..." my voice falters, the question sticking in my throat like broken glass. "What about bodies?"

The lieutenant's expression shifts almost imperceptibly. "We've recovered several remains from the water. Though none of them match your description. I'm sorry."

Hope and dread war within me. No body means there's

still a chance, however infinitesimal, that Alex survived. But it also means he could be drifting somewhere in the cold Atlantic, alone and beyond our reach.

"I need to see the site," I say suddenly, pushing myself up from the couch. "Take me there."

"Vesper," Oz catches my wrist, gentle but firm. "That's not possible."

"I'm afraid he's right," Lieutenant Wilson says. "The search area is restricted to Coast Guard personnel. And with night operations suspended until dawn—"

"Then I'll wait until dawn," I counter, desperation giving my voice a brittle edge. "I need to be there."

Z rises beside me, his arm sliding around my waist. "What she means is that we appreciate being kept informed of any developments." His eyes meet mine, a silent plea to stand down. "We understand you're doing everything possible."

The officer nods, her demeanor snapping back to composed efficiency. "I'll have updates sent directly to you as the search continues." She produces a business card, which Oz takes. "If your friend regains consciousness and can provide more details about what happened, please contact me immediately."

After she leaves, I collapse back onto the couch, the momentary surge of adrenaline evaporating as quickly as it came. The harsh lights make my head pound, each throb a reminder that this nightmare is real.

"I can't just sit here. I can't...I need to do something."

"Right now, the best thing we can do is be here for Talon. He's going to need us when he wakes up."

"And Alex needs us now," I counter, tears threatening again. "He could be out there, hurt, alone."

"If Alex is out there," Z interrupts gently, "he's doing everything in his power to get back to you. You know that. But right now, we focus on what we can control."

The logic is sound, but it does nothing to ease the ache spreading through my chest. I try to breathe through the rising panic, sharp and relentless, threatening to pull me under.

The minutes crawl by with excruciating slowness, each tick of the wall clock landing like a hammer against my nerves. Z can't stay still, pacing the length of the waiting room before sinking back beside me, only to repeat the cycle. Oz hasn't moved from his place by the window, his silhouette as still and unyielding as stone.

I bite my thumbnail until it bleeds, the metallic tang on my tongue grounding me. A brutal reminder that I'm still here, still breathing—while Alex might not be. Every time I close my eyes, I see him in the water, reaching for a surface that never comes. I force them open again, fixing my gaze on the ugly pattern in the waiting room carpet to keep the images from overtaking me.

"St. James Family?"

My head snaps up. A woman in blue scrubs stands in the doorway. The three of us rise in unison, instinctively drawing closer.

"That's us," Oz says.

She nods, checking her clipboard. "The surgery was successful."

Relief crashes into me so hard my knees nearly give out.

"Dr. Patel was able to repair the tissue damage and thoroughly clean the wound to reduce the risk of infection. He's in recovery now," she continues, glancing back at the chart. "His vitals are stable, but we're monitoring him closely for complications from the hypothermia and blood loss."

"When can we see him?" The question bursts from me, my voice cracking.

"We can allow one visitor at a time for now," she replies, her expression softening as she takes in my desperate state. "Just for a few minutes until he's moved to a regular room. He'll need to stay overnight. Possibly a couple of days."

Before either twin can speak, I step forward. "I'll go." It's not a request. "I need to see him."

Z and Oz exchange a quick glance, having one of those silent conversations only twins can manage. Oz nods slightly. "Of course. We'll be right here."

The nurse gestures for me to follow her through a set of double doors. The recovery ward is quiet.

"He's still groggy from the anesthesia," she warns, stopping before a partially drawn curtain.

I nod mechanically, steeling myself for what awaits beyond that thin fabric barrier. Nothing could have prepared me for the sight of Talon lying there, his skin nearly as white as the sheets beneath him. Tubes snake from his arms, monitors beeping a steady rhythm that should be reassuring but only amplifies the fragility of his condition. The broad shoulders that carried me when I couldn't walk are now swallowed by the hospital gown, making him look smaller somehow, diminished.

I approach the bed silently, afraid that even my breathing might disturb him. His left shoulder is heavily bandaged.

"Talon," I sob, reaching for his hand. His fingers are cold, so cold, and I clutch them between both of mine, trying to transfer my warmth into him. "I'm here."

His eyelids flutter open at the sound of my voice. "Vesper." My name comes out as a rasp, his throat raw from the breathing tube they must have used during surgery.

"Alex," he croaks, his fingers suddenly gripping mine with surprising strength. "He—"

"Shh," I soothe, though my heart hammers painfully against my ribs. "Don't try to talk."

"No," Talon struggles, his voice strengthening with urgency. "You need to know." He attempts to sit up, wincing as pain shoots through his injured shoulder. The monitors beside him beep more rapidly in response.

"Please, Talon. You need to rest."

"He saved me, Vesper." The words tumble out, each one a blade slicing deeper into my heart. "They had us surrounded. The boat was dead in the water. He—" his voice cracks, "—he pushed me overboard."

I can't breathe. The sterile hospital air turns thick, unbreathable as Talon's words paint a vivid, terrible pictures in my mind.

"He rammed our boat into theirs," Talon continues. "Explosion. So much fire..." His fingers tighten around mine with surprising strength. "He knew what he was doing, Vesper. He chose to—"

"Stop," I plea. "Please stop."

But Talon's grip only tightens. "He said to tell you he kept his promise." His voice cracks on the last word. "He made sure I came back to you."

As the words spill from his lips, my world shatters around me.

The promise I had begged him not to make come true. Alex *is* gone.

# Chapter 22

**LUCA**

NIGHTMARES DON'T END when you wake up. Not in this place. Not for me.

The haze of drugs is lifting slowly, the familiar cotton-mouth and dull headache my only companions as conscious-ness returns. My muscles feel like lead weights beneath the thin sheet covering my body. I've grown accustomed to this routine—the injections, the foggy aftermath, the gradual return to a reality that's arguably worse than the drug-induced oblivion.

I blink at the ceiling, pristine white like everything else in this sterile hell. My cell. My prison. Four walls, a bed bolted to the floor, a toilet without privacy, and a constant rotation of armed guards. Home sweet fucking home.

A sound shatters the silence. The mechanical whir of the door next to mine sliding open. My senses sharpen instantly, years of Rossi training kicking in despite the chemical fog still clinging to my brain. I hold still, controlling my breathing as I listen.

A thud. Heavy, like deadweight hitting the floor.

There are voices outside—two guards, maybe three. Their words are indistinct through the walls, but their tone is casual, bored even. Just another day at work for them. Just another body to process.

"...check on Rossi while we're here?" one asks, voice clearer now.

"Nah, he's still under. Doc said the new dosage would keep him out till morning."

Footsteps retreat down the corridor, followed by the heavy clank of the security door. Silence returns, but something has shifted in the air. A tension that wasn't there before.

The new arrival in the next cell. Another captive for The Collector's twisted menagerie.

I strain my ears, listening for any sign of life from the other side of the wall. Nothing at first, then, a soft moan. The sound twists something in my chest, a feeling I thought they'd drugged out of me months ago. Empathy.

"Hey," I press my lips close to the vent in the wall by my bed. "Can you hear me?"

Silence answers. I wait, counting my heartbeats, wondering if the drugs have finally cracked my mind completely. Then,    another moan, louder this time followed by a rustling sound, like someone struggling to move.

"Easy. The drugs take a while to wear off. Don't fight it."

I've become an expert on their chemical cocktails, learned to endure the surges rather than fight them. Survival lessons no one should ever have to master.

"Where?" A hoarse voice rasps from the other side.

I press my ear closer, desperate for human contact that isn't a guard or one of the technicians who treat me like a lab specimen.

"Where...where am I?"

"Hell," I answer simply. "Or the closest thing to it on earth."

My fingers trail along the smooth surface of the wall next to me, searching for weaknesses I know aren't there. I've examined every inch of this cell hundreds of times.

"How long...how long have you been here?"

"Not sure anymore. Months? Years? They keep me sedated most of the time."

The silence stretches between us, broken only by labored breathing from the other side. He's hurt, I realize. Or coming down from the same drugs they pump into me.

A sharp intake of breath from the other side. Then silence so complete I wonder if he's passed out.

"You there?"

"Yeah. I'm here."

Something in his tone makes me push myself up on my elbows despite the protest of my muscles. There's a familiarity there, buried beneath the pain and disorientation.

"You got a name?" I ask, pressing closer to the vent. Connection is currency here, more valuable than food or water.

A long pause follows. "Does it matter?"

"Probably not," I admit, settling back against my pillow. "But it's been a while since I've talked to anyone who isn't trying to stick a needle in me or milk me dry."

A sound comes through the vent, something between a cough and a bitter laugh. "Fair enough."

"So what'd they get you for?" I ask, falling into small talk that feels oddly appropriate. "What makes you valuable to The Collector?"

Another stretch of silence, this one heavier than before. I'm about to think he's passed out when his voice drifts through again. "A bargaining chip, I'm guessing."

"A bargaining chip," I echo, letting the words settle between us. "For what?"

His breathing has a rhythm to it now, measured, controlled. The kind of breathing you learn when pain is a constant companion and you're trying not to show it.

"Your sister."

I jolt upright, ignoring the wave of nausea that rolls through me. "What do you know about my sister?" My heart hammers against my ribs so hard I can barely hear over the rushing in my ears.

No answer comes from the other side of the wall.

"Hey!" I slam my palm against the cold concrete, pain shooting up my arm. "Answer me, goddammit! What do you know about Vesper?"

Still nothing. Panic claws up my throat as I press my ear against the vent again, straining to hear even the faintest sound of breathing.

"Please," I plea, desperation cracking my voice. "Please, if you know something, anything, about my sister…"

I slide to the floor, pressing my entire body against the wall as if I could somehow phase through it by sheer force of will. The mention of Vesper has shattered what little composure I've managed to maintain in this place. For months, I've survived on nothing but hatred for my father and uncle, and the desperate hope that Vesper somehow escaped the fate they planned for her.

"Come on," I plead, rapping my knuckles against the vent. "Don't do this. Talk to me."

A soft groan filters through the vent, followed by the unmistakable sound of retching. The drugs. I recognize the pattern, the sudden silence, the nausea, the temporary inability to maintain consciousness. Whoever is on the other side is losing the battle against the sedatives.

"She's coming. Your sister…is coming for you."

My breath catches in my throat, heart hammering against my ribs. "How do you know that? Who are you?"

Only silence answers in return. The tiny spark of hope flickers in my chest. "Come back. Please come back."

I won't give up. Not now. Not when there's finally something to hold onto besides hatred.

# Chapter 23

OSCAR

THREE DAYS of watching Vesper unravel at Talon's hospital bedside, and all I can think is that we're losing her faster than she lost Alex. Then we all lost Alex. Z has kept them both safe while I plan our next move. With Alex gone, our backdoor into tracking The Collector went with him. I have no idea how deep his trap was set. We can't risk going back to our place in Boston. Our only choice is one of our safe houses until I know how much The Collector knows.

Vesper sits quietly in Talon's now empty hospital room.

"The car's packed. We need to move." I keep my voice steady as I zip up the duffel bag of supplies for Talon's wounds that I nicked from a storage room. She hasn't slept more than two hours at a time since Talon told her what happened. Her skin has taken on an alarming pallor that makes my chest ache every time I look at her.

"Solnishko, we need to go."

She blinks slowly. "What?"

"The safe house," I remind her, trying to keep the worry from my voice. "Remember? We talked about this."

She nods mechanically, but I can tell the information isn't really registering. This vacant shell of Vesper terrifies me more than her tears or rage ever could. At least anger would be something to work with—something alive and burning.

"Where's Talon?" she asks, the first unprompted question she's offered all day.

"Z's helping him into the car." Her eyes drift toward the door, then back to me, that unsettling vacancy still present. "What about Alex?"

My heart constricts painfully. She's asked this same question a dozen times since it happened. Each time, the answer destroys her anew, as if she's hearing it for the first time.

"Solnishko..." I begin, the endearment catching in my throat.

"No," she interrupts. "Don't say it again. I know. I know." She presses her fingertips against her temples. "He's gone. I just...keep forgetting. Or hoping I dreamed it."

I rise, pulling her gently to her feet. Her body follows mine without resistance.

"The Coast Guard is still searching," I tell her, though we both know what they're searching for now. Not a survivor, but remains. "Lieutenant Wilson promised to call if they find anything."

Vesper nods again, that mechanical motion that's become her default response. We make our way down the hospital corridor in silence, her steps faltering occasionally. The doctors wanted to admit her for exhaustion, but we couldn't risk staying any longer. Not with The Collector's people potentially tracking us.

Outside, Z has the car idling near the entrance, Talon slumped in the back seat, pale but alert. He's still weak, his left arm in a sling, but the doctors cleared him for discharge as long as he follows the strict wound care instructions.

"How is she?" he mouths to me over Vesper's head.

I give a slight shake of my head. No change.

Z exits the driver's side, moving to help me settle Vesper into the back seat beside Talon. She goes without protest, her body collapsing against the leather. Talon immediately draws her against his side with his good arm. She curls into him with a small, broken sound that tears at something vital inside me.

"I've got you, princess. I've got you."

Z's stare catches my own. We've seen Vesper hurt, angry, terrified, but never filled with this hollow emptiness that seems to be consuming her from within.

"How long to the safe house?" I ask as we slide into the front seats.

"Three hours if we take the coastal route," Z replies, pulling smoothly away from the curb. "Two and a half if we cut inland."

"Coastal," I decide. "Less surveillance, fewer potential recognition points."

Z nods, adjusting our course. The hum of tires against asphalt fills the silence as we leave Newport behind. My eyes flicker to the rearview mirror every few minutes, tracking Vesper's reflection. She's curled against Talon, her face pressed into his neck.

"Any trace on Alex's backdoor protocols?" Z asks quietly, his voice pitched low enough that the two in the backseat can't hear.

I shake my head. "Nothing. Whatever he built, it died with him." The words taste bitter on my tongue. "He was the only one with all of the access codes."

"Fuck. So we're flying blind."

"Not completely blind," I counter, pulling out my phone to check for the hundredth time if there's any update from my contacts. "But our vision is severely limited. Alex was ten steps ahead of everyone. We're lucky if we're one step ahead now."

The coastal highway stretches before us, the Atlantic a somber gray-blue to our right. Every mile takes us further from the place we lost Alex, but the distance does nothing to ease the hollow ache in my chest.

"We should have found a way to go with them. Both of us. We could have provided backup, kept them safe."

"Don't," I warn, the single word sharp enough to cut. "We can't do this to ourselves."

In the rearview mirror, I see Talon shift in his seat, wincing as the movement jostles his injured shoulder. Vesper immediately places her hand on his chest, a reflexive gesture of comfort despite her own devastation. Even broken, she's still trying to hold us together. The sight makes something inside me crack.

"What's our next move after the safe house?"

"We regroup. Recover." I glance back at Talon and Vesper. "Then we find another way to locate Luca."

"Without Alex's tech..."

"We'll manage," I interrupt, not wanting to hear the doubt spoken aloud. "We have other resources."

The miles blur beneath our tires, each one taking us further from Newport and closer to the remote coastal property that will shelter us for the coming days. In the backseat, Vesper has finally drifted into an uneasy sleep, her head resting on Talon's good shoulder.

"Do you think he knew?"

"Knew what?"

"Knew what we'd become without him," Z clarifies. "How fragile this whole thing was."

I consider my brother's words, watching the road unfold ahead like a shadowed ribbon. The truth is, Alex had been our foundation in ways none of us fully appreciated—the quiet center around which we all orbited.

"Alex knew everything. That was his curse."

Z nods once, a sharp downward jerk of his chin. "And now it's ours."

The safe house appears ahead—a weathered Cape Cod-style home nestled against a rocky outcropping, hidden from the main road by a thick stand of pines. Z navigates the unmarked gravel drive with ease, killing the headlights as we approach. Security measures have become second nature, paranoia our constant companion.

"We're here," I announce softly, turning to find Talon awake despite the pain medication. Vesper remains asleep against him, breathing shallow but steady.

"Should we wake her?" Talon asks, his voice roughened by exhaustion.

"No," Z and I answer in unison. Let her have these moments of oblivion.

Z parks behind the house, positioning the car for a quick exit if needed. "I'll clear the perimeter," he says, already reaching for his weapon. "Stay here."

I nod, my palm resting on the grip of my own weapon, a constant presence at my side since we left the hospital. The car falls silent, broken only by Vesper's soft breathing and the distant crash of waves against the shore.

"She hasn't cried," Talon remarks. "Not once since they told us."

"I know." The weight of that knowledge settles like lead in my stomach. "It's not healthy."

"None of this is healthy. She's shutting down, Oz. I can feel her slipping away."

I turn in my seat to face him fully. "We won't let that happen."

"How?" The single word carries his grief, his guilt. "How do we fix this when we're all broken?"

Before I can answer, Z materializes beside the car. He gives a curt nod, signaling the all-clear, and opens the rear door.

"I'll take her," he says, carefully gathering Vesper into his arms. She barely stirs, her body limp with exhaustion, as Z lifts her against his chest.

Talon struggles to exit the car one-armed, pride holding him back until I move to his side. "Lean on me," I offer my shoulder. "The stairs are tricky in the dark."

His jaw tightens, but he accepts my help, his good arm gripping my shoulder as we make our way up the weathered porch steps. The hinges protest as I push open the door, revealing the interior of our temporary refuge.

The safe house is exactly as we left it the last time we were here—sparse furnishings draped in sheets, the air heavy with the scent of disuse and sea salt. Z has already disappeared down the hallway with Vesper, his footsteps fading on the wooden floors.

"Couch or bed?" I ask Talon, whose face has gone ashen from the short walk.

"Bed," he admits, the single word costing him. "Need to lie down."

I guide him toward the smaller bedroom off the main living area, helping him ease onto the edge of the mattress.

He hisses through his teeth as the movement jars his injured shoulder.

"Need your meds?"

"Not yet." He shakes his head, then gestures toward the hallway where Z took Vesper. "Stay with her tonight. She shouldn't be alone."

I nod, understanding the unspoken concern. Vesper's vacant stare has us all on edge. "Z will set the security protocols. Get some rest."

The floorboards creak beneath my feet as I move through the dim house. A soft glow emanates from the main bedroom, where I find Z settling Vesper onto the bed, her limbs arranged with careful precision.

"She didn't even wake when I carried her in," Z sighs.

"Exhaustion. Shock. Grief. Her body's shutting down what it can't process."

Z's calloused thumb traces the shadowed circle beneath her eye. I move to the opposite side of the bed, sinking down beside Vesper's sleeping form.

Vesper shifts, whimpering in her sleep. "Alex."

"I'll take the first watch," Z offers, already moving toward the window to check the perimeter again. "You should get some rest."

I don't argue. The past seventy-two hours have drained me physically and mentally. Each hour watching Vesper's silent suffering carving out another piece from my soul. I shed my jacket and shoes, stretching out beside her on the bed.

"Should we try to wake her?" I ask, watching the rapid movement beneath her eyelids. "She's dreaming."

Z shakes his head, letting the curtain fall back into place. "Let her sleep. Reality will be waiting soon enough."

He's right, of course. Whatever nightmare plays behind her closed eyes can't be worse than waking to the truth again. I settle deeper into the mattress, careful not to disturb her, and try to ignore the Alex-shaped void in our lives that seems to grow larger with each passing hour.

# Chapter 25

VESPER

THE WAVES DON'T CARE that he's gone. They just keep coming, relentless, smacking against the shore like nothing has changed.

I dig my toes into the cold sand, watching the first golden rays of sunlight stretch across the water. My body aches from another night of restless sleep, punctuated by dreams where Alex is reaching for me from beneath the waters, his mouth forming words I can never quite hear. I'm so tired of waking up gasping, clutching at empty air.

A week. Seven days of existing in this hollow space between breathing and living.

The Coast Guard stopped searching after a few days. No body was recovered. Just scattered debris and the official designation: *presumed dead.* Those two words echo in my head with every heartbeat. Presumed. Dead.

But presumed isn't certain. Presumed leaves room for hope, and hope is the cruelest thing of all.

I pull my knees to my chest, wrapping my arms around them as the morning chill seeps through my thin sweater. The safe house sits behind me on the rocky outcropping, windows still dark, except for the kitchen where Talon is probably making coffee, his movements still careful around his healing shoulder.

Footsteps crunch in the sand behind me, too heavy to be Talon's, too measured to be Oscar's. I don't turn around. I don't need to.

"Thought I might find you here, moya koroleva."

Z settles beside me, his warmth radiating against my side as he matches my posture, knees drawn up to his chest. He doesn't touch me, doesn't offer platitudes or demands. Just sits, a silent sentinel sharing my vigil.

The silence between us stretches, comfortable in its familiarity. Of the three remaining men in my life, Z understands the value of wordless company. Unlike Oscar with his careful planning or Talon with his need to fill empty spaces with comfort, Z knows when presence alone is enough.

"It's beautiful. The ocean. It shouldn't be allowed to be so beautiful right now."

Z's shoulder brushes mine, a gentle point of contact. "Nature doesn't stop for our grief."

"No," I agree. "Nothing stops."

Except me. I've been frozen in this moment for days,

unable to move forward. Suspended in the space between denial and acceptance. The others have tried to pull me toward acceptance, toward healing, but my fingers remain bloody from clinging to the jagged edges of hope.

"You should eat something," Z says after another stretch of silence. "You barely touched dinner last night."

I shrug, the movement requiring more energy than I have to spare. "Not hungry."

"Doesn't matter. Starving yourself won't bring him back, Vesper."

Nothing will. Alex is gone because of me. There's no other way around that bitter truth. He died because he was trying to bring my brother home. He died, and there's no way for me to apologize for our last conversation.

Z shifts beside me, his hand moving to cover mine where it rests in the sand. His skin is warm against my perpetually cold fingers. I should find comfort in the touch, but comfort feels like betrayal now, as if allowing any relief means accepting that Alex is truly gone.

"He wouldn't want you fading away like this."

A bitter laugh escapes me. "What Alex would want stopped mattering the moment he decided to sacrifice himself."

The words taste like ash in my mouth, sharp and acrid. I've cycled through every emotion since that night—denial, grief, rage. The anger is easiest to hold onto, burning hot enough to keep the hollow emptiness at bay, if only for a few moments.

"He made a choice," Z counters. "To save Talon. To protect you."

"I never asked him to die for me."

"No one ever asks for sacrifice, moya koroleva. That's what makes it a sacrifice."

The tide continues its relentless rhythm, each retreat leaving shells and debris scattered across the shore. Like the ocean gave Talon back but kept Alex for itself. A cruel exchange I never agreed to.

"I keep thinking about what we talked about before they left. He told me he couldn't love me the way the rest of you do."

Z's fingers tighten around mine, his breathing steady beside me. "Alex always believed he was more monster than man."

"He was wrong. He wasn't the monster he thought he was."

"No," Z says softly. "He wasn't."

Another swell crashes against the shore, reaching farther this time, the foam nearly brushing our feet before sliding back. I watch it recede, pulling sand and small stones with it, like it's still taking pieces of him.

"This feels familiar. It was on another beach that you brought yourself back from the brink, Vesper. When you escaped The Collector. When you chose to live despite everything that had been taken from you."

"That was a long time ago." I look back at the water. The memory feels distant, like it belongs to someone else—a stronger version of myself I can barely recognize anymore.

"It wasn't," Z counters firmly. "You survived then. You'll survive now."

I want to look away, to sink back into the comforting numbness I've wrapped around myself like armor, but Z won't let me.

"I had nothing to lose then. Now I've lost everything."

"Not everything." His thumb brushes across my cheekbone, wiping away a tear I didn't realize had fallen. "You still have us. Luca is still out there, Vesper. He needs you. Just like we do. You need to find your fight again."

"What if I can't?" The question emerges broken, vulnerable in a way I haven't allowed myself to be since the news came.

"Then we hold the pieces until you're ready to put them back together."

I rest my head against his shoulder, watching the ocean continue its endless dance with the shore. The numbness that's been my constant companion begins to crack, hairline fractures spreading through the protective shell I've built around myself.

"I'm so angry with him," I admit, the words burning on their way out.

"I know."

"And I'm angry with myself—for not being there. For letting you all convince me to stay behind."

"Your presence wouldn't have changed the outcome, Vesper."

But logic doesn't soften the guilt. It doesn't fill the Alex-shaped void hollowed out inside my chest.

"I miss him." The admission tears something open in me. "I miss him so much it hurts to breathe."

Z's arm tightens around me, a silent acknowledgment of my pain. We sit together in the steady hush of the sea, my grief finally breaking through the numbness that's consumed me for far too long.

"Vesper! Z!" Talon's voice cuts through the morning air, sharp with urgency. "Get back up here, now!"

Z tenses beside me, his body instantly alert. He cocks his head, listening to something in Talon's voice that I'm too worn out to catch.

"Something's wrong." He is already rising to his feet before his declaration registers, pulling me up with surprising gentleness despite the urgency in his movements. "Stay close to me."

"What is it?" I ask, stumbling as he guides me across the sand, his pace quickening with each step.

"Not sure, but Talon is on edge."

My heart thuds painfully against my ribs as we make our way up the rocky path to the safe house.

We reach the back door, and Z pushes it open carefully, ushering me inside with a protective hand at my lower back. The kitchen is empty.

"In here," Talon calls from the living room, his voice tight with something I can't identify.

My feet feel leaden, each step requiring conscious effort as we move through the narrow hallway. Z looks over at Talon. "What the fuck is going on?"

Oscar paces the length of the living room. I've never seen

him like this. Oscar—the calm one, the strategist, the steady force when the rest of us start to unravel. But now, his movements are erratic, barely restrained.

Clutched in his fingers is something small—a slip of paper, maybe, or...something else entirely.

"What's happening?"

Oscar stops abruptly, turning toward us. He holds out what I now see is a photograph, offering it to Z first. He takes it, his body going completely still as he studies the image. The blood drains from his face, and for a moment, I think he might be sick.

"Where the fuck did you find this?"

"On the doorstep. In an envelope addressed to Vesper. No postmark. Someone delivered it."

My stomach drops. "Let me see it."

Z hesitates, his fingers tightening on the photo. "Vesper, I don't think—"

"Show me." The command comes out sharper than I intend, a flash of my old self emerging through the fog. "Now."

The twins exchange a look loaded with silent communication before Z reluctantly passes me the photograph. The moment my fingers touch the glossy paper, the world tilts sideways.

It's a cell with industrial lighting. A metal bed bolted to the floor, a toilet with no privacy screen. But it's the figure slumped against the far wall that steals my breath.

Luca.

My brother's face is bruised, one eye swollen nearly shut,

but it's unmistakably him. His hair is longer than I remember, lank and unwashed, hanging around his gaunt face. But it's his eyes that gut me, the open defiance that peaks past the exhaustion.

"Luca." His name emerges as a gasp, my fingers trembling against the photograph. The room spins around me, and I grab the back of the couch to steady myself. "He's alive."

"Look at the corner," Talon points out. "Bottom right."

The date stamp in the corner shows yesterday's date.

"This—" My voice fails me. I try again, clutching the photo so tightly the edges cut into my palm. "This can't be real."

"And there's something else. Turn it over."

My fingers are numb as I flip the photograph, revealing a small black square in the center of the white backing. A QR code.

Talon's jaw clenches as he studies it over my shoulder. "Wait here," he orders, already moving toward the hallway. He disappears into his bedroom, returning moments later with one of the burner phones we keep for emergencies.

"If we scan that, it could lead them right to us," Z warns, stepping closer to me as Talon powers up the device.

"They already know where we are," Oscar responds. "But this is also our only lead."

Talon positions the phone over the QR code, his breathing shallow as the scanner activates. A soft beep, then the screen fills with static before resolving into an image that steals the air from my lungs.

Luca hangs suspended from the ceiling, thick chains wrapped around his wrists, his toes barely brushing the concrete floor. His head lolls forward, chin resting against his chest, but I can see the shallow rise and fall of his breathing. He's alive. My brother is alive.

"My God."

A voice emerges from the phone's speaker—distorted, mechanical, deliberately inhuman. "Hello, Vesper." It's the voice of my fucking nightmare. The Collector.

My stomach lurches as the camera pans around Luca, lingering on the lattice of scars crisscrossing his back. Fresh wounds weep over old scar tissue. My knees buckle, Z's arm locks around my waist, holding me upright as the monstrous voice continues.

"We've kept him alive for you, Vesper, as a gift. As a thank you for your donation to my cause."

The camera zooms in on Luca's face. His eyes flutter open, glazed with pain but still burning with that stubborn Rossi defiance. The screen flickers, then shows a new angle of Luca. "Vesper," he croaks, her name a broken sound. Someone off-camera presses a cattle prod against his ribs. His body convulses, a hoarse scream tearing from his throat.

"Stop!" I scream, lunging for the phone, but Z holds me firmly in place. "Stop hurting him!"

A figure moves into frame, face hidden behind a smooth, featureless mask. The voice comes through distorted. "You have something I want. And we have something you want. I propose a simple transaction."

The camera jerks away from Luca's convulsing form, settling instead on a wall where a projection appears. It's a blueprint I recognize immediately. The Rossi mansion. My childhood home. The place where my nightmares began. A red circle appears over the east wing of the mansion where my father's private study is located. The place where deals were made, where enemies were broken, where family secrets were buried beneath layers of mahogany and blood money.

"Twenty-four hours from now. 10 pm. Any sign of your protectors, and what's left of your brother won't be recognizable."

Before I can react, Talon wrenches the phone from my grasp, his movements swift and decisive despite his injured shoulder. He removes the battery, then pries out the SIM card, crushing it beneath his heel.

"Tracking?" Oscar asks sharply, already moving toward the windows to scan the perimeter.

"Possibly." Talon's face is grim as he drops the dismantled phone into a glass of water on the coffee table. "They already knew where to find us. That's the bigger problem. Leave everything behind. We take nothing with us, including the car. They might have a tracker on it."

My body feels disconnected. Luca's scream echoes in my ears. My brother. Alive. Suffering. Because of me.

"We need to move. Now."

Oscar is already gathering equipment, his movements sharp and efficient despite the tension coiled in every muscle.

"If they delivered that photo in person, it means they've been watching the house."

The fog that's surrounded me for days suddenly burns away, replaced by a clarity so sharp it's almost painful. The hollow ache in my chest remains, but alongside it blazes something I thought I'd lost forever—purpose.

"I'm going after him." My voice sounds strange to my own ears, stronger, steadier than it's been since Alex died.

"We're going after him," Talon corrects, already checking the magazine of his handgun. "But we need a plan first."

# Chapter 25

LUCA

THE GUARDS HAVEN'T COME for me in days. Their absence isn't mercy, it's just another form of torture.

I trace the familiar crack in the wall beside my bed, following its jagged path with my fingertip. The sedatives they pump into me run on a timed schedule. Just as I start to feel the fog lifting, just as my thoughts begin to coalesce into something resembling clarity, another dose arrives through the automated system in the wall. A hiss, a cloud of mist, and I'm dragged back under.

My sense of time is fragmented at best. Days blur together, marked only by the cycles of drugged sleep and hazy wakefulness. But something's changed. The guards' focus has shifted to the cell next door, their heavy boots passing my door without stopping, their voices muffled as they cluster around my neighbor instead.

I press my ear against the vent, straining to hear any sign of life from the adjacent cell. Nothing but silence. Not even breathing.

"Hey," I rasp, my voice rough from disuse. "You still alive over there?"

The silence stretches, broken only by the soft hum of the ventilation system. Whoever claimed to know my sister hasn't spoken in days. Maybe they moved him. Maybe he died. Maybe he was never real at all. Just another hallucination courtesy of the drugs.

A distant metallic clang echoes down the corridor. My body tenses, the familiar sound triggering years of ingrained responses. The security door at the end of the hall. Two sets of footsteps. One heavy, deliberate, the other lighter, almost hesitant. Not the usual guard rotation.

I drag myself to the corner of my bed furthest from the door, back pressed against the wall. The strategic position offers the illusion of distance, though in this eight-by-ten cell, nowhere is truly safe.

The footsteps slow as they approach. Voices come from just outside my door. A man and a woman, their tones hushed but urgent.

"This is a mistake," the woman says, her voice carrying a clinical detachment that reminds me of the white coats who draw my blood.

"Orders from above," the man responds gruffly. "Just do your job."

A key card beeps, followed by the pneumatic hiss of my cell door sliding open. I squint against the sudden influx of hallway light, momentarily blinded after days in the dim illumination.

A woman in a lab coat enters first, clutching a tablet to her chest like a shield. Behind her looms one of the regular guards, Denny, I think they call him. Built like a concrete wall with about the same level of compassion.

"Subject appears coherent," the woman notes, clinically assessing me without really seeing me. "Surprising, given the dosage levels."

"Dosage levels aren't the problem," I mutter. "Rossi blood burns through your poison faster than you expect."

Something flickers across the woman's face, irritation, perhaps. She turns to Denny with a curt nod. "Hold him down."

Before I can react, the guard lunges forward, meaty hands clamping around my biceps. I struggle against his grip, but months of captivity have withered my strength. My resistance is pathetic, barely enough to make him adjust his stance.

The woman approaches, pulling a syringe from her lab coat pocket. The liquid inside catches the light, clear with a faint amber tinge. Not the usual sedative.

"What is that?" I demand, panic rising in my throat. "What are you giving me?"

She ignores my question, tapping the syringe and

expelling air bubbles with the detachment. With clinical precision, she plunges the needle into my neck.

Heat floods my veins. Unlike the sedatives that dull everything, this hits fast and hard. My muscles go rigid, then melt. The room tilts sideways.

"Secure him to his bed," she instructs Denny, her voice distant through the rushing in my ears. "We need to monitor his movements."

Rough hands shove me onto the narrow mattress, the frame creaking beneath the force. Cold metal clamps around my wrists and ankles as restraints click into place. My heartbeat thunders in my ears, too fast and too loud. Something's wrong. This isn't like the usual sedatives. My thoughts aren't clouding. they're racing, frantic, and sharp.

"What did you do to me?" I gasp, arching against the restraints.

The woman makes a note on her tablet. "Preparation for transport."

Transport. The word cuts through my panic like a knife. They're moving me. After months in this cell, they're taking me somewhere else. My mind races with possibilities, none of them good.

"Where?" I demand.

"That's not your concern." She checks my pulse, fingers cold and impersonal against my neck. "The compound will keep you conscious but compliant. You'll be able to walk, but unable to resist commands."

Denny smirks, adjusting the restraints tighter. "Boss wants you presentable. Got a family reunion planned."

Family reunion. The words echo in my fractured mind. Vesper. They're using me to get to Vesper.

"No," I growl, straining against the metal cuffs until I feel skin tear. "Leave her alone!"

The woman steps back, nodding to Denny. "Ten minutes until full effect. I'll prepare the transport team."

As the door hisses shut behind her, Denny leans over me, his breath hot with the stench of cigarettes and coffee. "I wonder if your sister is still as sweet as she was when she was here."

My stomach rolls. Vesper was here? Oh god. Had they... had they done things to her as they had me? The thought makes me retch.

"She's a pretty little thing. Especially when she is sedated. The things I could do to that pretty body of hers without her even knowing."

Rage flashes through me, temporarily overriding the chemicals in my veins. "You don't talk about her," I snarl, lunging against the restraints with enough force that Denny actually steps back.

"Easy, tiger." He chuckles, clearly enjoying my helplessness. "Save your energy. You'll need it for the show tonight."

The drug continues its relentless assault on my system, spreading numbness from my extremities inward while keeping my mind painfully alert. My thoughts race in frantic circles as I process what little information I have. Transport. Family reunion. Vesper.

I'd convinced myself she was safe. Far away from this nightmare. I imagined her in Russia, living in some palatial estate as Dmitri Petrov's wife. I hated the thought of my sister being sold off like property to cement our father's alliance with the Russians, but at least she'd be protected. The room is spinning as realization dawns. "My sister...she's not with the Petrovs?"

Denny's eyebrows lift, genuine surprise crossing his features before amusement replaces it. "You really don't know, do you? Your sister's been quite busy since your daddy tried to marry her off. She served her purpose for The Collector, and then he sold her like the fucking bitch she is."

A murderous rage blossoms in my chest, momentarily overpowering the chemical in my veins. I strain against the restraints with such force that the bed frame creaks.

"You're lying," I spit, even as dread pools in my stomach. "My father would have burned this place to the ground if she was taken."

Denny's smile is ugly, revealing tobacco-stained teeth. "Your father's dead, kid. Has been for a while."

My father is dead? For all his cruelty, all his sins, I'd always believed him invincible. The immovable center of our twisted family universe.

"You're full of shit," I manage, though uncertainty creeps in. How long have I been here? What's happened in the world outside these walls?

"Believe what you want." Denny shrugs, checking his watch. "But your sister's coming for you tonight, walking right into the trap set for her. The Collector always gets what he wants. She's the key to his future."

My mind races despite the drug's increasing hold. What could Vesper have that's worth all this?

"What does he want from her?"" I growl, fighting to keep my thoughts coherent as the edges of my vision blur.

Denny's smile widens. "Above my pay grade, but I hear it's special. One of a kind. Something only your sister can provide him. Now, rest up. You'll be seeing her real soon."

# Chapter 26

VESPER

I STAND at the window of our Boston apartment, watching the late afternoon light paint the city skyline in hues of amber and gold. With our safe house no longer safe, Oz decided that we were better off back in Boston. Closer to the meeting tomorrow, and better equipped. In the blink of an eye, we were on the road, heading back to our home base. To Alex's empty room.

"Perimeter's secure," Oz announces as he emerges from the bedroom hallway. "Security system is armed."

I nod without turning. Behind me, I can hear the familiar sounds of my men preparing for war—the metallic click of weapons being checked, and hushed conversations punctuated by the occasional curse. It should be comforting, but all

I can think about is the empty space where Alex should be standing, hunched over his laptop with that little furrow between his brows.

I press my fingers against the cool glass, feeling the vibration of the city below. My mind keeps replaying the image of Luca hanging there, the way his body convulsed when that cattle prod touched his skin. Twenty-four hours. That's all the time I have to save what's left of my family.

"Vesper."

The voice behind me is gentle, careful. I turn to find Talon standing there, his injured arm still in a sling, holding out a steaming mug of coffee. The rich aroma reaches me, but my stomach turns at the thought of consuming anything.

"No, thanks," I say, shaking my head. "I can't."

"You need something. You've barely eaten."

"I said no." The words come out sharper than I intended.

Talon doesn't flinch, just sets the mug down on the windowsill beside me. "It's here if you change your mind."

Oz and Z emerge from the hallway, joining us near the large table in the living room where maps and blueprints of the Rossi mansion are spread out.

"We've got three potential entry points," Oz begins, leaning over the table and pointing to the layout. "East wing has the heaviest security, but we might be able to bypass it if—"

"No," I interrupt, stepping away from the window. Three pairs of eyes turn to me, surprise visible in each of them.

"No?" Z repeats, straightening to his full height.

"I'm going alone," I state. The decision crystallized during our silent drive back to Boston.

"Absolutely not," Talon says immediately, shaking his head. "We're not letting you walk into a trap by yourself."

"It's not up for debate." I move toward the table, studying the blueprint with calculated detachment. "The message was clear. If they see any of you, Luca dies."

"And if you go alone, you both die," Oz counters, his voice tight with frustration. "Vesper, be reasonable."

"Reasonable? There's nothing reasonable about any of this."

"We understand your urgency, moya koroleva, but rushing in without proper planning is exactly what The Collector wants."

My fingers trace the red circle marking my father's study. "He wants something only I can give him. He said it himself."

The three men exchange glances, a silent communication passing between them that makes my skin prickle with irritation.

"This is about my family. The Collector took Luca and I, raped our bodies, harvested our family's legacy, and sold them to the highest bidder. This has never been just about me, but my entire family. The only way this ends is if I meet with him."

"That's not entirely true," Oz says, his voice quiet but firm. "It's about us too, Vesper. It's about all of us now."

I turn away, frustration building in my chest. "You don't understand what he's capable of."

"We understand exactly what he's capable of," Talon

counters, moving to stand beside me. His good arm reaches out, fingers brushing mine. "We've seen what he did to you. What he did to Luca in that video. We're not naive."

"Then you should understand why I have to go alone!" My voice rises, echoing against the apartment walls. "I've already lost Alex. I won't lose the rest of you, too."

The room falls silent at the mention of his name. It's the first time I've spoken it aloud since the beach with Z. The pain is still raw, an open wound that refuses to heal.

Z approaches slowly, as if I'm a wounded animal that might bolt. "Vesper, listen to me. The Collector isn't expecting you to come alone. He's expecting you to bring us."

I blink, confusion momentarily replacing my anger. "What?"

"Think about it," Oz continues, picking up his brother's thread. "He knows you well enough to understand you wouldn't leave Luca to suffer. But he also knows us. He knows we wouldn't let you walk into danger unprotected."

"It's a trap within a trap."

"Exactly," Talon confirms. "He's counting on us to accompany you, planning to eliminate all of us in one sweep."

The realization settles over me like a cold shroud. The Collector has always been ten steps ahead, manipulating every move on this twisted chessboard. My hand trembles slightly as I reach for the coffee mug Talon left, needing something to ground me.

"So what's your brilliant alternative?" I ask, taking a sip of the now lukewarm liquid. "If going together is walking into a trap, and going alone is suicide, what options do we have left?"

Oz leans forward, his finger tracing a path on the blue-print I hadn't noticed before.

We go in differently. Not the way someone would expect."

"The underground tunnel system," Z adds, tapping another section of the blueprint. "Your father had escape routes built throughout the property. Alex found them when he was researching the estate."

My breath catches at the mention of Alex's name again. Of course, he would have discovered my family's secrets, even the ones I didn't know existed. He was thorough like that, meticulous in his preparation.

"These tunnels," I begin, "I never knew about them."

"They were deliberately kept off the main house plans," Oz explains. "Your father didn't want anyone knowing all his potential escape routes."

I shake my head. "Of course, he didn't." The irony isn't lost on me that I am using my father's paranoia to save the son he never truly valued.

"The main tunnel entrance is beneath the greenhouse," Z continues, his finger tracing the path on the blueprint. "It leads directly to a hidden door in your father's study. The Collector may know about the tunnel system, but he won't expect us to use it. Not if he believes we're coming through the front."

"So I'm the distraction," I conclude. "I walk in through the front door while you three sneak in through the tunnels."

Talon's jaw tightens. "It's risky. You'll be exposed, vulnerable."

"I've survived that man before," I remind them. "I can do it again. Long enough for you to get to Luca."

Oz studies me, his mind visibly working through scenarios. "You'll need to keep him talking. Stall as long as possible while we navigate the tunnels and locate Luca."

"That won't be difficult." The memories of The Collector's fondness for monologuing flashing through my mind. "He loves the sound of his own voice."

Z moves closer, his expression grave. "If anything goes wrong, if you feel threatened in any way, you give us the signal."

Talon moves to a leather case on the coffee table, opening it to reveal a small black device. "This is one of Alex's designs. It's a subdermal tracker and panic button in one."

My stomach twists at the sight of it, another piece of Alex's brilliance that would live on without him. "Subdermal?"

"It needs to go under your skin," Oz explains, his expression apologetic. "The Collector will search you for electronics. This is the only way to ensure he won't find it."

I stare at the tiny device, no larger than a grain of rice. "Where?"

"Upper arm," Z answers. "Easy to access, but not somewhere he's likely to check closely."

"Do it," I say, already rolling up my sleeve. "Now."

Talon hesitates, glancing at the twins. "It will hurt."

"Everything hurts," I reply simply. "This one is just pain with a purpose."

Z retrieves a medical kit from beneath the sink. He returns to my side, setting the kit on the coffee table and extracting a sealed package containing what looks like a syringe with an unusually thick needle.

"This was developed for covert operatives," Oz explains, watching as Z prepares the area on my upper arm with an alcohol swab. The cold sensation makes me shiver. "Alex modified it to include both tracking and emergency signal capabilities."

I clench my jaw at the mention of his name again. "Will I be able to feel it?"

"After the initial insertion, no," Z answers, his fingers gentle against my skin as he identifies the ideal placement. "The casing is biocompatible. Your body won't reject it."

Talon moves to my other side, offering me his good hand. I take it as Z positions the injector against my arm.

"Deep breath," Z declares. "On three. One...two..."

The pain is sharp and immediate, a burning sensation that radiates outward from the injection site. I bite down hard on my lower lip, refusing to make a sound as the device slips beneath my skin. Z removes the injector and immediately applies pressure to the tiny wound.

"Done," he says, reaching for a small adhesive bandage. "The signal is already active."

Talon squeezes my hand before releasing it. "The tracker has a battery life of approximately forty-eight hours. More than enough time for what we need to do."

I flex my arm experimentally, feeling only a slight tenderness where the device now sits beneath my skin. "How does the panic button work?"

"Press here," Oz demonstrates on his own arm, indicating a spot about an inch above where Z inserted the tracker. "Hard pressure for three seconds activates the emergency signal. We'll all receive the alert immediately."

I nod, committing the location to memory. "And if I can't reach it?"

The three men exchange glances, the unspoken worry hanging heavy between them.

"Let's make sure it doesn't come to that," Talon says finally, his jaw tight with determination.

Z returns the medical supplies to their case. "We should go over the timing. Every second will count once we're on the property."

My attention drifts back to the blueprint spread across the table, tracing the path from the greenhouse to my father's study. Memories flood back, the scent of expensive leather and cigars filling my nose. How fitting that the room where he plotted so much destruction would become the stage for our rescue.

"Vesper?" Oz's voice pulls me from my thoughts. "Are you with us?"

I blink, refocusing on the present. "Yes. Sorry."

"As I was saying, Talon will be your driver. Zaire and I will already be there in the tunnels by the time you arrive," Oz repeats again.

I nod, studying the rough sketch of the tunnel system

again. "How will you get there ahead of us without being seen?"

"We'll go in separately, hours before your scheduled arrival," Z explains, tracing the route with his finger. "There's a maintenance access point half a mile from the property line, hidden in what appears to be an abandoned groundskeeper's shed."

"Alex discovered it during his initial research," Oz says quietly. "He mapped the entire system before..." He doesn't finish the sentence; he doesn't need to.

I force myself to focus on the blueprint, not the absence that seems to grow more profound with each passing hour.

"What if he moves Luca?" I ask, voicing the fear that's been gnawing at me since we saw the video. "What if he's not even in the house?"

"That's the problem. He may not even have Luca with him. It could be like the pickup at Martha's Vineyard. The house may be the initial contact point with a secondary location for the meeting. We can't plan for what we don't know, but the tracker in your arm will tell us where you are. We can follow you."

"Alex designed it to work even in areas with signal-jamming technology," Talon explains, his voice softening at the mention of Alex's name. "It piggybacks on multiple frequencies, including some military bands. Unless The Collector takes you deep underground or into the middle of the ocean, we'll find you."

I try to take comfort in that, but doubt still gnaws at me. What if he's anticipated this too? The memories of my time there flood back into my mind, taking me back to the place of my nightmares again. The walls are closing in around me.

"I need a minute."

I don't wait for their response before heading down the hallway. My feet carry me automatically toward Alex's room, the door still firmly closed since we returned to the apartment. No one has entered it. It's become a shrine of sorts, a testament to the hole his absence has carved in our lives.

My hand hesitates on the doorknob, trembling slightly. Taking a deep breath, I push it open and step inside.

The room is exactly as he left it—bed neatly made with military precision, laptop closed on the desk, a half-empty mug of coffee still sitting beside it. Time has frozen here, preserving everything in a painful stasis. I can almost imagine him walking through the door, eyebrow raised in that questioning way of his, asking what I'm doing in his space.

I move to his closet and slide the door open, revealing a meticulous row of shirts and suits—each one spaced evenly, like everything in his life: controlled, calculated. My fingers drift across the fabrics until they pause on a gray Henley— the one he wore at the beach house after they first pulled me from hell. I slip it off the hanger, press it to my face, and inhale. His scent still lingers, warm and familiar, and it punches the air from my lungs, tightening my throat with a grief I can't swallow down.

"Tell me I'm not making a mistake. That the meeting tomorrow will not cost me everything."

The silence that greets my plea feels like another loss. I clutch his shirt tighter.

"It should have been me. It should have been me on that boat."

A soft knock at the open door makes me turn. Talon leans against the doorframe, his injured arm cradled against his chest.

"He wouldn't agree with that sentiment," he says quietly.

I don't bother wiping away the tears tracking down my cheeks. "He's not here to argue, is he?"

Talon steps into the room, his presence gentle despite his size. "No. But I am."

"You nearly died too," I remind him, fingers still wrapped in Alex's shirt. "Because of me."

"Because of The Collector," he corrects, moving closer. "Don't give yourself credit for his evil, Vesper."

I shake my head, looking around the pristine room that still feels inhabited by Alex's presence.

Alex knew, you know. He knew something would go wrong. That night before you left, he told me if it came down to a choice between you coming back or him, he'd make sure it was you."

Talon's expression tightens with pain. "He never told me that."

"Of course not. That wasn't how Alex operated. He just did what he thought was best for us all. He sacrificed himself, Talon, and for what? I am meeting the very person responsible for taking him away from all of us tomorrow."

Taking a deep breath, I turn back to Talon. "You're right.

We can't let fear stop us from moving forward. Alex's sacrifice wasn't in vain, and we owe it to him to keep moving forward."

Talon nods in silent agreement, his grip on my hand reassuring me of our shared resolve. Together, we would honor Alex's memory by continuing the mission he believed in so deeply.

With a newfound sense of strength, I pick up the shirt from the bed, holding it close for a moment, before folding it neatly. As I place it back down, a sense of purpose settled over me.

"We'll find Luca."

Talon's expression softens. "We will," he affirms, squeezing my hand gently. "Together."

# Chapter 27

VESPER

I'VE WORN a path into Alex's carpet from my endless pacing, the fibers beneath my feet flattened from the hours of restless movement. His room, a silent reminder of what we've lost.

I run my fingers along his desk for the hundredth time, searching for something, anything, that might help us. Alex always had contingency plans. He wouldn't have left us completely unprepared for this moment, would he?

"Come on, Alex," I plea. "You must have known this could happen. You must have left us something."

Only silence answers me. I've torn through his notes, combed through files on the only unlocked laptop he left behind, but found nothing that could help us face The

Collector. The rest of his setup is locked. Nothing that could ensure we all walk away from this alive.

A soft knock interrupts my desperate search. I don't need to turn to know it's Talon.

"Vesper?" His voice is low, careful not to startle me. "Z and Oz are leaving."

Talon stands in the doorway, already dressed, his injured shoulder no longer in a sling, though I can tell by the way he holds himself that it still pains him. The black outfit makes his skin seem paler, highlighting the exhaustion etched into his features. He's pushing himself too hard. We all are.

I've always hated goodbyes, but this one tastes like ash in my mouth.

"Tell them to wait," I order. "Not yet."

"They're loading up now. They want to be in the tunnels before dawn."

I push past him, my bare feet silent against the hardwood floors as I rush down the hallway. The apartment feels too large, too empty. Without Alex's steady presence, everything feels unmoored.

I find Oscar and Zaire in the garage, loading duffel bags into a nondescript black SUV. They both look up when I enter.

"You weren't going to say goodbye?" I demand, crossing my arms over my chest to hide how badly my hands are shaking.

Zaire approaches me first. "Moya koroleva," he says, his voice a low rumble. "We thought it would be easier."

"Easier for who?" I snap.

"For us," Oscar admits, his voice uncharacteristically gentle. "Saying goodbye to you has never been easy."

The honesty in his admission catches me off guard, momentarily silencing the panic clawing at my throat. I take in the sight of them, dressed in black tactical gear, weapons strapped to their bodies, expressions set with grim determination. These men who have become my world are preparing to risk everything for my brother. For me.

"What if this is the last time?" The words escape before I can stop them, voicing the fear that's been haunting me since we formed this plan.

Z closes the distance between us. "It won't be."

"You don't know that. Alex thought he was coming back, too."

Pain flashes across his features before he masters it. "We're not going into a firefight, solnishko. We're infiltrating tunnels that haven't been used in years. Reconnaissance only, until you arrive."

Oz approaches, standing shoulder to shoulder with his twin. "We need to go now to ensure we're in position when you arrive. Time is our advantage."

I know he's right, but logic does nothing to ease the panic coursing inside of me.

"I can't lose you, too," I say, my voice barely audible. "Not after Alex."

Z's thumb brushes across my cheekbone. "You won't."

Before I can respond, he leans down, pressing his lips to mine. I clutch at his tactical vest, drawing him closer, memorizing the feel of him. The slight scratch of stubble against my skin.

"I will always come back to you, moya koroleva."

Oscar steps forward as Z reluctantly moves aside.

"We'll be waiting for you," he says. "Just follow the plan."

I reach for him, fingers curling into the fabric of his shirt. "Be careful. Both of you."

His lips find mine, the kiss unlike his brother's—more controlled but no less passionate. His hand cradles the back of my head, holding me with a gentleness that feels unexpected against the weapons strapped to his body.

"See you on the other side, solnishko," he speaks against my lips before stepping back.

The twins exchange a look. With a final nod, they climb into the SUV, the engine purring to life with a soft rumble. I stand rooted to the spot as they back out of the garage, watching until their taillights fade into the predawn shadows. Even after they're gone, I remain, staring at the empty space where they were, the ghost of their kisses still lingering on my lips.

The garage feels suddenly vast and empty. Cold. I wrap my arms around myself, the chill of the concrete seeping through my bare feet as I finally turn away. Each step back toward the apartment feels heavier than the last, as if gravity itself has intensified with their departure.

I find Talon at the top of the stairs. He tracks my movement as I climb toward him, reading the emotions I can't quite conceal.

"They'll be fine," he says, but the slight tightness around his mouth betrays his own worry.

"You don't know that" I reply, brushing past him into the hallway. "None of us know anything anymore."

He follows me. "The plan is solid. Alex would approve."

"Don't." The word comes out sharper than I intend. "Don't talk about what he would approve of."

Talon's expression softens. "Vesper..."

"I need to get ready." I cut him off, unable to bear the sympathetic tone of his voice. "We leave in six hours."

I retreat to my own room, closing the door with a decisive click that makes it clear I want to be alone. The silence envelops me immediately, thick and suffocating.

The bathroom mirror reflects a stranger—hollow-eyed, pale, with tension etched into every line of my face. I splash cold water on my skin, trying to shock some life back into my features. Today I need to look strong and confident.

I strip methodically, letting my clothes pool on the tile floor before stepping into the shower. The scalding water cascades over my skin, and I turn my face into the spray, letting it mix with the tears I can no longer hold back. Here, with the water drumming against my ears, I allow myself one final moment of weakness.

The steam wraps around me, fogging the glass until I'm just a blurred silhouette. I lean my forehead against the cool tile, letting water cascade down my spine.

I hear the bathroom door open, then close with a soft click. I don't turn around. There's only one person it could be.

Talon steps into the shower behind me, still fully dressed, his clothes immediately soaking through. His strong arms wrap around my waist, pulling me back against his chest. He says nothing, just holds me as the water beats down on both of us, his steady heartbeat a counterpoint to my ragged breathing.

"You shouldn't be getting your wound wet."

"Some things are more important." His lips brush my temple. "You are more important, princess."

I turn in his embrace, facing him. Water streams down his face, plastering his hair to his skin, soaking through his black t-shirt. The bandage on his shoulder is already soaked through, but he doesn't seem to care.

"I'm scared," I admit.

"I know. I am, too."

I press my face against his chest. I feel his heartbeat against my cheek, steady despite everything we've faced. Everything we still have to face.

"We should get you a new bandage." I pull back slightly to examine his shoulder.

"Later," he says. "Let me just hold you for now."

We stand there as the water gradually cools, neither of us speaking. Words feel inadequate in the face of what's coming. Instead, we communicate through touch—my fingers tracing the contours of his face, our foreheads pressed together as we breathe the same steamy air.

When the water finally runs cold, Talon reaches behind me to shut it off. The sudden silence is deafening, broken only by the rhythmic drip from the showerhead and our synchronized breathing.

"Come on," he says gently, reaching for a towel and wrapping it around my body. "Let's get you dry."

I let him lead me from the shower, leaving puddles in our wake. He guides me to sit on the edge of the bed, then kneels before me, taking a second towel to gently dry my hair. His movements are tender, careful.

"I need to be stronger than this."

"You are strong," Talon assures me. "Stronger than anyone I've ever known."

I shake my head. "Strong people don't fall apart in the shower."

"Is that what you think strength is? Vesper, you've endured more in the past few years than most people face in a lifetime. You're still standing."

"Barely."

Talon sets the towel aside. "Do you know what I see when I look at you? I see a woman who survived The Collector once already. Who escaped and built a new life. Who's willing to walk back into hell to save her brother." His thumb traces circles on my palm. "That's not weakness, princess. That's the kind of strength most people can't even imagine."

Something shifts in my chest at his words—not healing exactly, but a momentary easing.

"I don't want to lose anyone else," I confess.

"Then we don't lose," he says simply, as if it's a decision we can make.

His certainty steadies me, creates a moment of stillness in the chaos of my mind. I let myself believe him, just for this breath, this heartbeat.

I surge forward, closing the distance between us, capturing his lips with mine. My desperation pours into the kiss, fingers gripping his wet shirt, pulling him closer. His mouth responds instantly, yielding then demanding, matching my intensity with his own.

When he suddenly tenses against me, a small sound escaping his throat, I pull back immediately.

"God, I'm sorry," I breathe, my fingers hovering over the wet bandage on his shoulder. "Your wound...I wasn't thinking."

Talon's smile is strained but genuine. "Worth it," he says, his voice husky. "Though maybe we should get this bandage changed before we continue."

"Let me," I say, rising from the bed. I find the medical supplies we keep in the kitchen, bringing them back to where he now sits on the edge of the mattress.

He peels off his soaked shirt, revealing the sodden bandage beneath. I work carefully, my fingers gentle as I remove the wet dressing. The wound is healing well, the angry redness fading to pink around the edges, but it still looks painful. A stark reminder of how close I came to losing him, too.

"Does it hurt much?" I ask softly as I clean around the edges with antiseptic.

"Not anymore," he lies.

I apply the fresh bandage with methodical care, smoothing the edges with my fingertips.

"Thank you," he adds as I secure the last piece of medical tape.

"I should be thanking you. For everything."

Talon captures my hand, bringing it to his lips. "No thanks needed, princess. Not between us. Vesper, I know this isn't the right time. But before we walk into whatever's waiting for us today, I need you to know something."

I go still, my hand freezing against his chest.

"I love you." The words hang in the air between us, simple yet profound. "Not just because we're in this impossible situation, not just because of what we've been through together. I love you for who you are. Not for your name, or your family's legacy, but for the woman standing in front of me who has endured so fucking much and is still fighting, not only for herself, but for us too."

My breath catches in my throat as he continues.

"I haven't had much love in my life. My father made sure of that." Something crosses his face before he pushes it away. "But with you, with us, I've found something I never thought possible."

In this moment, with his heart laid bare before me, I see the boy he must have been—starved for affection, desperate for connection, learning to hide his wounds behind charm and easy smiles.

"Talon—" I begin, but he shakes his head.

"You don't have to say anything. I just needed you to

know, in case..." He doesn't finish the thought, doesn't need to.

"In case nothing goes the way we plan," I finish for him.

I lean forward, pressing my lips to his with a gentleness that softens the desperation that came before. This kiss isn't born of fear or need, but an acknowledgment of what lies between us—fragile yet unshakable.

"I love you, too," I breathe against his mouth. The words feel simultaneously inadequate and enormous.

Talon pulls me closer, careful of his injured shoulder, until I'm nestled against his chest. His heartbeat thrums beneath my ear, steady and reassuring. We stay like that, suspended in time, neither of us wanting to acknowledge the hours ticking away or our upcoming confrontation with The Collector.

"We should get ready. We have a long day ahead."

I nod against his chest but make no move to pull away.

"Just a few more minutes," I reply, needing to hold onto this moment of peace.

His arms tighten around me in silent agreement. We breathe together. I memorize the feeling, his skin against mine, the lingering dampness from our shower, the faint scent of antiseptic from his bandage mingling with his natural musk.

When I finally pull away, it's with reluctance heavy in my limbs. I feel his stare follow me as I move to my closet, pulling out the outfit I've selected for today's confrontation. Simple, practical—black jeans, a henley, and boots with concealed steel toes that Zaire had given me. Nothing that could be used as a weapon against me, nothing The Collector would find suspicious.

"What time is it?"

"Just after seven," he answers. "We have three hours before we need to leave."

I pull my damp hair into a tight braid, securing it at the nape of my neck. When I turn back to Talon, he's watching me with an intensity that makes my breath catch.

"What?" I ask, suddenly self-conscious.

"I'm memorizing you," he admits. "Just in case."

"Don't," I sob, the word catching in my throat. "Don't talk like that."

Talon rises from the bed, his movement careful as he favors his injured shoulder. He closes the distance between us in two strides.

"I'm not planning on anything happening to either of us. But I've learned that memories are sometimes all we have to hold onto."

I reach up, tracing the line of his jaw with my fingertips, "We should eat something," I say finally. "You need your strength."

Talon nods, pressing a kiss to my palm before stepping back. "I'll make us breakfast. You finish getting ready."

After he leaves, I stand motionless in the center of my room, listening to the familiar sounds of him moving through the kitchen. It's so mundane, so normal, it makes my chest ache with longing for a life where this is all we have to worry about. Breakfast. Coffee. Each other.

Not whether or not we will make it through today.

# Chapter 28

VESPER

THE ROSSI MANSION looms ahead like a beautiful nightmare, its towering columns and sprawling grounds a gilded cage I once called home. From the passenger seat, I watch it grow larger through the windshield.

"Are you ready?" Talon asks, his voice tight with tension as he navigates the winding drive. His grip on the steering wheel is ironclad, and his injured shoulder remains carefully rigid beneath his tailored suit.

I don't answer immediately. How do you tell someone you're walking willingly into hell? That you calculated the cost of your soul and found it a fair trade for your brother's life?

"As ready as I'll ever be," I finally reply, my fingers unconsciously tracing the small bump on my upper arm where Alex's tracker sits beneath my skin. The thought of him stirs a sharp ache in my chest, but I shove it down, lock it away. I can't afford to break—not when Luca's life hangs in the balance.

"Remember, we stick to the plan. I drop you at the entrance, then circle around to the rendezvous point. Z and Oz should already be in position in the tunnels."

"I know," I say, trying to keep the tremor from my voice. "We've been over this a dozen times."

"And we'll go over it a dozen more if that's what it takes to keep you safe," he says, a muscle twitching in his jaw. "The moment anything feels wrong..."

"I activate the tracker," I finish for him. "I know the plan, Talon."

The gravel crunches beneath our tires as we round the final curve of the driveway. The mansion's façade comes into full view. Security lights automatically illuminate the manicured grounds.

My stomach knots as memories flood back—my father's study door always closed, the hushed conversations that stopped when I entered a room, the parade of men in expensive suits with cold eyes who would pat my head before disappearing behind those heavy oak doors.

"They're watching us." He nods subtly toward a security camera mounted discreetly among the climbing roses. "Have been since we passed through the gates."

I straighten my spine, smoothing my expression into controlled indifference. "Good. Let them see exactly what they expect—a desperate sister coming to save her brother."

The car slows as we approach the circular driveway in front of the main entrance. Massive stone steps lead up to double doors flanked by Doric columns. Two men stand at attention on either side of the entrance, their suits unable to hide the bulges of the weapons beneath.

"This is where we part," Talon says, bringing the car to a stop. His hand finds mine, squeezing once, hard. "Remember, princess, no matter what happens in there, we're coming for you."

I turn to him, memorizing the lines of his face. "I know." I lean forward to press my lips against his. The kiss is brief but fierce, a promise and a goodbye wrapped into one. "Stay safe."

"You too." His voice cracks slightly as I pull away, his fingers reluctant to release mine.

I step from the car into the cool evening air. The crunch of gravel under my boots echoes in the silence as I approach the stairs. Behind me, Talon's car idles for a moment longer than necessary before pulling away, the sound of the engine fading as he circles around to the eastern edge of the property.

One of the guards steps forward as I reach the bottom of the stairs. "Identification," he demands, his voice flat, emotionless.

"Vesper Rossi," I reply, my tone equally cold. "I believe I'm expected."

He nods once, stepping aside to allow me passage.

"We've been instructed to search you before entry," the second guard states, moving forward with mechanical precision.

I raise my arms without protest, forcing myself to remain still as his hands pat down my body with impersonal efficiency. The search is thorough but not invasive. The real inspection, I suspect, will come later when I'm face to face with The Collector.

"She's clean," the guard announces, stepping back.

The massive doors swing open silently, revealing the marble foyer. Crystal chandeliers cast prismatic light across gleaming floors.

"This way, Miss Rossi." A new figure emerges—tall, lean, with the careful movements of someone trained in violence. "The Collector is waiting for you."

I follow without comment. The house is eerily quiet, our footsteps echoing against marble and hardwood. Paintings of Rossi patriarchs line the hallway.

We turn down a corridor I know all too well, heading toward my father's study. The mahogany door looms before us, the intricate carvings along its frame depicting scenes from Dante's Inferno, my father's twisted idea of humor. My escort pauses, knocking twice before pushing it open.

"Miss Rossi has arrived," he announces, stepping aside to allow me entry.

I cross the threshold, the familiar scent of leather-bound books and aged whiskey washing over me. The study remains unchanged—walls lined with first editions behind glass, the massive desk dominating the center of the room, leather chairs positioned strategically for intimidation rather than comfort.

But it's the figure standing by the window that draws my attention. He is tall, impeccably dressed in a tailored charcoal suit, his back to me.

"Vesper," he says, his voice sending ice through my veins. "How kind of you to accept my invitation."

The Collector turns slowly, his face hidden behind the same expressionless covering from the video. I force myself to breathe, to appear calm, even as primal fear claws at my insides. This man had stripped away everything I was—reduced me to flesh, bone, and terror—and now he sits at my father's desk. The same chair my uncle died in not all that long ago.

"Where's my brother?" I demand.

He smiles. "Direct to the point." He gestures to the chair across from him. "Sit."

"I'll stand, thanks." I keep my voice even, refusing to give in to even the smallest of his power plays. "I didn't come here for pleasantries."

The Collector tilts his head, studying me through the smooth, vacant eyeholes, silent and calculating.

"Still defiant," he muses, his tone almost appreciative. "After everything you've lost, everything you stand to lose, you refuse to bend." He steps around the desk, his movements fluid and controlled. "I've always admired that about you, Vesper."

I force myself to hold my ground as he approaches, though every instinct screams at me to retreat. The subdermal tracker in my arm suddenly feels heavy, a reminder of what's at stake. Stall. Buy time. Give the twins a chance to find Luca.

"You said this was a transaction," I say coolly. "I'm here. Where's my brother?"

He stops just beyond arm's reach, close enough that I can smell his cologne. "All in good time. We have much to discuss, you and I."

"I have nothing to discuss with you," I say, my voice sharper than I intend. "I came alone, as directed. It's time for you to hold up your end of the deal. Give me my brother."

The Collector's voice slices through the air, laced with amusement so cold it raises the hairs on my arms. He turns away, gloved fingers drifting across the edge of my father's desk like he owns the place.

"So impatient," he murmurs, tone patronizing. "Do you know how many deals were made in this very study, Vesper? Hundreds—maybe thousands. Your father was quite the negotiator."

He moves to the painting behind the desk—a Caravaggio, if I remember right—and traces the ornate frame with a kind of reverence that makes my stomach turn.

"Every transaction that built the Rossi empire happened right here," he continues, voice coated in unsettling nostalgia. "Deals that secured your family's power, your wealth, your reputation. Always in the Rossi's favor."

My patience thins with every word. "I didn't come here for a history lesson."

"No?" He tilts his head. "But history is exactly why we're here. Your family's. Yours. *Ours*."

I dig my nails into my palms, using the sharp sting to stay focused. Every second he wastes is another chance for Oz and Z to move through the tunnels. Keep him talking. Keep him distracted.

"Then let's talk about that history," I say, tone steady. "Starting with why you're so obsessed with my family."

He exhales, something close to a sigh, though it carries a weight that feels far too pleased. "Obsessed is such an adolescent word. I prefer...*invested*. Deeply invested."

"Is that why you took me? Why you went after my brother?"

He doesn't answer right away. Instead, the room seems to contract around his silence, heavy and crawling. When he finally speaks, it's with a voice like velvet stretched too tight over something sharp.

"Because you were always the missing piece. And your brother...was leverage."

"I took you because I saw an opportunity to topple the Rossi empire. To right the wrongs done unto my family."

He turns back to face me, one gloved hand resting on my father's desk as if he has every right to touch it.

"Your grandfather was a thief, Vesper. Did you know that? Not the kind that robs homes in the dead of night, oh no, Elio Rossi was far more sophisticated." His voice drips with venom. "He stole through contracts and handshakes, through promises made and conveniently forgotten."

I keep my expression neutral, though my mind races.

This revelation feels significant, a piece of the puzzle I've been missing. My paternal grandfather had been dead for years when I was born. My parents rarely talked about him at all. My mother, especially.

"Have you ever heard your father speak of the Vasilyev family?" The Collector asks, his head tilting slightly as he studies my reaction.

I search my memory, trying to recall if I'd ever heard the name mentioned in hushed conversations or angry arguments. "No," I answer honestly. "He never mentioned them."

"Of course he didn't. Why would he burden his precious daughter with the knowledge of those his family destroyed?" He moves toward the liquor cabinet, pouring himself a measure of amber liquid without offering me any.

"Dima Petrov was cut from the same cloth as your grandfather," he continues, swirling the whiskey in his glass. "A man who took and took until there was nothing left for anyone else. He slaughtered his way to the throne of Russia, leaving corpses and broken families in his wake."

He takes a sip. "The Petrovs and the Rossis, two dynasties built on the bones of better men. Your father and Victor Petrov merely continued what their fathers started."

Something in his tone shifts, a personal hatred seeping through the careful control he usually keeps in place.

"The Vasilyev family ruled Russia for generations," The Collector says, his voice taking on a haunting, reverent quality. "We were the true kings, not through divine right, but through blood, sacrifice, and cunning. We built an empire that stretched from St. Petersburg to Vladivostok."

His fingers tighten around the glass. "Until Dima Petrov decided he wanted it all."

I remain silent, watching as he paces before the fireplace, his shadow dancing grotesquely across the study walls.

"He came in the night," The Collector continues. "With men loyal only to money, not honor. The Vasilyev compound burned. Women, children, it didn't matter to him. Dima wanted no challengers to his new throne."

The realization hits me like a physical blow. "You're a Vasilyev," I breathe.

His eyes lock onto mine through the smooth covering, burning with an intensity that makes me step back without meaning to. He lifts the disguise with deliberate slowness.

The face beneath is handsome in a harsh, unforgiving way—high cheekbones marred by scars, a strong jaw, and bright green eyes. Eyes like my mother's...like mine.

"Mikhail Vasilyev," he introduces himself with a slight incline of his head, a mockery of gentlemanly courtesy. "Your mother never mentioned me, did she?"

The room tilts beneath my feet as pieces lock into place. "That's not possible," I gasp, though the evidence stands before me, unmistakable in the curve of his cheekbone, the set of his jaw. Features I've seen in photographs of my mother's youth. Features I see in Luca.

"I'm your grandfather," he says. "Your mother was Elizaveta Vasilyev before she became a Rossi."

My legs threaten to give way beneath me. I grip the back of the leather chair for support, my mind reeling with implications. "You're lying."

"Am I? Look at us, Vesper. The resemblance is undeniable."

I stare at him, seeing the ghost of my mother in his features, the echo of Luca, even pieces of myself.

"After the Petrov massacre," he continues, moving toward my father's desk with the confidence of someone reclaiming what was always theirs, "a handful of us survived. We scattered, went underground, and bided our time. But Dima was relentless in his hunt."

The Collector—Mikhail—runs his fingers over the polished wood of my father's desk. "In order to get my revenge for what the Petrovs did to my family, I made a deal with Elio Rossi for the most precious thing in my life."

"My mother," I gasp.

"My daughter," he corrects, something possessive coiling through his tone. "I traded her to Elio Rossi for protection from the Petrovs—for the promise that one day, we would destroy them together." His mouth twists, the bitterness in his voice unmistakable. "Your grandfather took my daughter and my revenge in the same breath."

My grip tightens on the back of the chair as the weight of his words sinks in. My mother—always cold, always distant—is suddenly cast in a different light. Not just distant. Dispossessed. An unwilling bride bartered away as part of a political alliance. The pieces of my family history shift, falling into a more disturbing pattern.

"She hated him," I whisper, memories rising unbidden— her tight smiles, the way she flinched from my father's touch. "She always hated him."

"As she should have," Mikhail says with a grim nod. "Antonio Rossi was no better than the Petrovs. Power-hungry. Ruthless. He married my daughter for her bloodline, nothing more."

"If you were really her father," I snap, "why didn't you help her? Why leave her in a marriage she despised?"

Mikhail's face hardens. "Help her?" he repeats, voice turning cold. "I tried. When I learned the kind of man Antonio truly was, I sent men to extract her. She refused to leave."

"I don't believe you."

"Believe what you will. Elizaveta chose to stay for you and your brother. She knew what Antonio would do if she tried to take his children." His expression hardens. "By then, I had lost everything. My family, my power...even my own daughter chose the Rossi name over her birthright."

The revelation hits me like a physical blow. "So my mother is the reason you became The Collector? You turned your rage against her choice into...this?"

"Your mother was merely the catalyst, Vesper. The Rossis betrayed me, just as the Petrovs destroyed my family. I watched as these families—these dynasties built on blood and betrayal—continued to thrive while everything I loved turned to ash." "My bitterness became purpose. I decided I would dismantle them all, piece by precious piece. The children of the families who destroyed mine would become my greatest commodity."

I feel sick as understanding dawns. "You take their children...to sell them."

"Not just any children." His smile is chilling. "The sons and daughters they cherish. I take what these families value most—their legacy, their future. And I profit from their desperation."

"That's monstrous." The word feels inadequate for the horror before me.

"Monstrous?" Mikhail approaches me slowly. "What's monstrous is what these families did to mine. What your father's family did to your mother. What the Petrovs did to generations of Vasilyevs." He stops just inches from me. "I simply turned their own tactics against them."

"And Luca and I? What was your plan for us?"

Mikhail regards me with something almost like pride. "You were special cases. My own blood. I had different plans for you."

"Which were?"

"To use you as I was used." He shrugs, as if discussing a business transaction rather than human lives. "Your father's empire has grown too powerful. Victor Petrov's influence is too vast. I needed leverage against both."

He steps closer, and it takes everything in me not to recoil. "You were to be my crowning achievement, the granddaughter who would dismantle both dynasties from within."

"And Luca?"

"Insurance."

"But you sold me? If you needed me that badly, why did you let me go?"

A cruel smile twists Mikhail's lips. "I never truly let you go, Vesper. I merely...repositioned you."

"What does that mean?" I demand, my stomach clenching.

"What better vengeance than watching my own granddaughter dismantle the Petrovs from the inside out? It's revenge served exactly how I wanted it. All it took was the right buyer...or should I say, buyers."

A chill runs through me. "You knew who was buying me."

"Of course I did." His smile is cold, calculated. "The Second Sons. A collection of cast-offs and spares, building their own power base in opposition to Victor Petrov. The four individuals who tried to keep you from your destiny."

"You planned this," I gasp. The realization dawning with horrifying clarity. "You arranged my sale to the Second Sons knowing they'd protect me from Victor."

"I arranged everything," Mikhail confirms, setting his glass down on my father's desk with deliberate precision.

"But why?" I demand, struggling to keep my voice steady as rage and horror war within me. "Why this elaborate game?"

"Because the best revenge is the one where your enemies destroy themselves."

My hands tremble with horror, with the sickening realization that my entire life has been orchestrated by the man standing before me.

"And what about Luca?" I demand, forcing strength into my voice. "What role does my brother play in your grand revenge fantasy?"

"As I told you, granddaughter, he's my insurance policy."

"He's a human being."

"He's a Vasilyev," Mikhail corrects. "As are you. Despite your father's surname, the blood that flows through your veins is mine. Royal blood. Blood that belongs on the throne of Russia."

"What exactly are you proposing?"

Mikhail steps closer, his expression shifting into something almost paternal. "A simple exchange. Your brother's freedom...for your cooperation."

"My cooperation in what?"

"Reclaiming what's rightfully mine." He gestures expansively. "The Petrov empire. The Russian throne. It's your birthright, Vesper. Your destiny."

I stare at him, momentarily speechless. "You want me to...what? Stage a coup against Victor Petrov?"

"Exactly."

"You're insane," I spit, but the words lack conviction as my mind races through the implications. "Victor Petrov has an army, billions in resources, and decades of entrenched power. I can't just walk in and take the throne."

"Not alone, no," Mikhail concedes, circling me like a predator. "But you won't be alone. You'll have me, my resources, my connections. And most importantly—" a malicious smile forms on his face, "—your son, and my heir to both families."

"You can't have him," I snarl.

"Then you can't have your brother. Without your cooperation, I have no reason to keep him alive."

The words hang in the air between us like a garrote,

choking off any response I might have formed. I swallow hard, forcing myself to think past the blind panic threatening to consume me.

"You claim to care about family legacy," I say, measuring each word carefully. "Yet you're willing to murder your own grandson if I don't comply?"

Mikhail's expression doesn't change. "I've spent decades rebuilding from the ashes, Vesper. I've sacrificed everything—comfort, morality, even my humanity—to reach this point. One grandson is a small price to pay for the restoration of the Vasilyev dynasty."

"Show me proof that Luca is still alive," I demand, playing for time. "Recent proof. Not some pre-recorded video you could have filmed days ago."

"Cautious. Good." He reaches into his jacket, retrieving a sleek tablet. His fingers dance across the screen before he turns it toward me.

The image that appears steals my breath, Luca, strapped to a metal chair, his head lolling forward. A digital time-stamp in the corner shows today's date and current time. As I watch, a gloved hand enters the frame, gripping my brother's hair and yanking his head up. "Say hello to your sister," a voice commands off-screen.

Luca focuses slowly on the camera. "Vesper?"

His voice is weak, raspy from disuse or screaming. I can't tell which. But he's alive. My knees nearly buckle with relief. The feed cuts abruptly, Mikhail's finger sliding across the screen with casual cruelty.

"Satisfied?" he asks, tucking the tablet away. My face

must give me away because he doesn't give me a chance to answer. "No? Maybe you need a little more incentive? The Collector pauses, turning towards the closed office door. "Bring him in."

My heart slams into my ribs, time suspended as the door crashes open.

A guard shoves a figure through the doorway, the man stumbling forward before catching himself against the wall. His head is bowed, blond hair matted with dried blood. But I'd know that silhouette anywhere.

Alex.

He's alive.

# Chapter 29

VESPER

"ALEX?" His name tears from my throat, raw and disbelieving.

His head lifts at the sound of my voice. "Vesper." Just my name, but undeniably his voice.

My body moves before my mind can process, lurching forward only to be caught by Mikhail's iron grip on my arm. "Not so fast, granddaughter."

"Let me go!" I snarl, struggling against his hold as I drink in the sight of Alex—alive, breathing, standing before me. His face is bruised, one eye swollen nearly shut, his lip split and crusted with blood. But he's alive. Somehow, impossibly alive.

"Touching," Mikhail observes coldly. "I thought you

might appreciate this particular reunion. Consider it a gesture of goodwill. I had him fished out of the Atlantic despite how many of my men he killed with that stunt of his."

My mind reels, trying to process the impossible. Alex is alive, standing before me, his body a testament to the violence he's endured. I force myself to think past the shock, past the overwhelming relief threatening to drown me.

"Why?" I manage to ask. "Why keep him alive?"

Mikhail's lips curve into that terrible smile. "Insurance upon insurance, my dear. I've found redundancy to be quite valuable in my line of work."

I can see him cataloging every detail of my appearance, assessing for injuries, for signs of mistreatment. Even now, beaten and captive, he's trying to protect me.

"He's been rather...resistant to questioning," Mikhail continues, releasing my arm but positioning himself between us. "Loyal to a fault. A rare quality these days."

"Let him go," I hiss.

"Let him go?" Mikhail shakes his head. "You misunderstand the nature of our negotiation. Mr. Rafner here isn't part of what's being offered. He's merely...additional motivation."

I force myself to look away from him, to focus on Mikhail's face, my grandfather's face, with its terrible familiarity.

"You want me to help you take down Victor Petrov," I say carefully, buying time as I process this new reality. "In exchange for Luca's freedom. And Alex? What do you want in exchange for him?"

Mikhail glances over his shoulder at Alex's battered form. "He remains with me. Insurance that you'll fulfill your end of our arrangement."

"No deal," I say immediately, my voice stronger than I feel. "Both of them or nothing."

Mikhail's expression hardens. "You're not in a position to negotiate, Vesper."

"Aren't I?" I step closer, confidence in my stance. "You need me. If I'm truly the key to your grand revenge against the Petrovs, then I have leverage."

"Don't," Alex rasps, speaking for the first time since saying my name. "Vesper, don't do this."

The guard behind him strikes him across the back of the head, sending him staggering forward. I flinch, a small sound escaping my throat as Alex catches himself on the edge of the desk.

"I admire your spirit," Mikhail says. "But don't mistake my indulgence for weakness. I could kill them both right now and still proceed with my plans. It would simply be...less elegant."

"Then why don't you? Why keep any of us alive if you don't need us?"

A flicker of something—respect, perhaps—crosses his face. "Because blood matters, Vesper. Legacy matters. The Vasilyev line continues through you...through your son."

"Leave my son out of this," I warn, ice in my veins at the mention of my child.

"Impossible. He is the culmination of everything I've worked toward, a Vasilyev, Rossi, and Petrov blood in one heir. The boy who will unite three dynasties under one rule. Under my tutelage."

Alex makes a strangled sound, lurching forward only to be restrained by the guard.

"You're never getting near my son," I say, each word sharp and deliberate, laced with venom.

Mikhail smiles, unperturbed. "We shall see." He gestures toward Alex. "Perhaps Mr. Rafner would like to share his thoughts on the matter." He turns to address Alex directly. "Tell her what becomes of those who defy me."

Alex's jaw tightens, a muscle twitching beneath the bruising.

"I've already told you my answer. Both of them, or no deal."

Mikhail studies me for a long moment, his head tilted slightly as if seeing me anew. "So much like your mother. That same stubborn pride..."

He moves to the window, gazing out at the grounds. The silence stretches between us, heavy with unspoken threats. My mind races, calculating how much time has passed.

"Very well." Mikhail turns his back to face me. "A compromise, then. Your cooperation, and the return of both your brother and Mr. Rafner at the conclusion of our business. In exchange, I won't kill Petrovs in the tunnels. Mr. St James, I believe, is circling the property."

My blood freezes in my veins. The twins. Talon. He knows they're here.

"What are you talking about?" I force confusion into my voice, but Mikhail's cruel smile tells me he isn't fooled.

"Please, Vesper. Did you really think I wouldn't know about the tunnels? About your little rescue team making their way beneath our feet right now?" He gestures casually, and a guard moves to a panel beside the bookcase, pressing buttons on a keypad.

A monitor descends from the ceiling, splitting into four separate feeds. My heart sinks as I recognize Z and Oz making their way through the narrow passageway, weapons drawn, their faces set with determination. Another camera shows Talon circling the perimeter as he approaches the greenhouse.

"I've let them get quite far," Mikhail remarks conversationally. "It seemed prudent to see what you would do. Whether you'd honor our meeting or attempt something...foolish."

Alex silently shakes his head, pleading with me.

"So what now? You kill us all and proceed with your plans regardless?"

"That would be wasteful," Mikhail says, sounding almost disappointed. "No, I think a demonstration is in order." He turns to the guard. "Flood tunnel section C."

"No!" I lunge forward, but the guard restrains me with brutal efficiency, his arm like a steel band across my chest. On the monitor, a wall of water surges through the tunnel, rushing toward the twins who have no idea what's coming. They have seconds at most.

"Stop this! I'll do whatever you want!" My voice cracks with desperation. "Please!"

Mikhail raises his hand, and the guard at the panel pauses, finger hovering over the button. The water on the screen halts its advance, held back by whatever mechanism controls the flood system.

"Your word, Vesper. I want your sworn oath that you'll cooperate fully. No tricks, no attempts at escape. Swear it on your son's life."

"I swear," I relent, defeat washing through me like the water that nearly claimed Z and Oz. "I swear on my son's life. Just don't hurt them."

Mikhail studies me for a long moment, searching for any sign of deception. Finding none, he nods once. "Release her."

The guard's arm drops away, and I stagger forward, catching myself on the edge of the desk.

"Call them off," Mikhail orders, gesturing to the monitor where the twins have paused, sensing something wrong though they can't see the wall of water held in check just around the bend. "Now that you understand. Let's discuss the details."

"Your terms," I say, straightening my spine. "All of them. Now."

"You have seventy-two hours to kill Victor Petrov, his son, and your dearly beloved cousin, Bianca. Upon their deaths, you relinquish your claim to the Rossi family legacy and sign over your son to me. In exchange, your brother and Mr. Rafner will go free."

"Is that all?"

"Of course not, granddaughter. You will marry a man of my choosing. Someone with the connections and resources we need. Someone loyal to me to preserve our bloodline. You and your future husband will build me an army of heirs."

Alex makes a strangled sound of protest, earning him another brutal blow from the guard. Blood trickles from the corner of his mouth as he glares at Mikhail with naked hatred.

I can't look at Alex. If I do, I'll break, and that will kill us all. Instead, I focus on the monster wearing my grandfather's face, the architect of my family's destruction.

"And if I refuse?" I ask, though we both know it's an empty question.

"Then I flood those tunnels with your friends still inside them," Mikhail answers smoothly. "I execute Luca while you watch. And Mr. Rafner..." He glances at Alex with clinical detachment. "Well, I believe you've seen his handiwork. Imagine those skills applied to him, day after day, until there's nothing left but meat and bone."

My stomach lurches at the image his words conjure. I force myself to breathe, to think past the blind panic threatening to consume me.

"How do I know you'll keep your word? That you'll let any of us live once I've done what you want?"

Mikhail's smile is thin, reptilian. "You don't. But what choice do you have?"

None. That's the terrible truth of it. I have no choice, no leverage, nothing but the desperate hope that I can find a way out of this trap once I'm inside it.

"What you're asking is impossible."

"Then make it possible. Once you infiltrate the Petrovs, I will provide you with the army you need. Everything up until that point is on you, granddaughter. If you're anything like your bastard father, you'll figure it out."

I swallow hard, mind racing.

"I want proof of life for Luca every day. Alex, too."

"Reasonable requests," Mikhail concedes with a slight nod. "I'm not an unreasonable man, Vesper. Just a determined one."

"And my friends in the tunnel and outside, you let them go. Unharmed."

His lips curve into that terrible smile. "I'll allow them to retreat. Whether they choose to do so is their decision, not mine."

On the monitor, Z and Oz have stopped moving, clearly sensing the trap. They stand back-to-back, weapons ready. Talon has reached the greenhouse, crouched as he studies the entrance.

"Call them," Mikhail orders, nodding to a guard who produces a phone. "Tell them to leave. Be convincing."

The guard passes me a phone, and I take it with trembling fingers. One call to save their lives, to surrender any hope of rescue. The alternative doesn't bear thinking about.

I dial Z's number from memory using the guard's phone, pulse pounding as it rings. Once. Twice. It goes to voicemail. Shit.

I call again. Same result.

He doesn't recognize the number. Of course he doesn't.

My fingers fly over the keypad as I shoot off a quick text:

> It's Vesper. Pick up the damn phone. Now.

Almost immediately, I hit redial.

This time, he answers on the second ring.

"Vesper?" His voice is tense, cautious. "Are you okay?"

"Yes," I say, though my voice is too tight to sound convincing. "You need to leave. Now."

"What?" His tone shifts, all suspicion and edge. "What the fuck's going on?"

I meet Mikhail's cold stare as he watches me, one finger hovering over the control panel. "It's a trap. He knows you're there. There's a flood mechanism—" My voice cracks. "Please, Z. Get Oz and go back. Tell Talon to retreat, too."

"We're not leaving without you," Z seethes.

"You have to," I plead, desperation bleeding into my tone. "I will meet you back at the apartment. I'll explain everything."

"He's watching you right now on security cameras. If you don't leave, he'll drown you both, and kill Luca and Alex on the spot."

Silence stretches across the line, and I can almost see Z's jaw clench, his expression tightening with barely restrained anger.

"Alex?" Disbelief evident in his voice.

"He's alive," I confirm. "But not for long if you don't get out of here. Please, Z. Trust me."

The line goes dead. On the monitor, Z and Oz exchange

tense words before reluctantly turning back, retreating the way they came. Talon's feed shows him receiving a call, his expression tightening before he disappears from view.

"Satisfied?" I hand the phone back to the guard.

"Quite," he replies. "You've made the right choice, granddaughter."

"I didn't have a choice," I correct him. "You made sure of that."

"A lesson your father never learned. There are always choices, Vesper." He gestures sharply to the guard behind Alex. "Take him. We're done here."

The guard grabs Alex roughly, yanking him toward the door. Alex's face contorts with pain. "Vesper, listen to me!" He struggles against the guard's grip, digging his heels into the carpet.

"Shut him up," Mikhail orders coldly.

The second guard moves forward, but Alex twists violently, smashes free just long enough to lurch toward me, desperation etched across his battered face. "You're the key! The key to everything!" Alex shouts as the guards recapture him, one landing a vicious blow to his ribs that doubles him over. Still, he fights, his voice growing more frantic. "You're the key, Vesper!"

A guard's fist connects with his jaw, silencing him momentarily. Blood trickles from the fresh split in his lip as they drag him toward the door.

"Get him out of here," Mikhail snarls, visibly unsettled by Alex's outburst.

I lunge forward instinctively, but Mikhail's iron grip

catches my arm, holding me in place. "He's not yours yet, granddaughter."

I watch helplessly as Alex vanishes through the doorway, his desperate face locked on mine until the last possible moment. The door slams shut with a finality that echoes through the study.

Mikhail releases my arm, straightening his suit jacket. "He's quite devoted to you," he observes, returning to the desk. "Such loyalty is rare. Too bad his bloodline comes with no political power. A child sired by him would be strong. Nevertheless, there are other options to consider."

My throat constricts around words I can't form. Alex is alive. The knowledge should bring relief, but instead it carves a fresh wound alongside the existing scar. He's alive and suffering because of me.

Mikhail picks up the tablet from the desk, handing it to me with a sharp, businesslike air. "As promised," he says. "You'll receive a link to their video feeds once daily. Your proof of life."

I take the tablet, my fingers feeling numb against the cold surface.

"The link will only be active for a 15-minute window each day. Miss that window, and you won't see your brother."

The weight of his words hangs in the air as he meets my gaze. "This tablet is your lifeline, Vesper. To them. And to me. When you're ready to make your move, you'll use this to contact me."

I clutch the tablet to my chest, as if I could somehow pull them through the screen and into safety.

"Remember, Vesper. Seventy-two hours. If Victor Petrov, his son, and Bianca still draw breath when that clock runs out, I will personally ensure everyone you've ever loved dies. Slowly. Painfully. Starting with your brother and ending with Alex Rafner."

I clutch the tablet tighter. "I understand."

"I hope you do." He turns to face me. "This is your destiny, granddaughter. The restoration of the Vasilyev legacy. Once it's done, once you've fulfilled your purpose, they'll be free." His lips curve into that terrible smile. "And you'll have served a greater purpose than your mother ever did."

The comparison to my mother sends a chill through me. I wonder how many times he made similar promises to her, how many times he betrayed her trust.

Mikhail gestures to a guard standing silently by the door. "Bring the car around. Take my granddaughter back home." He approaches me, placing his hands on my shoulders in a mockery of familial affection. "I suggest you use your time wisely. And, don't bother trying to run. There is no place on this Earth where I won't be able to find you. I think I've proven that to be true already.

# Chapter 30

ALEX

PAIN IS a familiar friend by now, but the fear...that's the part that's killing me.

They shove me into the back of the SUV, my already battered ribs screaming in protest as I slam against the leather seat. The guard follows, jamming the barrel of his gun into my side just hard enough to make me wince. Unnecessary. Where the fuck does he think I'm going to run in this condition?

"Don't try anything stupid," he grunts, as if I haven't heard that warning a dozen times already.

I say nothing, conserving what little energy I have left. My body is a catalog of injuries—three broken ribs, a dislocated shoulder they'd popped back in without anesthesia, split lip, bruised kidney. The list goes on. But it's not my physical state that has me spiraling into rage and terror as the vehicle pulls away from the Rossi Mansion.

It's Vesper. Standing there in her father's study, facing down the monster who I now know shares her blood.

Her grandfather. The fucking Collector is her grandfather.

The revelation still twists in my gut like a knife. How many times had I combed through her family history, searching for any connection, any leverage against The Collector? The answer had been hiding in plain sight all along. Her captor came from within.

The SUV lurches over a pothole, sending pain radiating through my chest. I bite back a groan, refusing to give my captors the satisfaction. The guard beside me smirks, enjoying my discomfort.

I need to think, to plan. Mikhail Vasilyev has just handed Vesper a death sentence. Kill Victor Petrov and his family, or watch everyone she loves die. The impossible choice.

But she's not alone in this. Not as long as I'm breathing. I may be a captive, but if she can figure out what I was trying to tell her, then she will have the keys to the entire fucking kingdom. With Talon, Oz, and Zaire at her side, it might be just enough to make the impossible, possible. Though I can't help them directly, there's one thing I can do.

I can keep her brother alive.

The SUV takes a sharp turn onto a gravel road. The place they took me from had asphalt. This isn't where we came from.

"Where's Luca Rossi being held?"

The guard snorts. "Shut up."

"Just wondering if we're neighbors," I continue, keeping my tone casual despite the way my heart hammers against my broken ribs. "Been a while since I've had company."

"I said shut up." The guard jams the gun harder into my side.

I swallow a gasp, letting my head fall back against the seat. Worth a try. I need to know if Luca is at the same facility. If he is, there might be a chance...

My thoughts scatter as the vehicle takes another sharp turn, this time sending me sliding across the leather seat until I collide with the door. Pain explodes through my shoulder, but I grit my teeth against it. Focus, Rafner. Stay conscious.

Through the tinted windows, I catch glimpses of dense forest. We're heading somewhere remote. Not surprising for a man who specializes in making people disappear. The guard's phone buzzes, and he answers with a curt "Yes, sir," before hanging up.

"Change of plans," he announces to the driver. "Taking him to Facility B."

My pulse quickens. Facility B. A designation implies multiple locations, multiple facilities where Mikhail keeps his "collection." Which means Luca could be at Facility A, C, or God knows where else. The realization sinks like a stone in my gut. Finding him just got exponentially more difficult.

The SUV slows as we approach what appears to be an abandoned industrial complex, all concrete and rusted metal. The kind of place that's been forgotten by time and mismanaged municipal records.

Two armed guards emerge from a nondescript door as our vehicle pulls to a stop. The guard beside me grabs my arm, his fingers digging into bruised flesh.

"Move," he orders, hauling me out of the SUV with unnecessary force.

My legs buckle when my feet hit the ground, my body betraying me after days of malnutrition and abuse. I stumble, catching myself against the vehicle's frame before they can drag me to my feet again. The evening air is cold against my face, carrying the scent of pine and something chemical.

"Welcome to your new home, Rafner," one of the guards says, a cruel smile twisting his lips. "Hope you like the accommodations better than the last place."

They march me toward the building, each step painful. The concrete structure looms before us, windowless and forbidding.

The metal door groans as it opens, revealing a hallway that clashes starkly with the building's rough exterior. The space beyond is sterile and over lit, flooded with harsh recessed lighting. It feels like a hospital—if hospitals were designed by people who preferred causing pain over healing it.

"Move," the guard grunts, shoving me forward.

My shuffling steps echo against the polished concrete floor as they lead me deeper into the facility. We pass a series of identical doors, each fitted with a small observation window and an electronic lock. I count them silently—one, two, three, four—mapping the layout out of habit. If I ever get a chance to escape, knowing the terrain could mean the difference between freedom and death.

At the sixth door, they stop. One guard swipes a keycard, punches in a code, and the lock disengages with a sharp beep. The door swings open to reveal a cell nearly identical to the one I was held in before—pale walls, a narrow cot bolted to the floor, and a stainless steel toilet with no privacy. The only difference is a small vent near the ceiling, likely for air circulation rather than escape. They're not that careless.

"Home sweet home," the guard sneers, shoving me inside hard enough that I stumble and crash to my knees on the concrete floor.

The impact sends lightning bolts of pain through my already battered body, but I refuse to make a sound. I won't give these bastards the satisfaction.

"The Collector wants you kept alive," the second guard informs me, his tone clinical. "But he didn't specify what condition you needed to be in. Remember that."

The door slams shut behind them, the electronic lock engaging with a finality that echoes in the sterile space. Alone, again. I allow myself a moment of weakness, slumping against the wall as my body catalogs each pain point. Breathing hurts. Moving hurts. Existing hurts.

But I'm alive, which means there's still hope.

I drag myself to the cot, each movement a careful negotiation with my broken body. Once seated, I force myself to breathe through the pain, methodically assessing my surroundings. The cell is approximately eight by ten feet. Temperature controlled. No visible cameras, though that doesn't mean they aren't watching. The vent is too small for escape, barely large enough for adequate air circulation. The bed is bolted down, the frame welded to supports embedded in the floor. Even the thin mattress has been designed to prevent concealing anything inside it.

Professional. Thorough. Just like everything else The Collector, Mikhail. does.

I run my fingers along the wall nearest the bed, searching for imperfections, for anything that might offer insight into where I am or who might be nearby. The concrete is smooth, almost polished. No markings, no signs of previous occupants. Nothing to indicate Luca might be close.

The sound of footsteps in the corridor pulls me from my examination. I force myself upright, ignoring the protest of my ribs. Never show weakness. That's the first rule of captivity. The electronic lock disengages with a soft beep, and the door swings open to reveal a woman in scrubs, a medical kit in her hands. Behind her stands a guard, weapon drawn.

"Against the wall," the guard orders.

I comply, turning to face the wall with my palms on the cool cement. No sudden movements. The woman's footsteps approach, hesitant but determined.

"I'm going to check your injuries," she states, her voice clinically detached. "Don't move."

Cold fingers probe my ribs, and I bite back a hiss of pain. She works methodically, checking each wound with impersonal efficiency. Not a doctor, the touch lacks the confident precision, but someone with medical training. A nurse, maybe, or an EMT that Mikhail keeps on payroll for his "collection."

"Three fractured ribs," she reports to the guard. "Shoulder shows signs of improper reduction. Possible internal bleeding. He needs X-rays."

"Not authorized," the guard replies flatly. "Just patch him up enough to keep him alive."

She sighs, barely audible, but there, before continuing her examination. Her fingers pause at a particularly tender spot on my back, and I can't suppress a wince.

"This kidney contusion is concerning."

"Not my problem," the guard responds. "Hurry it up."

She opens her medical kit, the clasps clicking loudly in the silent cell. I hear the tear of packaging, then feel the cool press of an antiseptic wipe against the cut on my face.

"This will hurt," she warns, moments before I feel the sharp sting of sutures being placed at my temple. The pain is clarifying, focusing my scattered thoughts. I focus on my breathing. Pain is information. I use it.

"Turn around," she instructs after finishing with the sutures.

I comply, facing her for the first time. She's younger than I expected, maybe early thirties. Her eyes avoid mine as she cleans the split in my lip.

"Are there other prisoners here?" I ask quietly.

"Quiet," the guard snaps from his position by the door.

The woman continues working, wrapping my ribs. Her

touch is clinical but not cruel. a small mercy in this place devoid of compassion.

"He needs fluids and proper nutrition," she tells the guard as she packs up her supplies. "And those ribs need to be monitored for pneumothorax."

"Noted," the guard replies disinterestedly. "You done?"

She nods, casting one final glance at me, still avoiding direct eye contact, before turning to leave. "I need to see the man in the next cell. Collector's orders."

"Fine, but make it quick. I need a smoke."

The door closes behind them with that now familiar electronic beep, leaving me alone once more. The woman's words echo in my mind. "I need to see the man in the next cell." Could it be Luca? The timing of our transfer, the urgency in her voice when she mentioned him, it can't be a coincidence.

Ignoring the protest of my battered body, I move to the wall separating my cell from the next, pressing my ear against the cool concrete. Nothing. The walls are too thick for normal sound to penetrate.

I shift my attention to the small vent near the ceiling. It's too small for escape, but sound might travel through the ventilation system. Dragging the thin blanket from the cot, I bunch it beneath the vent to give myself a few extra inches of height, then brace myself against the wall as I stand on it. The vent is just barely within reach when I stretch upward, my fingers brushing the metal grate while I try to ignore the pain radiating through me.

I listen carefully for the sound of the woman who just

entered my cell or the guard. Nothing. I take my chance, knowing they can't kill me if they want Vesper's cooperation. More pain, I can handle just fine.

"Hello?" I call out, my mouth as close to the vent as I can manage. "Luca? Can you hear me?"

I wait, straining to hear any response through the ventilation system. Nothing but the soft hum of circulating air. I try again, a little louder this time.

"Luca Rossi? If you can hear me, make any sound."

I hold my breath, listening intently. For a moment, there's only silence. Then, a faint tapping. Three distinct knocks against what sounds like the same metal vent on the other side of the wall.

My heart rate quickens. "Once for yes, twice for no. Are you Luca Rossi?"

One knock. Clear. Deliberate.

Relief floods through me so powerfully my knees nearly buckle. "Are you injured?"

One knock, followed by what sounds like a muffled cough.

"Your sister is coming for you," I say, the words scraping through my raw throat. "She knows you're alive."

Another knock, faster this time, urgent. I can almost feel his desperation vibrating through the metal vent.

"Listen to me carefully," I continue, straining to keep my voice audible to him but not to any potential microphones. "The Collector is your grandfather. Your mother's father. That's why he took you both."

Two rapid knocks, followed by what sounds like muffled cursing.

"I know it's hard to believe, but it's true. He's using you as leverage to force Vesper to kill Victor Petrov and his family." I pause, checking the hallway for any signs of movement. "She has seventy-two hours. If she fails, he'll kill us both."

One slow, deliberate knock. He understands the stakes.

"But we're not dead yet. As long as we're alive, there's a chance."

My muscles scream as I maintain this awkward position, but I push through the pain. This connection to Luca is too valuable to lose over physical discomfort.

"Tomorrow, they will put you on a video feed. Vesper will see it. Make sure she knows you're alive, but don't try to communicate anything else. The Collector will be watching for any coded messages." I pause, listening for any response from Luca's side. One deliberate knock comes through.

Suddenly, a new pattern of tapping begins. It's methodical, purposeful. I focus intently, counting each distinct tap. One...three...fifteen...eight...One tap for A, three for C, fifteen for O...letters. He's spelling something.

W-H-O A-R-E Y-O-U?

I open my mouth to respond when footsteps echo in the corridor outside. Heavy boots against concrete, the jangling of keys.

"Shit," I mutter, carefully lowering myself from my makeshift platform. My ribs scream in protest as I hurriedly straighten the blanket and return to the cot, arranging myself as if I've been resting all along.

The electronic lock disengages. I steady my breathing, schooling my expression into one of exhausted compliance as the door swings open to reveal two guards.

"Dinner," one announces flatly, sliding a tray across the floor with his boot. The meager meal, some kind of gray stew and stale bread, isn't worth the pain it would take to retrieve it immediately.

I remain motionless on the cot, feeling their suspicious stares. Did they hear me? Are there microphones in the vents?

"The boss wants you healthy enough to stay alive."

The first guard crouches down as if trying to discern any signs of defiance or rebellion. I meet his stare head-on with a careful mask of defeat.

Reluctantly, I push myself up from the cot, my every movement a pained reminder of the bruises and wounds that mar my body. I shuffle towards the tray, the smell of the stew turning my stomach, but hunger gnawing at my insides.

As I reach for the tray, the second guard shifts uncomfortably, his hand hovering near the stun baton at his belt. I know the consequences of disobedience, of defiance. The boss's reach is long, his punishments unforgiving.

I take a tentative bite of the bread, the taste dry and bland on my tongue. The guards watch me closely. After a few moments of tense silence, the first guard stands, his expression unreadable. "Finish your meal," he orders, his voice a low growl that brooks no argument.

I nod, swallowing the lump in my throat, and force

myself to take another bite. The guards linger for a moment longer before finally ordering me to slide the tray back over and retreating, the sound of the lock sealing me once again in my cell.

Alone once more, I sit back on the cot, the taste of stale bread lingering in my mouth. The guards' words hang heavy in the air, a stark reminder of the fragile line I walk between survival and surrender in this unforgiving world.

# Chapter 31

ZAIRE

THE RAGE in my blood won't settle. It's been almost two hours since we left her there, alone with that monster, and every minute feels like another betrayal.

"We need to go back," I growl, pacing the length of our apartment for the hundredth time. The walls are closing in, suffocating me with each pass. "She could be dead already for all we know."

"She's not dead." Oz's voice cuts through my spiral, his tone maddeningly calm as he sits at the kitchen table. "The Collector wants something from her. He won't kill her until he gets it."

I slam my fist against the wall, welcoming the sharp pain

that shoots up my arm. "That's supposed to make me feel better? That he's keeping her alive to use her?"

Talon looks up from his position by the window, his injured shoulder still held carefully rigid. "Z, we all feel the same way. But rushing back in there half-cocked will just get her killed for sure."

"So we just wait?" I snarl, rounding on them both. "Sit here on our asses while she faces that psychopath alone?"

"We follow her instructions," Oz says, rising to his feet with that lethal grace that mirrors my own. "She told us to trust her. To wait for her here."

I laugh, the sound bitter even to my own ears. "And when has Vesper ever made decisions that prioritize her own safety?" I demand. "She'd sacrifice herself in a heartbeat if she thought it would save us. You both know that."

Oz's jaw tightens, but he doesn't argue. He can't. We've all witnessed Vesper's self-destructive loyalty firsthand.

"She said Alex is alive," Talon says quietly, the words hanging in the air between us like smoke.

I freeze mid-step, the impossible truth still refusing to settle in my mind. "If she's right, if he's really..." I can't finish the sentence, hope too dangerous a thing to voice aloud.

"Then The Collector has been playing us from the start," Oz concludes, his mind already racing ahead. "Alex's 'death' was staged to fracture us, to weaken our defenses."

"And it worked," Talon mutters. "I should have made sure. Should have searched longer, found some proof—"

"None of us could have known," I cut him off, unwilling to let him shoulder that burden alone.

The apartment door clicks open, and we all freeze, weapons drawn before conscious thought. Vesper steps through, her face a blank canvas that chills me more than any display of emotion could. She looks...untouched. Physically, at least. But those green eyes that have haunted my dreams since the day we met are dead. Empty. Like someone extinguished the fire that's always burned there, even in her darkest moments.

"Vesper," I breathe, holstering my weapon and crossing the room in three long strides.

She flinches when I reach for her, a tiny, instinctive movement that stops me cold.

"Don't," she commands, her voice hoarse as though she's been screaming. Or forcing herself not to. "Please, just...don't touch me right now."

I step back, giving her the space she's asking for. Behind me, I sense Oz and Talon exchanging glances, the same worry coursing through all of us.

"Are you hurt?" Talon asks, his voice gentler than I've ever heard it.

Vesper shakes her head and moves past us into the apartment. She sets a sleek black tablet on the coffee table, then lowers herself onto the couch. Her movements are mechanical, controlled—like she's piloting her body from somewhere far away.

"He's my grandfather," she says flatly, staring at nothing. "The Collector. Mikhail Vasilyev. My mother's father."

The revelation lands like a physical blow. Oz curses softly in Russian, while Talon makes a strangled sound of disbelief.

I want to reach for her again, to ground her with my touch, but the memory of her earlier flinch stops me cold. Instead, I lower myself onto the coffee table across from her, positioning myself directly in her line of sight.

"Vesper, talk to us," I urge, keeping my voice steady despite the storm raging inside me. "What happened in there?"

She finally focuses on me, but it's like looking at a stranger wearing Vesper's face. "He wants me to kill Victor, Dmitri, and Bianca. I have seventy-two hours."

"What?" Talon exclaims, moving closer. "That's suicide. Victor's compound is impenetrable. Not to mention in fucking Russia."

"He has Luca," she continues in that same hollow voice. "And Alex. They're both alive."

Oz approaches cautiously, his mind already piecing together the implications. "You saw Alex? You're certain it was him?"

"It was him." Her fingers clench into fists on her lap, the first real sign of emotion since she walked through the door. "They've been...hurting him while we thought he was dead."

Oz moves to sit beside Vesper, careful not to touch her. "Did he give you any specifics? A timeline beyond the seventy-two hours?"

She shakes her head, reaching for the tablet on the coffee table. "This is my 'lifeline' to him. And to them." Her fingers tremble as she swipes across the screen. "I get proof of life once a day. A one-hour video feed that expires at the end." The screen is blank.

The guilt is a living thing writhing in my gut. We abandoned him, mourned him, while he suffered. I force the thought away, focusing on the immediate threat.

"What else does this Mikhail want?" I press, sensing there's more she hasn't told us.

A tremor runs through Vesper's body, almost imperceptible if I wasn't watching her so closely.

"He wants my son. To raise him as the heir to his new empire. He wants..." Her voice falters. "He wants me to marry someone of his choosing. Someone with connections."

The rage that floods through me is blinding, a red haze that threatens to consume everything in its path. I'm on my feet before I realize it, a string of Russian curses tearing from my throat. Something inside me snaps.

"Fuck this!" I roar, slamming my fist through the drywall. The plaster crumbles, dust billowing around my bloodied knuckles. "We're not playing his fucking game!"

My vision narrows to a crimson tunnel as I tear through the apartment, upending the coffee table, sending the tablet skittering across the floor. The sound of my own pulse drowns out whatever Oz is shouting at my back.

"Z, stop!" Talon grabs my arm, but I shake him off with enough force to send him stumbling backwards into the wall.

"We abandoned Alex," I snarl, rounding on him. "We left him there while that monster tortured him. And now we're supposed to sit here with our thumbs up our asses while Vesper sacrifices herself again?"

I grab the nearest object—a lamp—and hurl it across the

room. It shatters against the wall, glass exploding in a spray of light and rage, raining down like sharp, glittering confetti from a nightmare.

"We should have burned that fucking mansion to the ground with everyone inside it." My voice is barely recognizable, a guttural growl that tears at my throat. "We're going back. Tonight. I'll kill every last one of them myself."

Oz steps into my path, his face a mirror of my own, but with that infuriating control I've always envied. "Zaire, enough. This isn't helping."

"Get out of my way, brother. I will do this with or without you."

"And get us all killed in the process?" Oz steps closer. "They're alive, Z. Both of them. That's what matters right now."

"Alive and imprisoned by a psychopath!" I spit back.

"Because Vesper made a deal to keep us safe." Oz's voice drops lower, forcing me to focus on his words. "She bought us time by agreeing to his terms. If we storm in there now, we destroy any chance of getting them out alive."

I turn away, unable to face the logic in his argument. My breath comes in ragged gasps as I fight to contain the storm building inside me, threatening to tear me apart from within. The wall I punched throbs in rhythm with my heartbeat, blood seeping between my knuckles.

"Seventy-two hours," Oz continues, pressing his advantage. "That's what she negotiated. Three days to figure out a counter-move."

"What counter-move?" I demand, whirling back to face

him. "You heard her. He wants her to assassinate Victor fucking Petrov and marry some puppet of his choosing. There's no counter-move to that kind of insanity."

"There's always a move," Oz insists. "We just haven't found it yet."

I glance at Vesper, still seated on the couch. Something in Vesper's posture shifts, a subtle tension that draws me back from the brink of my rage. I force myself to breathe, to push down the violent impulses screaming for release.

"Did Alex say anything to you? Anything that might help us?"

"He tried," she says, her fingers tracing the edge of the tablet. "Right before they dragged him away. He was fighting them, desperate to tell me something."

I move closer, careful not to crowd her. "What did he say?"

"That I'm the key. The key to everything, according to him." She shakes her head, that momentary spark fading completely. "But I don't know what the hell he was talking about. I'm not the key to anything. I'm the reason all of this is happening."

The self-loathing in her voice pulls me back from my spiral of rage. I kneel before her, close but not touching.

"That's not true," I tell her firmly. "None of this is your fault."

"Isn't it? My grandfather orchestrated everything, my sale to you, Alex's death, Luca's captivity, all because of who I am. Because of the blood in my veins."

"Blood doesn't define you, Vesper." I reach for her hand,

relieved when she doesn't pull away this time. "Your choices do."

Something shifts in her expression—a flicker, a barely visible crack in the emptiness she's worn like armor since walking through that door.

"I have to do this. I don't see another way."

"There's always another way," Talon interjects, moving to sit on her other side. "We just need to find it."

Oz has already shifted into strategic mode, pacing the room with calculated steps as he processes everything we've learned. "Victor Petrov's compound is heavily fortified," he says, thinking aloud. "But every stronghold has vulnerabilities."

"It's not just about getting in," Vesper counters, her voice stronger now. "It's about getting close enough to kill him, his son, and Bianca. Three separate targets, likely in different locations."

I squeeze her hand gently. "You're not seriously considering this."

"What choice do I have?" She pulls her hand from mine, rising to her feet with a sudden burst of energy that seems to surprise even her. "He has my brother. He has Alex. And if I don't at least make him believe I'm trying to fulfill my end of the bargain, they're both dead."

The air in the apartment thickens with tension, each of us processing the impossible situation from different angles. Vesper begins pacing, her movements jerky and unpredictable, like a wounded animal searching for escape.

"We need to think clearly," Oz says, his voice cutting

through the heavy silence. "The Collector, Mikhail, he's been planning this for decades. Every move calculated, every contingency accounted for."

"Except Alex," I counter. "He couldn't have anticipated Alex building that backdoor into his systems. The one that died with him when—" I stop, correcting myself. "The one we thought died with him."

Vesper freezes mid-stride. "The key. What if that's what Alex meant? Not me, but something I have. Something I know."

Talon straightens, wincing as his injured shoulder protests the movement. "Like what? A password? Access codes?"

"I don't know," she admits, frustration coloring her voice. "But Alex wouldn't have said it if it wasn't important. He was desperate to tell me something specific, even while they were beating him."

My blood boils at the image her words conjure, but I force myself to focus. "What exactly did he say? Word for word."

"'You're the key, Vesper. The key to everything.'" She shakes her head. "That's all he said."

Oz sits up suddenly. "Wait. Vesper, you're the key."

"Yeah, we got that far, but what does it mean?"

"No," Oz shakes his head emphatically, wincing slightly at the movement. "Alex said he found files on Mario's computer. Blackmail material on the other families. Leverage we can use for their help. He has it on a flash drive. He extracted it before we left."

"So?" I ask, impatience bleeding into my voice.

Oz stands now. "Vesper is not just the metaphorical key. She's the literal key. You can unlock it."

"Biometric encryption," I breathe, the pieces falling into place. "Alex would have secured the data with the highest level of protection."

"Oz," Talon nods eagerly. "Not just any biometric lock, one keyed specifically to you. Your fingerprint, retinal scan, maybe even DNA."

Vesper stares at him. "But where would he keep something like that? I searched his room. I didn't find anything."

"Not in his room," Talon interjects. "He would have kept it somewhere more secure. Somewhere only you would think to look."

I watch as something shifts in Vesper's expression, the first real animation I've seen since she walked through that door. Her brow furrows in concentration.

"The basement," she says suddenly. Vesper is already moving, heading toward the hidden stairwell that leads to the apartment's lower level. We follow her.

I haven't set foot down here since before Newport, since before we lost him. The air is cooler here, carrying the faint metallic scent of blood that never quite washes away, no matter how thoroughly he cleaned. I feel the familiar tightening in my chest as we descend the stairs, not fear exactly, but a visceral respect for what happens in this space.

Vesper moves with newfound purpose, her footsteps echoing against the concrete as she crosses to the center of the room. The overhead lights flicker on automatically, motion sensors responding to our presence. Everything is meticulously organized, with chains bolted to support beams. A butcher's playground, designed for maximum efficiency.

"What exactly are we looking for?" I ask.

"I don't know yet. But Alex wouldn't have told me I was the key if he didn't think I could figure it out." I watch her as she moves through the basement, her fingers trailing along surfaces, cataloging every detail. "Come on, Alex. Give me some sort of sign. What am I looking for?"

I watch Vesper as she methodically sweeps the basement, her movements becoming more fluid as purpose replaces the hollow emptiness that has consumed her for days. This is the Vesper I know, focused, determined, refusing to accept defeat even when the odds are stacked impossibly against her.

"Think, Vesper," Oz encourages, keeping a respectful distance as she works. "If Alex encrypted something specifically for you, it would be somewhere meaningful. Somewhere that connects to you both."

"This is pointless. I have no idea where to look."

"Think about the last time you were down here. Before they left for Martha's Vineyard. Did he say or give you something?"

"He said a lot of things. Mostly about him being expendable. Nothing about how to find the key."

I watch as Vesper's frustration builds. "Tell me where to fucking look, Alex!" she screams into the void.

Her voice echoes off the concrete walls, the raw emotion

in it hanging in the air like smoke. Then silence falls, heavy and oppressive, broken only by her ragged breathing.

I move toward her, instinct overriding caution, but Oz catches my arm with a subtle shake of his head. Let her work through this.

Vesper stands motionless in the center of the room.

"Why did you think about the basement?" Talon interrupts the silence. "Why this space, Vesper?"

"This is where he told me about his demons," she sighs, her voice heavy. "Where he revealed and demonstrated what was buried beneath the surface." She moves to the metal exam table in the center of the room. "He killed Natasha right here, after forcing her to admit what she'd done." She pauses, glancing around once more. "Over there," she says, nodding toward Alex's weapon cabinet, "he confessed to me the night before his trip to Martha's Vineyard that he could never be with me because he feared he would destroy me. He believed his life was expendable."

"Expendable," I echo, the word catching in my mind like a burr. Alex never did anything without purpose—every word, every action calculated for maximum effect. "What exactly did he say about being expendable?"

"He said he wasn't like the rest of you. That he was the expendable one." Her voice grows stronger as she continues, "He told me if it came down to a choice between him or Talon coming back, he'd make sure it was Talon."

"He knew," Talon breathes, realization dawning across his features. "He fucking knew something might go wrong. He was preparing you."

Vesper moves toward the weapons cabinet with renewed purpose, her fingers tracing the metal edge of the door. "This is where we were standing when he said it." She pulls the door open.

"Nothing here," she mutters, frustration creeping back into her voice.

"Wait," Oz interjects, stepping closer. "The cabinet itself. Check for false bottoms, hidden compartments."

Vesper kneels, running her fingers along the interior of the cabinet, feeling for irregularities. Her movements become more frantic as she finds nothing, desperation bleeding through her careful control.

"Damn it, Alex," she hisses, slamming her palm against the metal in frustration. The cabinet resonates with a hollow sound that makes us all freeze.

"That didn't sound right," I say, dropping to my knees beside her. "Hit it again."

Vesper strikes the cabinet floor once more, and again we hear that strange, echoing quality. Not solid. Not quite empty either.

"There's something in there," Talon confirms, leaning in despite his injured shoulder.

Oz pushes forward. "The floor panel, check for seams, anything that might indicate a hidden compartment."

Vesper's fingers trace the metal flooring, feeling along edges until, "Wait." Her nail catches on something almost imperceptible. "There's a seam here."

We watch as she works her fingernail into the tiny gap, trying to pry up the panel. After several tense seconds, she sits back on her heels with a frustrated sound.

"It won't budge."

"Let me," I offer, pulling a knife from my boot. I slide the thin blade into the seam, working it carefully around the perimeter until I hear a faint click. The panel shifts slightly beneath my touch.

"There," I mutter, wedging my fingers into the newly created gap. With a metallic groan, the false bottom lifts, revealing a shallow compartment beneath.

Vesper gasps, reaching inside to extract a small metal case no larger than her palm. It's sleek and black, with no visible seams or openings, just a small depression on its surface sized for a fingertip.

"Biometric lock," Oz confirms, moving closer to examine it. "Fingerprint scanner, from the looks of it."

Vesper stares at the case. "You really think this is what Alex meant? That I'm literally the key to this?"

"Only one way to find out," Talon says gently.

She takes a deep breath, then presses her index finger to the depression. For a moment, nothing happens. Then a soft blue light pulses beneath her fingertip, scanning the unique whorls and ridges of her print. It flashes green, but doesn't unlock.

"Well, that didn't work." Talon takes it from Vesper, studying it. "No retinal scanner. DNA?"

"So I need to prick my finger? How would he have gotten a blood sample from me?" She pauses. "You know what, it's Alex. He probably has my entire DNA mapped."

She takes the device from Talon, studying it. "Where would I even put it?"

"Try kissing it," Talon suggests. I turn to stare at him. "What?" he shrugs. "Saliva has DNA?"

"I don't even want to know how you know that."

"It's worth a try, and far less invasive."

Vesper takes the device and presses her lips to it. The light turns green, followed by a barely audible click as the case unseals itself.

"It worked," she blurts out, awe and grief mingling in her voice.

With careful movements, she opens the case. Inside lies a small flash drive, matte black with no markings, nestled in custom-fitted foam. Beside it rests a folded piece of paper.

Vesper lifts the note with trembling fingers, unfolding it to reveal Alex's sharp, angular handwriting. The room falls into a heavy silence.

*Show them who you really are, Vesper.—A*

The note trembles in Vesper's hands. I watch as she traces his signature with her fingertip.

No one speaks for a moment, the weight of Alex's foresight settling over us like a heavy fog. Even now—held captive and broken—he's still ten steps ahead of everyone else. The thought fills me with equal parts hope and dread.

# Chapter 32

LUCA

THE DOOR CRASHES open like a thunderclap, making me flinch despite myself. After all this time in this hellhole, you'd think I'd be used to it.

"Move, Rossi." The guard's voice is emotionless as he yanks me from my cell, his fingers digging into my bicep hard enough to leave fresh bruises alongside the fading ones.

I stumble into the hallway, the lights harsh after the dimness of my room. My bare feet slap against the cold tile as they march me down a corridor I've never seen before. This is new. This is different. And different has never meant good in this place.

"Where are you taking me?"

The guard doesn't answer. Of course, he doesn't. They never do.

We stop at a metal door halfway down the hall. He punches a code into the keypad, then shoves me inside with enough force that I stumble, catching myself against the wall. The room is larger than my cell, two beds instead of one, a small table, even a window, though it's covered with metal grating.

The door slams shut behind me. Thirty-seven seconds pass in silence before it opens again.

Another body is thrust inside, this one taller, lankier. He catches himself with more grace than I managed, turning immediately to face the door as it closes. When he turns around, recognition jolts through me like an electric shock.

"Alex?" The name escapes my lips before I can stop it. Alex Rafner from St. Jude's Academy—platinum blond hair now matted with blood, ice-blue eyes rimmed with exhaustion, but unmistakably him.

Recognition flickers across his battered face. "Hey, neighbor."

Neighbor? Why the hell would he say that unless...fuck, he's the guy on the other side of the wall. My brain struggles to process this revelation. The man I've been communicating with through the vents is someone I actually know. Or knew, a lifetime ago, when we were just teenagers at St. Jude's.

"You're the one who's been talking to me?" I manage, my voice hoarse from disuse. "Through the vents?"

Alex nods, his movements careful, controlled. He's

clearly in pain, though he's trying not to show it. "Good to finally see your face, Rossi. You look like shit."

A strangled laugh escapes me. "You're one to talk."

His face is a tapestry of bruises in various stages of healing—purple fading to green around his left eye, a fresh split in his lip crusted with blood, a row of neat stitches at his temple. The way he's holding himself suggests broken ribs, maybe worse.

"What the fuck happened to you?"

"The same as you, I suspect. Guards with a penchant for violence?"

He moves toward the unoccupied bed, each step measured as if calculating the exact amount of energy required. I notice the careful way he holds his torso, broken ribs, probably. I've had them before. The Collector's guards aren't exactly gentle.

"How long have you been here?" I ask, moving to sit on my own bed.

"Hard to tell. Time works differently in this place. After I rammed a boat into your grandfather's guards, it got a little hazy after that."

"You rammed a boat in his guards?" I can't keep the incredulity from my voice.

Alex shrugs, then immediately winces at the movement. "Seemed like a good idea at the time."

"And how'd that work out for you?"

He gestures to his battered body with his less injured arm. "I'm here, aren't I?"

"Why are they putting us together?" I ask, suspicion

immediately replacing shock. Nothing happens here without purpose, without calculation.

"Motivation for your sister. Her daily proof of life for both of us." Alex eases himself onto the edge of the bed with a barely suppressed wince. "The Collector wants her compliance. Seeing both of us alive, but suffering, is the perfect leash."

I study him more carefully, trying to reconcile this battered man with the quiet, reserved classmate I barely knew at St. Jude's. Back then, he was just another privileged kid, brilliant but distant, existing on the opposite side of my limited social circle. He had sidled up with the Petrovs immediately upon his enrollment. Not that it stopped me from casually observing him in the classes we shared together.

"Don't take this the wrong way, but you were solidly on Team Petrov the last time I saw you."

"Still am. Well, Oscar and Zaire. Their uncle, not so much." A ghost of a smile touches his lips before fading. "It's complicated."

"We're sharing a cell in some psychopath's private dungeon. I think we're past complicated."

"We've been protecting her."

"We?"

"The Petrov Twins, Talon St. James, and I. We call ourselves The Second Sons."

"That a stupid fucking name," I blurt out.

Alex's mouth quirks up in the barest hint of a smile. "Not my choice."

A moment of silence stretches between us, filled with the hum of the ventilation system and distant footsteps in the corridor. I take the opportunity to really look at Alex, not just his injuries, but the man himself. He's changed since St. Jude's. The lanky teenager has been replaced by lean muscle, his once-boyish features hardened into something more vicious.

Alex had always been attractive, even during those awkward years when we were both still figuring ourselves out, all sharp edges and restless energy. Back then, I told myself it was just admiration. Normal. Harmless.

But now...

Now there's nothing boyish about him. There's a calm brutality in the way he moves, a quiet strength that draws the eye before I can think to look away. My gaze lingers longer than it should on the cut of his jaw, the line of his throat, the way his shirt clings.

I shift, jaw tight, willing the heat under my skin to settle. It's stupid. I don't even know if he's into—

No. Doesn't matter. Shouldn't matter.

But I still can't stop looking.

And worse, I think he notices.

Shit.

I lean back against the wall, studying him. There's something different about him from what I remember. Back then, he was always hunched over a laptop, avoiding eye contact, speaking only when absolutely necessary. This Alex carries himself differently, like a weapon at rest.

"So my sister..." I begin, unsure how to phrase the question burning in my mind. "You've been what, her guardians?"

"It started that way. Your grandfather sold her to the highest bidder once he was done with her. We got her out."

The implication hangs in the air between us. I feel my jaw tighten. "You bought my sister?"

"Yes?"

"Let me get this straight. My apparently long lost grandfather kidnapped my sister, and then sold her to you?" I seethe through gritted teeth. "Is that what you are telling me?"

"That about sums it up," Alex shrugs. "Some details and context are missing, but pretty spot on to where we find ourselves now."

"Details and context," I echo, feeling my hands ball into fists. "I'd fucking love to hear those. You bought my fucking sister."

"We saved her life. An alternative buyer would have used her as a broodmare to stake a claim to your family's legacy. So yes, we bought her. And then we gave her back her freedom."

"That's a convenient story."

"It's the truth. You can ask her when you see her in a few days."

"You mean when she kills Victor Petrov and his family?" The words taste bitter on my tongue.

"He deserves it," Alex shrugs. "But, I think she'll enjoy killing your cousin Bianca more, considering she is passing off Vesper's son as her own.

I feel like I've been sucker-punched. "Vesper has a son?"

"Not by choice."

"Who's the father?" I finally ask.

"Dmitri Petrov," Alex says, his voice flat. "It wasn't consensual."

"He raped her?" Something cold and vicious unfurls in my chest.

"With the help of your darling new grandfather, they took her eggs," Alex shifts on the bed to find a less painful position. "I think you can draw the conclusion from there."

"I'll kill him."

"Get in line, Luca. Though let's be honest, Vesper will beat us both to it if we make it that far,"

I try to process this information, but my mind keeps snagging on the same impossible fact. "My sister has a child," I say it aloud, testing how the words feel. "I'm an uncle."

"Yes," Alex confirms, watching me carefully.

I stand and pace the small confines of our shared cell, energy suddenly coursing through me despite my weakened state. The pieces are clicking together with sickening clarity, my capture, Vesper's torment, and now this impossible task set before her.

I stop pacing and face him. "Do you think she can do it?"

Alex considers the question. "Yes. She's not the same person you remember. The Collector made sure of that."

I sink back onto the bed, trying to reconcile the sister I knew with this new version Alex describes. "What did he do to her?"

Alex's expression tightens. "It's not my story to tell. But she survived. She always survives."

"So you and my sister," I say after a moment, keeping my voice casual. "How complicated is 'complicated'?"

"Would you believe me if I said I'd die for her?"

"I believe you've already tried," I reply, nodding toward his injuries.

A ghost of a smile touches his lips. "Fair assessment."

"And the others? The Petrovs and St. James?"

"The last thing I want to do is dive into your sister's sex life with her brother."

Sex life? Jesus, is Vesper sleeping with one of them? More than one? All of them? How the fuck did that happen? He has to be messing with me. Vesper's naive, innocent, or well, was. I can't see her going down the non-traditional route when it comes to relationships.

"Are you saying...?"

"She's well-protected and cared for. The three of them circle around her like her own personal pack of protectors. If we make it out of this, and you get to see her again, you'll understand what I mean."

The way he hesitates before choosing that word tells me everything I need to know. I feel a strange mixture of protectiveness and resignation wash over me. My sister, always the center of gravity, pulling others into her orbit whether she means to or not.

"Tell me what she's like?" The question slips out before I can reconsider. "Vesper, I mean. Now."

"She's..." He pauses, searching for the right words. "Stubborn as hell, smarter than she gives herself credit for. Savage when cornered."

I nod, picturing my sister, the one I remember, not this hardened version he describes. "And the scars? The ones that don't show?"

Alex's jaw tightens. "Deep. But healing, I think. Before all this—" he gestures vaguely to our surroundings, "—she was starting to find herself again. To trust."

"And now?"

"Now she's probably burning the world down looking for us." A ghost of a smile touches his lips. "The Collector thinks he's using us to control her, but he's just given her something worth fighting for."

I absorb this, trying to reconcile the sister I remember with the woman Alex describes. "She always protected me, you know. Even when we were kids. I was supposed to be the one protecting her this time. And look how well that turned out for both of us," I gesture at our cell with my good hand. "Some protector I turned out to be."

"Don't underestimate your importance to her. The only reason she's playing along with your grandfather's game is you."

I snort, wincing as the movement jars my ribs. "And you."

"Primarily you," he corrects. "I'm just...additional motivation."

There's something in his tone I can't quite place—not quite bitterness, not quite resignation. Before I can question it further, the electronic lock on our door beeps. We both tense, instinctively shifting into more defensive positions despite our injuries. Four guards enter, batons extended at their sides.

"I hope your sister enjoys the show, Rossi. I know we will."

# Chapter 33

VESPER

THE TRUTH DOESN'T ANNOUNCE itself with fanfare. It slips in quietly, like a thief in the night, stealing your breath before you even realize what's been taken.

I stare at the tablet screen, my finger hovering over the notification. A link. Unassuming. Anonymous. The promised daily proof of life that makes me both desperate to click and terrified of what I'll see.

"Vesper?" Talon's voice pulls me back from the edge of panic. "What is it?"

"It's him." My voice sounds foreign to my own ears. "The daily check-in."

The guys abandon Oscar's computer, where they've been hunched for the past three hours, poring over the encrypted files from Alex's flash drive. They approach me with synchronized caution, like hunters circling wounded prey. Their concern would be touching if it didn't feel so suffocating.

"Do you want privacy?" Oz asks, assessing my mental state, measuring my capacity for what might appear on that screen.

I shake my head. "No. Stay." The word comes out more desperate than I intended. "Please."

Z settles beside me on the couch, close enough that I can feel his warmth. Always so careful with me now, as if I might shatter at the slightest contact. Maybe I would.

"Whatever we see, we face it together."

I press the link before I can reconsider, my heart pounding against my ribs as the screen fills with static. When it clears, my breath stutters. The image sharpens into a sterile room—stark and clinical in its emptiness—save for two figures slumped against opposite walls.

"Luca." I lean closer to the screen. My brother's head is down, but I'd know him anywhere. His chest rises and falls with shallow breaths, the only reassurance he's still alive.

And across from him, Alex. My stomach lurches at the sight of him. Whatever they've done to him in the hours since I saw him at the mansion has left its mark. His face is a mottled canvas of fresh bruises blooming over the old ones, one eye swollen completely shut. Blood trickles from his split lip, dripping onto his torn shirt. He's barely conscious, leaning sideways against the wall.

"Jesus Christ," Talon mutters behind me.

Four guards circle them like vultures, batons slapping

rhythmically against their palms. The sound echoes through the tablet's speakers, a metronome of threatened violence.

"Smile for your sister, Rossi," one of the guards barks, prodding Luca with his baton. "She's watching you."

Luca's head jerks up, immediately finding the camera. Recognition flashes across his face, followed quickly by defiance.

"Vesper," he mouths, no sound accompanying the shape of my name on his lips.

One of the guards moves toward Alex. "Your turn, Rafner. Say hello to your girlfriend."

Alex's single good eye narrows with sheer determination, locking onto the camera. His cracked and bleeding lips part, struggling to shape my name, but instead, a tortured, guttural gasp escapes as the guard viciously yanks his hair, twisting it with cruel force that clumps rip from his scalp.

"Stop it!" I cry out uselessly, knowing they can't hear me.

"Easy," Z mutters beside me, his hand hovering near mine but not touching. "They're doing this to provoke you."

The guard releases Alex with a contemptuous shove that sends him slumping against the wall again. Another guard approaches Luca, crouching to his level with mock familiarity.

Luca lunges forward suddenly, spitting directly in the guard's face. The reaction is immediate and brutal, a backhand that snaps my brother's head to the side, followed by a vicious kick to his ribs that leaves him doubled over, gasping.

"No!" I hear myself scream, surging forward as if I could

reach through the screen and shield him. Z's arm finally wraps around my waist, anchoring me as I watch helplessly.

"That's enough!" Alex's voice, ragged but suddenly strong, cuts through the chaos. Despite his battered state, he manages to push himself upright, drawing the guards' attention away from Luca. "You want to hurt someone? Try me."

The guard laughs, abandoning Luca to stalk toward Alex. "Always the hero, aren't you, Rafner? Let's see how heroic you feel after this."

He raises his baton, but before it falls, Luca's voice stops him.

My brother's attention is fixed on the camera, desperation etched across his bruised features. The guard's boot connects with Luca's stomach, cutting off his words. But he doesn't look away. His focus is steady on the camera, on me, mouthing something I can't quite catch before another blow sends him sprawling.

Alex struggles against the wall, using it to lever himself into a more upright position. His good eye finds the camera again, and through the blood and bruising, I see something burning there.

His entire body shudders under the pressure of consciousness, but his focus is resolute. I watch, transfixed and horrified, as he fights through the haze of pain to mouth words he needs me to understand. They're slow and deliberate, his determination carving clarity from the chaos.

"Remember," he seems to say, but his struggle to form the words is palpable. The effort costs him, each letter shaped with excruciating slowness. His chest heaves, ribs visibly contracting as he forces air through his battered lungs.

The screen flickers for a moment, threatening to steal this fragile connection. I grip the tablet harder. His lips continue their agonizing movement, a rehearsal of his earlier plea to me. reminder, I cling to now more than ever. One of the guards swings wide. His fist connecting with Alex's jaw. He falls slack against the wall.

"Your grandfather wants us to remind you of the terms. The clock is ticking." He taps his wristwatch meaningfully. "Sixty-five hours left." The screen goes black, leaving only my own reflection staring back at me, wild-eyed, pale with fury and fear. The tablet slips from my trembling fingers, Z catching it before it hits the floor, and places it back on my lap.

"Seven minutes," Oz states, checking his watch. "The feed lasted exactly seven minutes." His mind is already working, cataloging details while I sit frozen, the images of Luca and Alex's broken bodies burned into my retinas.

Talon crouches in front of me, his expression grave. "Vesper, look at me."

I can't.

"Vesper." His voice is firmer now, his hand gently tilting my chin upward until I have no choice but to look at him. "They're alive. Focus on that."

I pull away from both of them, standing abruptly. The room spins for a moment, grief and rage making me light-headed. I need to move, to act, to do something besides sit here while the men I love suffer.

"Oz, keep working on the files," Z interrupts, his voice leaving no room for argument. In one fluid motion, he rises from the couch and grabs me, lifting me effortlessly against his chest.

"What the hell are you doing?" I demand, struggling against his hold, but his arms are like steel bands around me.

"Something you need." His jaw is set in that stubborn way I know too well as he strides toward the stairs, carrying me like I weigh nothing.

I pound against his chest. "Put me down! We don't have time for whatever this is!"

Z ignores my protests, descending the stairs to the basement level. Instead of turning toward Alex's workspace, he continues past it to the door at the end of the hallway—the gym.

The moment we cross the threshold, I'm hit with the familiar scent of leather and sweat. The space is dimly lit, the punching bags hanging in the corner, the sparring mats empty and waiting.

He finally sets me down. "Hit me," Z says, stepping back and spreading his arms wide.

I stare at him, anger momentarily giving way to confusion. "What are you talking about?"

"Hit me."

"Why would I hit you? Are you crazy?"

"You need to get it out, Vesper. The rage, the fear—it's poisoning you from the inside out."

"I don't have time for this," I snap, turning toward the door, but Z moves faster, blocking my path.

"Yes, you do," he counters. "You think clearly when you're fighting. Always have. Right now, your emotions are clouding your judgment, and we need you sharp. Alex and Luca need you. That's the only fucking way we get through this."

"My judgment is fine," I hiss, trying to sidestep him.

Z shifts with me, his movements fluid. "No, it's not. You're spiraling, moya koroleva."

"Get out of my way," I warn, my hands clenching into fists at my sides.

"Make me."

The challenge in his voice ignites something primal inside me. Without conscious thought, I lunge forward, throwing a wild punch toward his jaw. Z sidesteps easily, letting my momentum carry me past him.

"You can do better than that," he taunts softly.

I whirl around. This time, my attack is more focused—a brutal combination Talon drilled into me, unrelenting.

Z blocks the first blow, but the second catches him in the ribs. He grunts, a sound of approval, as he circles me.

"That's it," he praises me. "Channel it."

I advance again, throwing my entire body into each strike. My fist connects with his shoulder, his chest, but he absorbs the impacts without retaliating, becoming a living punching bag for my rage.

"Fight back!" I demand, frustration building as he continues to merely defend.

"Not until you show me you mean it." His voice is maddeningly calm. "You're still holding back."

Something inside me snaps at his words. The dam I've built around my emotions crumbles, and everything I've been suppressing since walking into my father's study floods through me—the terror of seeing Alex alive when I'd mourned him as dead, the helplessness of watching Luca suffer, the sickening revelation of my grandfather's twisted plans.

My next attack is vicious, primal. I feint left, then drive my knee toward his midsection. Z barely blocks in time as I follow with an elbow strike that grazes his jaw.

"There she is," he murmurs, satisfaction threading every word as he finally begins to fight back.

We move across the mat in a brutal ballet, neither of us holding back now. Z's size and strength are matched by my speed and desperation. Sweat clings to my skin, my breathing growing ragged as we circle and strike. For these precious moments, there is only the fight—no Collector, no impossible deadline, no tortured loved ones. Just the clean, clarifying violence of bodies in motion.

Z catches my wrist as I aim for his throat, using my momentum to spin me against his chest. His arm locks around my waist, pinning me against him.

"Better, but still not your best."

I drive my heel into his instep, simultaneously throwing my head back. The crack of my skull connecting with his jaw is satisfying, as is his grunt of pain when he releases me. I whirl to face him, dropping into a fighting stance.

Z wipes blood from his split lip, a menacing smile spreading across his face. "Now we're getting somewhere."

We clash again, the tempo increasing with each exchange. Z lands a blow to my ribs that steals my breath, but I counter with a sweep that nearly takes his legs from under him. The physical pain is almost welcome, a sharp, clean contrast to the emotional agony that's been consuming me.

When he catches me in another hold, I don't fight it immediately. Instead, I let my body go slack for just a second, feeling his grip loosen in response before I explode into motion, bursting free and landing a solid hit to his solar plexus.

Z doubles over. "Nice shot," he wheezes, a glint of pride on his face.

I don't give him time to recover. I lunge forward, using my momentum to drive him backward. We tumble together, his back hitting the mat with a satisfying thud as I follow him down. My thighs clamp around his waist, pinning his hips while I capture his wrists, pressing them to the mat above his head.

"Yield," I demand, my chest heaving with exertion.

Z stares up at me, something shifting in his expression. The playful challenge transforms into something more primal.

Before I can process what's happening, he surges upward, his lips capturing mine in a kiss that's nothing like the careful, measured touches he's been giving me since we found out Alex was alive.

I freeze for a heartbeat, shock slicing through me. Then something breaks open in my chest, and I'm kissing him back just as fierce, just as desperate. My grip on his wrists loosens, fingers sliding into his hair, yanking him closer.

His hands seize my hips, rough and unyielding, dragging me against him with bruising intent.

The kiss is blood and salt, his split lip, my bitten tongue, sweat beading on overheated skin. It's messy, violent, and exactly what I need. For the first time since that hellish meeting with my grandfather, I feel something other than fear—desire, raw and consuming, burning everything else to ash.

Z rolls us, reversing our positions in one smooth motion. He settles between my thighs, his mouth trailing from my lips to my jaw, down the column of my throat, leaving a smoldering ache in his wake.

"Tell me to stop," he rasps against my pulse, his teeth grazing the sensitive skin there. "If this isn't what you want, say it."

I answer by dragging his mouth back to mine, my legs wrapping around his waist to erase the space between us. There's no gentleness here, no room for guilt or grief, just the desperate hunger to feel *alive* again.

His fingers slide beneath my shirt, palms hot as they skim up my ribs. When his thumbs brush the underside of my breasts, I arch into him, a sound tearing from my throat, part moan, part sob, all need.

"I need this," I gasp against his mouth. "I need to feel something that isn't—"

Z snaps, his restraint fracturing. He grabs my shirt by the collar and yanks, ripping it straight down the middle in one vicious tear. Before I can react, his fingers hook beneath the band of my bra and wrench it apart, the clasp giving way under the force. Cool air rushes over my bare skin, nipples tightening instantly as he tosses it aside.

"Fuck," he breathes, his gaze hungry. "Look at you."

His hands find my breasts, rough and greedy, kneading with a firm rhythm, thumbs circling my nipples until I'm writhing beneath him. Then his mouth replaces his touch, latching onto one hardened peak. I cry out, back arching off the mat as his teeth graze sensitive flesh, the sting of it sharpening everything, grounding me with need.

"Mark me," I plead, yanking him closer. "Make me *feel* it."

He utters a low curse against my skin, then bites down just hard enough to steal my breath before soothing the sting with a slow flick of his tongue. One hand moves to my other breast, pinching and rolling the nipple between his fingers, pressure delicious and deliberate, *claiming*.

"Like this?" he asks, his voice a graveled rasp as he sucks a bruise onto the swell of my breast.

"Yes," I gasp, arching into the sweet pain of his mouth. "Don't stop."

Z trails bites and kisses down my stomach as his hands work at my jeans. He tears open the button with impatient fingers, yanking the denim down my legs with such force I hear a seam rip. I kick off my shoes to help him, desperate to feel his skin against mine.

When I'm left in only my underwear, Z pauses, rising to his knees to stare down at me. His chest heaves with each breath, his split lip bleeding again from our kisses.

"Your turn," I demand, reaching for the hem of his shirt.

He pulls it off in one smooth motion, revealing the sculpted planes of his torso. The familiar sight of his tattoos sparks a rush of heat low in my belly. My fingers trace the lines of ink, following them down to the waistband of his sweatpants where his arousal strains against the fabric.

Z hisses when I palm him through the thin material. "Careful, moya koroleva," he warns, voice strained. "I'm barely holding on as it is."

"Then don't hold on," I challenge, hooking my fingers into his waistband and dragging them down along with his boxer briefs. His cock springs free, hard and flushed against his stomach, the sight making my mouth water with want.

Z kicks the clothing away impatiently, now gloriously naked above me. His hand slides between my thighs, fingers finding the damp cotton of my underwear. He pushes the fabric aside and strokes through my folds. The calluses on his fingertips create a delicious friction that has me arching off the mat. "I need to taste you."

Before I can respond, he's tearing my underwear off with a sharp rip of fabric. His broad shoulders push my thighs wider as he settles between them, his hot breath hitting my core in a way that makes me shiver with anticipation.

"Please," I gasp, beyond pride or patience.

Z's eyes flash as he looks up at me from between my legs. "Since you asked so nicely."

The first stroke of his tongue nearly unravels me. He groans against me, the vibration rippling through my core as he devours me with relentless focus. His grip on my thighs is unforgiving, holding me steady as I writhe beneath him, completely at his mercy.

"Z, fuck." My words dissolve into incoherent sounds as he slides two thick fingers inside me, curling them to hit that spot that makes my vision blur. His tongue circles my clit with merciless precision, alternating between broad strokes and targeted flicks that have me climbing rapidly toward release.

"You're close, moyo koroleva, aren't you?"

I nod, unable to form words as pleasure builds inside me like a gathering storm. His fingers curl deeper, finding that spot while his mouth works relentlessly against my most sensitive flesh. The pressure builds and builds until I'm balancing on the knife's edge of release.

Suddenly, he pulls away, withdrawing his fingers and mouth just as I teeter on the precipice. My body jerks in protest, a desperate whimper tearing from my throat.

"What are you—" I gasp, trying to pull him back.

Z hovers above me, keeping just enough distance that I can't find the friction I desperately need. "Not yet. I want you to be desperate first."

His fingers return, circling my entrance with maddening lightness, never quite giving me what I need. "Z, please," I beg, writhing beneath him, trying to force his touch where I need it most.

"Patience," he admonishes, lowering his head to capture my nipple between his teeth. The sharp sensation makes me cry out, my back arching off the mat.

He builds me up again with devastating skill, fingers and

tongue working in tandem until I'm once more teetering on the edge. My thighs begin to tremble, my breath coming in short, desperate pants, and then he stops again, leaving me empty and aching.

"Goddamn it!" I slam my fist against the mat in frustration. "Stop teasing me!"

Z looms over me, his expression shifting with primal satisfaction. "You wanted to feel something else," he reminds me, his fingers trailing up my inner thigh with feather-light pressure. "This is what you're feeling instead. Need. Want. Desire. Desperation."

I hook my leg around his waist, using the leverage to flip us as I straddle him, pinning him to the mat as I position myself above his straining cock.

"My turn," I growl, sinking down onto him in one fluid motion.

The sensation of him filling me is exquisite, a breathtaking blend of pleasure and pain that wipes every other thought from my mind. For this moment, there's no Collector, no impossible mission, no countdown ticking away the hours. There is only this. Z's powerful body beneath mine, the delicious stretch of him inside me, the way his fingers grip my hips with bruising force, grounding me in something raw and real.

"Fuck," he hisses, his head thrown back as I begin to move. "Vesper—"

I set a brutal rhythm, using him with single-minded purpose, chasing the high coiling in my gut. He slides his palms up to cup my breasts, thumbs brushing over my nipples with just enough pressure to draw a gasp from my lips. When he pinches, I cry out, my pace stuttering.

Z takes the opening, surging up to claim my mouth in a bruising kiss before flipping us with ease. He hooks one of my legs over his shoulder, the shift in angle making every thrust hit harder, each one a jolt of pleasure that ripples through my core and fans the ache blooming in my limbs.

"On your knees," he rasps.

I obey without hesitation, rolling onto my stomach and pushing up onto all fours. He positions himself behind me, one hand steady on my hip, the other tangling in my hair at the nape of my neck, tugging just enough to arch my spine and bare everything to him.

"This is what you need, isn't it?" His breath is hot against my ear as he lines himself up. "To lose control. To let someone else take over."

"Yes," I gasp, pressing back against him, needy and breathless. "Please."

He thrusts into me in one hard, claiming stroke that punches the air from my lungs. His grip tightens, holding my head back as he finds a brutal rhythm. Each snap of his hips drives me forward, the mat burning beneath my palms as I scramble for purchase.

Then suddenly, his fist tightens in my hair and yanks me upright against his chest. My back arches sharply, the shift making every stroke feel sharper, fuller. His other arm snakes around my throat, applying just enough pressure to make my pulse hammer against his skin.

"Fuck, I can feel you quivering around my cock. You like this, don't you?"

I can't answer, can barely breathe as his fingers tighten just enough to restrict my airflow without cutting it off completely. The edges of my vision begin to blur, spots dancing at the periphery as oxygen becomes precious. The sensation is terrifying and exhilarating all at once, complete surrender, complete trust.

"Good girl. I want to feel your body arching for air, trembling under my control...knowing every second that you're mine." He thrusts, matching the rhythm of my beating heart. Thud. Thrust. Thud. Thrust. Over and over again.

"You feel that?" he growls, his mouth at my ear, hips relentless. "That helpless little flutter in your chest? That's mine now. Just like the rest of you."

My breath stalls—sharp, desperate—his hand a vice of dominance around my throat, and he feels it, groans against my skin like he owns every quiver, every gasp. Each thrust feels more intense, more consuming, as if Z is claiming not just my body but something more essential. The pressure in my core builds to an almost unbearable level, my muscles clenching around him as I teeter on the edge.

"Let fucking go, baby." His voice is rough and filthy in my ear, each word scraping down my spine like a live wire. "Let go of everything, Vesper. The pain, the fear, all that control you cling to...I want it gone. I want you wrecked. Ruined. *Mine.*"

His hand tightens in my hair, his other gripping my throat, owning every breath, every whimper.

"Don't hold back. Not tonight," he snarls, hips snapping into mine. "Scream for me. Shatter for me. Give me every dirty, desperate piece of you."

His hand releases my throat just enough for me to gasp a desperate breath, and something inside me fractures. The careful control I've maintained since walking into my father's study—since learning my grandfather's identity, since seeing Alex alive—splinters into a thousand sharp-edged pieces.

I scream. The sound tears from my throat, primal and raw, unleashing everything I've been holding back. Z pounds into me mercilessly, giving me exactly what I need—oblivion, release, a moment where I don't have to be strong or calculated or brave.

"That's it. Give me everything. All of it."

My orgasm rips through me with violent intensity, my body convulsing around him as pleasure blurs everything else. I'm dimly aware of sobbing his name, of my nails sinking into his forearm hard enough to draw blood. Z follows with a guttural roar, his hips slamming into mine one last time as he spills inside me.

We collapse together onto the mat, a tangle of sweat-slicked limbs and ragged breathing. Z's arms wrap around me, pulling me against his chest as aftershocks ripple through me.

For several moments, we lie in silence, my breathing gradually slowing to match the steady rise and fall of Z's chest beneath my cheek. The world outside this room seems distant, temporarily held at bay by the sanctuary of his arms.

"Thank you." My body aches in a dozen different places, each twinge a reminder that I'm still here, still fighting, still alive. "For knowing what I needed even when I didn't."

He presses his lips to my temple, the gesture unexpectedly tender after everything we'd just done. "I always know what you need, moya koroleva. It's my job."

"Your job, huh?"

"One of many services I provide," he replies, a hint of his usual arrogance returning to his voice. His hand moves to my hip, thumb brushing over what will surely become a bruise by morning. "Did I hurt you?"

I shake my head against his chest. "Not in any way I didn't want."

His arms tighten around me, something protective in the gesture. "Good."

We should move. Should clean up, return upstairs where Oz is undoubtedly making progress on Alex's files. But I can't bring myself to leave this moment, this brief respite.

Movement overhead interrupts the moment. footsteps crossing the floor above us, then the creak of the basement door opening. Z tenses beneath me, his body instantly alert as the footsteps descend the stairs.

"Z? Vesper?" Talon's voice echoes down the hallway, drawing closer. "You guys good? I heard noises."

Z shifts me off him with surprising gentleness before calling back. "We're fine. Just working through some tension." His voice carries that familiar edge of humor.

Talon appears in the doorway, taking in our disheveled

state with a raised eyebrow. Torn clothing around us, Z's split lip, the bruises already forming on both our bodies.

"Is that what they are calling it these days?" he smiles. Talon leans against the doorframe, but I catch the subtle way he stares me for signs of genuine distress. "Though you might want to borrow Z's shirt, Vesper. Yours seems to have met with an unfortunate accident."

I glance down at the tattered remains of my clothing scattered around us and feel the flush rise to my cheeks. Not embarrassment exactly, we're long past that, but awareness of how completely I'd surrendered to the moment.

"Oz sent me to find you."

The reminder of why we're here, of what's at stake, crashes back like a bucket of ice water. I sit up, wincing slightly as my muscles protest the sudden movement. Z immediately reaches for his discarded shirt, handing it to me with gentle efficiency.

"What did he find?" I ask, pulling the shirt over my head, covering enough to preserve what little modesty I have left.

"We have the blackmail. We have what we need."

# Chapter 34

OSCAR

I CAN ALWAYS TELL when my brother has fucked someone senseless. It's in the way he moves like a predator who's just fed but is still prowling for more. As I watch him emerge from the basement with Vesper trailing behind him, I can't help but smirk at Talon, who's already pulling out his wallet.

"Don't even start," I say, holding out my hand as Talon slaps a fifty into my palm. "I've shared a womb with the man. I know his post-coital strut when I see it."

Talon shakes his head, glancing back toward the stairs where Z and Vesper disappeared. "Could've been a hardcore training session. She looked like she needed to blow off steam."

"Oh, she blew something alright." I pocket the cash, turning back to the laptop where I've been scouring Alex's files.

Talon drops into the chair opposite me, wincing as his injured shoulder protests the movement. "You're a sick bastard, betting on your brother's sex life."

"Says the man who took the bet." I don't look up from the screen, my fingers continuing their rhythmic dance across the keyboard. "Besides, it's not about the sex. It's about knowing what she needs." Vesper has been spiraling. It was only a matter of time until she spiraled out of control. Z just realized it sooner than the rest of us.

Vesper reappears a few minutes later wearing fresh clothes and her hair still damp from what I'm guessing was a quick shower to wash off the evidence of their "training session." There's something different about her now. subtle shift in her demeanor that only someone who's been watching her as closely as I have would notice.

"Better, solnishko?" I ask, studying the way she moves across the room with more fluidity than before, the rigid tension noticeably diminished.

She nods, a faint flush coloring her cheeks. "Yes. I needed to...clear my head."

Z appears behind her, his split lip and the fresh bruise blooming along his jawline telling their own story. He catches my knowing look and responds with a barely perceptible shrug, neither confirming nor denying what transpired downstairs, but not bothering to hide his satisfaction either.

She seems lighter than I've seen her since before this

nightmare began. The haunted, hollow look since her meeting with The Collector hasn't disappeared entirely, but it's been pushed back, replaced by something sharper, more focused. Z's methods may be unorthodox, but I can't argue with results. Despite the pang of jealousy that he's able to give her that and not me.

"I've made progress with the files," I tell her, gesturing toward the laptop. "Mario had a lot of blackmail on the families."

"Which families?"

"Most of the American families," I answer, turning the laptop so she can see the organized folders. "Some of the European ones, too."

Vesper leans over my shoulder, her scent, a mixture of her vanilla shampoo and something distinctly Z, tickling my nostrils as she studies the screen. Her finger traces the list of family names, each one representing a potential ally...or enemy.

"And Russia?"

I sigh, leaning back in my chair. "A few, but not as many as I would have liked."

The disappointment is evident in her expression. "So what do we do with this information?" She looks between the three of us.

"We rally them to join our cause," I say, my mind already mapping out potential alliances. "Your grandfather didn't just terrorize his own grandchildren. There are others. Dozens. If they help us, it could mean getting their missing family members back."

Z moves closer, his hand coming to rest on Vesper's lower back in a gesture that seems unconscious. "You're suggesting we build an army."

"I'm suggesting we build a coalition," I correct him, though the distinction may be semantic. "The Collector has been playing these families against each other for decades. What if we show them they have a common enemy?"

Talon nods slowly, understanding dawning across his features. "The enemy of my enemy is my friend," Talon finishes, leaning forward with renewed energy. "We turn The Collector's own tactics against him."

"Exactly," I nod, scrolling through the files. "Mario had dirt on nearly every major family. Enough leverage to force cooperation if needed."

Vesper's fingers hover over the screen, tracing the names of powerful families who've suffered under The Collector's reign of terror. "But will blackmail really make them fight for us? We need loyalty, not reluctant allies who might turn on us at the first opportunity."

"Not blackmail," I clarify. "Common cause. Mario has been watching The Collector closely. Some of these files have names, dates, and proof of which ones are still alive."

Z's expression darkens. "And which ones aren't."

"We offer them something more valuable than money or power," I continue. "We offer them closure. Or better yet, the chance to get their loved ones back."

Vesper straightens, "How many?"

"Fourteen confirmed still alive, including your brother.

Mario didn't have the locations, though, so that is a problem, but it's a start."

"Fourteen families who might help us."

I nod, already calculating odds and alliances in my head. "Plus, whatever other information we can extract from these files. Mario was thorough."

"But we still have the same problem," Talon interjects. "Even with allies, how do we get to Victor Petrov? His compound might as well be on the moon for all the good fourteen crime families will do for us."

Vesper stills. "Then we get him to open the doors by giving him what he wants, Rossi-Petrov heirs."

"Absolutely not!" Z's roar drowns out everything else as he lunges forward, his face contorted with rage.

"That's suicide—" Talon shouts, rising from his chair so quickly that it topples backward.

"We're not using you as bait—" I start, my voice colliding with my brother's furious objections.

The three of us talk over each other, our protests colliding into a chaotic roar that fills the apartment. Z paces like a caged animal, gesturing wildly as he curses in Russian, while Talon's voice rises to match his, sharp and unrelenting. I'm already running through alternate scenarios in my head, rattling them off one after another—but no one's listening. No one's hearing anyone.

"ENOUGH!" Vesper slams her palm against the table with such force that my laptop jumps.

The room falls silent instantly. She stands tall, chin

raised, that familiar steel in her spine that I've always admired.

"It's the only way. Victor Petrov wants his dynasty secured more than anything. Yes, he has my son now, but he will want more security. More heirs. Bianca can't give him that. I can."

"Absolutely fucking not," Z seethes, crossing the room to tower over her. "I am not selling you off to my uncle. Not now, not ever."

Where most people would crumble under his rage, she only seems to grow stronger, more resolute.

"Think about it," she says. "Really think about it. Bianca and Mario needed my son. They needed a true Rossi heir to secure their position. Victor doesn't know about him yet. What better way to topple his empire and legacy than from within?"

Z shakes his head violently. "No."

"It gets us through the door," she continues. "I become the Trojan horse."

I lean forward, the pieces clicking together in my mind. "It's not the worst plan," I admit, earning a murderous glare from my twin. "Strategically speaking, it gives us access we wouldn't have otherwise."

"You too?" Z spins to face me, betrayal etched across his features. "Have you both lost your fucking minds?"

Talon clears his throat. "Let's hear her out before we dismiss it entirely."

Vesper nods gratefully at him before turning back to Z.

"We could have a timeline of ten years, and we will never be able to get that close to him, Z. This is the only way."

"Ten years or ten minutes, it doesn't matter," Z argues. "You're not offering yourself to Victor Petrov."

I watch the tension between them build. Z's protective rage versus Vesper's iron determination. It's a standoff neither will easily concede.

"What exactly are you proposing?" I ask, cutting through their silent battle. Strategy demands clarity, and right now we need specifics, not emotions.

"I contact Victor directly. I tell him everything. Mario and Bianca deceived him, how they had me taken by The Collector, and harvested to produce his grandson."

"And then what?" Talon asks.

"Then I offer him what he truly wants," Vesper says, her chin lifting with resolve. "A legitimate alliance through marriage. Myself to Dmitri, just as was originally planned before I was taken."

The silence that follows is deafening. I can practically hear the gears turning in everyone's heads, especially Z's, whose face has gone frighteningly blank.

"It's actually brilliant," I admit, earning a murderous glare from my twin. "Victor would never expect it. After everything that's happened, you offering yourself will seem like a legitimate surrender rather than a trap. You're the head of the Rossi family now," I stand, moving to the center of our small group. "It would get you through the front door."

"And then what?"

"I give my grandfather what he wants. The keys to the Petrov kingdom."

The pieces fall into place in my mind like a strategic chess game unfolding. I rise from my chair, a plan crystallizing with clarity. Vesper is a fucking mastermind. This plan...is a masterclass of deception.

"Wait," I say, my voice cutting through the tension. "That's exactly what we need to do. We play them against each other. The Collector wants Russia, he wants the Petrovs destroyed. It's been his endgame for decades." I begin pacing, the excitement of this strategy energizing me. "And Victor? He's obsessed with legacy, with heirs, with continuing the Petrov/Rossi bloodline."

Z's expression shifts from rage to interest as he follows my logic. "So we tell Victor about his grandson..."

"And about who orchestrated everything," I finish, nodding. "When Victor discovers what happened with your son, he'll want blood."

Talon leans forward, understanding dawning on his face. "Victor already hates The Collector from their past conflicts. This would be personal."

"We don't just offer Victor an alliance. We offer him revenge. We turn Victor's rage away from us and toward my grandfather."

"Let them destroy each other," Z repeats, something like approval flickering across his face.

"It's brilliant," I admit, the tactical advantage becoming clearer with each passing second. "We don't need to kill Victor, Dmitri, or Bianca ourselves.  just need to make Victor believe The Collector is his true enemy."

"My grandfather thinks I'm coming to kill Victor, but instead I'll be revealing everything—how The Collector engineered my abduction, how he arranged for my son's conception, how he's been plotting against the Petrovs for decades."

"Victor will do the rest," Talon adds, his tactical mind already mapping the fallout. "He'll mobilize everything he has against The Collector."

Z's tension hasn't fully dissipated, but I can see him recognizing the potential. "And while they're tearing each other apart..."

"We rescue Luca and Alex," Vesper finishes, her voice stronger than I've heard it in days. "And my son."

I move to the laptop, pulling up a new document. "We need to prepare exactly what information to reveal and what to withhold. Victor needs to believe this is about his family's honor, not just another power play."

"He'll want proof," Talon warns, coming to stand beside me. "Victor doesn't trust easily."

"We have proof," I say, pulling up another folder on the laptop. "The records from the clinic show your male embryos being sent to Russia, the money trail from Mario making the storage payments. The photos of you while captive. I can transmit enough of it to whet his appetite, with the rest available when we meet face to face."

"Say he agrees, how do we get there? It's not like I have a passport lying around."

"We get him to send a plane for you and for us."

Z's jaw works silently as he processes this new approach, his expression torn between tactical approval and visceral rejection of anything putting Vesper in Victor's path.

"Once we're in the air, we contact your grandfather and get the ball rolling there. All the while, our coalition is lying in wait."

Z crosses his arms over his chest. I recognize that stance. The same one he's had since we were children, whenever he sees holes in my plans.

"This is insanity. You're assuming Victor will act rationally when he learns about his grandson. You're assuming The Collector will focus his rage on Victor rather than punishing Vesper for her betrayal. You're assuming fourteen crime families with generations of blood feuds between them will suddenly join hands and sing Kumbaya because we ask nicely."

I sigh, recognizing the valid concerns beneath his skepticism. "We're not asking them to become best friends."

"No, you're asking them to risk their lives based on blackmail and promises," Z interrupts, pushing away from the wall. "These aren't rational actors, Oz. These are men who've built empires on vendettas and violence. What happens when the Gambinos remember the Lucchesis killed their underboss in '97? What happens when the Irish decide they'd rather see the Italians burn than help them? All it takes is one betrayal, one family tipping off The Collector or Victor, and we're all dead."

He's not wrong. The fragility of our plan becomes more apparent with each objection he raises.

"What's your alternative?" Vesper challenges, stepping toward him. "Our deadline gets closer and closer by the second. We don't have time to discuss this in a committee meeting, Zaire. need to execute it now."

"I don't have an alternative," Z admits, his voice tight with frustration. "That's what makes this so fucking infuriating."

I watch the conflict play across his face.

"Then help us make this work," Vesper says, her tone softening as she moves closer to him. "Find the holes in our plan so we can patch them. Make it airtight."

Z's jaw works silently as he stares down at her. "You realize what you're proposing? Walking into the lion's den with nothing but your wits and our word that we'll be there to back you up?"

"I trust you," she says simply. "All of you."

"Fine, but we're doing this my way," Z insists, his voice leaving no room for negotiation. "If we're playing both sides, we need fail-safes. Multiple extraction points. Weapons cached where Victor's security won't find them."

I nod, already mapping contingencies in my head. "We'll need to contact our people in St. Petersburg. The ones Uncle Victor doesn't know about."

"The Second Sons have operatives throughout Russia," Talon adds, moving to the kitchen where we keep our secure satellite phone. "I can activate them within hours."

Vesper watches us shift into planning mode.

"What about my grandfather? He'll expect updates. Progress reports on my mission to kill Victor."

"We feed him just enough to keep him believing you're following his plan."

"Photos," I suggest, moving back to the laptop. "Staged reconnaissance shots of Victor's compound. Travel documentation. Enough breadcrumbs to maintain the illusion."

"And when he realizes I've betrayed him?" Vesper's question hangs in the air, heavy with implications none of us want to voice.

"By then it won't matter," Z says with cold finality. "Because by then, Victor will be hunting him, not us."

"I'll start contacting the families," I say, already mentally sorting through the list. "I have direct lines to most of the underbosses, and where I don't, Talon does. We'll need to be careful about how we approach them. Give them just enough information to pique their interest without revealing our entire hand.'

Vesper nods, her fingers drumming against the table as she processes. Then she turns to Z, her expression shifting to something more hesitant.

"How do we get in contact with your uncle?" she asks.

Z goes still. I recognize the conflict behind his eyes, hatred for the man who destroyed our family, warring with the tactical necessity of involving him.

Z runs a hand through his hair, tension evident in every line of his body. "Normally, we'd request a meeting through our father," he says, his voice tight with barely contained rage. "But he's exiled himself to some godforsaken island in the Mediterranean, drinking himself into oblivion."

I consider our options, mentally cataloging the

remaining Petrov connections we've maintained despite our estrangement from the family. "What about Dmitri?" I suggest watching Z's reaction carefully. "We can use him to put us in contact. Play the remorseful nephews who want to return to the family with their tails tucked between their legs." The idea leaves a bitter taste in my mouth, but strategy often requires swallowing pride. "That might work."

Vesper looks between us, her brow furrowed in that way that always means she's cutting through unnecessary complications. "Why don't I just call him?" she asks, her directness catching us all off guard. "You have his number, right? Seems more direct than intermediaries. You're his nephews."

The simplicity of her suggestion momentarily stuns us into silence. Z stares at her as if she's suggested we walk into a nuclear reactor without protection.

"Just call Victor Petrov?" Talon repeats, incredulity coloring his voice.

"Yes," Vesper says, unfazed by our collective shock. "Direct approach. No games."

"You don't just call Victor Petrov. The man has layers of security, gatekeepers, protocols."

"Actually," I interject, my mind already working through the logistics, "it's not the worst idea."

Z turns his glare on me. "Have you lost your mind?"

"Think about it," I continue, unperturbed by his reaction. "What's Victor's greatest weakness? His pride. His ego. A direct call from the head of the Rossi family, a woman he believes was stolen from him, would appeal to that ego."

Talon nods slowly. "The unexpectedness of it might work in our favor. Victor appreciates boldness, even from his enemies."

"This is insane," Z mutters, but I can see his resistance weakening.

"Do we have his number?" Vesper asks.

My brother's jaw works silently for a moment before he reluctantly pulls out his phone. "I still have his private line. He never changed it.  thinks it's a power move, letting us know we could call but never would."

"Until now," Vesper says, her hand outstretched for the phone.

Z hesitates, his thumb hovering over the screen. "Vesper, once we do this, there's no going back. You understand that, right? Victor isn't just some garden-variety psychopath."

"We don't have a choice. The clock is ticking, and I am not wasting another second. Make the call."

# Chapter 35

VESPER

THE SOUND of Victor Petrov's phone ringing echoes through our apartment like a death knell, each tone more ominous than the last. I hold my breath, watching Z's face harden into something cold and unrecognizable as he waits for the connection.

The line clicks. A gruff voice answers in rapid Russian, the syllables sharp as broken glass.

Z's responds in English, his accent suddenly thicker than I've ever heard it. "This is Zaire Petrov. I need to speak with my uncle."

A beat of silence, then the voice switches to heavily accented English. "Zaire? This is...unexpected."

"Put him on." The command in Z's voice is unmistakable. voice of a man who expects to be obeyed despite years of estrangement.

I move closer, my heart hammering against my ribs as a muffled exchange takes place on the other end. Z's breathing carefully measured.

Oz and Talon position themselves on either side of me, a protective formation we've fallen into without discussion. The seconds stretch like hours until finally, a new voice comes through the speaker, deep and authoritative.

"Nephew." The single word carries decades of history, dripping with equal parts disdain and curiosity. "I trust you have an excellent reason for ignoring your exile from this family."

Z's jaw tightens, a muscle working beneath the skin.

"I have someone here who wishes to speak with you." Z's voice remains steady, though I can see the tension in every line of his body. "The head of the Rossi family."

Victor's laugh is like gravel being crushed underfoot. "Mario knows how to contact me directly. Why is he using you as a mediator?" His tone sharpens. "What have you done, nephew?"

Z's eyes meet mine, a silent question. I nod once, stepping forward to take the phone from his hand. Our fingers brush during the exchange, his skin cool against my feverish touch.

"This is Vesper Rossi," I say, forcing strength into my voice.

"Miss Rossi." Victor's tone shifts subtly. "I had heard rumors of your...reemergence. Though I find it curious you're in my nephew's company. I have to admit it is quite surprising that you are assuming the head of your family, considering your uncle is very much alive."

"Actually, that is no longer the case. He's dead. I killed him myself."

The silence that follows is charged with an electric tension that makes the hair on my arms stand on end.

"Did you, now?" Victor's voice has dropped an octave, carrying a blend of skepticism and intrigue. "That's quite a claim from a woman who's been missing for years."

"It's not a claim. It's a fact." I keep my voice steady, channeling the steel that's become my armor. "Mario was a traitor. To my family, to yours, and to the agreements our families made."

Z moves closer, his body a warm presence at my back as he listens. His breath tickles my neck as he leans in to hear Victor's response.

"And what would you know of those agreements, Miss Rossi? The alliance your father brokered on your behalf was fulfilled by your cousin. Your services are no longer required. Bianca has already provided me with my heir."

"You mean, I provided you with an heir?"

"I oversaw the birth myself, Miss Rossi. You were not present."

"I wasn't the birth mother, but I assure you, Victor, I am that boy's mother. You've been deceived from the moment you consented to her marriage to Dmitri."

I can almost hear Victor's breathing change through the phone.

"Explain yourself." His tone brooks no argument.

"Bianca isn't a Rossi. She doesn't have a drop of my family's blood running in her veins," I continue.

"This is a serious accusation, Miss Rossi." Victor's voice has taken on a blunt edge.

"I have proof. Records from my captivity. Records of the medical torture I was put through to produce your grandson under the direction of my uncle for the benefit of his bastard daughter and your alliance."

"Do you?" Victor's tone is glacial. "Because from where I sit, this sounds like the desperate fabrication of a woman who abandoned her responsibilities and now regrets it."

I feel Z's hand tighten on my shoulder, silently urging me to stay calm. I take a deep breath, steadying myself.

"I didn't abandon anything," I reply, keeping my voice level despite the anger bubbling beneath the surface. "I was taken. Abducted by the man you know as The Collector."

Victor's dismissive scoff crackles through the speaker. "A convenient story. The Collector is a myth used to frighten children and weak men."

"He's very real. And I have the scars to prove it."

"What you have, Miss Rossi, is audacity." His voice hardens. "You disappear for years, then suddenly resurface with my estranged nephews at your side. Don't be shocked. Where one goes, so does the other. Now, you're claiming some elaborate conspiracy? This is nothing more than a transparent attempt to worm your way into my family's good graces now."

Oz moves closer, his expression tense as he watches me. I press on.

"The DNA tests are ready to be sent to you," I say, playing the strongest card I have. "Medical records from the fertility clinic showing the extraction of my eggs, the creation of embryos using Petrov sperm, and the implantation into Bianca. Records of payments from Mario Rossi's private accounts to keep it all hidden."

"You expect me to believe my son was deceived? That I was deceived?"

"I expect you to verify everything I'm saying," I counter. "I'm offering to send you the proof. All of it. Right now."

Z 's body heat radiates against my back as he listens. His breath tickles my ear as he whispers, "Good. Keep pushing."

"And what would you gain from this...revelation, Miss Rossi?" Victor's voice drips with suspicion. "If what you say is true, and that remains to be seen, why come to me now?"

I exchange glances with Oz, who gives me an encouraging nod.

"Because I want what is rightfully mine. My son," I say, allowing raw emotion to bleed into my voice. "I want my place at the table."

"Your place at the table," he repeats, each word measured carefully. "You believe you're entitled to that after all this time?"

"I'm not just entitled to it. I'm demanding it." My voice gains strength as I continue. "That boy is my flesh and blood. My Rossi legacy. The rightful continuation of our families' alliance that Mario perverted for his own gain."

Z's hand slides down to the small of my back as I push forward.

"You've always prided yourself on legacy, Victor. On blood. On the purity of the Petrov line." I pause, letting my next words land with precision. "Wouldn't you want to know if your grandson, your heir, isn't being raised by his true mother?"

"You have one minute to convince me this isn't an elaborate game, Miss Rossi."

"Check your email. Oz is sending the first documents now."

Oz nods, hitting send on his laptop with a theatrical flourish. We wait in tense silence, the only sound in the room our collective breathing.

"These could be fabricated," he says finally, though there's a new note in his voice, uncertainty where before there was only dismissal.

"That is just the tip of the iceberg, Victor. I have videos, photos, and financial records. I have enough proof for my claim."

The line falls silent, and I can almost see Victor sitting in his palatial office, turning over the evidence we've provided, his mind working through all the angles. The silence stretches until I wonder if he's hung up.

"What exactly are you proposing, Miss Rossi?" His voice, when it finally comes, has lost its dismissive edge. Now it carries the careful consideration of a chess master evaluating an unexpected move.

I take a deep breath, feeling Z's hand press more firmly against my back in silent support.

"The political alliance as originally contracted," I say steadily. "A marriage between me, as the head of the Rossi family, and Dmitri. It's your only way to guarantee true-born Rossi-Petrov heirs."

Z's hand tenses against my spine, but he remains silent. We've rehearsed this, planned for it, yet the words still taste like ash in my mouth.

"A bold proposal," Victor says, the faint sound of ice clinking against glass coming through the line. "Especially considering Dmitri is already married to your cousin."

"My false cousin," I correct him. "And marriages can be...dissolved when they're built on lies."

Victor chuckles, the sound devoid of humor. "And in return for this generous offer? What do you get out of this arrangement, Miss Rossi?"

"Revenge on the people who did this to me."

"Your uncle is already dead."

"Yes, that is he, but I want revenge on the man who held me captive for years. Medically raped me over and over again for your family's benefit."

"Who?"

"The Collector."

"The Collector is a myth."

"Turns out, he's not."

"The Collector," Victor repeats, a new edge to his voice. "You claim to know his identity?"

"I don't claim anything. I know exactly who he is." I

steady myself against Z's solid presence behind me. "Mikhail Vasilyev."

The silence that follows is so absolute that I can hear my own heartbeat thundering in my ears. Even through the phone, I can feel the temperature drop at the mention of that name.

"That's impossible." Victor's voice has lost all its calculated coolness, replaced by something raw and visceral. "Mikhail Vasilyev is dead. His entire bloodline was wiped out decades ago."

"Not all of it," I counter. "Considering I am his granddaughter." Silence falls again. "Is it safe to assume that I have your attention now, Victor?"

The sound of shattering glass comes through the speaker, followed by rapid Russian that even Z looks startled to hear.

"Proof. I need absolute proof."

"DNA doesn't lie, Victor. My mother's. Mine. My son's." I pause, letting the implication sink in. "Your grandson carries Vasilyev blood."

"That is impossible." Victor's voice trembles with barely contained rage. "Elizaveta Rossi was not—"

"My mother was Elizaveta Vasilyev before she became a Rossi," I cut in, pressing our advantage while he's off-balance. "Sold by her father to secure protection from your family. A sacrifice he's been plotting to avenge ever since."

Another string of Russian curses crackles through the line. Z's eyes widen slightly at whatever Victor is saying.

"My grandfather orchestrated everything," I continue

relentlessly. "My abduction. The harvesting of my eggs. The creation of your grandson. All to infiltrate your family from within."

"If what you say is true..." Victor's voice is cold, calm—like still water hiding sharp rocks beneath. "Then your own blood betrayed you. Why should I trust you now?"

"Because I want what you want. The destruction of Mikhail Vasilyev. I want my family's legacy back. I want the power to protect my son. You can give me those things, and I can give you Mikhail."

A pause stretches across the line, taut with calculation.

"You understand what you're proposing. An alliance against your own blood."

"Mikhail Vasilyev may share my blood, but he is not my family." The words burn with a truth I've only recently come to understand.

"You mentioned proof," Victor says, the sound of a lighter flicking open coming through the speaker. "I want all of it. Every document. Every recording. Every trace of this...conspiracy."

"Of course," I reply, nodding to Oz, who's already preparing the secure file transfer. "But I won't send everything electronically. The most damning evidence comes with me, in person."

"You expect me to bring you to Russia based on partial evidence and your word?" His laugh is sharp, disbelieving.

"I expect you to act in your own self-interest," I counter smoothly. "The safety of your grandson. The integrity of your bloodline. The chance to finally eliminate Mikhail Vasilyev."

Victor says nothing. "This deal is only on the table for twenty-four hours, Victor. Take it, and protect your family's legacy, or don't, and live with the knowledge you were sold a bill of goods for a daughter-in-law. The choice is yours."

"Very well," Victor says after a long pause, his voice hardening into something cold and final. "A plane will be waiting for you at Hanscom Field in two hours. The pilot will have clearance for my nephews as well."

My heart hammers against my ribs. worked. I catch Z's eye, the slight widening of his pupils the only indication of his surprise.

"Thank you," I begin, but Victor cuts me off.

"Do not mistake this for trust, Miss Rossi. Consider it...professional curiosity." Ice clinks against glass as he takes a drink. "And know this, if you are lying to me, if this is some elaborate scheme, I will personally ensure that you suffer in ways that will make your time with The Collector seem like a pleasant memory. Your death will be measured in weeks, not moments."

I swallow hard, knowing his threat isn't empty. "I understand."

"Good. Then we have nothing more to discuss until you arrive." The line goes dead before I can respond.

I lower the phone slowly. "We're in."

"Holy shit," Talon breathes. "You actually did it."

Z takes the phone from my hand, his fingers brushing against mine. "That was..." He shakes his head. "You played him exactly how you needed to."

"Not exactly," I counter, already heading toward the

bedroom to pack. "He's still suspicious. We need to make sure our evidence is airtight before we get there."

"How long until your grandfather expects an update?" Oz asks, already moving to his laptop where he's compiling the files we'll need.

"Soon." I glance at the black tablet sitting on the coffee table, its sleek surface reflecting the overhead lights. "He'll want to know my progress toward eliminating Victor."

"Then we give him what he wants," Z says, his expression hardening. "We tell him you're on your way to Russia. Let him think his plan is working."

I nod. "He'll want video confirmation. Proof I'm following through."

"So we give him a show," Talon suggests. "Record something on the plane that makes it look like you're committed to his mission."

"It needs to be convincing," I warn. "He's not easily fooled."

Z's hand comes to rest on my shoulder, his touch steadying. "Then we'll make it convincing."

"I hope you're right, Z. Because if this plan fails, if he sees through our charade, I fear the consequences will be dire."

# Chapter 36

VESPER

THE PETROV FAMILY crest gleams on the side of the Dassault Falcon X like a warning sign.

"Holy shit," I exclaim as we approach the sleek aircraft waiting on the tarmac. The private jet is a monument to wealth and power, its polished exterior reflecting the afternoon sun. It's the kind of luxury that's meant to intimidate, to remind anyone who approaches that they're stepping into Victor Petrov's domain.

Z walks beside me. Oz flanks my other side while Talon brings up the rear.

A flight attendant in a crisp uniform stands at the base of the jet stairs. His expression remains neutral as we approach, but I catch the flicker of recognition when he notices the twins.

"Miss Rossi," he greets me with a slight bow, his accent thick but his English crisp and deliberate. "Mr. Petrov sends his warm regards."

Then he spots Talon, and his expression sharpens.

"We do not have a fourth party on our manifest. He cannot be allowed to board."

"I'm afraid that's not possible," I say, stepping forward with a confidence I don't entirely feel. "Mr. St. James is my head of security. Where I go, he goes."

The attendant's jaw tightens. "My instructions were quite clear, Miss Rossi. Three passengers only."

"Then your instructions are incorrect," I reply, my voice dropping to the cold, commanding tone I've been practicing. voice of a woman who expects to be obeyed. "Contact Victor if you must, but understand that delaying me will only irritate him further."

Z shifts beside me, his body language subtly changing to support my stance. "My uncle doesn't appreciate waiting, Sergei," he adds, surprising me by using the attendant's name. "Especially not for something as trivial as a passenger manifest."

The attendant, Sergei, hesitates. I can see the mental calculation happening behind his carefully neutral expression. risk of disobeying Victor's explicit instructions versus potentially angering him by delaying our arrival.

"One moment," he finally says, retreating a few steps to speak into his earpiece in rapid Russian.

"Nice touch. Very mafia princess. It's a good look for you."

I resist the urge to smile, keeping my expression impassive as Sergei returns.

"Mr. Petrov has approved the additional passenger," he announces stiffly. "Please, follow me."

The interior of the jet is expensive and masculine. Six plush seats face each other in the main cabin, with a private bedroom visible through a partially open door at the rear. Everything about the space screams wealth and power. the crystal decanters of amber liquor secured in a custom cabinet, to the Petrov crest embossed on the napkins.

"Please make yourselves comfortable," Sergei says, gesturing to the seats. "We'll be departing shortly."

Z moves through the cabin with the casual familiarity.

"Been a while since you've been on the family jet?" I ask quietly as I take the seat beside him.

"Last time I was on one of these, I was sixteen," he replies, his voice barely audible. "Our father was shipping us off to St. Judes."

Oz settles across from us, already scanning the cabin with methodical precision. "The layout's been updated, but it's essentially the same aircraft," he observes.

Talon remains standing, taking his head of security role seriously. "How many crew members?" he asks Sergei.

"Three flight crew, sir. Two pilots and myself. All vetted personally by Mr. Petrov," Sergei adds with a hint of pride. "I primarily served on your uncle's personal aircraft."

"Victor's personal staff," Oz adds, exchanging a meaningful glance with his brother. "Interesting choice for our retrieval. Kitty must be stateside."

"Who's Kitty?"

"His mistress. The one he hides from our aunt on the other side of the world."

I settle into the buttery leather seat, feeling the subtle power play unfolding around me. Victor sending his personal crew isn't just courtesy. surveillance. Every word, every gesture will be reported back to him.

"Would you care for refreshments before takeoff?" Sergei asks, moving toward the bar.

"Vodka," Z replies without hesitation. "Stolichnaya Elite, if my uncle still keeps it stocked."

"Of course, sir." Serge selects a frosted bottle from a hidden compartment. "Miss Rossi? Gentlemen?"

"The same," I say, watching as he pours four crystal tumblers with the clear liquid.

Talon finally takes a seat beside Oz, though his posture remains alert. "How long is the flight?" he asks, accepting his drink with a nod.

"Approximately ten hours, sir," Sergei answers, handing the last glass to Oz." We'll be taking a direct route across the Atlantic, avoiding European airspace where possible."

"Victor's paranoia hasn't changed, I see," Oz remarks, swirling the vodka before taking a measured sip. "Still avoiding the NATO radar."

Sergei's expression remains carefully neutral. "Mr. Petrov prefers discretion in all matters."

"I'm sure he does." I raise the crystal tumbler to my lips.

The vodka burns a clean path down my throat, warming my chest. Despite the circumstances, I can't help but appreciate its quality—smooth with just enough bite to remind you of its potency. Like Victor himself, I imagine.

The jet engines whine to life, the vibration humming through the floorboards. A disembodied voice announces our imminent departure in both Russian and English, instructing us to secure our seatbelts for takeoff.

Z downs his vodka in one gulp, his throat working as he swallows. When he sets the empty glass down, there's a new tension in his jaw. "Nine hours in a metal tube with my uncle's eyes and ears," he says quietly, just for me. "This should be fun."

I reach for his hand beneath the polished table between us, giving his fingers a brief squeeze. "We knew this was coming," I remind him.

The plane takes off with ease, as we climb higher and higher into the air until it levels off at cruising altitude.

It makes contacting my grandfather a tad harder. Every inch of this aircraft is likely bugged, cameras hidden in the glossy wood panels, microphones embedded in the plush leather seats. Victor's paranoia ensures we're being watched from every angle. Mikhail expects an update within hours, yet I can't exactly pull out the black tablet and start recording a progress video while surrounded by Victor's staff.

"Sergei," I call, my voice carrying the authoritative edge I've been practicing. "I'd like to freshen up."

"Of course, Miss Rossi. The lavatory is at the rear of the aircraft, just before the private suite."

I rise, smoothing the wrinkles from my skirt. "Thank you."

The lavatory is predictably luxurious—Italian marble and gold fixtures, plush hand towels embroidered with the Petrov crest. I lock the door behind me and lean against the sink, finally allowing my composure to slip for just a moment. The face staring back at me from the mirror looks foreign.

This might be the only semi-private space on the entire aircraft. Even so, I scan for cameras, checking corners and light fixtures. Finding nothing obvious doesn't mean they aren't there, but I have no choice but to take the risk.

I pull the black tablet from my purse, powering it on with trembling fingers. The screen illuminates with a soft blue glow, reflecting in the polished marble. I have mere minutes before my absence becomes suspicious.

Opening the recording function, I position myself against the wall, making sure the luxurious surroundings are visible in the frame. Evidence I'm on a private jet, headed to Russia. Evidence I'm following Mikhail's orders.

"I'm en route to St. Petersburg. I've gained his trust enough to secure passage on his private jet. When we land, I'll be taken directly to his compound."

I lean closer to the camera, allowing determination to harden my features. "Join me in Russia. You'll have what you want soon enough."

The lie tastes bitter on my tongue. Mikhail needs to

believe I'm committed to his revenge, that I'm willing to sacrifice everything, including myself, to fulfill his twisted legacy.

I stop the recording, quickly reviewing it before sending it through the encrypted channel Mikhail established. The moment the confirmation appears, I delete all traces from the screen and power down the tablet, returning it to my purse.

My hands grip the marble countertop as I steady my breathing. Each lie, each calculated move, brings me closer to Alex and Luca.

A soft knock at the door startles me.

"Miss Rossi?" Sergei's voice filters through. "May I offer you anything further?"

"I'll be right out," I call, splashing cold water on my face and reapplying my lipstick with precision. Had you asked me if I ever thought I'd be willingly on a flight to Russia to play a game of chess with monsters, I'd have said you were crazy, but here I am.

When I return to the main cabin, Z's eyes find mine immediately, a silent question in their silver depths. I give him an almost imperceptible nod as I retake my seat beside him."

"Everything alright?" he asks, his voice pitched low enough that only I can hear.

"Yes, I hate flying. I'll be okay once my stomach settles," I lie, accepting a fresh glass of vodka from Sergei. "This should help. Thank you, Sergei."

The flight attendant hovers nearby, his attentiveness

bordering on surveillance. "Dinner will be served in three hours."

"Thank you, Sergei," I say, setting my vodka down untouched, "I think I'll rest before dinner. The past few days have been...taxing." I rise from my seat, smoothing my skirt with deliberate calm. "Is the private suite available for use?"

Sergei hesitates. "The suite is typically reserved for Mr. Petrov himself, but as he is not aboard..." He gives a small nod. "Yes, of course, Miss Rossi. Shall I prepare it for you?"

"That won't be necessary." I glance at Talon, who immediately understands his role. "Mr. St. James will take care of my needs." The irony of my words is not lost on me, nor on Talon, who fights back a smile.

"Yes, Miss Rossi," Talon adds, already on his feet. His expression is all business as he follows me toward the rear of the aircraft.

Sergei's lips thin slightly, but he steps aside. "As you wish."

I feel Z and Oz watching us as we move toward the private suite at the back of the plane. The door closes behind us with a soft click, and Talon immediately begins a methodical sweep of the space, checking under furniture, running his fingers along moldings, and examining light fixtures.

The suite is opulent even by Petrov standards. queen-sized bed dominates the space, with burgundy silk sheets and pillows embroidered with gold thread. A small sitting area occupies one corner, complete with a private bar and entertainment system.

"Clear?" I ask quietly as Talon finishes his sweep.

He nods, holding up a finger to his lips before pulling a small device from his pocket. He activates it, waiting for the green light to blink before relaxing slightly.

"Signal jammer, courtesy of Alex," he explains in a hushed tone. "It'll buy us maybe ten minutes before it raises flags with the flight systems. They'll think it's interference, but we shouldn't push our luck."

I sink onto the edge of the bed, the silk sheets cool beneath my fingertips. "Did you see Sergei's face when I asked for the suite? Victor must use this room for more than just sleeping."

"I don't want to think about what's happened on these sheets," Talon grimaces, remaining standing with his back to the door. "Did your message get through to your grandfather?"

"Yes. He thinks I'm headed straight into Victor's lair to assassinate him." I rub my temples, feeling the beginnings of a headache forming. "I invited him to join me there."

A soft knock interrupts my spiral of worry. Talon immediately pockets the jammer

"Enter," I call, slipping into the poised demeanor I've been rehearsing.

Z slips into the suite, his movements fluid as he closes the door behind him. "Sergei's watching," he offers, crossing to sit beside me on the bed. "Figured I'd give him something to report back to my uncle."

"How thoughtful," I reply, loud enough to be heard through any listening devices. "Joining me for a private conversation about our future alliance?"

Z's lips quirk as he leans closer, his breath warm against my ear. "Something like that."

The door opens again, and Oz slips in with the same fluid grace as his twin. He locks it behind him.

"Sergei is practically vibrating with curiosity," he chuckles, moving to join us.

"Let him wonder," Z remarks, shifting to make room for his brother on the bed. "It gives Victor something to think about besides our motives."

Oz settles beside me, his thigh pressing against mine in the limited space. The three of us huddle together on Victor's bed.

"I swept for bugs," Talon says, nodding toward his pocket where the jammer rests. "We've got a few minutes of privacy before the interference becomes too obvious."

"We need to talk about what happens when we land," I say, keeping my voice low despite Talon's assurance of temporary privacy. "Victor's not going to let us stick together once we're on his territory."

Z's jaw tightens. "He'll separate us immediately. Standard protocol for anyone entering his compound, even family."

"Especially family," Oz corrects, his analytical mind already mapping scenarios. "He'll want you alone, Vesper. As soon as you hand over the evidence about your son and Bianca's deception."

My stomach twists with anxiety. "How long do you think we'll have before he isolates me?"

"Minutes," Z answers bluntly. "The moment we step off

this plane, we'll be escorted to separate vehicles. He'll want to question each of us individually, look for inconsistencies in our stories. With Talon posing as your security, and considering his injury, he may let him stay with you."

Talon leans against the wall, arms crossed over his chest. "And once he confirms the evidence is real, you'll become his most valuable asset. The mother of his true heir, the key to his dynasty's future."

"And his revenge against my grandfather," I add. "He'll want to keep me close, use me as bait."

Oz nods, his expression grim. "We'll be cut off from each other."

'Which is why we need a fail-safe. A way to communicate when we're separated." Z pulls out a box from his suit jacket, depositing on my lap. I open it to find a gold watch. Diamonds encircling the watch face.

"Let me," Z offers, lifting the timepiece from its box and securing it to my wrist. The diamonds sparkle under the fluorescent lighting of the jet cabin.

"I mean it's pretty, but how does a watch help me?" I peer up at Talon, who taps his watch meaningfully.

"These aren't just for telling time. They're encrypted and connected to each other through a private network Alex designed. Short text messages only, but they'll bypass Victor's security systems."

"Assuming he doesn't confiscate them the moment we land," I point out, my mind racing through contingencies. "Victor isn't stupid."

"He'll search us," Oz agrees. "Strip us down, take

anything that could be used to communicate or as a weapon."

Z's hand finds mine, his fingers interlacing with mine in a gesture that feels more possessive than comforting. "We've prepared for this. The watches look like standard luxury timepieces, Patek Philippe, nothing suspicious. A digital watch might raise his suspicions, but this will hopefully fly under his radar. Even if he has them examined, the communication function is buried deep enough that a standard security sweep won't find it."

"And if that fails?" I press. "What then?"

Oz's lips curve into a cold smile. "We're his nephews, Vesper. Blood. He may hate us, but family means something to Victor. He won't kill us outright, not without cause. Not when he could use us against you."

"That's not as reassuring as you think it is," I mutter, anxiety churning in my stomach.

Talon checks his own watch. "Time to turn off the jammer." He reaches into his pocket and pulls out the device. The green light disappears as he puts it back into his pocket. "So what do we do with the eight hours and change until we get to Russia?"

"I have some ideas," I smile.

The way Talon's eyebrows shoot upward makes me laugh despite the tension coiling in my chest. "What exactly do you have in mind, princess?"

I lean back against the silk pillows, spreading my arms across Victor's bed with deliberate provocation. "When are we going to get this much time without someone interrupting us? I mean, you said we should give him a show." I trail my fingers suggestively along the bedspread. "I say we do."

"You want to give Sergei something to report back to my uncle?"

"Why not?" I challenge, reaching up to slowly unbutton the top of my blouse. "Victor already thinks I'm trying to seduce my way into his family. Might as well lean into the role."

Oz watches me, a slight smile playing at the corners of his mouth. "She has a point," he shrugs.

Talon moves first, a wolfish grin spreading across his face as he locks the door with deliberate finality. The click echoes in the suite like a promise.

"Always the pragmatist," Talon says as he shrugs out of his jacket with fluid grace. The motion pulls at his injured shoulder, but the flicker of pain is quickly buried beneath the calm composure he wears like a second skin. "Though I'm not sure Victor will appreciate us desecrating his bed."

"That's half the appeal," I say, slowly working open my blouse, one button at a time. With each release, more skin is revealed, a quiet, deliberate invitation. I don't rush. I want them to feel the weight of every second, to ache for what comes next. Three pairs of eyes track my movements, hungry, waiting.

"We're heading straight into chaos," I continue. "And I don't know what's waiting on the other side. What I *do* know is I want this. Tonight. With the men I love. Might as well join the mile high club while we wait."

Zaire moves first, of course. Always the one who loses control for me. He grips my hand, halting the motion of the next button as he steps in close, his mouth inches from mine.

"You really think I'm going to let you say something like that and walk away untouched?"

I arch a brow. "Wasn't planning on walking anywhere. We're on a plane, remember?"

He crashes his mouth to mine, hot, hungry, claiming. His hand slides into my hair, the other locking tight at my waist as he drags me flush to him. The kiss turns hard and messy. It takes everything I have to pull away from him.

"Then let's make sure you remember it," he rasps.

"I want to feel it tomorrow," I shoot back, already reaching for the next button. "Every bruise. Every ache. I want Victor to see your marks on my skin like the badges they are. I want him to know that I may be coming to him to sell myself, but he can't take away what we have together."

Oz moves with a calm, dangerous precision that makes my pulse skip every time. He slips in behind me on the bed, rough palms sliding beneath the hem of my blouse to stroke bare skin, claiming territory inch by inch.

"If we're giving Victor's little spy a show," he murmurs against my neck, breath hot and full of promise, "we might as well make it unforgettable."

His mouth finds the spot just below my ear, tongue flicking, teeth sinking in. I gasp, hips twitching. At the same moment, Zaire's mouth crashes into mine, devouring me. I'm caught between them—one branding my skin, the other stealing breath like it belongs to him.

My body lights up like dry tinder, nerve endings sparking, blood roaring.

Talon watches, still as a blade. Then he moves, silent and
sure, sinking to his knees at the edge of the bed. His touch
traces a path up my calves, deliberate, spreading me open as
he pushes my skirt higher with maddening control.

"Last chance, princess," he murmurs, his fingers teasing
slow circles just shy of where I burn. "Because once I start
tasting you, I'm not stopping until you're shaking so hard
you forget your own fucking name."

I rip my mouth from Z's, gasping, a raw tremor ripping
down my spine like lightning.

"I'm not backing out," I snarl, my voice thick with need.
"I want all of you. Mouths. Cocks. Hands. I want to feel
everything. Take me. Break me. Make me yours."

Talon's smile is pure sin. "Then hold on tight, baby.
Because we're going to take you apart."

Zaire's fingers make quick work of the buttons I'd left
undone, tearing the blouse open with a controlled urgency
that sends a jolt straight to my core. The fabric slips from my
body and hits the floor, leaving me half-naked between three
men who look like they're ready to devour me.

Oz's hands slide around from behind, fingers sinking into
the lace of my bra as he palms my breasts with a possessive
hunger. His thumbs roll over my nipples until they're stiff
and aching, the rough drag of lace only heightening the
sensitivity. I arch into his touch with a needy gasp, and Z
steals the sound from my lips with another punishing kiss.

Below, Talon's fingers hook into my panties and drag

them down my legs at a torturous pace. The air hits my soaked skin, and I shiver, exposed, open, throbbing. He spreads my thighs wide, slow and deliberate, like he's peeling me apart just to savor the view.

"Let's give Sergei something to jerk off to," Talon mutters, his breath searing against the inside of my thigh. His gaze locks with mine, and then he dives in.

The first stroke of his tongue wrecks me. My back arches, head dropping against Oz's shoulder as a helpless cry escapes me. Talon doesn't ease in. He feasts. Tongue fucking me with ruthless precision, lips dragging over every slick inch, building pressure fast and sharp.

Z's mouth trails down my throat, teeth grazing the sensitive column before he bites down on the spot that turns my legs to liquid. Behind me, my bra slips free with a flick of his fingers, and then Oz is back, his touch rougher now, tweaking my nipples until I'm gasping, spine arching toward him.

"You feel that?" Oz rasps against my ear, his breath hot and uneven, fingers rolling and tugging without mercy. "That's what it's like when you belong to us. Every fucking inch of you—shaking, dripping, begging for more."

I can't form words. I'm too far gone, lost in the collision of mouths and touch.

I'm surrounded, drowning in sensation. Talon's mouth between my thighs, wicked and relentless. Z's lips mapping my collarbone, each kiss a brand. Oz molding my breasts to his palms, his teeth grazing my earlobe. Every nerve sparks. Every inch of me burns.

"Look at you," Zaire rasps, lifting his head just enough to watch my face twist with pleasure. "This is what it looks like when your kings worship their queen."

Talon's tongue is merciless, circling my clit with slow, lethal precision. No teasing. No hesitation. Just a calculated unraveling. He grips my thighs tightly, fingers digging into soft flesh to hold me wide open, forcing me to take it all, every flick, every devastating stroke of his tongue.

I grind down on his mouth, chasing the high with reckless need. Greedy. Wild.

Behind me, Oz and Z touch like they're mapping me. brush of fingers down my sides, each graze of knuckles over my breasts sending jolts of heat straight to where Talon is wrecking me.

"Tell us what you need, solnishko," Oz breathes into my ear, voice a wicked promise. His teeth scrape along the sensitive line of my neck, and I shudder. Pleasure pulses low and deep, close to boiling over.

"More," I gasp, dragging him closer. "I need more. I need all of you."

Z's mouth finds the corner of mine, lips curving into a wolfish smile. "Our queen has spoken."

And they move, focused on me like soldiers trained to tear me apart. My body is lifted, shifted, repositioned with ease, like they've done this before, like this is what they were made for. Hands and mouths everywhere. The rip of fabric. The thud of clothes hitting the floor.

Talon rises, his bare chest flushed, cock hard and heavy, the thick head already glistening. The scar across his shoulder catches the light, a brutal, beautiful mark of loyalty. Oz shrugs out of his shirt next, all lean muscle and clean skin.

They're fucking breathtaking. Powerful. Wild.

And they're all mine.

"Get over here," Zaire commands, his voice low and wrecked, thick with hunger. He positions himself against the headboard, legs spread, cock hard and waiting. His hand wraps around my wrist as he pulls me onto his lap. My back is flush to his chest, his cock pressing against my entrance, hot and thick with promise.

He grips my hips, holding me steady. "Nice and slow." He lowers me onto him inch by inch. The stretch is glorious—deep, burning, just enough to steal my breath—and I moan, body shuddering as he fills me completely.

"That's it, moya koroleva. Take every fucking inch. You were made to ride this cock."

Oz kneels in front of us. His expression is pure sin, fingers trailing up my thighs before sliding between them. He presses his thumbs to our joined bodies, teasing, stroking, spreading slick warmth everywhere.

"Fucking beautiful," he mutters, watching me come undone. He leans in, kissing me slowly at first like he's savoring the way I tremble for him. Then he presses harder, his tongue pushing past my lips like he owns every inch of me, starting with my mouth.

When Oz pulls back, Talon moves in from the side. He grabs my neck, turning my face to him with firm control.

"My turn," he says, voice rough and possessive, and then

he's on me. His kiss is hard and claiming, teeth catching my bottom lip as he swallows every sound I try to make.

I'm lost in them. Z's cock driving up into me with expert force, Oz's fingers circling my clit with maddening precision, Talon's mouth claiming mine like he's marking me from the inside out. Every part of me is touched, taken, consumed.

Z hisses against my shoulder, hips snapping up with bruising strength.

"Look at you," he pants. "Bouncing on my cock like it's the only thing keeping you alive. Show them who you fucking belong to."

My cry is swallowed by Talon's mouth, but I ride him harder, drowning in pleasure, in them, in this.

And I've never wanted anything more.

Oz watches, his hand wrapped around his own length, stroking in time with Z's thrusts. The sight of him pleasuring himself while watching us is impossibly erotic, adding another layer to my building pleasure.

Talon breaks our kiss to trail his lips down my neck until he reaches my breast. His mouth closes around my nipple, teeth grazing the sensitive peak before soothing it with his tongue.

I'm overwhelmed, suspended in a web of pleasure woven by these three men who have become my world. My head falls back against Z's shoulder, a symphony of moans and gasps escaping my lips as they drive me higher, closer to the edge with each touch, each thrust, each command.

Z's rhythm falters slightly as he watches Talon's mouth

on my breast, his grip on my hips tightening. "Fuck," he hisses, his voice strained. "The things you do to me, Vesper."

Oz rises from his position, moving to stand at the edge of the bed. His hand cups my cheek, turning my face toward him as he positions himself before my lips. "Open for me, solnishko," he murmurs, his thumb brushing across my lower lip.

I comply without hesitation, parting my lips to welcome him. The girth of him on my tongue, the salt-sweet taste, the groan that escapes him as I take more of him in, it all adds to the maelstrom of sensation threatening to consume me. Beneath me, Z's thrusts grow more urgent, each upward snap of his hips hitting harder, pushing me closer to the edge with every movement.

Talon's mouth moves to my other breast, his hand sliding between my legs to circle my clit with devastating precision. The multiple points of pleasure. Z filling me, Oz's length sliding between my lips, Talon's skilled fingers and mouth, all push me toward the precipice with alarming speed.

"She's close," Talon declares, feeling the telltale tremors beginning to course through my body. "Aren't you, princess?"

I can only moan in response, the sound muffled by Oz's cock as my body tenses, hovering on the edge of release. The pressure builds and builds.

"Show us how good we make you feel."

The dam splinters. Pleasure slams into me, raw and over-whelming, my body convulsing around Z as my orgasm rips through me. My vision blurs at the edges, stars bursting behind my eyelids as I cry out around Oz, the sound muffled but unmistakable. Z follows with a guttural groan, his hips snapping upward as he spills inside me, his grip on my hips so tight it'll leave bruises.

I collapse back against Z's chest, gasping for breath as aftershocks ripple through my body. Oz withdraws from my mouth, his expression hungry and unsatisfied as he watches me tremble in the aftermath.

"Don't get too comfortable," Talon warns as he trails his fingers up my sweat-slicked thigh. "We're just getting started."

Z's arms wrap around me, his chest still heaving against my back. "I want him to see what we do to your body. I want him to know that we own you, despite what he thinks. His teeth graze my earlobe. "You are ours. Our pretty little plaything that takes our cocks so fucking well."

Before I can respond, Oz is already pulling me from Z's lap with gentle insistence, guiding me onto all fours atop the silk sheets.

"Mine," he growls, settling behind me. His touch sweeps over the curve of my ass before he grips my hips.

"Ready for me, solnishko?"

I nod, unable to speak as he pushes into me with one deep, smooth thrust. My gasp catches in my throat. I'm still stretched and dripping from Zaire, and the sudden fullness ignites a fresh surge of pleasure that tears through my already oversensitive body.

Oz sets a maddeningly controlled pace. Each stroke is

slow and intentional, designed to make me feel every inch. Zaire's earlier urgency fades behind it, igniting a new kind of fire deep within me.

"Your cunt feels like fucking heaven, solnishko," he groans behind me. "Tight, wet, greedy. I'll never get enough of this."

Talon kneels in front of me, his cock thick and hard, gripped in his hand. "Show me what that pretty mouth can do, princess."

I open for him without hesitation, wrapping my lips around him and sucking with the same hunger Oz is feeding behind me. I take him deep, cheeks hollowing as I bob my head in rhythm with Oz's thrusts. I am stretched between them, used from both ends, and I have never felt more wanted. More undone.

The position leaves me vulnerable and exposed. Every nerve is alive with sensation, every inch of me claimed. It's overwhelming. The kind of surrender that sends heat flooding through my veins, fierce and all-consuming.

Zaire leans against the headboard, chest heaving, sweat glistening across his skin. "Look at her," he says to his brother, voice hoarse with pride. "Taking both of you like she was fucking made for it."

Oz's rhythm falters slightly at his twin's words, his fingers digging into my hips. She was made for this," he agrees. "Made for us."

"You need to see this," Talon groans, his voice strained as he fights for control. "The look on her face when she's being filled from both sides...it's fucking art."

I'm caught between them, suspended in pleasure as Oz's pace increases, his controlled rhythm unraveling into something raw and primal. Each thrust drives me forward onto Talon, creating a relentless loop of sensation that has me moaning around his length.

Z moves from his position at the headboard, sliding beneath me with serpentine grace. His hands cup my breasts, fingers pinching my nipples with just enough pressure to make me gasp.

"We're going to ruin you for anyone else," he promises, his breath hot against my ear as he twists beneath me.

Oz's rhythm stutters as he nears his peak, his fingers biting into my flesh with bruising force. "Fuck," he hisses, his control finally fracturing. "I can't—"

He drives into me one final time, burying himself to the hilt as he comes with a guttural groan. The sensation of him pulsing inside me triggers another climax that tears through me like lightning, my body clenching around him as stars burst behind my eyelids.

Talon pulls out of my mouth just as the cry rips free from my throat. His eyes are wild with hunger, his cock still hard and untouched while Oz collapses against my back, breath ragged and spent.

"I've waited long enough," Talon rasps, voice thick as he guides me into position. Oz slips free, leaving my limbs heavy and boneless, pleasure-drunk and aching. Talon lifts me with effortless strength, laying me on my back like I'm something precious he intends to claim fully. He spreads my thighs wide, his grip firm and possessive, like he already owns every inch of me.

"I want to see your face when I make you come."

Zaire shifts beside me, dragging his fingertips up my slick stomach. His touch is lazy but full of intent as he watches Talon settle between my legs.

"Think you can take more, *moya koroleva*?" His voice curls against my ear like silk soaked in sin. "Or have we finally found the edge of what that wicked little body can handle?"

I turn to him even as my thighs tremble. "I haven't met a limit yet."

He hooks my legs over his shoulders, lining up with my entrance, and flashes a wicked smile.

"That's my girl."

He slams into me with one hard thrust, bottoming out in a single, brutal stroke that makes me cry out, my back arching off the sheets. The stretch is intense, bordering on too much. My cunt is still raw and sensitive from being wrecked by Z and Oz, but I take him anyway. I want it. I need it.

Talon doesn't give me time to adjust. He starts moving immediately, pounding into me with controlled, punishing force.

"You've had two cocks in you, princess," he snarls, voice thick with possession. "And you're still so fucking tight for me. Like your body knows who it belongs to."

Every thrust pushes me closer to the edge, pleasure razor-sharp and laced with the burn of overstimulation. I'm wrecked, drenched, marked by all of them. And I wouldn't stop it if I could.

The sensation is overwhelming, each nerve ending singing with overexposed pleasure as Talon fills me completely. I clutch at the silk sheets, trying to ground myself against the storm threatening to sweep me away.

"Look at me," Talon commands. "I want to see those pretty eyes when you fall apart for me."

I force my heavy lids open as he establishes a rhythm that's both punishing and controlled. Every thrust lands exactly where I need him, his focus etched into the way he angles his hips for maximum impact.

Z stretches beside me, his fingers lazily skimming across my collarbone, eyes fixed on the fading bruises and bite marks painting my skin.

"She's not walking into that court unclaimed," he murmurs, a slow smile curling his lips. "She's walking in marked—claimed—and there's nothing Victor can do to take that away."

Oz appears on my other side, his breathing still slightly labored as he recovers. His fingers tangle in my hair, turning my face toward him so he can claim my mouth in a kiss that's surprisingly gentle compared to the intensity of Talon's movements between my thighs.

"Our queen," Oz smiles against my lips. "Carrying all three of us inside her when she faces my uncle."

I'm surrounded, claimed, marked by these three men who have become my world. The knowledge that I'll walk into Victor Petrov's domain bearing their seed, their scent, their bruises...it's both terrifying and thrilling. A secret power I'll carry with me into the lion's den.

Talon's pace increases, his control slipping as he drives into me with mounting urgency. My oversensitive body responds despite my exhaustion, pleasure building once more.

"One more." His fingers find my clit with unerring precision. "Give me one more, princess."

The dual stimulation is almost too much to bear, my nerve endings screaming with overstimulation. I writhe beneath him, caught between pleasure so intense it borders on pain and the desperate need for release.

"I can't," I gasp, tears pricking at the corners of my eyes as my body trembles on the precipice.

Oz's hand replaces Talon's between my legs, his long fingers circling my swollen clit with devastating accuracy. "Give us what we want, solnishko. What you need," he urges, his breath hot against my neck. "Surrender to us."

The combined assault of all three men, Talon's relentless thrusts, Oz's skilled fingers, Z's mouth and hands marking my body, pushes me over the edge into an oblivion so complete it feels like I'm shattering. My back arches off the bed, a scream tearing from my throat as pleasure crashes through me with devastating force. Talon follows immediately, his rhythm faltering as he buries himself deep inside me with a guttural groan, his body shuddering with release.

I collapse against the silk sheets, utterly spent, my limbs too heavy to move as aftershocks ripple through my oversensitive body. Talon carefully withdraws, pressing a gentle kiss to my inner thigh before moving to stretch beside me.

"Fuck," Z breathes, his fingers tracing the marks they've left on my skin with possessive satisfaction. "If Sergei wasn't sure what we were doing in here before, he certainly knows now."

A breathless laugh escapes me as I lie surrounded by the three men, their bodies forming a protective cocoon around mine. "Mission accomplished." I rasp, my voice hoarse from screaming.

Oz's fingers brush damp strands of hair from my face, his touch unexpectedly tender. "Rest, solnishko. We have hours yet before we land."

I nestle into their embrace, savoring the temporary sanctuary of their arms. Tomorrow we'll step off this plane and into Victor Petrov's domain, where every word will be a potential trap, every gesture scrutinized. But tonight, cocooned between these three men on Victor's own bed, I allow myself to relax even just for a little bit.

# Chapter 37

ALEX

PAIN HAS A RHYTHM, if you listen closely enough. The steady metronome of agony keeping time with each heartbeat.

The guards yank us from our cell without warning, my broken ribs flaring in agony as I'm hauled upright. I catch Luca's gaze for a split second, just enough to exchange a silent message before black fabric drops over my head, plunging everything into darkness.

"Move," a voice snarls, followed by a shove between my shoulders.

I shuffle forward, relying on everything but sight. Ten steps straight, then a turn to the right. The floor shifts beneath my feet, from smooth tile to rough concrete. We're headed toward the loading bay. I count thirty-three more steps. The air opens up, echoing differently now. Higher ceilings. The low rumble of an engine confirms it.

"Step up," the guard barks, pressure pressing between my shoulder blades.

I lift my foot and feel the cold edge of metal beneath it—a van, judging by the height. Behind me, Luca stumbles, followed by a grunt as someone manhandles him up behind me.

"Sit," comes the next command, and I'm shoved down onto a hard bench, the surface unyielding against my spine.

The metal floor vibrates beneath my feet as the engine idles. I count four distinct breathing patterns besides Luca and myself. least four guards are accompanying us. Heavy boots shuffle around as they position themselves. Something cold, metal clicks around my wrists—handcuffs. I test the restraints subtly, solid, no give. Professional work.

The van lurches forward suddenly, throwing me against the restraints. Pain explodes through my ribcage, but I swallow the groan that threatens to escape. Never show weakness. Not to these people.

"Alex?" Luca's voice comes from my right, low and cautious. "Any idea where they're taking us?"

I tilt my head in his direction, though the hood makes it pointless. "Could be anywhere. Transfer to another facility. Something worse."

"Shut up back there," a guard barks, followed by the distinct sound of a baton tapping against metal.

I fall silent, but my mind races through possibilities. The

timing is suspicious.  24 hours since Vesper's meeting with Mikhail. Is this part of his "proof of life" promise? Or something else entirely?

The van takes a sharp turn, sending us sliding against our restraints. Luca hisses in pain beside me.

"You okay?" I whisper when the guard's attention seems elsewhere.

"Been better," he replies through what sounds like gritted teeth. "Any chance this is a rescue?"

"Doubtful. Your sister needs more time."

The road beneath us changes—smoother now, likely asphalt rather than the gravel drive of the facility. We're on a public highway now. We're being moved long-distance, not just between buildings on the compound.

The minutes stretch into what must be hours, the rhythm of the road hypnotic beneath the roar of the engine. My body settles into the pain, finding that strange meditative state where agony becomes just another sensation to catalog rather than something to fight against.

A new sound penetrates my awareness. Distant at first, then growing louder with each passing second. The distinctive whine of jet engines, the roar of a plane passing low overhead.

My blood turns to ice.

"Do you hear that?"

"An airplane," he confirms.

The van slows, turning onto what feels like a service road —the suspension bouncing over potholes, jostling my broken ribs. The plane sounds grow louder, almost deafening now. We're near an airport. Too near for coincidence.

My mind connects the pieces with sickening clarity. Vesper must have made her move against Victor Petrov. The 72-hour deadline...she's acted faster than Mikhail anticipated. And now we're being transported, insurance policies to be cashed in or discarded depending on her success.

"They're taking us to the airport," I declare, leaning closer to Luca. "Russia. They're sending us to Russia."

"Why Russia?" Luca's voice is strained, fear bleeding through the forced calm of his words.

"Because that's where she'd be going. Vesper must have found a way into Petrov territory. She's making her move against Victor."

"So soon?"

"It's the only explanation for why they're moving us now." I feel the van slowing, turning in what must be a wide arc. "Mikhail wouldn't risk transporting us unless something's changed."

The van comes to an abrupt halt. Doors slam open at the front, followed by the sound of boots on pavement. The back doors wrench open, letting in a blast of cold air that cuts through my thin clothes.

"Out," a voice commands as hands grab my arms, yanking me forward.

My feet hit pavement, knees buckling before strong hands steady me. The hood is ripped from my head, the sudden brightness blinding. I squint against the light, forcing my eyes to adjust.

We're on a private airfield. A sleek Gulfstream waits on the tarmac, its engines already spooling up, stairs extended from its fuselage. Armed men form a perimeter around us, their faces hidden behind balaclavas, weapons held at the ready.

Luca stands beside me, blinking into the harsh daylight as the guards bark orders and herd us toward the waiting transport. His face is pale beneath the bruises, the kind that look worse in the sun. Sickly purples and fading yellow marks mapping every hit he didn't dodge.

He moves stiffly, jaw clenched like he's holding something back. Pain. Rage. Probably both. He's quieter than I remember. Harder too. Back at St. Jude's, he was always the golden boy. His sister's protector, and his father 's perfect heir. I was the fuse waiting to be lit on the other side of the divide.

Oscar and Zaire were the only ones who didn't care about the blood on my hands. They accepted me into their circle without hesitation, no judgment, no questions. Talon was the same. But Luca? He watched me. Always.

Like prey watching a predator, trying to figure out when I'd make my move or if I would at all.

He thought I didn't notice. But I always did. Even then, there was something sharp in the way he looked at me. Like he wasn't sure whether to keep his distance...or get closer just to understand what made me tick.

And maybe part of me wanted him to.

That's why I can't stop noticing him now. Noticing the way he doesn't flinch, even when the guard shoves him forward. The way he stays on his feet, even after everything.

I remind myself this isn't about him. It's about Vesper. She's the reason we're here. The reason they're keeping us breathing. She's the one I promised myself I'd protect, no matter the cost. Still, I catch myself glancing at Luca again.

We're nothing alike. And yet...here we are.

"Move," a guard snaps, the butt of his rifle slamming into my shoulder, forcing me forward.

The wind howls across the tarmac, sharp and bitter, thick with the stench of jet fuel and oncoming rain. Overhead, the engines scream like warnings, the roar vibrating through my ribs. Each step sends a fresh jolt of pain through my body, but I stay upright. I have to. One stumble, one crack in my armor, and they'll bury me in a shallow grave before we ever touch down in Moscow.

Beside me, Luca moves with that same stiff precision. Blood crusts along his temple.

"Mikhail's taking no chances," I mutter, just loud enough for him to hear. "This is a one-way trip to Russian soil."

He glances at me. "Why?"

"Because if Vesper pulls it off, we're leverage."

I pause as we reach the foot of the stairs, the metal steps slick with rain. The wind cuts through my shirt like knives.

"And if she doesn't..."

I don't finish. I don't have to. Because the answer hangs between us like a noose.

If she fails, we're already dead.

# Chapter 38

VESPER

MY THIGHS BURN with each step down the airplane stairs—a delicious reminder of what I've been doing for the past nine hours. Sergei waits at the bottom, his expression tightly controlled, professional disdain written in every line of his posture as he extends a hand to assist me.

"Miss Rossi," he says stiffly, his accent thicker now that we're on Russian soil. "Welcome to Saint Petersburg."

I accept his hand with a gracious smile, feeling the way he barely touches my fingers, as if I'm contaminated. The biting Russian air stings my cheeks as I descend.

Talon follows close behind, his warmth at my back a comforting presence as we reach the bottom of the stairs. He leans in, his lips brushing my ear under the pretense of steadying me. "I think our flight attendant friend heard every minute of our little party. He hasn't been able to look at me since I left the bedroom."

I press my lips together to suppress a laugh at Sergei's rigid posture as he leads us toward the waiting vehicles. "I think you might be right. He practically sprinted down the aisle when Z asked for fresh towels."

Three black SUVs wait on the tarmac, engines idling, exhaust creating ghostly plumes in the cold air. Z and Oz descend the stairs behind us, their expressions hardening as they step onto Russian soil. I catch the subtle shift in their posture as they shed the playful lovers from the plane and don the armor of Petrov heirs returning to hostile territory.

"Miss Rossi," Sergei gestures to the first vehicle, "you and Mr. St. James will ride in the lead car. Mr. Petrov has arranged separate transportation for his nephews."

And so it begins. The separation Victor planned, designed to isolate and interrogate us individually. I glance at Z, meeting in a moment of silent communication.

"Of course," I reply smoothly, turning back to Sergei. "I expected nothing less from a man of Victor's...thoroughness."

Sergei's lips thin at my familiar use of his employer's name, but he says nothing as he opens the rear door of the first SUV. I slide into the plush leather interior, Talon following close behind. The door closes with a solid thud that feels unnervingly final.

The driver sits rigidly behind the wheel. In the passenger

seat sits a man I immediately recognize as security. His eyes meet mine in the rearview mirror, assessing and cold.

"Miss Rossi," he says in heavily accented English, "I am Alexei. Mr. Petrov has assigned me as your security detail during your stay."

My handler, then. The unspoken meaning is clear. I won't be going anywhere without Alexei tracking my every move.

"How thoughtful," I reply. "Please convey my appreciation to Victor for his...concern. It comforts me to know that he cares that much about my well-being."

Alexei's expression doesn't change as he turns to face forward again. The convoy begins to move, pulling away from the private airfield in formation. Through the tinted windows, I watch as Saint Petersburg materializes—ancient spires and onion domes silhouetted against the gradually darkening sky.

"Pretty city," Talon remarks beside me, his casual tone belying the tension I feel radiating from him.

"It was once called the Venice of the North," Alexei offers unexpectedly. "Built on islands and canals by Peter the Great. He wanted Russia to have a window to Europe."

I lean closer to the window, watching golden lights shimmer on the waterways as we cross one of the city's many bridges. The city has an ethereal beauty—a haunting elegance that seems fitting for the Petrov family's seat of power.

"Will we be going directly to Victor's estate?" I ask, careful to keep my tone conversational.

"Mr. Petrov is eager to meet with you, Miss Rossi. We will be traveling to the Winter Palace immediately."

I struggle to keep my expression neutral. The Winter Palace, not one of the properties Z and Oz had briefed me on. They'd expected Victor to bring us to the family compound outside the city, or perhaps the business headquarters in the financial district. This is an unexpected deviation.

"The Winter Palace?" I repeat, glancing at Talon, whose subtle frown confirms my concern. "I thought that was a museum now."

A ghost of a smile crosses Alexei's stern features. "The original Winter Palace houses the Hermitage Museum, yes. Mr. Petrov's residence is a...private homage to the original. Built to similar specifications but with modern amenities."

Of course, Victor Petrov would build himself a replica of the czars' imperial residence. The man's ego truly knows no bounds.

"I see." I turn my attention back to the passing cityscape. "And my associates? Will they be joining us there?"

"All in good time, Miss Rossi," Alexei replies, his tone making it clear the conversation is over.

I feel Talon tense beside me, his hand subtly shifting to rest closer to mine on the leather seat. silent gesture of support and protection. The dim interior of the SUV conceals the way my fingers absently brush against the diamond-studded watch on my wrist. Our only lifeline if we're separated.

Dawn breaks over St. Petersburg as we wind through streets that grow increasingly grand. Elegant buildings in pastel yellows and blues line the wide boulevards, their architecture whispering of imperial glory and old-world wealth. The convoy turns onto a private road flanked by iron gates that swing open at our approach, revealing an expanse of manicured gardens, their edges silvered with early morning frost.

And then I see it. Victor's homage to the Winter Palace rises before us—a sprawling edifice of turquoise and white, adorned with gilded accents that catch the first rays of sunlight. It's smaller than the original, perhaps a third of the size, but no less imposing with its neoclassical columns and intricately carved balustrades.

"Subtle," Talon mutters under his breath, just loud enough for me to hear.

The convoy stops at a circular driveway, and immediately a dozen men in suits emerge from the palace entrance, forming a reception line that feels more like a gauntlet. Alexei exits first, circling the vehicle to open my door.

"Mr. Petrov awaits you in the grand hall," Alexei says, extending his hand to help me from the vehicle.

I step onto the cobblestone driveway, the chill Russian air cutting through my clothes as I take in the full grandeur of Victor's palace. The waning light catches on countless windows, making the building shimmer like a mirage. I straighten my spine, ignoring the pleasant ache between my thighs as I adopt the posture of someone worthy of this reception.

"Follow me," Alexei directs, stepping aside to allow me passage.

I glance back at the other SUVs, where Z and Oz are being escorted in different directions. Z's eyes find mine briefly, his expression unreadable to anyone but me. The slight tightening around his mouth is the only indication of his concern before guards lead him toward the eastern wing of the palace.

Talon stays close as we ascend the marble steps, his presence reassuring at my back. The massive doors swing open to reveal an entrance hall that steals my breath. ceilings painted with mythological scenes, marble columns rising like ancient trees, and a floor inlaid with intricate mosaics depicting the Petrov family crest.

"Impressive, isn't it?" says a voice that makes my blood freeze.

Victor Petrov stands at the top of a sweeping staircase, his imposing figure silhouetted against a massive stained-glass window. Even from this distance, I can make out the resemblance to Z and Oz. The same strong jawline, the same commanding presence, though where the twins radiate barely contained wildness, Victor exudes calculated control.

He descends the stairs with unhurried grace, each step measured and deliberate. He's taller than I expected, well over six feet, with broad shoulders encased in what I recognize as a bespoke suit. His hair is silver at the temples, styled impeccably.

"Vesper Rossi," he says, my name rolling off his tongue with an accent thicker than his nephews'. "At last we meet."

I force my lips into a smile, extending my hand with

more confidence than I feel. "Victor. Thank you for your hospitality."

He takes my offered hand, but instead of shaking it, he raises it to his lips. His eyes never leave mine as his lips brush my knuckles.

"The pleasure is mine," he replies, releasing my hand.

His attention slides to Talon. "And this is your...security detail?"

"Talon St. James," I confirm, watching as the two men size each other up like wolves from rival packs.

"American?" Victor notes, his tone making the word sound like an insult. "Interesting choice. He looks a little fragile for security, no?"

Talon doesn't rise to the bait, maintaining professional composure as he inclines his head in acknowledgment. "Mr. Petrov."

Victor's attention returns to me. "You've had a long journey," he says after a moment. "Perhaps you'd like to freshen up before we discuss the matter that brings you to my home?"

The polite suggestion carries his command. I recognize the tactic, giving me time to grow anxious, to second-guess myself while he interrogates Z and Oz separately.

"I'd prefer to address our business immediately. Time is precious, after all," I counter smoothly,

"My private study, then. We can speak freely there." He gestures toward a corridor branching off from the grand entrance.

I follow him across the mosaic floor, conscious of Talon's

footsteps behind us. Victor leads us down a hallway lined with portraits. Generations of history seem to press down on me as we walk further into the palace, the opulence growing more intimate yet no less impressive.

Victor stops before a set of double doors inlaid with intricate marquetry depicting the Russian imperial eagle. He places his palm against a nearly invisible scanner camouflaged within the wooden design.

"Security," he explains, catching my glance. "Some traditions evolve with the times."

The doors swing open silently, revealing a study that could have belonged to a czar. Rich mahogany paneling lines the walls, interspersed with shelves of leather-bound books and artifacts that belong in museums. A massive desk dominates one end of the room, its surface bare except for a single laptop and a crystal decanter of amber liquid.

"Please," Victor gestures to a seating area near a fireplace where flames leap behind a protective glass screen. "Make yourself comfortable."

I choose an armchair positioned to keep both Victor and the door in my line of sight, a precaution that doesn't escape his notice. His lips curve slightly as he takes the seat opposite me, unbuttoning his suit jacket.

"Mr. St. James," Victor addresses Talon without looking at him, "I'm sure you understand that what Miss Rossi and I must discuss requires privacy."

Talon begins to balk at the idea, allowing to let his control over his role crack slightly.

"I'll be fine," I assure him.

Talon's jaw tightens, but he offers a curt nod, professional despite his obvious reluctance. "I'll be right outside the door if you need me, Miss Rossi."

The heavy doors close behind him with a soft click that sounds unnervingly final. Victor studies me for a long moment before he reaches for the crystal decanter.

"Vodka?" he offers, pouring himself a measure. "Distilled from wheat grown on Petrov land, using water from our private spring. A family tradition for generations."

"Please," I reply, keeping my expression calm despite the nervous energy coursing through my veins.

Victor pours a second glass before he hands it to me. Our fingers brush momentarily, his skin cool and dry against mine. I resist the urge to wipe my hand on my skirt afterward.

"To new alliances," he proposes, raising his glass.

I mirror his gesture. "To truth."

The vodka burns a clean path down my throat, warming my chest even as my mind remains ice-cold with focus.

"You've made quite extraordinary claims, Miss Rossi," Victor begins, setting his empty glass aside. "Claims that, if true, would suggest a level of deception I find...personally offensive."

"Not claims. Facts."

Victor's expression remains impassive. He leans forward slightly, the gesture somehow more threatening than if he'd slammed his fist on the table.

"Facts require evidence, Miss Rossi. The files you sent were...intriguing, but hardly conclusive."

I reach into my handbag, withdrawing a small USB drive. It feels disproportionate to its size—this tiny device carries enough information to topple empires—or at least one man.

"Everything is here," I say, placing it on the polished surface of the side table between us. "Medical records from the fertility clinic. DNA profiles. Financial transactions linking Mario to both the clinic and my grandfather." I pause, letting my next words land with precision. "And video footage of my time in captivity."

Victor makes no move to take the drive. "You understand my skepticism, no? The idea that my son—that I—could be so thoroughly deceived..."

"Pride makes for effective blindfolds," I reply, watching his jaw tighten at my audacity. "Especially when the deception aligns with what you want to believe."

"You have your father's directness."

"Thank you for the comparison. Though I hope to avoid his fate."

Victor's expression shifts, just a micro movement of muscles around his eyes, but it's enough to confirm he knows exactly what happened to my father.

"Unfortunate business," he declares, finally reaching for the USB drive. He turns it over in his long fingers, examining it like a jeweler appraising a gem. "Your father was a man of honor. At least in his dealings with me, but these things happen. Health is a fickle thing."

"That it is, but the age of old men running my family is long gone."

"The age of old men is over, you say?" He pockets the

USB drive without looking at it, his attention fixed solely on me. "Yet here you sit, seeking alliance with perhaps the oldest man of them all."

"Not seeking," I correct him, maintaining eye contact. "Offering. There's a distinction."

"Semantics, Miss Rossi. But I appreciate your...candor."

He rises with fluid grace that belies his age, moving to a panel in the wall. When he presses his palm against it, the panel slides open to reveal a concealed safe. I watch as he inserts the USB drive into a standalone private computer system.

"You'll forgive my precautions," he says without turning. "In my experience, gifts from estranged family members often contain surprises."

"A sensible approach," I reply, using his distraction to subtly adjust my watch, ensuring the communication function is active. "I'd expect nothing less."

I remain still, my breathing measured despite the thundering of my heart as Victor works on the computer. Everything hinges on his reaction to what he's about to see. "These records," he says, his voice deceptively calm, "you obtained them from your grandfather?"

"No," I admit. "I acquired them after killing Mario. They were extracted from his personal laptop."

Victor moves back to his seat, lowering himself with the controlled movements of a man restraining violence. "The medical procedures documented here—the harvesting of your eggs, the embryo creation, the implantation into Bianca —you're saying my son was complicit in this?"

"Dmitri was deceived as thoroughly as you were," I reply, choosing my words carefully. "You needed a male heir, and what better way to guarantee it than by gender selecting the embryo. That is what happened, isn't it?"

Victor's lips thin.

"I thought as much," I smirk. "They played you for a fool, all because of your obsession with a male heir, Victor. A convenient explanation, just enough to keep you from questioning why IVF was necessary."

Victor's fingers drum once against the arm of his chair, the only outward sign of his agitation.

I steady my breathing, forcing my voice to remain calm despite the tension crackling through the air.

"My eggs. Petrov sperm. Implanted in a woman with no Rossi blood whatsoever." I lean forward slightly. "The boy who bears your name carries my DNA, not Bianca's. The true Rossi-Petrov bloodline you've always wanted."

Victor's hand tightens around his empty glass. For a moment, I think he might shatter it in his grip.

"And this...elaborate deception was orchestrated by Mikhail Vasilyev? Your grandfather?"

"With Mario's eager participation," I confirm. "My grandfather orchestrated my abduction, my...harvesting. Mario provided the false daughter, the perfect puppet to complete their plan."

Victor rises abruptly and crosses to the fireplace, tension coiled in every step.

"Mikhail was always cunning," he says at last, his tone distant, like he's sifting through memories better left untouched. "We were young once, allies even, before the families turned on each other."

"I'll be honest, Victor. My mother hardly ever mentioned him. I didn't meet my grandfather until recently—and when I did, everything shifted."

Victor turns, his expression grim. "She was right to keep you from him. Mikhail has never cared for balance or strategy. Only revenge."

He moves back to his desk with slow, deliberate steps. The room feels smaller as he settles into the high-backed leather chair, the position elevating him above me in a subtle power play.

"If what you say is true—" he begins.

"It is," I interrupt, earning a sharp look that would make lesser people flinch.

"If it is true," he continues, "then verification is simple enough."

His long fingers hover over the desk phone, pressing a button. When he speaks, the Russian flows from his lips like silk, his tone commanding but calm. I catch only fragments —words for "bring" and "immediately"—my limited Russian, insufficient to grasp the full meaning.

The tension in the air thickens as we wait, neither of us speaking. Victor watches me with unnerving intensity.

The heavy doors swing open a moment later. I glimpse Talon in the hallway, his posture tense as he tries to see past the two burly guards who enter. My heart stutters when I spot a petite figure between the guards—Bianca.

My cousin steps into the room, her hair swept into an

elegant chignon paired with an expensive designer dress. She freezes mid-step when she sees me, her eyes widening with recognition before darting to Victor in confusion.

"What's happening? Why is...why is she here?" she questions, her voice small as she takes another hesitant step forward.

The color drains from her face as she stares at me, her manicured hand rising to her throat in a gesture both defensive and stunned. Gone is the confident woman I remember from my father's study. Bianca looks fragile, uncertain—like she's seeing a ghost. Her own personal bogeyman, the one about to destroy her life for stealing mine.

"Cousin," I greet her, forcing warmth into my voice despite the circumstances. "It's been a long time."

"You shouldn't be here," she hisses, glancing nervously at Victor. "You disappeared."

I lift my hand to my chest. "It doesn't appear that I did, cousin. What is it that they say? The stories of my disappearance are greatly exaggerated, or is that about death? Either way, here I am."

"Sit," Victor orders her. Bianca sheepishly complies, settling herself into the chair next to mine.

"I don't know what she's told you," Bianca begins, her voice trembling slightly despite her obvious attempt to appear composed. "But whatever it is—"

"Is it true that you are not Mario Rossi's biological daughter?" Victor cuts her off.

I watch as the blood drains from Bianca's face, her lips parting in silent shock.

"I...I don't..." she stammers, her fingers twisting the expensive fabric of her dress.

"A simple question," Victor continues as he rises. "One with a simple answer. Yes, or no."

"You dare question my identity," Bianca's voice sharpens. Gone is the simpering fool. What remains is cold, calculated steel. "I am Bianca Rossi. Daughter of Mario Rossi. This—" she gestures at me with a sneer, "—this is nothing but a desperate ploy from a woman who abandoned her responsibilities and now regrets it. She's lying to you. Can't you see? She disappeared for years and now suddenly reappears with these...these fabrications? This woman wants what I have. My position. My husband. My son."

The vehemence in her voice is impressive. If I didn't know better, I might believe her myself.

"Call my father," she insists. "He will verify it."

"Your father is in no position to answer anything, Bianca," I interject. A wide smile forms on my face. "He's dead. I shot him myself."

She stills. "You...you killed my father?" She shoves herself from her seat, launching herself towards me. "You fucking bitch!"

"Enough," Victor cuts her off, his voice sharp as a blade. He rises from behind his desk, towering over all of us as he gestures to one of the guards. "So it is true. You deceived me, Bianca."

"I am a Rossi!" Bianca screams, her voice cracking with desperation. "You have no proof! Just the words of a woman who abandoned her family!"

Victor's expression doesn't change as he studies her. I watch his hand slip beneath his desk, the movement so smooth it's almost imperceptible.

"I have all the proof I need."

The gunshot is deafening in the confined space of the study. I flinch instinctively as crimson mist erupts from the back of Bianca's head, spattering across the antique wallpaper behind her. Her body crumples instantly, collapsing in a heap at my feet. Warm droplets of her blood speckle my cheeks and hands.

For a moment, I can't process what I've just witnessed. Bianca's eyes remain open, frozen in that final moment of terrified realization, but the light behind them is already gone. A pool of blood spreads beneath her head, seeping into the intricate pattern of the Persian rug.

"Such a waste," Victor remarks, lowering the pistol with casual indifference. He glances at the guards who haven't moved a muscle. "Clean this up. And inform my son his marriage has been...terminated."

My heart hammers against my ribs as I force myself to remain still, to betray no emotion despite the horror unfolding before me.

I can't tear my gaze away from her face. The woman who stole my life, now just an empty vessel on expensive carpet.

"Miss Rossi!" Talon's voice cuts through my shock, his footsteps pounding in the hallway outside. "Vesper!"

The doors burst open as he fights his way past the guards, his face twisted with alarm. He freezes when he sees the scene. Me, still seated, splattered with Bianca's blood,

Victor, standing calmly with the gun still warm in his hand, and Bianca's body sprawled between us.

Victor places the pistol on his desk with deliberate care, the metal making a soft click against the polished wood. He straightens his cuffs before walking toward me with measured steps.

"My apologies for the...theatrics," he says, extending his hand to help me up. "Some problems require immediate solutions."

I stare at his offered hand, noting the absence of blood spatter on his immaculate suit. Somehow, he'd managed to execute Bianca without getting a single drop on himself. I place my trembling fingers in his, allowing him to pull me to my feet. My legs feel unsteady beneath me as I step carefully around Bianca's body.

"Come," he says, extending his hand to help me up. His palm is warm and dry as it envelops mine, pulling me to my feet with surprising gentleness. "You shouldn't have to witness the...unpleasantness of cleanup."

I allow him to guide me away from Bianca's body, my legs moving mechanically. The smell of gunpowder and copper fills my nostrils, making my stomach roil.

"My guards will escort you to suitable quarters where you can refresh yourself," Victor continues, his tone as casual as if we're discussing dinner plans rather than standing over a corpse. "You will dine with me within the hour. We have much to discuss about our new alliance."

# Chapter 39

VESPER

I STARE at my reflection in the bathroom mirror, Bianca's blood drying in rust-colored flecks across my cheeks and neck. My hands tremble as I grip the marble countertop, the diamond-encrusted watch on my wrist catching the light. I've seen death before, delivered it myself, but the casual way Victor executed her, like swatting an annoying insect, has left me shaken to my core.

The bathroom door opens behind me, and Talon steps in. "They're listening," he mouths silently, tapping his ear before turning on the shower. The rush of water creates a shield of noise as he moves closer.

"Are you alright?" he asks softly, his hand warm against the small of my back.

I shake my head, words failing me as the enormity of what we've walked into finally hits. Victor Petrov shot Bianca without hesitation, without trial. His own daughter-in-law executed, and in the next breath, invited me to dine with him. Victor Petrov may be a bigger monster than my own grandfather. What would he do to me if he discovered our deception?

"I need to get this off me."

Talon reaches for a plush hand towel, wetting it under the faucet before gently turning me to face him. With tender care, he begins to wipe away the blood from my face. Each gentle stroke removes another spatter of Bianca's life from my skin, but nothing can erase the image of her crumpling to the floor.

"You should shower. I'll stand guard at the door."

I nod, suddenly desperate to wash away every trace of this nightmare. "Thank you."

As Talon turns to take up his position at the door, I shed my blood-stained clothes, letting them fall to the marble floor in a heap. The hot water scalds my skin as I step under the spray, but I welcome the pain to ground me in the present, to wash away the shock threatening to paralyze me.

I scrub until my skin turns pink, watching as the last traces of Bianca's blood swirl down the drain. Steam fills the massive shower enclosure, clouding the glass walls and creating a momentary illusion of safety.

Wrapping myself in one of the plush towels, I step out of the shower, my mind racing with contingency plans. I need to contact Z and Oz to confirm they're safe and warn them.

A soft knock at the outer door catches my attention. Talon motions for me to stay where I am as he answers it. I freeze, watching through the partially open bathroom door as Talon speaks in hushed tones with someone in the hallway. My pulse quickens, imagining Victor's guards coming to escort me to dinner—or worse.

When Talon steps back into view, he's holding something that makes my breath catch. A designer dress sways gently from a satin hanger in his grip, its midnight blue fabric shimmering under the chandelier light. It's exquisite, and clearly meant for me.

"Compliments of your host." His expression is unreadable as he holds up the garment. The dress is a masterpiece of understated elegance, with a plunging neckline and a slit that would reach mid-thigh. "Victor thought you might appreciate something...fresh to wear."

I step forward, my fingers brushing against the silky material. "He works quickly."

"Efficient monsters usually do," Talon mutters. "There are shoes to match. And jewelry."

As if on cue, I notice the velvet box sitting on the bed behind him. My stomach churns at the thought of Victor selecting these items for me. This isn't hospitality, it's ownership. Marking me as his property before I've even agreed to our alliance.

"How thoughtful." It takes everything I have not to roll my eyes when I open the box and find a brilliant diamond necklace with inlaid rubies. He's wasting no time spoiling the broodmare to his empire.

Talon peers at it over my shoulder. "Subtle. Nothing says 'welcome to the family' like a collar of diamonds and blood."

I lift the necklace from its velvet nest. The central ruby is the size of my thumbnail, surrounded by diamonds that catch the light. It's breathtaking and suffocating all at once.

"Help me?" I turn my back to Talon and lift my damp hair. His fingers brush my neck as he takes the necklace, the touch sending an involuntary shiver down my spine.

"Just so we're clear," he declares as he fastens the clasp, "we're still sticking to the plan, right? Even after..." He doesn't finish the sentence. He doesn't need to.

The necklace already feels like a noose around my neck. "Yes."

"I know." Talon's jaw tightens. "I just wanted to make sure we're on the same page."

The diamonds lie cold against my skin as I drop the towel and step into the midnight blue dress. It fits as if it were made for me specifically. The thought is unsettling. I had assumed this dress belonged to my recently departed cousin, but she and I weren't even remotely close in size or body type. The idea that Victor had a dress waiting for me makes my skin crawl with fresh horror.

"How would Victor even know my size?" I turn to examine the fit in the mirror.

"Maybe he had you measured while you slept on the plane," Talon suggests, only half-joking.

A chill runs through me at the thought. I shake my head and cross the room to where my bag sits on an antique writing desk. I need to focus on something I can control.

Opening the bag, I find The Collector's tablet exactly where I left it nestled. My fingers tremble slightly as I power it on, the screen casting an eerie blue glow across my face. I pull up the message I sent from the jet's bathroom, checking for any response.

Nothing. The screen remains stubbornly empty of notifications.

"He hasn't replied." A knot of unease tightens in my stomach. My grandfather is many things, but negligent isn't one of them. His silence is deliberate.

"Maybe that's a good thing," Talon says, moving closer to look over my shoulder. "Gives us more time to maneuver."

A sharp knock at the door makes us both freeze.

"Miss Rossi?" A voice calls from the corridor. "Mr. Petrov requests your presence for dinner in fifteen minutes."

"Thank you," I call back, smoothing the midnight blue fabric of my dress. "Please inform him I'll be there shortly."

Heavy footsteps retreat down the hallway as I turn to Talon, my heart hammering against my ribs.

"Let's not keep our host waiting." I run my fingers through my damp hair, arranging it into loose waves that cascade down my back. "How do I look?"

"Like a queen walking into battle."

I lift my chin despite the gaudy mass of jewels around my neck. "Then let's go to war."

The halls of Victor's palace stretch before us like a labyrinth, each corridor more opulent than the last. Talon offers his arm, a silent support as we follow a guard whose expression remains unreadable. My heels click against the marble floors, the sound echoing through the vast, gilded spaces.

We descend a grand staircase, the steps wide and shallow, forcing a measured pace that feels ceremonial. At the bottom, a woman in a crisp uniform awaits.

"This way to the dining room, Miss Rossi," she says, her accent thick.

The dining hall materializes behind massive double doors. A cavernous space dominated by a table that could seat thirty but is set for only six. Crystal chandeliers cast prismatic light across gilded surfaces, illuminating priceless artwork and tapestries that line the walls. Victor stands at the far end, resplendent in evening attire.

Victor notices me the second I enter. A smile curves his lips as he strides toward us with the confidence of a man who's never questioned his own power.

"Vesper." My name rolls off his tongue with a familiar ease that makes my skin crawl. "You look exquisite."

Before I can respond, he's beside me, his fingers closing around my wrist as he detaches me from Talon's arm with smooth efficiency. The gesture is subtle but unmistakable—a transfer of possession.

"Come," Victor guides me toward the head of the table, his hand at the small of my back. "You'll sit here, to my left. The position of highest honor for a guest in my home."

I allow myself to be maneuvered into place, the heavy chair pulled out with a flourish by a waiting servant. Victor's hand lingers on my shoulder as I'm seated, his fingers tracing the edge of the necklace he provided, branding me.

Talon moves to take up his position along the wall, his expression carefully neutral as he surveys the room.

"Mr. St. James," Victor calls, not bothering to look in Talon's direction as he takes his own seat at the head of the table. "That won't be necessary. Join us." He gestures to the chair directly next to mine.

Talon hesitates for just a heartbeat before acquiescing, taking the offered.

The massive doors at the far end of the dining hall swing open again, and my breath catches as Oscar and Zaire enter. They've been transformed.  are their travel-worn clothes, replaced by impeccably tailored suits that highlight the elegance of their Petrov heritage.

"Ah, my nephews. How kind of you to join us."

Oscar moves with fluid grace to take the seat directly across from Talon. His lips form a silent question—Okay? I give him an almost imperceptible nod, hoping my expression conveys more confidence than I feel.

Z takes the remaining seat beside his brother, his posture deceptively relaxed, though I can see the tension in his body. The family resemblance between the three Petrov men is striking in this setting.

"Drinks?" Victor gestures to a servant. "The Petrov Reserve, bottled on the day of my grandson's birth."

The servant moves efficiently, pouring the clear liquid into crystal glasses. I notice Victor glance at his platinum watch, a flash of irritation crossing his face as he checks the time. His fingers drum once against the polished table.

"Shall we begin?" I suggest reaching for my glass.

"Not yet." Victor's tone remains pleasant, but there's an edge to it now. He adjusts his cufflinks, an unnecessary gesture that speaks volumes about his growing impatience. Another glance at his watch confirms what I already suspect, someone important is missing.

The silence stretches uncomfortably as servants bring out the first course—delicate plates of caviar nestled on beds of ice. Victor finally takes his seat at the head of the table with a barely suppressed sigh.

"My son," he announces, "is late. As usual."

As if summoned by his father's displeasure, the doors swing open once more. Dmitri Petrov strides into the dining hall with unhurried confidence.

The years have hardened Dmitri into something foreign. He's filled out since I last saw him, his once-lanky frame now muscled and imposing beneath his tailored suit. His features are a striking amalgamation of his cousins. His hair is cropped shorter than I remember, accentuating the sharp angles of his jawline. A thin scar bisects his left eyebrow.

Dmitri moves with grace toward his designated spot, watching me with every step. There's no warmth in his gaze —only calculation, curiosity, and something shadowed I can't quite name.

He settles between his father and Oscar. The three generations of Petrov men form a visual dynasty across the table. His movements are measured as he unfolds his napkin and places it in his lap, all while keeping that unwavering focus on my face. It's as though he's trying to reconcile the woman before him with the girl he once knew—the one who vanished before their arranged marriage could be fulfilled.

"Vesper," he finally says, my name rolling from his tongue with a hint of his father's accent.

"Dmitri," I reply.

His gaze drops to the necklace resting against my throat, his expression flickering briefly before returning to careful neutrality.

Victor clears his throat. "Now that we're all present," he says with pointed emphasis, "we can begin." He lifts one elegant hand, signaling the servants who line the walls.

They spring into action. The soft clink of fine china and the gentle ring of crystal glasses fill the room as the first course is placed before each of us.

I lift my fork, feeling Victor's gaze pressing against my skin as I sample the delicate blini topped with glistening black caviar.

No one speaks. The only sounds are the gentle scrape of silver against china and the occasional crystalline note of a glass being set down. Talon's knee presses against mine beneath the table. A silent reminder that I'm not alone.

Z sets his glass down with a soft clink. The servants reappear as if summoned by the sound, whisking away our barely-touched appetizer plates with efficiency.

Attendants emerge from hidden doors, bearing silver platters that steam in the chandelier light. They place a portion of what appears to be venison, surrounded by roasted root vegetables, before each of us.

Victor lifts his knife and fork, the silver catching the light.

"I find myself in a rather unexpected position," Victor says, voice calm but laced with weight. "This morning, I executed a woman who deceived me for years...only to discover the rightful Rossi heir seated at my table."

"It seems fate has corrected its own mistake. The alliance that should have been formed years ago can now proceed as originally intended."

I feel Z tense across the table.

"A union between our families," Victor continues, dabbing his lips with his napkin, "through the marriage of my son Dmitri to Vesper Rossi."

The words hang in the air. Dmitri's expression remains unreadable, though his eyes never leave my face.

"Now that his first wife is no longer with us," Victor adds with chilling casualness, "there are no obstacles to this arrangement. The paperwork is already being prepared."

Z's fork clatters against his plate, the sharp sound slicing through the silence of the dining hall and pulling every gaze to him. His face is tight, unreadable, a muscle twitching in his jaw as he calmly picks the utensil back up. The air around him hums with barely restrained tension.

"Are you unwell, nephew?" Victor inquires.

"Fine, Uncle," Z responds, his voice strained. "The meat is...exceptional."

Victor chuckles humorlessly. "There is, however, one matter we should address before proceeding further." He sets down his knife and fork, folding his hands on the table's edge. "Your...relationships with my nephews and your security guard. Do not deny it, Miss Rossi," Victor continues, swirling the vodka in his glass. "Sergei was quite thorough in his report of your activities aboard my jet. Quite thorough indeed."

Dmitri's head snaps toward his father, then back to me, his jaw clenching visibly.

"While I appreciate your...enthusiasm for forging alliances with the Petrov bloodline," Victor says, his tone dripping with mock civility, "I must insist that such arrangements cease immediately upon your marriage to my son. A Petrov bride comes to her marriage without complications. My son does not share well, do you, my boy?"

"No, Father. I do not."

"I wasn't aware my personal relationships were already under your jurisdiction," I reply, keeping my voice steady despite the hammer of my pulse. "Our alliance hasn't even been formalized."

"Everything within these walls is under my jurisdiction, Miss Rossi. Including you, now that you've accepted my hospitality."

I force myself to take a sip of water, buying precious seconds to compose my response. "I appreciate the clarification. Though I wonder, does your son share your views on ownership?"

"My father and I are in complete agreement on matters of family."

"How fortunate," I reply, setting my glass down with deliberate care.

Z clears his throat, drawing his uncle's attention. "Speaking of family matters," he says, his tone carefully neutral despite the tension radiating from him, "I'm curious about my nephew. When might we meet him?"

Victor's expression shifts, calculation replacing condescension. "In due time. The boy is at our country estate, away from...distractions."

"Surely his mother deserves to see him," Talon interjects, speaking for the first time since the meal began.

"Mr. St. James," Victor replies, his tone glacial, "I don't recall asking for your input."

"And yet, you've received it," Talon replies, meeting Victor's stare with unwavering calm. "Vesper deserves to see her son."

The tension in the room thickens to something almost tangible. I place my hand on Talon's arm, both a warning and a show of solidarity.

"My security chief speaks out of concern for me," I say smoothly, redirecting Victor's attention. "But he raises a valid point. When can I expect to meet my child?"

Victor studies me over the rim of his glass. "Soon enough. Once certain...arrangements are finalized."

"You mean once I'm legally bound to your son," I clarify. "Using my child as leverage seems beneath a man of your stature, Victor."

A ghost of a smile plays at the corner of his mouth. "Not leverage, my dear. Insurance. In my experience, mothers are unpredictable when reunited with children they've never known. I prefer to ensure your full commitment to our arrangement first."

"And what exactly does this arrangement entail?" I ask, keeping my voice level even as anger coils tight in my gut.

Victor gestures to a servant who immediately steps forward with a velvet box. He places it on the table between Dmitri and me.

"My son has something for you," Victor says, nodding to Dmitri.

Dmitri reaches for the box, his movements deliberate as he opens it to reveal a ring that makes my breath catch. The diamond at its center is enormous, at least five carats, surrounded by smaller rubies that match the necklace around my throat. It's ostentatious, a physical manifestation of Petrov wealth and power designed to be seen from across a room.

"A fitting symbol of our alliance," Dmitri says, his voice revealing nothing as he removes the ring. He extends his hand across the table, palm up, clearly expecting me to place my hand in his.

I hesitate just long enough for tension to thicken the air before slowly extending my left hand. Dmitri's fingers are warm and dry as they close around mine, his grip firm as he slides the ring onto my finger. It's heavy and constricting.

"Perfect fit," Victor remarks with satisfaction. "Just as I knew it would be."

Across the table, Z's expression goes completely blank—that unsettling stillness I've come to recognize as a warning sign, the calm that conceals his most volatile emotions. Oscar, meanwhile, studies his plate with unusual intensity, as if it holds the answers to questions no one wants to ask.

"The wedding will take place tomorrow at noon. I've arranged for the priest to come to the family chapel on the estate. I'll send out the necessary invitations to the Russian families and close friends."

The announcement lands like a grenade at the table. My fingers tighten around my water glass as I process his words.

"Tomorrow? That seems rather...expedient." The lie spills from my lips easily. I had anticipated the expedition. With my grandfather's own timeline, acceleration is fine by me. Victor just doesn't need to know that.

"Dragging things out serves no purpose. Especially considering how eager I am for more heirs. The Petrov legacy must be secured. On that note," Victor continues, setting down his utensils with deliberate precision, "I've taken the liberty of arranging for a physician to examine you this evening. To verify that your...entanglements haven't resulted in complications."

My stomach lurches. "Complications?"

"Pregnancy," Victor clarifies with brutal directness. "Terminating one would only cause unnecessary delays." He takes a sip of vodka, watching me over the rim of his glass. "Consider it my wedding present."

Talon's hand moves to his thigh, where I know he keeps a concealed weapon. I press my foot against his under the table, a silent warning. We can't afford a confrontation. Not yet.

"How considerate," I say, my voice dripping with false gratitude as I set down my fork. "Though I assure you, such measures are unnecessary."

"Indulge me. I prefer certainty in all matters related to my family's bloodline considering your recent revelations about your cousin."

"Of course," I acquiesce, forcing a smile that feels like shattered glass. "Whatever puts your mind at ease."

Victor's attention shifts to Dmitri, something passing between father and son in that silent exchange. "You've been uncharacteristically quiet, my son. Are you not pleased with your bride-to-be?"

Dmitri studies me across the table. "She's everything you promised, Father." His voice reveals nothing of his thoughts. "I look forward to...continuing our family's legacy."

"It occurs to me, Vesper, that your grandfather should be present for tomorrow's ceremony. I think it would be...appropriate for him to witness. His granddaughter fulfilling her destiny. Joining our families as was originally intended. Arrange it."

Dmitri's eyebrows lift slightly. The first genuine reaction I've seen from him all evening.

"As you wish, Victor," I force from my lips.

"Please, we are family now, child. You may call me father."

# Chapter 40

VESPER

I'VE EXPERIENCED many forms of violation in my life, but this might be the most civilized.

Two female guards escort me back to my quarters, their expressions blank as they flank me through Victor's palace. My new ring weighs heavy on my finger, the massive diamond catching the light with every movement. beautiful shackle. Neither woman speaks as we walk, the only sound is the rhythmic click of our heels against the marble floors.

"Where's Talon?" I ask, trying to keep my voice casual despite the anxiety churning in my stomach.

"Mr. St. James has been relocated to more appropriate accommodations," the taller guard responds without looking at me. "Mr. Petrov felt it unsuitable for your security detail to remain in your personal quarters."

Of course he did. First, Oz and Zaire. And now, Talon. Isolation at its best.

When we reach my door, the guards position themselves on either side, a clear indication they won't be leaving. The message is unmistakable. I'm no longer a guest but a prisoner in gilded shackles.

"The physician will arrive momentarily," the shorter guard informs me as she opens the door. "Mr. Petrov requests your full cooperation."

I step into my room and freeze. Where my luxurious bed once stood now sits a gynecological examination chair, its stirrups extended like metal arms waiting to embrace me. Beside it, a small table holds an array of medical instruments, neatly arranged. The sight sends ice coursing through my veins.

A sharp knock at the door startles me from my horrified contemplation. Without waiting for my response, the door swings open to reveal a mountain of a man, his shoulders nearly touching both sides of the door frame as he enters. His coat stretches tight across his broad chest, and a stethoscope hangs around his neck like an afterthought.

"Miss Rossi," he greets me, his Russian accent so thick it turns my name into something almost unrecognizable. "I am Dr. Lebedev. I will examine you now."

There's no warmth in his assessment, no bedside manner, just the cold efficiency of a man accustomed to following orders without question.

"Please remove clothing from waist down and sit at the end of the table," he instructs, gesturing toward the stirrups with a meaty hand. "We will be quick."

I remain frozen, my heart hammering against my ribs. The doctor sighs, impatience flickering across his broad features.

"I will give privacy," he says, moving toward my bathroom. "Two minutes."

The bathroom door closes behind him with a soft click. I glance toward the main door where I know the two guards stand just outside, ready to intervene if I resist.

My fingers tremble as I approach the chair, bile rising in my throat. This is just another tactic. Victor's way of asserting control, a silent reminder that my body now belongs to the Petrov empire. *You've survived worse,* I tell myself. *Much worse.*

With stiff, mechanical movements, I slide off my underwear, leaving the midnight blue dress pooled around my hips as I perch on the edge. The cold metal bites into my skin, and a violent shiver rips through me. I fix my gaze on the ceiling, forcing each breath to remain steady as I count the delicate swirls etched into the plaster overhead.

Then, vibration. Soft, almost imperceptible, against my wrist.

The watch. Our encrypted line.

I angle my wrist, eyes scanning the message scrolling across the diamond-studded face.

STAY STRONG. WE'RE WORKING
ON IT. – Z

The words hit harder than any touch, solid ground beneath my feet when everything else threatens to collapse. I'm not alone. Not completely.

The bathroom door creaks open. Dr. Lebedev steps out, latex gloves already in place, his movements swift despite his size. He stations himself at the foot of the chair.

"Feet in stirrups," he commands, not bothering to look at my face.

I comply, swallowing my revulsion as I place my feet in the cold metal supports. The vulnerability of the position makes my skin crawl, memories of the clinic during my captivity threatening to overwhelm me.

"This will be cold," Dr. Lebedev warns, his voice devoid of empathy.

The shock of the cold speculum makes me flinch despite my determination to remain stoic. I keep my eyes fixed on the ceiling, retreating into my mind as the doctor's clinical examination proceeds. His touch is impersonal, mechanical, just another man handling my body without my consent.

I hear the door opening, but assume it's one of the female guards checking on the examination's progress.

"We are not done here," the doctor bellows from between my legs.

"Leave us." The voice attached to that command chills my blood. I shift, just enough to see Dmitri standing in the doorway. "Get out," Dmitri commands, his voice quiet yet carrying such authority that Dr. Lebedev immediately withdraws the speculum and straightens.

The doctor nods stiffly, stripping off his gloves and gathering his instruments. He moves past Dmitri, the door closing behind him with a soft click that echoes in the sudden silence.

I scramble to close my legs, fighting against the stirrups that hold them apart. Humiliation burns through me, hot and suffocating as I struggle to maintain what little dignity I have left. Dmitri watches me, his expression unreadable as he steps further into the room. With a few short steps, he's at my spread feet

"Get your hands off me," I snap, trying to push myself out of the chair, but Dmitri moves with unexpected speed.

His hand shoots out, pressing against my knee, stopping my attempt to close my legs. "Not yet," he says, his voice low and controlled. "I want to see what my wife's blood bought me."

"Don't you dare," I hiss, struggling against his grip, but he's stronger than he looks, his fingers digging into my skin as he forces my legs to remain spread in the stirrups.

"Stop fighting," Dmitri commands, stepping between my legs where the doctor stood moments before. "If we're to be married tomorrow, I should know what I'm getting, shouldn't I?"

I twist against his hold. "I am not merchandise to be inspected."

His fingers press harder, bruising my skin as he leans closer. "Everything in this house belongs to my father. Soon, you'll belong to me." His free hand moves toward my inner thigh, and I recoil from his touch.

"I belong to no one," I spit, summoning all my strength to kick out with my right leg, wrenching it free from the stirrup. My heel connects with his shoulder, sending him stumbling back a step.

Dmitri recovers quickly, his expression shifting from shock to something darker as he straightens. The blow didn't injure him—only caught him off guard.

"I like it when they fight back," he snarls. "Breaking you will almost be worth the cost."

I yank my other leg free from the stirrup, scrambling backward until my back hits the raised portion. My dress is bunched around my waist, my dignity in tatters, but my eyes never leave his face as I reach for anything I could use as a weapon.

"Did you fight my cousins when they fucked you? Did you let your security guard stick his dick inside of you like a fucking whore, Vesper?"

His words hit like physical blows, but I refuse to show how they affect me. Instead, I reach for the only weapon within reach, a metal speculum from the doctor's abandoned tray.

"Touch me again and I'll gouge your eyes out," I say, calm and cold, each word honed to cut through the heat of my rage.

Dmitri studies me, his head tilting slightly as if seeing me for the first time. To my surprise, he laughs, a sound devoid of humor that raises gooseflesh along my arms. "You think

I'm the monster here? My father just executed my wife. The mother of my—" He stops abruptly, jaw clenching as something like grief flashes across his features before hardening into rage.

"Your wife was a fraud," I remind him, still clutching the speculum. "And that boy is my son."

"A son you've never met. A son deprived of his mother because of you."

"I. Am. His. Mother."

"She's gone because of you!" Dmitri snarls, lunging forward with unexpected speed. His fingers clamp around my wrist, twisting until pain shoots up my arm. The speculum clatters to the floor as he wrenches it from my grasp.

I refuse to cry out, even as his grip tightens to the point of agony. His face contorts with rage, features twisting into something barely recognizable as he raises his hand, palm open and ready to strike.

"Dmitri!" Victor's voice cracks like a whip from the doorway. "Lower your hand. Now."

Dmitri freezes, his arm still raised, fingers still digging into my wrist. His breathing comes in harsh pants.

"Release her," he commands. When Dmitri hesitates, Victor's expression hardens. "I won't ask again."

The pressure on my wrist vanishes as Dmitri drops my arm. I immediately pull my dress down to cover myself, the humiliation burning hotter than the pain.

Victor moves with surprising speed for a man his age, crossing the room to grab his son by the collar. "Out," he hisses, shoving Dmitri toward the door with enough force to make him stumble. "We will discuss your behavior later."

As Dmitri disappears through the doorway, Victor eyes the disheveled state of my dress and the red marks deepening on my wrist.

"My apologies for my son's...enthusiasm," he says with chilling formality. "He's taking his wife's death rather personally, it seems."

I yank my dress down further, desperate to cover myself. "Get out."

Victor's eyebrows rise fractionally at my tone. "This examination will happen, Miss Rossi. One way or another."

He turns toward the door, his movements unhurried as he steps into the hallway. I hear his voice, low and commanding, followed by heavy footsteps. My stomach drops as Dr. Lebedev reappears.

Victor shoves the doctor back inside. "Do your fucking job. Properly this time."

The door slams shut, leaving me alone with the doctor again. He approaches the examination chair, latex gloves snapping as he pulls them on.

"Please don't do this."

"Orders," he says simply, gesturing toward the stirrups. "Will be quick."

I bite back a sob as Dr. Lebedev's clinical touch invades me once more. His examination is thorough but impersonal, his breathing steady while mine comes in ragged gasps. I focus on a single point on the ceiling, counting each second that passes. One, two, three...

The watch vibrates against my wrist again. I can't look at it now, can't risk drawing attention to it. Instead, I retreat into myself, building walls around my consciousness brick by brick.

"Is normal," Dr. Lebedev announces after what feels like an eternity. He withdraws his instruments and steps back, stripping off his gloves with a snap that makes me flinch. "No pregnancy. Get down now."

I move mechanically, lowering my legs from the stirrups. My muscles protest, cramped from tension and the unnatural position. My feet touch the cold floor, legs trembling as I stand.

Dr. Lebedev's eyes dart to the door, then back to me. His massive frame suddenly seems to shrink as he hunches forward.

"Listen carefully," he speaks in unexpectedly clear English, all traces of his thick accent vanishing. "We have less than a minute."

He moves to open his medical bag, but instead of retrieving more instruments, he pulls out a sleek handgun. The metal gleams under the chandelier light as he presses it into my palm.

"From your grandfather," he says, closing my fingers around the weapon.

I stare at the gun, then at the doctor's face, understanding failing to penetrate my shock. "What? My grandfather? I don't—"

"Quiet, woman." Dr. Lebedev glances nervously at the door.

My mind reels as I clutch the cold metal. "But the examination...you just—"

"Had to be convincing. Victor watches everything. Hide it."

"Are you even a doctor?" I gasp.

The door handle turns, and Dr. Lebedev instantly transforms back into the hulking, accent-heavy physician, as he snaps his medical bag shut.

"All done," he announces loudly as the female guard peers in. "Patient healthy. I go now. You bring chair."

With trembling fingers, I shove the gun between my breasts, the cold metal pressing against my skin as I tuck it into the built-in bra of Victor's gifted dress.

The female guard marches in. She doesn't speak as she begins collapsing the stirrups. I back away, pressing myself against the far wall, willing my heartbeat to slow as the gun shifts against my skin.

She wheels the chair toward the door, metal legs squeaking against marble floors. The sound grates against my raw nerves, but I maintain my composure, keeping my expression blank as she exits. The door closes with a definitive click, followed by the unmistakable sound of a lock engaging.

Alone at last.

My watch vibrates against my wrist with insistent urgency. I lift it to eye level, my breath catching as I read the scrolling message.

OPEN BALCONY DOOR. - O

My heart pounds against the cold metal of the gun as I move toward the doors. I unlatch them, the cool night air rushing in as I push them open. The Petrov estate stretches below me, manicured gardens illuminated by strategic lighting that leaves few places for concealment.

I step onto the balcony, scanning the shadows for any sign of Oscar. The floor is cold beneath my bare feet, a quiet reminder of my vulnerability. The diamond ring on my finger catches the moonlight, scattering fractured rainbows across the marble balustrade.

"Up here."

The words come from above. I tilt my head back to see Oscar perched on the roof overhang, his dark clothing blending with the night sky. He moves with feline grace, dropping silently to the balcony beside me.

"Are you hurt?" His eyes scan my body, lingering on the bruises forming around my wrist. "I heard Dmitri's voice."

"I'm fine," I lie. How did you—"

"Later," he cuts me off, glancing behind us. "We have three minutes before the security sweep reaches this section."

His fingers brush my cheek, the gentleness of his touch nearly undoing my fragile composure.

"I wish I could stay." His thumb traces the edge of the bruise forming on my wrist.

I nod, swallowing the lump in my throat. "Z?"

"Z was losing his shit when he heard what happened. We practically had to restrain him."

"What else is new?" I manage a weak smile, trying to

inject lightness I don't feel. "Tell me he's not planning to storm Victor's bedroom with guns blazing."

"Worse. Had they not disarmed us, this would have been over much faster," Oz's expression hardens. "Talon's with him now, keeping him from doing anything stupid. But we need to move fast."

I reach between my breasts, withdrawing the gun. "My grandfather's doctor slipped me this. He's apparently been working for Mikhail all along."

"Victor's being played from all sides." A grim smile touches his lips. "Good. We can use that. He reaches into his jacket, pulling out the signal jammer. "Talon didn't get a chance to leave this. Contact your grandfather, insist that he bring your brother and Alex tomorrow. Everything else is in place."

A distant sound makes him tense. His head whips toward the garden below as he spots movement among the hedges.

"Security patrol. I've stayed too long already."

My heart clenches at the thought of being alone again in this gilded prison. I grab his arm, suddenly desperate. "Oscar, I—"

He pulls me against him, cutting off my words with a kiss that's both tender and fierce. His lips move against mine with urgent passion, saying everything words cannot. He pulls away against both of our wishes. "Be brave, just a little bit longer, solnishko. Tomorrow ends this nightmare."

Before I can respond, he's gone—swinging over the balcony edge with fluid grace. I rush forward, gripping the cold railing as I watch his silhouette descend the building's intricate exterior. He disappears into the neatly trimmed topiaries below, vanishing without a trace.

The night air feels colder without him. I retreat into my room, closing the balcony doors behind me.

Tomorrow ends this nightmare. The gun presses against my skin, cold and reassuring as I cross the room.

The tablet. I need to contact my grandfather now.

My fingers close around the sleek device hidden in my bag. I clutch it to my chest, scanning the room for surveillance cameras I know must be there. The bathroom is my only hope for privacy.

I slip inside, locking the door behind me. I turn on the shower, letting steam fill the space as I perch on the edge of the massive tub. I activate the jammer Oscar left behind, the small device blinking green to indicate it's working.

Ten minutes. That's all I have before someone might get suspicious.

I power on the tablet. My finger hovers over the contact icon, and hesitation grips me. What if the doctor was lying? What if this is another of Victor's tests?

No. I can't afford doubt now.

I type quickly.

Need to speak immediately.

The message shows as delivered, and I hold my breath, counting seconds in my head. One, two, three...

The tablet vibrates in my hands, the screen illuminating with an incoming call. My grandfather's name flashes across the display, making my heart stutter. I accept the call, and his face materializes on the screen.

"I see you received my gift."

I touch the spot where the gun rests between my breasts. "Your doctor was quite...thorough in his delivery."

"He comes in handy." A thin smile stretches across Mikhail's face. "What news do you have for me that requires a call?"

I swallow hard, forcing my voice to remain steady. "Bianca is dead. Victor shot her right in front of me when she couldn't deny your accusations."

Mikhail's expression doesn't change. "As expected. Victor's always been predictable in his rage."

"I'm to marry Dmitri tomorrow at noon," I add, watching carefully for his reaction.

My grandfather's face hardens. "That was not our arrangement," he says, each word cutting like a blade. "You were to eliminate Victor, not bind yourself to his bloodline."

"I didn't have a choice. You wanted him dead, and offering myself in her place is the only way I could get close to him." The steam from the shower swirls around me as I lean closer to the screen.

"By becoming a Petrov bride?" He spits the words like venom. Mikhail's face contorts with rage. "I gave you purpose. I gave you power. And this is how you repay me? By marrying the son of the man who destroyed our family?"

"I have no intention of actually marrying Dmitri," I snap. "The ceremony is a means to an end—your end. Victor's end. All of it."

Mikhail's expression shifts, calculation replacing the simmering tension in his eyes as he studies my face through the screen.

"Explain yourself."

"I need you there tomorrow," I say, leaning closer to the tablet. "In person. It's the only opportunity we'll have with both Victor and Dmitri in the same place, vulnerable. You promised me an army, Grandfather. I need it now."

"After all these years underground, you want me to just show up at Victor Petrov's doorstep?"

"That's exactly what I expect." I press my palm against the cold gun hidden in my dress. "Your men are already inside these walls. Your doctor proved that. How many others have you planted in Victor's household over the years?"

"Enough to keep me informed."

"Then use them. Tomorrow, when I'm standing before Victor and his son, when all eyes are on the bride, that's when we strike." My heart pounds against my ribs, but my voice remains steady. "But I can't do it alone. I need you there. Not just your men, but you."

"Why?" The question is sharp, suspicious.

"Because Victor needs to see your face when it all falls apart. He needs to know who orchestrated his downfall."

A cold smile spreads across Mikhail's face. "You truly are my blood after all."

"I want Luca and Alex there, too."

His smile vanishes instantly. "They're freed after you kill Victor. You know what our arrangement is, granddaughter."

"And you've not sent me my proof of life today. You have not honored your side of the arrangement."

"You question my honor?"

"I question everything about you," I reply without hesitation. "Bring them tomorrow, unharmed, or Victor will know you are still alive. I'll make sure the world knows Mikhail Vasilyev is still alive. I'll tell every family you've robbed of their children what you've done. If you give me what I want, you'll have your Russian seat before sundown. You wanted me to be strong, grandfather. Reap the fruit of your efforts."

"Very well," he finally concedes, the words seemingly dragged from him. "Your brother and his companion will attend."

"How generous of you."

"But know this, Vesper, if you don't kill Victor, I will execute them in front of you." The call ends abruptly. The screen dimming.

# Chapter 41



SLEEP REFUSES TO COME, chased away by the phantom ache of Dmitri's fingers bruising my wrist, the memory of his calculated stillness as he stood between my forcibly spread legs. Every time I blink, his face flashes behind my lids. The gun tucked beneath my pillow offers hollow comfort against the ghosts that linger in the shadows.

By the time pale gray light filters through the curtains, I've memorized every crack in the ceiling, every swirl in the molding. The bruises on my wrist have deepened to an ugly purple—a bracelet of possession I can't remove.

A sharp knock at the door makes me flinch.

"Enter," I call, my voice steadier than I feel as I slide the gun under my pillow.

The door swings open, revealing a procession of servants carrying silver trays laden with breakfast, garment bags, and an array of beauty products. They flood into my room, transforming the space into a bridal preparation chamber without a single word exchanged.

I'm whisked away from my bed, stripped of my nightgown, and subjected to their ministrations without so much as a "good morning." Three women work on my hair simultaneously, tugging and pinning while another scrubs my face with cleansers.

"Too pale," one mutters in Russian, slapping rouge onto my cheeks with enough force to sting.

"Hold still," another commands as she lines my eyes with kohl, her breath hot against my face.

I remain silent, a living doll. My compliance is calculated —each moment bringing me closer to the endgame, to freedom. To my family.

When they finally unveil the dress, my breath catches. It's a monstrosity of satin and lace, dripping with crystals and pearls that must weigh ten pounds alone. The bodice is structured with visible boning, the neckline cut so low it borders on obscene.

"Arms up," the head stylist orders, and I comply as they lower the massive creation over my head.

The adornments of crystals and pearls press against me, but the real torture begins as they lace the back. Each pull of the ribbons forces the air from my lungs, squeezing my ribs until breathing becomes a conscious effort.

"Tighter," someone instructs, and I grip the bedpost as they cinch me further. "Mr. Petrov specified the waist measurement," explains the head stylist, yanking the laces with brutal efficiency. "He wants perfection."

Of course he does. I bite the inside of my cheek, tasting blood as they secure the final knot.

"The veil," announces a severe-looking woman, approaching with what appears to be a cloud of tulle and crystal. It descends over my elaborately styled hair, cascades down my back.

Through the shimmering veil, the world takes on a dreamlike quality, appropriate for this nightmare masquerading as a wedding day. They position me before a full-length mirror, stepping back to admire their handiwork.

The woman staring back at me is a stranger.

"Beautiful," sighs one of the stylists. "Like a true Petrov bride."

I want to tell her there's no such thing. Every Petrov bride is either a prisoner or a corpse. Sometimes both.

"The necklace," the head stylist declares, approaching with a velvet box. "Mr. Petrov was most insistent."

Inside rests a diamond collar even more elaborate than the one from yesterday. Three rows of flawless gems, culminating in a ruby pendant the size of a robin's egg. The symbolism isn't lost on me. Yesterday's necklace was a taste. This is the full leash.

"It's heavy," I remark as they fasten it around my throat.

"Tradition," one of them responds dismissively. "Every Petrov bride wears this on her wedding day."

I wonder how many of those brides survived to see their first anniversary.

They start fussing again, but I excuse myself to the bathroom, dragging the monstrosity of a dress with me. Once inside, I pull the gun given to me by Mikhail's doctor and secure it into bands of my garter before returning to the women ready to fuss even more.

A sharp knock at the door silences the room. The stylists freeze, exchanging glances of barely concealed panic before the eldest moves to answer it.

Victor Petrov stands in the doorway, resplendent in a black tuxedo adorned with military-style medals across his chest. His silver hair is slicked back, emphasizing the sharp angles of his face. For a man his age, he exudes power and virility that's both impressive and terrifying.

"Leave us," he commands, and the stylists scatter without a backward glance.

Victor steps into the room, his gaze sweeping over me. "Turn around," he instructs, making a small circular motion with his finger.

I comply, pivoting slowly, the weight of the dress making every movement feel heavy, intentional. The veil swishes softly against the marble floor as I complete the turn and face him again.

"Acceptable." His attention lingers on the necklace, a flicker of satisfaction crossing his face. "The diamonds were my grandmother's. She wore them when she married into the Petrov name, as did my wife. As will you."

"How many brides have worn this necklace to their execution?"

Victor's lips curve into something approximating a smile. "Only the ones who deserved it." He approaches with measured steps, reaching out to adjust the veil where it frames my face. His fingers brush against my cheek. "I trust there will be no...complications today," Victor continues, straightening one of the diamond pins in my hair. "You've proven yourself remarkably adaptable thus far. It would be a shame to see that resourcefulness go to waste."

His fingers pause at the back of my neck, just above the diamond collar. "You witnessed Bianca's fate yesterday." The pressure of his touch increases slightly. "Remember what happens to those who are no longer useful to me."

I swallow hard, the diamond collar suddenly feeling tighter around my throat.

"The Petrov family has no room for ornaments, only assets," he continues, his voice almost gentle. "Assets that appreciate in value, like you and the children you'll bear. The others...well, you can guess the rest."

I meet his stare through the veil, refusing to flinch despite the warning in his touch. "I understand, Victor."

"Father," he corrects, his fingers tightening slightly against my neck.

"Father," I repeat, the word tasting like poison on my tongue.

Seemingly satisfied, he releases me and steps back, checking his watch. "It's time."

Victor calls out to the guards stationed outside of her room. "Take her to the car."

The door swings open immediately, revealing two men in suits who enter with military precision. They flank me, not touching but close enough that escape would be impossible.

"I'll see you at the chapel," Victor says, straightening his cuffs with meticulous attention. "Try not to disappoint me."

He leaves without a backward glance, his footsteps fading down the marble corridor. The guards move closer, one extending his arm in a mockery of a gentlemanly escort.

"This way, Miss Rossi."

I take his arm with as much dignity as I can muster, the constricting bodice making each breath shallow and deliberate. The second guard follows close behind as we move through Victor's palace.

Servants pause in their duties as we pass. They look on in awe and happiness. Their expressions are a lie, a mask as false as my own. I wonder how many of them are my grandfather's spies, watching and waiting for the moment when this farce implodes.

Outside, a white Rolls Royce gleams in the morning sun, its polished surface reflecting the palace like a distorted mirror. The chauffeur holds the door open, his white-gloved hands steady as I'm helped into the plush interior.

"Your security detail will follow in a separate vehicle," the guard informs me before closing the door with a soft thud.

I'm alone for the first time since the preparations began. My fingers immediately go to my thigh, confirming the gun is still secure in my garter. The cold metal against my skin is a stark reminder of what's at stake today.

My watch vibrates against my wrist. The only allowance given since it nearly covered the bruise from Dmitri. I glance down, angling it beneath the voluminous skirts to read the message scrolling across its face.

IN POSITION. STAY STRONG. -T

The car pulls away from the palace, rolling down the long driveway. Through the tinted windows, I watch Victor's stronghold recede into the distance, gleaming like a mirage against the late morning sky. The chapel appears on the horizon, its golden domes catching the sunlight like beacons.

The car rolls to a stop before the chapel steps, its golden domes even more imposing up close. The chauffeur opens my door, and I steel myself for whatever awaits. Instead of Victor's guards, I'm greeted by a sight that makes my heart stutter. Oscar and Zaire stand side by side on the marble steps, both resplendent in tailored tuxedos.

Z's attention settles on me through the veil, his face composed, though the tension simmering beneath is impossible to miss.

Oscar steps forward and offers his hand to help me out of the car. He moves closer, adjusting my veil with unexpected tenderness.

"Like a fucking cupcake. The most beautiful, savage cupcake I've ever seen."

I grip Oscar's arm tighter than necessary as I find my balance on the steps. "What are you doing here?"

"Uncle's orders," Z replies, his lips barely moving as he takes my other arm. "We're to walk you down the aisle and give you away."

Oscar's fingers press against mine in silent reassurance. "His way of reminding us that you belong to Dmitri now."

"Poetic."

Z and Oz lead me up the steps to the closed door of the chapel. The massive wooden doors loom before us, carved with religious scenes that seem to mock the unholy union about to take place within.

"Ready?"

I nod, unable to form words as my heart thunders against the restrictive bodice. The doors swing open, revealing the interior bathed in golden light from stained glass windows. Rows of wooden pews line either side of a center aisle. At the far end stands the altar, where Dmitri waits in black, his father at his side.

But it's not them who capture my attention.

Three rows back on the left, I see him. Luca. My brother. He sits stiffly, his expression carefully composed. But when our eyes meet, the fierce love shining there nearly undoes me.

Seeing him this close after all these years is killing me. Every instinct screams to run to him, to throw my arms around him and never let go. But I can't. Not yet. I have to stay the course. I have to see this through.

Beside him is Alex, tall and solemn, tension radiating from every line of his body.

And behind them, my breath stutters. Sits Mikhail. My grandfather's thin frame curls into the pew like a spider in its web, his pale stare locked on me. He nods once, barely more than a twitch, his lips curved in something that could almost be a smile.

Music swells from hidden speakers, a traditional wedding march that sounds more like a funeral dirge. Z's fingers tighten around my arm as we begin to walk. My dress trails behind me like chains, each step deliberate, forced.

Eyes follow us. Victor's men, the carefully selected guests permitted to witness this farce, and my grandfather's spies, scattered like shadows among the crowd.

Dmitri stands at the altar, unmoving. His expression is blank, revealing nothing of the rage I saw yesterday. The bruises on my wrist pulse in sync with my racing heartbeat beneath Oscar's steady grip. My future husband watches our approach with that same sharp, ravenous focus—the kind that doesn't just see everything...it consumes it.

Victor looms beside him, positioned strategically above the proceedings on the raised platform. From his elevated perch, he commands a view of every corner of the chapel, every face, every potential threat. The military medals on his chest catch the light, creating the illusion of blood spatters across his immaculate jacket.

When we reach the steps leading to the altar, my feet falter. Z's hand tightens around my arm, steadying me as I struggle for breath against the vise of my bodice. His touch lingers a moment longer than necessary, a silent promise, a reminder that I'm not alone.

The priest steps forward. His Russian accent cuts through the chapel.

"Who gives this woman to be married to this man?" the priest intones, his face impassive as he delivers the ancient question.

Z's fingers dig into my arm for a heartbeat before he forces himself to loosen his grip. I feel his reluctance like a physical thing, his body rigid with tension beside me.

"We do," Oscar says, his voice even, but there's a barely contained tension beneath the calm—tight, volatile, ready to snap.

The twins share a glance—quick, charged, full of meaning they don't speak aloud—before each of them reaches for me. Z's thumb brushes lightly over my wrist, a fleeting touch. Oscar gives my fingers a soft, reassuring squeeze.

Then, together, they place my hands into Dmitri's waiting grasp.

The moment Dmitri's skin touches mine, I fight the urge to recoil. His fingers close around mine with possessive strength, the pressure just shy of painful.

"The bride and groom will now ascend," the priest announces, gesturing toward the altar steps.

Dmitri tugs me forward, the abrupt movement making

me stumble slightly on the first step. His grip tightens, steadying me with a roughness that makes Victor's lips twitch with what might be approval. I force my feet to move, each step taking me closer to a future I have no intention of living.

Behind us, I hear Z and Oz take their positions at the foot of the altar steps, their presence a small comfort as I face the two Petrov men who intend to own me.

The priest begins the ceremony in Russian, his voice echoing through the chapel's vaulted ceiling. I understand enough to follow along—declarations of holy union, promises of fidelity. Words that mean nothing in this mockery of marriage.

Victor's silver stare sweeps over the assembled guests, lingering briefly on my grandfather. If he recognizes Mikhail, he gives no indication.

I steal a glance at Luca and find him already looking at me. He looks thinner than the last time I saw him. But he's alive. My brother is alive. That truth settles like steel in my spine, just as Dmitri's fingers tighten around mine.

"We will now exchange vows," the priest announces in accented English, gesturing for Dmitri to begin.

Dmitri turns to face me, lifting my veil. His features remain unreadable, lips pulling into a faint curve that could be mistaken for a smile by anyone who didn't know better.

"I, Dmitri Victor Petrov," he begins, his voice echoing through the chapel, "take you, Vesper Rossi, to be my wife." The words fall from his mouth with the smoothness of something long rehearsed, completely devoid of warmth. "I vow to protect what is mine, to strengthen our bloodlines, and to ensure our legacy endures through the children you will bear me."

Every word drips with possession. No love. No hint of partnership. Just legacy and control. He doesn't flinch or falter as he continues, delivering vows that sound more like a business agreement than a promise made before God.

"Your family's strength will become Petrov strength. Your body will nurture Petrov heirs. Your loyalty will belong solely to me and the empire we will build together."

The chapel remains silent as his final words hang in the air. Victor nods with approval.

"And now, the bride," the priest prompts, turning his face toward me.

I take a measured breath, the corset restricting my lungs as I prepare to speak.

"I, Vesper Rossi," my voice carries clearly through the chapel, stronger than I feel, "take nothing from you or your family."

A collective gasp ripples through the assembled guests. Dmitri's fingers tighten painfully around mine as Victor's expression darkens to thunderous rage.

I yank my hands from Dmitri's crushing grip and take a deliberate step back.

"I will not be another decoration in your family's collection of broken women," I continue, my voice gaining strength with each word. "I will not bear children to continue your legacy of violence and control."

The chapel erupts. Victor's face contorts into something

almost unrecognizable, twisted with such raw rage that spittle gathers at the corners of his mouth. "What is the meaning of this?" he hisses through gritted teeth.

"This is your reckoning, Victor."

The chapel falls into stunned silence at my declaration. Victor's face contorts with rage, a vein pulsing at his temple as he takes a menacing step toward me.

"Guards!" he barks, his voice echoing through the sacred space.

Armed men materialize, weapons drawn, as they converge on the altar. Behind me, I hear the unmistakable sound of guns being cocked—my grandfather's men revealing themselves among Victor's security detail.

"I wouldn't," comes Mikhail's voice, calm and cold as he rises from his pew. "My men have been in your household for years, Victor. Did you really believe I'd let you live after what you took from me? Do you think I'd give you my granddaughter?"

Recognition flickers across Victor's face as he truly registers who my grandfather is. "Mikhail," he breathes, disbelief and rage tightening his jaw and stiffening his posture.

"Get her!" Victor roars.

Dmitri lunges, but Z is faster. He vaults up the altar steps and slams his fist into his cousin's jaw with a sickening crack. Dmitri stumbles back, blood spilling from his split lip.

Oz appears at my side, a gun already in his hand. He fires once. The shot hits Dmitri square in the chest. Blood blossoms across his crisp white shirt as he collapses.

"Dmitri!" Victor bellows, his voice tearing through the air like a war cry. "Kill them! Kill them all!"

Pandemonium erupts. Victor's men surge toward Mikhail's with ruthless force. Bullets rip through the stained-glass windows, the thunderous blasts sending vibrant, razor-edged shards raining down on the terrified wedding guests.

I can't move. I'm frozen, caught in a surreal tableau of chaos and vengeance. The aisle is littered with shattered glass and slick with crimson.

And then I see him.

Victor's face shifts—no longer cold and calculating, but contorted with something I never expected: grief. Real, gut-wrenching grief.

He shoves past his own men, falling to his knees beside Dmitri's body.

"My son," he chokes, and the rawness in his voice stills the room for a breath.

He gathers Dmitri into his arms, cradling him with a tenderness that feels almost impossible amid the carnage. Blood soaks his immaculate suit as he presses one shaking hand to the wound, the other cupping Dmitri's pale face. His silver head bows low, whispering something I can't hear over the gunfire still cracking around us.

For the first time since I've met him, Victor Petrov looks broken, vulnerable, a father losing his only child. His hand strokes Dmitri's hair back from his face with trembling fingers, watching his legacy dissipate in front of him.

"Get her out!" Talon's voice cuts through the mayhem as

he fights his way toward us, his movements fluid and brutal as he takes down two of Victor's guards. "I've got Luca and Alex."

I rip away the veil, tearing it from my head as the chapel dissolves into warfare. I reach beneath my skirts, fingers closing around the cold metal of the gun.

"Vesper, move!" Z shouts, tackling me as bullets spray across the altar where I stood seconds before. The impact knocks the breath from my already constricted lungs as we crash to the floor.

"Can you run in this fucking monstrosity?"

"No," I gasp, struggling against the unyielding corset. "I can't breathe, let alone run."

Z's knife appears in his hand. With swift movements, he slashes through the laces binding my torso, the bodice immediately loosening as blessed air fills my lungs. "Better?"

"Much," I manage, taking my first full breath since they'd laced me into the dress hours ago.

Oz drops beside us, his gun raised as he fires over the altar rail. "We need to move."

"Not without my brother or Alex."

"Talon is getting them. We have to get you out."

"I'm not leaving without them!" I grab Z's arm, my fingers digging into his sleeve. "Not after everything we've done to get here."

A bullet shatters the altar beside us, sending splinters of wood flying. Z shields me with his body, his muscles tensing as fragments pepper his back.

"Trust Talon," Oz urges, firing another round over the rail. "He'll get them out. We have a plan for this."

I spot Victor through the chaos. He's still cradling Dmitri, but something in his posture has shifted—stiff, coiled, dangerous. His head lifts, scanning the battlefield until his focus lands on me. The hatred etched across his face chills my blood.

"You," he mouths, the word clear even across the distance.

He gently lowers Dmitri to the ground, arranging his son's limbs with tender precision before rising to his feet. Blood stains the front of his immaculate suit, turning the military medals into grotesque ornaments as he draws a gun from beneath his jacket.

"We need to move. Now." Z's voice cuts through my horror as Victor begins advancing, shooting his own men when they get in his way.

Z grabs my hand, dragging me toward a side exit as bullets scream past us.

Oz covers our retreat, his movements swift and merciless as he takes down two of Victor's men closing in on our position.

"Move!" Z shoves me forward as we dash between pews, the heavy wedding dress hampering my every step despite the loosened corset. I stumble, the massive skirt tangling around my legs as gunfire erupts to our right.

A bullet tears through Z's shoulder, spinning him sideways. Blood sprays across my dress as he staggers against me. Oz whirls around, rushing to his twin's side just as another shot rings out. The bullet catches him in the chest, sending him crashing into the nearest pew.

"No!" My scream tears through the chaos as both men fall.

I lunge toward them, but a powerful arm clamps around my waist, yanking me backward with brutal force. Cold metal presses against my temple, the unmistakable pressure of a gun barrel against my skin.

# Chapter 42

VESPER

"DROP YOUR WEAPONS, MIKHAIL," Victor snarls, pressing the gun harder against my head. "Or watch your precious granddaughter's brains paint this holy ground."

My heart hammers against my ribs as I stare down at Oscar and Zaire sprawled on the chapel floor. Blood pools beneath Z's shoulder, spreading across the marble like spilled wine. Oz lies motionless, his chest barely rising with each shallow breath. Their bodies, broken because of me.

"Look what you've done," Victor hisses in my ear. "All this unnecessary death. All because of you."

Mikhail stands twenty feet away, his weapon trained on Victor. His face reveals nothing.

"You always had a flair for the dramatic, Victor," Mikhail calls out, his voice slicing through the smoke-filled chapel. "Taking hostages, making threats. The same tired tactics for forty years."

Victor's arm tightens around my waist, the barrel of the gun digging harder into my temple. "And yet, here we are. You, about to lose another woman you claim to love. Like mother, like daughter, I suppose."

I scan the room in a panic, searching for Luca and Alex. Through the haze and debris, I spot movement near the side entrance. Talon crouches behind an overturned pew, shielding my brother with his body while Alex lays down cover fire. Relief floods me. alive. At least, for now.

"Put down your weapon, Mikhail," Victor demands again. "Or I swear I'll kill her where she stands."

My grandfather's thin lips curve into something that might be a smile. "Go ahead."

The chapel goes still. Even the gunfire halts, the moment hanging thick in the air as Victor stiffens behind me.

"What did you say?"

"I said, go ahead." Mikhail's voice is eerily calm, his focus unmoving. "Kill her. One less liability for me to manage. So long as her son is still alive, I'll still achieve my goals."

Ice floods my veins as the meaning of his words sinks in. My own grandfather is willing to sacrifice me and has perhaps intended this all along.

"You heartless bastard," Victor breathes, genuine shock coloring his voice. "Even I wouldn't—"

"What? Sacrifice your family? You killed your daughter-in-law, Victor. It seems you're not above anything. You were forcing your own son to re-marry the woman responsible for his wife's death within hours of it happening. Is her body even cold?"

"That's different. Bianca was—"

"A pawn. Just like Vesper. Just like your son." Mikhail takes a deliberate step forward, his weapon never wavering. "The only difference is that I'm honest about it. I learned long ago that blood is just blood. Useful only when spilled for power."

The gun at my temple trembles slightly as Victor processes my grandfather's betrayal. I feel his chest rise and fall against my back, his breathing accelerating with disbelief.

"She's my weapon," Mikhail corrects him coldly. "As was her mother before her. As was her brother until he proved too weak. All a means to an end. Your end. So kill her, and when I kill you, I still get what I want."

All this time, the promises of family, of revenge shared— nothing but manipulation to position me exactly where I stand now. My heart would shatter if I hadn't anticipated this moment. The cold calculation in Mikhail's eyes, the casual way he dismisses my life, it confirms what I've suspected since our first meeting. My grandfather never saw me as family, only as a tool to be wielded against his enemies. A disposable one at that.

"You're both the same," I spit. "Two old men playing games with lives that aren't yours to take."

Victor's grip falters for a fraction of a second—just enough. I drive my elbow backward with every ounce of strength I possess, catching Victor in the solar plexus just as Talon had taught me. His breath explodes from his lungs as he doubles over, the gun jerking away from my temple. I twist in his grasp, my hand already reaching beneath my skirts for the weapon strapped to my thigh.

"You think I didn't know?" I hiss, my fingers closing around the cold metal. "That I didn't see exactly what you both are?"

Mikhail's expression shifts almost imperceptibly.

"Clever girl," he chortles. "But still just a girl playing games designed by men."

"No," I counter, my voice steadier than I feel. "A woman ending games that should have died with your generation."

I wrench free from Victor's grasp as I stumble backward. My gun is already in hand, aimed squarely at his chest. His eyes widen, not with fear, but disbelief. For a man who thrives on absolute control, it's my rebellion that cuts deepest.

"You won't shoot me." Victor straightens to his full height despite the pain in his abdomen. "You don't have the stomach for it."

"I killed Mario Rossi," I remind him, my finger steady on the trigger. "What makes you think you're different?"

A commotion to my left pulls my attention for a split second—just long enough for Victor to lunge. His hand clamps around my wrist, twisting hard until pain shoots up my arm. The gun jolts in my grip but I manage to hold on as we struggle, locked in a vicious rhythm amid the wreckage of what should have been my wedding.

"Vesper!" Talon's voice cuts through the chaos. He's moving toward me, Alex and Luca close behind, their faces contorted with determination.

"Stay back!" I shout, knowing Victor or my grandfather will not hesitate to kill them.

"You think you're so clever," Victor snarls. His grip tightens around my wrist as he forces my gun hand toward the ceiling. "But you're just another foolish girl who thinks she can change the world."

His other hand shoots toward my throat, fingers closing around the diamond collar he gifted me. The pressure cuts off my air as he uses the necklace like a leash, dragging me closer with vicious intent.

"This is what happens to little girls who bite the hand that feeds them," he hisses, spittle flying from his lips as madness overtakes calculation.

"I'm not a little girl," I rasp, voice strained through Victor's chokehold.

My body shifts—just slightly, just enough. A twist of my hips, a lean into his hold that disguises the motion of my free hand slipping to the torn bodice of my dress. My fingers find the blade Z stashed there when he cut me loose.

In one smooth, desperate motion, I drive the steel between Victor's ribs. It slides in with sickening ease, the resistance barely a breath.

His gasp catches mid-snarl. The pressure on my throat

weakens as a bloom of red spreads like a stain across his immaculate white shirt.

"Impossible," he breathes, eyes wide as he staggers back a step.

"Very possible." I twist the blade. "Bleed for me, Victor. Like all the other women your family destroyed."

The crimson blooms across his chest, staining the silk like a violent flower unfurling. His knees buckle. I catch him as he collapses, lowering him to the marble floor of the chapel.

I kneel beside him. His breaths come in wet, ragged pulls, lungs filling with the price of his legacy. I lean in, my voice a low hiss against the chaos still thundering around us.

"Tell me where my son is," I demand. "Tell me, and I'll protect him from my grandfather with my dying breath."

Victor's focus shifts to me. For a heartbeat, there's something almost human behind it. Blood bubbles at the corner of his mouth as he lifts a trembling hand, his fingers brushing my cheek with a gentleness that feels entirely out of place.

"My hunting lodge."

I press my palm against the wound in his chest, not to save him but to ease his passing. For all his cruelty, for all the lives he's destroyed, in this moment, he's just a dying man trying to save his grandson.

"I'll find him," I promise. "And Mikhail will never touch him."

A ghost of a smile touches Victor's bloodless lips. "You

are...stronger than I...gave you credit for," he manages, each word a struggle.

His hand falls away from my face as the light fades from his eyes. Victor Petrov—the man who built an empire on fear and violence—dies with my name on his lips. With Victor's death, it only leaves my grandfather and me.

I rise from Victor's lifeless body, picking up my discarded gun near his body. My dress and skin painted like a bloody war bride.

"You worthless, manipulative bastard," I snarl, stepping over Victor's corpse toward Mikhail. "You were going to let him kill me."

Mikhail's thin lips curl into what might pass for a smile on another man's face. "But he didn't. And you proved yourself worthy of your bloodline after all."

The gun in my hand feels like an extension of my body as I level it at his chest. "Worthy? You think this was about proving myself to you?"

"Lower the weapon, granddaughter." He speaks as if addressing a petulant child.

I keep my gun trained on Mikhail's chest, my finger steady on the trigger. "I'm done taking orders from you."

"Fine, we'll do this the hard way."

He snaps his fingers, and suddenly his men surge forward. Three of them grab Luca, who thrashes wildly, landing a solid punch before they wrench his arms behind his back. Talon drops two of Mikhail's men with brutal efficiency before someone smashes the butt of a gun against his temple, sending him to his knees. Alex fights like a cornered animal, breaking one man's nose before four others over-whelm him.

"Stop!" I scream as they force my brother and the others to their knees.

Mikhail's expression remains impassive. "Lower your weapon, or I'll give my men the order to kill them all. Starting with your precious brother."

One of his men presses a gun to Luca's temple. My broth-er's eyes meet mine, fierce and unafraid despite the blood trickling down his face.

"Don't you dare give in to him, Vesper," Luca calls out. "He'll kill us anyway."

I think of Z and Oz, bleeding on the chapel floor. Of Victor's final words. Of my son, waiting at a hunting lodge I've never seen.

"Five seconds," Mikhail says coldly. "Four."

"Three..." Mikhail continues, his voice steady as a metronome marking the seconds until my brother's execution.

"Two..."

"One..."

I lower my weapon, a smile spreading across my face as I do. Mikhail's expression shifts, confusion replacing triumph as he registers my unexpected reaction.

"You've come to your senses, child. Good."

"No," I smile. "You misunderstand, Grandfather. I don't need this gun." From the corner of my eye, I see movement above us. "Not when I have them," I say, pointing upward.

Mikhail follows my gesture just as dozens of figures rise

from the chapel's balcony—men and women with weapons trained on his men below. Our reinforcements. Their faces are hard, determined, marked by the same hunger for justice that's driven me.

"What is this?" Mikhail hisses, his composure cracking for the first time.

"Your reckoning, Mikhail," I answer.

The color drains from Mikhail's face as he takes in the armed figures surrounding us from above. Men and women of all ages stand shoulder to shoulder, weapons steady in their hands as they aim at his men below. Some wear the haunted expressions of those who've lost everything. Others burn with the hard, unyielding focus of vengeance long denied.

"Did you really think I'd walk into Victor's stronghold without a plan?" I spit. "While you were scheming to use me as bait, I was building my own army—every family you've destroyed, every mother, father, sister, and brother left grieving because of you."

Mikhail's men shift, the unease rippling through their ranks as they realize they're surrounded—and outnumbered. The guard holding Luca loosens his grip for a split second, just enough for my brother to slam an elbow into his gut and twist free.

Chaos erupts.

Talon surges up, driving his shoulder into the nearest guard and wrenching the weapon from his hands. Alex moves with brutal efficiency, dropping two of Mikhail's men before they can even react.

"This ends now. Put your weapons down or die along with him. Your choice."

To my surprise, Mikhail's men hesitate, looking to their leader for direction. The old man stands alone now, abandoned by his guards as they assess the overwhelming odds against them.

"You ungrateful child," he spits, his face contorting with rage. "After everything I gave you—"

"Everything you gave me?" I interrupt, taking a step closer. "You gave me torture. You gave me captivity. You gave me the fear that my son would grow up without a mother."

My voice rises, echoing through the bullet-riddled chapel. "You turned me into a weapon, yes. But not the one you intended."

Mikhail's pale eyes flick between the armed figures above and the chaos erupting below. For the first time since I've known him, he looks every bit his age—frail, cornered, desperate.

"You've lied to me from the beginning. Used me. Manipulated me. Violated me—for your revenge." My voice shakes, but I don't lower the gun. "I'm done being a fucking pawn on your chessboard."

"Everything I did was for our family," he snaps, the edge in his voice returning. "The Vasilyev name was going to die with me. I needed an heir worthy of our legacy."

Movement behind me pulls my attention. Luca limps toward us, supported by Alex. Blood stains the side of his suit, but there's a fierce determination in his eyes as he fixes our grandfather with a look sharp enough to cut glass.

"I was never supposed to be your heir," I say coldly, keeping the weapon steady. "I was meant to be a vessel. Just like my mother. Just like Luca. Just like every child you've stolen and broken."

Luca's gaze meets mine, and in that instant, the years of silence, pain, and betrayal fall away. Despite the blood and bruises, he straightens his spine and nods—wordless, but solid. We are done being pawns.

Mikhail's face hardens, revealing the monster beneath. "You ungrateful bitch. I gave you purpose when you were nothing but a broken toy. I showed you who you truly are."

"Yes, you did." My finger tightens on the trigger. "And I'm not what you wanted me to be."

A movement to my left distracts me. Z is struggling to sit up, pressing his hand against his bleeding shoulder. Relief floods through me at the sight of him alive, fighting. Oz stirs beside him, his breathing labored but steady. They're hurt, but they're alive.

Mikhail seizes the momentary distraction, his hand darting beneath his jacket. I react instantly, muscle memory taking over as I squeeze the trigger. The bullet hits my grandfather in the stomach. He staggers backward, shock registering on his face as his hands clutch at the wound. Blood seeps between his fingers, staining his immaculate suit.

"You shot me," he gasps, the reality of his situation settling in as he slides down against the pew, leaving a crimson smear in his wake.

"Yes, I did," I reply, watching him with the same cold

detachment he showed me. "How does it feel to be at someone else's mercy?"

I approach him as he slumps against the pew, clutching his stomach.

"You think this is over? My organization will hunt you down. They'll find your son. They'll—"

I watch his own men dropping their weapons. "Your men are abandoning you. Look at this legacy you built. Not even those you've paid to protect you will stand by your side now.

Footsteps sound behind me as Alex, Luca, and Talon move to flank me.

"No, they won't," Luca interrupts. "Your organization is finished."

I feel something cool press into my palm. Talon's fingers brush against mine as he discreetly transfers a syringe filled with clear liquid. I close my hand around it, understanding immediately.

I lower myself to one knee beside my grandfather, feigning concern as I lean closer. My free hand slips beneath the folds of my dress, concealing the syringe from the view of anyone watching.

"Watching you die will never take away the pain from the destruction you've caused, but it will help," I say loud enough for the room to hear, keeping my voice steady while I fix him with a cold, unwavering stare.

"What are you doing?" he sputters, confusion cracking through his composure.

I reach for his hand, as if to offer comfort, and gently turn it over to expose his wrist. "Ensuring justice."

The needle slides into his vein with smooth precision, my thumb pressing the plunger before he can react.

He jerks slightly, eyes going wide as he feels the liquid entering his bloodstream. "What have you—"

"Not poison," I say quietly, almost kindly. "They need you dead, and I need you alive just a little while longer." I lean closer, my lips nearly touching his ear. "All they'll know is that the man responsible for their pain is gone."

For the first time, real fear crosses Mikhail's face. Not fear of death, but of erasure. Of losing the legacy he's sacrificed everything to build. His body begins to slacken, muscles giving in to the sedative. His eyelids droop, panic still flickering in the depths of his dulling gaze.

Within seconds, he goes limp, head lolling to the side, his empire unraveling faster than he can stop it.

"It's done," I announce, rising to my feet. "Mikhail Vasilyev is dead."

A collective exhale ripples through the chapel. The armed figures in the balcony lower their weapons, some crossing themselves in silent prayer, others embracing as decades of fear dissolve in an instant.

I look up at the balcony where dozens of faces stare down at us. These people have lost everything to my grandfather's obsession. Children stolen, bodies violated, futures shattered. They deserve more than just Mikhail's apparent death.

"This isn't over," I call out, "What my grandfather built

still exists. The facilities where he kept your loved ones, the labs where he stole pieces of you, they're still operating."

I step forward, the bloodied wedding dress trailing behind me like a battle flag as I address the assembled families.

"I know what was taken from you. I know because it was taken from me, too." My hand moves instinctively to my abdomen, to the internal scars hidden beneath. "But I swear to you, on everything I hold dear, I will find every single facility. Every lab. Every hidden bunker where The Collector kept his prizes."

A woman's voice calls down from above. "My daughter was taken five years ago. We never found her body."

"I will find her," I promise, holding her tear-filled stare. "If she's alive, I'll bring her home to you. If her genetic material is still stored somewhere, I'll return it to your family. And if she was sold—" my voice hardens, steady with purpose, "I'll hunt down whoever bought her and make them pay."

A murmur ripples through the chapel, low and rising. Grief-stricken families who moments ago clung to despair now sit straighter, eyes fierce. The chapel now thrums with something more powerful than vengeance. Hope. Fueled by rage, yes, but hope all the same.

I move through the wreckage—shattered glass, blood-slick tile, the stench of gunpowder clinging to the air—until I reach him.

Alex.

He's holding Luca upright, one arm braced around him like its instinct. His chest rises and falls in steady, measured breaths, but his eyes...they're darker than I remember. Distant.

He looks up when I stop in front of him. No smile. No relief. Just the quiet intensity that's always surrounded him like a second skin. Only now, it feels heavier. Sharper. Like the edges inside him have finally cut through to the surface.

"You stayed alive," I say softly. My voice cracks before I can stop it. "You kept him safe."

Alex doesn't flinch, doesn't look away. "I did what I had to do."

He transfers Luca into my arms, careful, efficient. But I feel it—something in him falter. Just for a second.

"I brought him back," he says.

But he doesn't finish the thought. He doesn't need to.

*At what cost?* I see the rest of it in his eyes. The ghosts. The shift. Whatever lines he hadn't crossed before, he's crossed them now—and there's no coming back from it. Not for him. Maybe not for any of us.

I study him in the silence that follows. He looks the same. Same scars. Same cold, steady calm. But the man I once knew—the one who watched the world from a distance, always holding something back—is gone.

What's left is something colder. Quieter. And I don't know if he even realizes it yet.

I press a kiss to Luca's temple and look toward the bloodied figure crumpled at the edge of the altar.

"He's ready for you," I say, meaning Mikhail. But I'm not really looking at him. "He's ready for The Butcher."

I'm looking at Alex. At what he's become.

And I wonder if this was always inevitable.

"As far as anyone needs to know, yes."

Luca's fingers tighten on my arm, sudden intensity flashing across his battered face. "I need to know he can't hurt us anymore, Vesper. I need to be sure."

I pull him closer, my lips brushing against his ear. "He'll wish he were dead by the time Alex is finished with him. He will extract every piece of information we need about his organization, every person still in captivity, every family waiting for justice."

A shudder runs through Luca's body, part relief and part horror at what I'm implying. "And then?"

"That's for you to decide," I remark. "You are the head of our family, Luca. It's your call."

Luca's hand tightens around mine. "No, Vesper. It's not my call." He shakes his head, a strange mix of relief and certainty washing over his features. "I was never meant to be the head of this family. You are."

I stare at him. "They'll never accept me. I'm just a woman."

"The woman who orchestrated the downfall of two crime empires in a single day." Luca gestures at the bullet-riddled chapel, at Victor's cooling body, at our sedated grandfather. "The woman who built an army from the broken pieces our grandfather left behind."

My throat tightens as I struggle to find words. "But you—"

"I never wanted this," Luca admits. "I've spent years pretending to be something I'm not. You were born for this,

Vesper. Not me. Our family will be in far better hands with you leading it than me."

I search his face for any sign of doubt, but there's only steadfast certainty in his eyes. Something shifts in his expression, a vulnerability I've rarely seen in my brother.

"There's another reason," he admits quietly, glancing briefly at Alex. "Our world, this life...it's never had room for men like me. The families will accept you with your three men far more readily than they'll ever accept who I truly am."

All these years, the pressure on him to conform, to be the heir our father wanted. The expectation to marry, produce children, and continue the bloodline, while hiding his true self.

"Luca..." I begin, but he shakes his head.

"It's okay, V," he smiles faintly. "You will lead our family into something better than what our father and grandfather built."

I glance at Alex, who's watching Luca with quiet intensity. And suddenly, the truth is undeniable. My brother has spent his entire life fighting wars no one else could see.

"Are you sure?" I ask.

"Never been more certain of anything." He squeezes my hand. "The old guard is dying, Vesper. Let them die with their prejudices."

A sound escapes me—half breath, half disbelief—surprising us both. It's sharp, almost out of place in this blood-soaked chapel, surrounded by bodies and shattered glass. The absurdity of it all settles over me like a punchline delivered too late.

"What?" Luca asks, his brow furrowing.

"Nothing," I murmur, shaking my head and squeezing his hand. "It's just...when I woke up this morning, I didn't expect to become the head of a crime family before lunch."

"You mean, *two*." Luca's lips twitch, and then he's grinning, the expression tugging painfully at his battered features but no less real.

Alex glances between us with something like stunned amusement, clearly wondering if we've lost our minds.

"I think there's two men over there who want to see you," Luca mentions, nodding toward Oz and Zaire.

I support Luca as we make our way toward Z and Oz. My brother leans heavily against me, his breathing labored but determined. Z struggles to his feet as we approach, grimacing through the pain of his shoulder wound. Blood has soaked the entire left side of his tuxedo.

"Took you long enough," he manages, the corner of his mouth lifting in a pained smirk. "I was starting to think you were going to let that old bastard walk out of here."

"Never," I promise, reaching out to touch his face, reassuring myself he's real and alive beneath my fingers. "How bad is it?"

"I've had worse," Z dismisses, though the pallor of his skin tells a different story. He nods toward Oz, who's now sitting up with Talon's help. "He took one to the chest. Vest caught most of it, but he's got at least two broken ribs."

Oz coughs, wincing as he presses a hand to his sternum. "Three, minimum," he corrects, his voice raspy but determined. "Worth it to see Victor's face when you pulled that trigger."

I scan the chapel, taking in the carnage we've created. Bodies litter the once-pristine floor. Blood stains the marble like abstract art, pooling around fallen forms and broken glass. In death, it's impossible to tell which side they belonged to. Blood is just blood, after all.

Talon appears at my side, his jacket torn and bloodied but his movements sure as he helps support Oz. "We need to get out of here," he says, scanning the devastation around us. "Police will be here soon."

"Not in this part of Russia. Victor owns the local authorities. They won't come without his order."

I turn toward Victor's body, sprawled beside his sons on the altar steps. Even in death, he looks imperial. A fallen king surrounded by the ruins of his kingdom. The diamond necklace weighs heavy against my collarbone, I reach up and snap the clasp, letting Victor's diamond collar fall to the floor beside his corpse.

"My son," I remind him. "Victor told me he is at a hunting lodge. Do you know where that is?"

Z pushes himself fully upright, swaying slightly before steadying himself. "I know the place. It's his private retreat."

"Then that's where we're going," I declare.

"You're not going anywhere except a hospital," Luca protests, eyeing the twins' injuries with growing concern. "All of you need medical attention."

"We have a doctor." I shift to look in the direction I had last seen the good doctor, only to find his lifeless body draped across a pew. "Correction, we *had* a doctor."

"We've come too far to stop now," I say, scanning the room for any survivors loyal to Victor. "We'll get another doctor. They can't be that hard to find with the kind of cash Victor probably has in his sock drawer. But first, we find my son."

Z nods, his face set with unwavering determination despite the blood soaking through his sleeve. "The hunting lodge is about two hours north."

"How many men?" Talon asks, already calculating the odds.

"Protecting his only heir? A half a dozen, maybe more," Z replies. "Elite security. They'll die before letting anyone near the boy."

"Then they'll die," I state simply.

Luca studies my face, perhaps seeing something there that concerns him. "Vesper, you're not thinking clearly. Look around you—we're all injured. We need to regroup, come up with a plan."

"I have a plan. Find my son and kill anyone who stands in my way," I counter, checking the ammunition in my gun.

"She's got a point," Oz manages, wincing as the effort sends pain shooting through his ribs. "We didn't come this far to wait."

Alex returns to our group, wiping his hands methodically on a handkerchief. There's blood under his fingernails, but his expression is calm, almost satisfied. "Mikhail has been secured. We can drop him off on our way to get your son. Does the estate have a dungeon?"

Oz and Zaire glance at each other. "Would a holding cell do?"

Alex considers their answer before nodding. "I can make it work."

"What about the mess?"

Alex smiles, opening his mouth. "I have a…"

"The fuck you do," Talon interjects. "We are on the other side of the planet right now, and you are telling us with a straight face that you have someone who can clean up this mess. Dude, I know you're like some technological god, but there is no way."

Alex's smile widens. "You underestimate the reach of proper planning, my friend. I've had assets in place across three continents for years."

"This particular contact is a former Spetsnaz. Very discreet. Very thorough." Alex looks around the chapel. "Good thing he offers bulk discounts."

"Of course he is," Talon mutters, shaking his head in disbelief. "Next, you'll tell me you have a helicopter waiting on the roof."

"Helicopter, no." Alex smiles back at him. "Don't be ridiculous. It's a Learjet at Pulkovo. I can get a helicopter if you'd like, though."

Talon throws his arms up in exasperation. "Why am I even surprised? What else are you hiding? A submarine? A secret moon base?" His voice rises with each suggestion, the stress of the day finally cracking his usually unflappable demeanor.

I can't help the small smile that forms despite everything. There's something oddly comforting about Talon's indignation in the midst of all this blood and chaos.

"I think we should focus on the task at hand," I interject, watching as Z struggles to stay upright. The blood loss is taking its toll, his face growing paler by the minute. "My son is waiting."

Oz clears his throat, wincing as the movement jostles his broken ribs. "The hunting lodge has a panic room," he says, his voice strained but clear. "Victor had it installed after an assassination attempt in the early 2000s. Biometric scanner for access. Victor's handprint or retinal scan is the only way in."

My focus drifts to Victor's corpse. "Then we'll bring Victor with us."

Z lets out a short, harsh sound that might've been a laugh if it hadn't ended in a grimace. "That's my queen. Always thinking."

"We need to be practical," Oz cuts in, voice steady despite the strain. "Everyone's bleeding, we're exhausted, and storming a secure location with half-dead men isn't a strategy—it's suicide."

I turn to argue, but he lifts a hand.

"The mansion is fifteen minutes away. We regroup there. Patch ourselves up, gear up properly, and go in with enough blood in our veins to actually fight."

"He's right," Talon adds. "Victor's estate is fully stocked

—armored vehicles, weapons, medical supplies. Everything we'll need."

My instinct screams at me to run, to tear the world apart until my son is safe. But logic wins out. I glance around—the blood, the bruises, the way Z can barely stay upright. We won't save anyone if we die on the way.

"What about Victor's loyalists?" I ask. "His staff, the guards. We can't show up like this and declare he's dead. The ones protecting my son—those are his elite. They won't just fall in line. If they suspect he's gone, they'll disappear with the kid."

A slow smile creeps across my lips as the pieces click into place.

Z raises a brow. "What are you thinking, *moya koroleva*?"

"Victor's dead. So is Dmitri. By their own rules of succession, everything passes to me—through my son. And until he's of age...I hold the crown."

Talon's brows knit as he works through it. "So what you're saying is—"

"What I'm saying is, we don't go in as rebels." I meet Oscar's eyes, steady and sure. "We walk in as rightful heirs. And we take what belongs to us."

Oscar studies me for a beat, pain and pride written across his face. "You or Z want it?" I ask.

He exhales, sharp and quiet, and shakes his head with a small, pained smirk. "The Petrov empire was never meant for us, solnishko. Z and I spent our lives running from it."

He glances toward his twin, something unspoken passing between them.

"Besides," he adds, voice lower now. "You've earned it more than either of us ever did."

Z nods, his complexion pale with blood loss but his expression sharp. "Uncle will be rolling in his grave knowing a woman, especially you, is taking control. Makes it all the sweeter."

"Then it's settled," I declare, stepping over broken glass toward the chapel doors. "Let's go claim what's ours. It's time I meet my son."

# Chapter 43

## VESPER

THE PALACE STAFF and guards bent the knee far more easily than I could have imagined. Clearly loyalty didn't run as deep with Victor's staff as he imagined. Though the men guarding my son will likely be far more loyal than the servants at the Winter Palace. After a few hours of patching everyone up, we leave for the hunting lodge.

The drive to the northern hunting lodge stretches before us like an eternity compressed into miles. Though the twins insisted on accompanying me despite their injuries, I can see the pain etched into the tight lines around Z's mouth each time we hit a bump in the road. Oz isn't much better, his breathing shallow to avoid aggravating his broken ribs.

As the Russian countryside blurs past the windows, my mind drifts to the child waiting at the end of this journey— my son. The thought still feels surreal, almost dreamlike. What will he look like? Will he have my green eyes, or Dmitri's deep, shadowed orbs staring back at me? Blonde hair like mine, or rich chestnut like his father's?

I press my forehead to the cool glass, watching my breath fog the surface. Will he have Dmitri's jawline? My stubborn chin? I try to picture him, but the image shifts and refuses to settle.

Will I even recognize him as mine when I see him? Or will he be a stranger who shares my blood?

The most terrifying question lurks beneath all the others. Will I be able to love him instantly? He's half Petrov, created from my stolen eggs and the DNA of a family I've just decimated.

"You're thinking too much," Z's voice cuts through my spiraling thoughts.

"Hard not to," I admit, turning away from the passing landscape to face him. "I've dreamt about him, wondering what this moment would feel like. What if bringing him into this world is a mistake?"

"You're scared," he finishes for me. "That's normal, moya koroleva."

I shake my head, forcing back the tears threatening to form. "What if he hates me? What if he's bonded with his caretakers? What if—"

"What if he's perfect?" Z says, his hand finding mine

despite the obvious pain the movement causes him. "What if he has your smile and your spirit? What if this is the beginning of something beautiful instead of the end of something terrible?"

His fingers tighten around mine. The simple contact pulls me back from the edge of panic.

"I don't know how to be a mother," I confess. "I wasn't exactly given the best examples."

Oscar leans forward from the seat behind us, his face appearing between the headrests. "You don't have to know everything right away, solnishko. No one does."

"He's right," Talon adds from the driver's seat. "Kids don't come with instruction manuals. We'll figure it out together. Unlike most kids, this one has an incredible mother, and three men who will love and protect him like he's our own."

"They're not wrong," Luca chimes from the third row next to Alex. "He has a hell of a lot better chance than we did, Ves."

I appreciate their attempts at comfort, but the fear gnaws more than they understand.

"We're almost there," Talon announces, slowing the vehicle as we turn onto a narrow road flanked by towering pines. "Ten minutes out."

The forest grows denser around us, ancient trees swallowing the last traces of daylight. Snow begins to fall in gentle flurries, dusting the landscape in a deceptive blanket of innocence. In the distance, I catch glimpses of a structure through the trees—sharp angles and chimney stacks rising above the canopy. The hunting lodge looms ahead, a sprawling construct of timber and weathered masonry, as if it had grown from the forest itself.

Talon pulls off a couple of hundred feet from the lodge in a dense tree line. We funnel out, some easier than others, and stand behind the SUV while he surveys the lodge ahead. Alex deploys a drone that he confiscated from The Winter Palace.

"Security patrol, two o'clock," Talon points out beside me, his breath forming small clouds in the frigid air.

"How many?" My fingers tighten around the grip of my gun.

"I count eight external," Z responds, his voice tight with pain despite the field dressing on his shoulder. He refused to stay behind, insisting that a "scratch" wouldn't keep him from finishing what we started. The stubborn fool. "Four on rotation, four at fixed positions."

"And inside?"

"Based on the thermal imaging, at least four more," Alex replies. "Clustered near the east wing. That's likely where they're keeping him."

My heart pounds against my ribs at the thought of my son, a child I've never met, just yards away behind those walls.

"Is it just me, or does that seem like overkill for an infant?" Luca remarks. "He's a few months old. It's not like he can crawl away."

"Two words: Victor's heir. Paranoid bastard, remember?" Z snaps back at my brother.

"I'm just saying that it's over the top. Our parents gave us one guard and a nanny. Not an entire army to guard us."

"Victor wasn't guarding a baby," Alex interjects. "He was guarding the future of his bloodline. Plus, he was a psychopath. It tracks."

I swallow hard, the reality of my son's existence still surreal despite everything we've sacrificed to get here. A child conceived in captivity, born to a woman who wasn't his mother, raised by people who stole him before I ever held him. After today, my son will only know me as his mother and the love of the men around me. God, I hope that's enough.

"We need to move," I say, pushing aside the emotion threatening to overwhelm me.

I pull Victor's severed hand from the insulated bag at my side, grimacing at the cold, waxy texture of his skin. The ultimate key card.

"Remember," Oscar warns, "we go in quiet. No gunfire unless absolutely necessary. We don't know where exactly the child is, and I won't risk a stray bullet."

Z checks his pistol, his movements slightly hampered by his injured shoulder. "Four teams. Talon and I take the perimeter guards on the east and north. Alex and Luca handle the west and south. Oz and Vesper move directly to the east wing once we clear a path."

I nod, the plan we formulated during the drive north solidifying as the moment approaches. My body thrums with a strange combination of exhaustion and hyper awareness.

"The moment we're spotted, they'll move him to the panic room," Alex reminds us, checking his own weapon. "So stealth is paramount until we secure the child."

"We'll need exactly seven minutes to neutralize the external security," Talon adds. "You two wait for our signal before approaching the east entrance."

I feel Oscar's hand squeeze mine briefly, a gesture so gentle it nearly shatters the composure I've been desperately maintaining.

"We'll get him, solnishko. Today your son comes home."

Z clears his throat, drawing our attention back to the task at hand. "Comms check," he says, tapping the earpiece nestled against his skull. One by one, we confirm our connections.

"Alpha team moving," Talon relays, his voice clear in my earpiece as he and Z slip away. The snow muffles their footsteps as they disappear among the trees, heading toward the eastern perimeter.

I watch them go, a knot of anxiety tightening in my stomach. Z's injury makes him vulnerable, but I know better than to voice my concern. He'd sooner cut off his other arm than stay behind while we retrieve my son.

"Beta team following," Alex confirms, nodding once to Luca before they, too, vanish into the twilight. My brother moves with newfound purpose, his steps lighter since our escape from the chapel. Freedom looks good on him, even as he heads into danger.

Oscar and I remain crouched in the tree line, watching as our teams position themselves around the lodge. The wind picks up, sending icy fingers through my hair and numbing my cheeks. I should feel the cold more keenly, but all I register is Victor's severed hand in my bag and the rhythmic pounding of my heart.

"Your grandfather was a monster. But he was right about one thing."

I turn to him, eyebrow raised in question.

"You are remarkable," he continues. "You've taken over your family, toppled the largest crime family in the world, and now, you're getting your son back."

"Thank the men who believed in me enough to help," I retort, touched by his words despite the gravity of our situation. "You all sacrificed everything."

Oscar's lips curve into a pained smile. "Not everything. Not yet."

A crackle in our earpieces interrupts the moment. "Alpha team in position," Talon's voice comes through, steady and professional. "First guard neutralized. Moving to the second target."

"Beta team approaching south fence," Alex confirms seconds later. "No complications."

I check my watch, counting down the minutes until we can move. The waiting is excruciating. My fingers brush against the outline of my weapon.

"What will you name him?" Oscar asks suddenly, his question catching me off guard.

I blink, realizing that I've never allowed myself to think

that far ahead. Names meant attachment, and attachment meant vulnerability, which I couldn't afford until now.

"I don't know," I admit, watching my breath form crystalline clouds in the frigid air. "I've been so focused on finding him that I never thought about it."

"You'll know when you see him," Oscar says softly. "The right name will come to you."

A soft crackle in our earpieces interrupts the moment. "Perimeter secured," Z's voice comes through. "East entrance clear. You're good to move."

I exchange a glance with Oscar, both of us immediately shifting into action mode. We rise from our crouched positions, keeping low as we move across the snow-covered clearing toward the lodge. My heart thunders in my chest, each step bringing me closer to the child I've fought so desperately to reach.

"Stay behind me," Oscar orders as we approach the east entrance—a service door partially concealed by ornamental shrubbery. Despite his injuries, he positions himself protectively in front of me.

The door is secured with both a keypad and a biometric scanner. I remove Victor's hand from the insulated bag, suppressing a shudder as I press the cold, stiff fingers against the glowing panel. For a heart-stopping moment, nothing happens. Then a soft beep and the lock disengages with a mechanical click.

"We're in," I relay into my comm as Oscar eases the door open, weapon raised.

The interior of the lodge is warm after the biting cold

outside, the air heavy with the scent of pine and wood smoke. We move silently through a utility corridor, passing a laundry room and storage closets.

"Thermal readings show two heat signatures in the room at the end of this hall. One adult-sized, one small."

My son. My breath catches in my throat.

"And the other guards?"

"Moving toward the west wing. Looks like Alex and Luca's distraction is working."

We advance down the corridor, our footsteps silent on the plush carpet.

A soft cry pierces the silence—high-pitched, unmistakably infantile. The sound stops me in my tracks, a physical force slamming into my chest. My son's voice. The first time I've ever heard it.

Oscar's hand closes around my arm, steadying me as emotion threatens to overwhelm my focus. "Steady. We're almost there."

We reach the end of the hallway where a wooden door stands between us and my child. I press my ear against it, listening. The infant's cries have quieted to soft whimpers, followed by gentle shushing sounds. A woman's voice.

"A nanny," Oscar breathes.

"Or a guard. We need to be sure."

Oscar nods, positioning himself to the side of the door. I take a deep breath, forcing my racing heart to slow as I grasp the handle. With one fluid motion, I push the door open, weapon raised.

The room beyond is a nursery straight from a fairy tale.

Soft golden light spills from a crystal chandelier, illuminating hand-painted murals of Russian forests and mythical creatures. A massive crib carved from wood dominates the center, draped with silken canopies.

Beside it stands a woman in her sixties, silver-streaked hair pulled into a severe bun. She wears a simple black dress with a white apron, her weathered hands frozen in the act of tucking a blanket around the crib's occupant. Her eyes widen with alarm as she takes in my weapon, my blood-splattered tactical gear.

"Step away from the crib," I order in broken Russian.

The woman's expression hardens, her body instinctively shifting to shield the crib.

"Who are you?" she demands, voice steady, showing no fear despite the gun aimed at her chest. "Where are the guards?"

"They're indisposed," Oscar answers as he steps in behind me. "Move away from the child. Now."

Something flickers across the woman's face as she studies me—something sharp, assessing. Recognition settles in, followed closely by a quiet resignation.

"You're her," she says softly. "The mother."

My finger twitches slightly on the trigger. "Step away from my son."

She hesitates, glancing between Oscar and me before settling on my face again. "He looks like you," she murmurs, more to herself than to us. "I always wondered why the child's eyes were green when neither of his parents had them."

"Last warning," Oscar says, as he moves closer, weapon trained on the woman's chest.

With a resigned sigh, she takes two steps back from the crib. "I am not armed," she says. "I am only Irina, the nurse."

I keep my gun trained on her as I edge toward the crib, my heart threatening to burst from my chest. The soft whimpering grows louder as I approach, and for the first time, I catch a glimpse of my son.

Time stops.

He's perfect. Impossibly small yet somehow exactly as I'd imagined in my dreams. A dusting of dark hair crowns his head, his tiny fists waving in frustration at being disturbed. But it's his eyes that steal my breath—vibrant green, identical to mine, blinking up at me with innocent curiosity.

"Hello, little one," I coo, my voice cracking as I holster my weapon. "I've been looking for you for a very long time."

The baby stills at the sound of my voice, his tiny features scrunching in concentration. For a heartbeat, we simply stare at each other. His little mouth opens in an 'o' of surprise.

"He knows you," Irina declares from behind me.

My arms hover above the crib, suddenly unsure. I've killed without blinking, toppled empires with a word—but this? Reaching for something so small, so breakable, terrifies me more than anything I've ever faced.

"It's okay," Oscar says softly behind me. "He's waiting for you."

I inhale, then slide my arms beneath the tiny bundle. He weighs almost nothing, but the moment he rests against my chest, I feel the world shift. No battlefield ever made me feel this exposed. I cradle his head instinctively, surprised by how natural it feels…and how fiercely I already want to protect him.

The scent of him fills my senses, powder and innocence and something uniquely his own. His warmth seeps through my tactical gear, melting the last frozen fragments of my heart as I draw him closer.

"I've got you now," I sob against his downy hair. "No one will ever take you from me again."

His tiny hand escapes the blanket, five perfect fingers splaying before curling around my index finger with surprising strength. The connection is electric. physical manifestation of the bond that's drawn me across continents and through blood to find him.

"Remarkable grip." Oscar steps closer to peer down at the infant's face. His expression softens as he takes in the delicate features. "Strong like his mother."

I can't look away from my son's face. There's a depth in his expression, an intensity in his small features that feels far too knowing for someone so young.

"We need to move. The others can only hold position for so long."

I nod, reluctantly dragging my attention back to Irina, who watches us with a calm, unreadable expression.

"What is his name?" I ask. "What have they been calling him?"

Her lips press into a thin line. "Nikolai Dmitrievich Petrov. After Victor's father."

The name hits like a blow. The Petrov legacy, forced onto him before he ever had a voice. I shake my head, rejection immediate and final.

"That's not his name."

"What will you call him then?" Oscar asks, eyes fixed on the doorway, his posture alert.

I turn back to my son, memorizing every detail. A name rises, quiet but certain, as if it's been waiting all along.

"Matteo," I declare.

The baby blinks up at me, as if considering the sound of his true name. His fingers tighten around mine in what I choose to interpret as approval.

"Matteo," Oscar repeats, a smile warming his voice. "It suits him."

I turn to Irina, who stands watching us with that same unreadable expression. "Is there anything he needs? Formula? Supplies?"

Something softens in her weathered face. "There is a bag by the changing table. Everything is prepared. I...I always knew this day would come."

Oscar moves swiftly to retrieve the bag, checking its contents with efficient movements. "Looks complete. Formula, diapers, extra clothes."

"You prepared for this?" I ask Irina, studying her more carefully now.

"A mother's love is not something to be trifled with. Even Victor's power has limits. I have cared for him since birth. He is a good baby. Strong. Rarely cries unless he wants attention."

The sound of distant gunfire filters through the thick walls. My arms tighten instinctively around Matteo, who whimpers at the sudden pressure.

"What will you do with me?" Irina asks, her chin lifting slightly.

I study the older woman's face, searching for signs of deception or threat. Instead, I find only a weary resignation and something that might be relief.

"Did you care for him?" I ask her. "Truly care for him?"

Irina straightens her spine, dignity radiating from her despite her circumstances. "I have cared for him since the moment he arrived. Every feeding, every bath, every cry in the night—it was me who comforted him."

There's no boast in her words, only simple truth. My arms tighten protectively around Matteo, but I recognize the genuine concern when she looks at him.

"Let her go. Thank you for loving my son and protecting him until I found him."

"You would release me? Just like that?"

"You kept him safe," I reply. "That's worth something to me."

Oscar's head tilts slightly as he listens to his earpiece. "We need to move. Now. Security protocols have been triggered in the west wing."

"Go," Irina urges, suddenly animated. "Take the service corridor behind the kitchen. It leads to a garage with snowmobiles. The keys are in a box by the door."

I hesitate, studying her face. "Why help us?"

A ghost of a smile touches her weathered lips. "I have

raised many children for powerful men. None of them ever came looking for their babies themselves. This one deserves a mother who would burn the world to find him."

Matteo stirs against my chest, his tiny face scrunching with displeasure at the noise.

"Oscar, lead the way," I command, adjusting my hold on Matteo to keep one hand free for my weapon if needed. "Irina, thank you."

The older woman nods once, dignity in every line of her body. "Be good to him. He likes to be sung to when he cannot sleep."

My throat tightens with unexpected emotion. "I'll remember that."

"Here," she says as she grabs a thick blanket from the edge of his crib. "This will keep him warm."

I take the blanket, wrapping it around Matteo's tiny body before tucking him securely against my chest. "Thank you," I say again.

She nods, her weathered face softening as she looks at Matteo. "Go. Be the mother he deserves."

Oscar moves to the door, checking the corridor before motioning me forward. I follow close behind him, one hand supporting Matteo's head while the other hovers near my weapon. The service corridor is dimly lit, our footsteps muffled by thin carpeting as we navigate through the lodge's back passages.

"We have him. We're coming out now."

Matteo whimpers against my chest, his tiny body tensing at the sounds of conflict echoing through the lodge. I whisper soft reassurances as we move swiftly through the service corridor.

"Shhh, little one," I soothe. "I've got you now."

The kitchen appears ahead, industrial-sized and gleaming with stainless steel. Oscar pauses at the threshold, scanning for threats before motioning me forward. We slip through the space like ghosts, past hanging copper pots and marble countertops still bearing evidence of the evening meal's preparation.

"Garage access should be through here." Oscar pushes open a heavy door that reveals a short staircase leading down.

The temperature drops as we descend, concrete replacing wood beneath our feet. Three snowmobiles stand ready near a large rolling door, their sleek bodies promising swift escape across the frozen landscape.

"Keys," Oscar reminds me, nodding toward a metal box mounted on the wall.

I shift Matteo carefully, reaching for the box while keeping him secured against me. Inside, neatly labeled keys hang in orderly rows. I grab the set marked "Arctic Cat," tossing them to Oscar as a door slams somewhere above us.

"Hurry," I urge, following him to the nearest snowmobile.

Oscar mounts the machine despite his injuries, inserting the key and bringing the engine to life with a throaty rumble. Matteo startles at the sound, his tiny face scrunching in preparation for a wail.

"I know, sweet boy," I soothe, pressing his head gently

against my chest where he can feel my heartbeat. "It's loud, but it's taking us home."

The garage door begins to rise automatically as Oscar revs the engine. Cold air rushes in, carrying snowflakes that dance in the fluorescent light. I climb behind Oscar, one arm locked securely around Matteo while the other grips Oscar's waist.

"Hold tight," he calls over his shoulder, and then we're moving, shooting out into the night like a bullet from a chamber.

The wind tears at my face as we accelerate across the snow-covered clearing, Matteo tucked securely inside my jacket. Behind us, shouts echo from the lodge. Snow sprays from beneath our treads as Oscar pushes the machine to its limits, weaving between trees with reckless precision.

"Z, we're clear," I shout into my comm over the roar of the engine. "Southeast exit. Where are you?"

"Two clicks east of your position," Z's strained voice crackles through the comm. "Heading toward extraction point alpha."

The night air slices against my face as Oscar maneuvers the snowmobile through the dense forest. Matteo remains miraculously quiet against my chest, as if he understands the gravity of our escape. I press my lips to his forehead, tasting the sweetness of his skin beneath the wool cap Irina had tucked over his head.

"Luca and Alex?" I demand, squinting against the icy wind as we crest a small rise.

"Already at the rendezvous point. They torched the SUV.

It should draw their attention away from us long enough to get out." Talon's steady voice confirms.

Relief floods through me, but I don't allow myself to relax. Not yet. Not until we're all safely away from this place.

The snowmobile's headlight cuts through the night, illuminating our path through the pristine snow. Trees flash past in a blur, branches occasionally whipping close enough to sting. Oscar's body tenses beneath my grip as he navigates a particularly steep descent.

"How's the little prince?" he calls over his shoulder.

"Fast asleep against me," I breathe, wonder threading through my voice despite the chaos around us.

"Almost there," Oscar shouts over the engine's roar. The extraction point, a flat stretch of land just large enough for a helicopter landing, lies ahead, illuminated by portable lights.

My heart leaps at the sight of our team assembled and waiting. Luca stands beside Alex, a smile breaking across his face the moment he spots us. Talon kneels in the snow, checking his weapon while keeping a sharp eye on the perimeter. And there, leaning against a tree, shoulder freshly bandaged, is Z, his attention fixed on us.

The snowmobile slows and stops beside the idling helicopter, its rotors turning in slow, lazy circles, ready to roar to life at a moment's notice. The pilot, one of my grandfather's men who pledged loyalty to me after Victor's death, nods once from behind the glass.

"You got him," Luca breathes as I dismount, one arm still wrapped protectively around Matteo. He steps forward, voice trembling as he gently peels back the blanket to see the tiny face tucked inside. His breath catches. "He looks just like you."

"Ready to meet your family?" I murmur to Matteo, shifting him carefully so Luca can get a better look. My son blinks up at his uncle, wide-eyed and curious, not afraid, only watching, taking everything in

# Chapter 44

VESPER

I HUM SOFTLY as I pace the moonlit corridor, Matteo's tiny body warm against my chest, his wispy hair tickling my chin. The Winter Palace feels different tonight—less like a prison and more like a sanctuary, though I know better than to trust such feelings.

"Is he finally asleep?" Alex's voice, quiet but unmistakable, comes from behind me.

I turn, careful not to disturb Matteo. Alex stands at the end of the hallway. The moonlight streaming through the tall windows turns his platinum hair almost ethereal, like fresh snow under starlight.

"Just now." I continue my slow pacing. "He fought it for two hours."

Alex moves closer, his footsteps silent despite his size. Nothing about Alexander Rafner is accidental. "He has your stubbornness." Alex stops beside me, looking down at Matteo's sleeping face. There's something in his expression, something gentle that few people would believe possible from the son of the Butcher of Selfoss.

Becoming an instant mother hadn't come with an instruction booklet. Every day was a scramble of figuring out how to soothe, how to feed, how to keep Matteo calm. Some moments I felt like I was barely holding it together. But Talon...Talon seemed to have a gift. Somehow, he could lull Matteo to sleep with ease, like it was the simplest thing in the world. Oz and Zaire on the other hand...are a work in progress.

"I prefer to call it determination." I sway gently to maintain the rhythm that's finally lulled Matteo to sleep.

Alex's lips twitch, almost forming a smile. "Determination, then."

His large hand hovers near Matteo's head, hesitant, as if seeking permission. The juxtaposition is jarring. These same hands that I've seen rip flesh apart without flinching now ghost over my son's head with the delicacy of butterfly wings.

"You're good with him," I observe quietly.

Alex's icy blue eyes meet mine, something vulnerable flickering in their depths before disappearing behind his usual guarded expression. "Children deserve gentleness."

"Would you like to hold him?"

Alex stiffens. "I don't think—"

"He won't break," I assure him, already shifting Matteo carefully toward his chest. "And neither will you."

For a moment, I think he might refuse, but then his arms, capable of such violence, form a cradle. I transfer Matteo's sleeping form into them, our bodies momentarily close as we make the exchange. Matteo settles against him, tiny fingers curling reflexively against the soft fabric of his shirt.

"Support his head." I guide Alex's large hand into position with a light touch.

Alex stands still, as if afraid the slightest movement might shatter this moment, or worse, harm the precious bundle in his arms. But Matteo only sighs in his sleep, nestling closer to the warmth of Alex's chest.

"He trusts you."

"He shouldn't," Alex responds, "No one should."

I study his face—the sharp angles softened by the silvery light, the weariness settled in the tension around his mouth. "Trust isn't rational, Alex. It's instinctive." I pause, weighing my next words. "Matteo feels safe with you. Children sense things adults have forgotten how to recognize."

Alex's focus stays on Matteo, but there's a subtle shift in his features, something almost imperceptible loosening.

"Or he simply doesn't know better yet," he says, though the bite in his voice is absent.

I watch as he begins to sway gently, falling into the rhythm I'd used earlier. It's effortless, instinctual—the kind of motion that transcends logic, the one even the most broken seem to understand. Even the son of a monster.

"How's Luca?" I ask, leaning against the window frame. "Really."

Alex finally looks at me, his motion steady, Matteo nestled securely in his arms. A shadow flickers across his face, one I know too well.

"He has nightmares," he says after a pause. "Wakes up screaming. Thinks he's back in the facility. That they are..." His words catch, and he swallows them down.

It slices through me like glass. I'd seen the signs. exhaustion clinging to him, the way he tenses at sharp sounds, but hearing it out loud makes my chest ache. He's closed himself off, locked that trauma behind walls so thick not even I can reach him. And I should be able to. I survived the same hell. I'm one of the few who understands. But he's buried it deep, sealed it tight.

"He tries to hide it from you," Alex continues, shifting Matteo slightly as the baby stirs. "Doesn't want to worry you when you have enough to handle."

"And you know this because...?" I let the question hang between us.

"My room is next to his. I hear him through the walls."

"And you go to him," I realize, the pieces fitting together. The way Luca seems calmer around Alex, the subtle looks they exchange when they think no one is watching. They'd only been free a few days, but I noticed it right away."

"Sometimes," Alex admits. "When it's bad enough."

I remember the first time he touched me, how his massive hands hovered above my skin as if I were made of spun glass. Even now, with all we've been through, there's always that moment of hesitation in his movements around me.

"You've always been so careful with me. From the beginning. Like you might accidentally crush me if you weren't vigilant."

His throat works as he swallows. "I could."

"But you didn't," I counter softly. "That's the difference between you and the monsters who raised us."

Matteo stirs between us, tiny fists stretching before settling again. The moment hangs suspended, fragile and charged with possibility.

"I should take him back to his crib." Though I make no move to reclaim my son from Alex's arms.

"Not yet. Let me hold him a little longer."

I nod, my throat tight with unexpected emotion.

We stand together in the moonlight, three broken people forming something that feels close to whole. Alex's free hand rises slowly, hesitating before gently brushing a strand of hair from my face. His touch is feather-light, reverent.

"You've changed everything," he confesses. "For all of us."

I lean into his touch, allowing myself this moment of vulnerability. "We've changed each other."

His fingers linger at my temple, tracing a delicate path down my cheek. The gentleness in his touch belies the strength I know lies beneath. There's something different about Alex, a quieter intensity compared to Z's volatility or Oscar's calculated passion. Where they burn hot, Alex runs deep, like ice that can still sear the skin.

"The others," he begins, "they fit naturally into your world. I'm still..."

"An outsider?" I finish for him. "You're not. As much as we've tried, Alex, I've realized something over the last few days. Things work out for a reason. We didn't, and that's okay, because I'm not that person for you. But, I think we both know who is that person."

Alex's breath catches. "I don't know what you mean."

"I think you do." I keep my voice gentle, watching his reaction carefully. "The way you look at him when you think no one's watching. How you're always the first one there when the nightmares come..."

His jaw tightens, the muscles working beneath his skin. "He needs protection. After what he's been through."

"We've all been through hell, Alex." I reach up, my hand settling against his cheek, forcing him to meet my eyes. "But the way you are with Luca...it's different."

Silence stretches between us, fragile and charged. Matteo sighs in his sleep, oblivious to the tension surrounding him.

"He's going to need you when the time comes." I watch Alex closely, noting the way his jaw tightens.

"When the time comes for what?"

"When we go back to Boston."

I notice his fingers tighten gently around Matteo. "Aren't we all going back together?"

"I've asked Luca to run Russia as my proxy until Matteo comes of age. I can't be in two places at once, and I know my brother will keep Matteo's legacy safe until he's ready. I think you should stay here with him."

His fingers twitch at Matteo's blanket, betraying the conflict inside him. For a moment, I worry I've crossed a line, pushed too far into something neither of us is ready to admit.

"You've thought this through."

"I've had nothing but time to think with this little one keeping me up at night." I watch Alex settle Matteo more securely in his arms. "The truth is that the Petrov empire won't run itself, and someone needs to stay behind to make sure the transition goes smoothly. Someone I trust completely."

"And you trust Luca with this?"

"I trust both of you with this," I correct him. "Luca understands the business side, the politics of it all. But he needs…" I hesitate, searching for the right words. "He needs someone who understands what he's been through."

"Like you have with Zaire and Oscar," Alex observes quietly.

I nod, surprised by his perception. "They balance each other. Balance me."

"And Talon?"

"Talon is…Talon is my constant. My shield when I need protection, my sword when I need strength. He is the voice of reason."

Alex nods, a flicker of understanding passing across his features. "The four of you, then. A family."

"Yes." The word feels both simple and profound on my

lips. "But that doesn't mean you and Luca aren't part of it too. Family isn't just blood or proximity, Alex. It's a choice. We've all chosen each other in different ways."

Matteo stirs in Alex's arms, his tiny face scrunching before relaxing again. Alex adjusts his hold with surprising expertise, tucking the blanket more securely around my son.

"Are you sure this is what he wants? He's been away from you for years, Vesper. Family is what he needs right now."

"He's already agreed. I asked him yesterday. He said he would do it for me, for Matteo. For our family's legacy. But, I think, a part of him knows going back to Boston, to our family home, will not be easy."

"He didn't mention it."

"Perhaps he was waiting for the right moment." I rest my hand on Alex's forearm. "Or perhaps he was waiting to see if you would stay with him."

A muscle works in Alex's jaw as he processes my words.

"I will always love you, Alex, but you deserve to find what you're looking for, too."

"What if I don't know what I'm looking for?"

"I think you do." I reach out, my fingers brushing his arm. "Sometimes we find things we never knew we needed until they're right in front of us."

Alex shifts Matteo in his arms, the movement so natural it seems he's been holding babies his entire life rather than mere minutes. "Your brother deserves better than me to protect him, Vesper."

"My brother deserves someone who understands him. Someone who doesn't flinch from the darkness because they've walked through it themselves. Someone who comes when the nightmares are at their worst. Someone who can build him up again when he finally shatters."

Emotion flickers across Alex's face—doubt, longing, fear.

"What if I'm too broken to be anything but a shadow at his side?"

"We're all broken, Alex. That's how the light gets in." I smile softly.

Matteo stirs against Alex's chest, his peaceful expression crumpling as his mouth forms a 'o' of displeasure. A soft whimper escapes his lips, quickly building toward something more insistent.

"I think our moment of peace is over," I reach for my son as his whimpers turn to tiny protests. Alex transfers him to my arms with that same careful precision.

Matteo's cries grow more determined as I settle him against me, his little face flushing with the effort of making his needs known. "I think someone might be hungry." I adjust him against my shoulder and pat his back soothingly. I turn toward the nursery, but pause, looking back at Alex, who stands illuminated in the moonlight, suddenly looking uncertain without Matteo in his arms.

"Alex, thank you. For everything."

He nods, that almost-smile touching his lips again.

I hesitate, watching him for a moment longer. "Will you think about what I said? About staying with Luca?"

Alex's expression grows distant, thoughtful. "I will."

"Good," I reply, meaning it. "Because he needs you. More than either of you realize."

# Epilogue

## LUCA - THREE MONTHS LATER

**THE DEAD DON'T SCREAM,** but I do.

I wake up with the taste of blood in my mouth, my own this time from biting my tongue. The sheets are drenched, clinging to my skin like a shroud as I gasp for air that won't come. The faces from my nightmare—Mario, my father, the nameless women in the facility—they're still there, burned onto the backs of my eyelids.

I'm drowning in sweat and terror when I hear the soft click of my bedroom door. My hand instinctively reaches for the knife I keep under my pillow.

Alex's massive frame fills the doorway. He doesn't turn on the light or speak immediately. Instead, he waits, giving me time to recognize him, to remember where I am. Who I am.

I force myself to breathe, counting silently to ten like Vesper taught me. In through the nose, out through the mouth. My heart still pounds against my ribs like it's trying to escape.

"Same dream?" he asks, stepping into the room.

I nod, not trusting my voice to form words yet. The sheets are still tangled around my legs, clinging like a damp weight I need to shed.

"You bit your tongue," Alex observes, his accent thicker in the dim light. He moves to the bathroom without turning on the lights, returning with a damp cloth that he offers without comment.

I take it, pressing the cool fabric against my mouth, tasting copper and shame. The nightmares are getting worse, not better. It's been months since we escaped, since Vesper reclaimed her son and brought down two empires in the process. I should be healing. Instead, I'm fracturing further with each passing night.

"Come with me."

I nod, grateful for the distraction. Anything to escape this room with its phantom screams and memories. I swing my legs over the side of the bed, the wood floor cool against my bare feet. Alex turns his back, giving me privacy as I pull on a t-shirt and sweatpants. My fingers tremble slightly as I tie the drawstring.

We move silently through the shadowed corridors of the mansion. Alex walks slightly ahead, his massive frame somehow managing to avoid every creaking floorboard. I follow in his footsteps, trusting his path through the quiet house. Even the night guards keep their distance when Alex moves through the halls.

Instead of heading to the kitchen where we usually sit after my nightmares, Alex leads me down a staircase I've never descended before. I hesitate at the top, my instincts flaring with warning.

"Alex, where are we going?"

He pauses, turning to face me. In the dim emergency lighting, his eyes look almost colorless. "There's something you need to see. Something I've been saving for you."

My stomach tightens with apprehension, but I follow him down the concrete steps. The temperature drops with each step, the air growing cooler and slightly antiseptic. This isn't part of the main house, —it's something else entirely.

At the bottom of the stairs, he places his palm against what looks like a plain section of wall. A hidden scanner glows green beneath his hand, and a door slides open with a pneumatic hiss.

"What is this place?"

"A medical facility. State of the art."

We step into a sterile corridor, bright LED lights flickering on automatically as we move forward. The walls are pristine, the floor polished concrete. It reminds me of the facility where Mario kept me, and my heart rate spikes again.

"Alex, I don't like this." My voice sounds small, childlike, and fearful.

"I know." His massive hand closes gently around my

wrist, his thumb finding my pulse point. "Trust me, Luca. Please."

His touch steadies the panic that threatens to consume me. I force myself to breathe as he guides me forward, past several closed doors with electronic locks, until we reach the end of the corridor. The final door is different, heavier, reinforced with what looks like blast-proof steel.

"Before we go in," Alex says, turning to face me fully, "you need to understand something. What's behind this door is my gift to you. For everything they took from you. For everything they did."

"What have you done, Alex?"

Instead of answering, he places his palm against another scanner. The heavy door unlocks with a series of clicks before sliding open.

The smell hits me first, sharp antiseptic layered with rotting flesh. My stomach clenches as Alex leads me inside.

The room is divided by a glass partition. On our side, medical monitors display vital signs—heart rate, blood pressure, and oxygen levels. On the other side...

My grandfather.

Mikhail is strapped to a hospital bed, tubes and wires threading through his frail body, tethering him to machines that keep him hovering just above death. The man who once loomed like a shadow over my entire life is barely a shell now. Sagging over sharp bones, his presence reduced to something sickly and fragile. His eyes are open, staring blankly at the ceiling with chilling awareness.

"He's been waiting for you," Alex says, his voice low and

steady in the sterile quiet. "For three months, I've kept him alive. For you."

I step closer to the glass, unable to look away from the wreckage of the man who orchestrated my torment. Mikhail's head turns at the sound, slow and deliberate. His stare locks onto mine with unsettling clarity. Recognition flits across his sunken features, chased quickly by something that might actually be fear.

"Can he hear us?"

"Yes." Alex moves to a control panel, pressing a button that casts sterile light across the observation room. "He can hear everything. Feel everything."

A tremor runs through me as I press my palm to the cold surface of the glass. Mikhail's eyes track the movement, his cracked lips parting in a soundless effort to speak. His throat moves, but nothing escapes.

"I've been careful," Alex says, stepping in close enough that his presence warms my back. "Keeping him suspended right at the edge. The damage from your bullet...he would've bled out in minutes without intervention. I didn't let that happen. I made sure he stayed."

"Why?" The question tears from me, raw and aching.

"Because some debts can't be settled with a clean death," Alex replies. His reflection in the glass is unreadable, but there's something alive and burning just beneath the surface. "He needed to suffer. The way he made you suffer. The way he made all of us suffer."

I stare at the broken figure behind the glass, searching for the monster of my nightmares in this frail shell of a man. My fingers press harder against the partition, leaving smudges on the pristine surface.

"What have you done to him?"

"Everything he deserves," Alex replies, his accent thickening with emotion. "And nothing that would release him too quickly."

He guides me to a small control panel embedded in the wall. My heart pounds against my ribs as Alex's fingers hover over the panel. "You can speak to him. Or you can administer various...treatments. The choice is yours, Luca. Always yours."

The power of this moment overwhelms me. The frail, withered creature who once controlled every aspect of my existence, now completely at my mercy. A man who trafficked in children, who authorized my torture, who manipulated my sister into becoming a weapon.

"I want to go inside," I hear myself say.

Alex studies my face carefully. "Are you certain?"

I nod, unable to articulate the storm of emotions churning inside me. Alex presses a sequence of buttons, and a section of the glass wall slides open. My stomach churns, but I force myself forward, step by deliberate step, until I'm standing beside the hospital bed.

Up close, Mikhail is even more grotesque. His skin has a waxy translucence that reveals the blue-green tracery of veins beneath. The bullet wound in his abdomen has been surgically maintained, kept open but prevented from healing completely, the edges red and angry against his yellowed skin. IV lines snake into his arms, delivering just enough fluids and nutrients to keep him alive.

"Hello, Grandfather," I say, surprised by the steadiness in my voice.

A trembling hand lifts slightly against its restraint, fingers curling as if trying to reach for me. I step back instinctively, the movement automatic after years of conditioning.

"He can't hurt you anymore," Alex reminds me, his massive frame positioned protectively at my back. "He can't hurt anyone."

I lean closer, studying the face that has haunted my nightmares. "Do you recognize me? The grandson you threw away? The one you called weak?"

Mikhail's lips move, forming words without sound. I can read them anyway: "Luca."

"Yes," I confirm, a strange calm settling over me. "I'm still here. I survived everything you did to me."

His throat works, struggling to produce sound. After several attempts, a raspy sound escapes, "Should...have killed...you."

"Yes," I agree, surprising myself with the calm acceptance in my voice. "That was your mistake. One of many."

I move closer, studying the medical equipment surrounding him. Each machine has a purpose, monitoring vital signs, administering fluids, managing pain. Or perhaps, withholding it. Alex has been methodical, as he is in all things.

"I dreamed of this moment," I tell Mikhail, tracing a finger along the cold metal railing of his bed. "When I was in that facility, when they were cutting into me, when I was screaming for help that never came, I imagined what I would do if I ever got my hands on you."

Mikhail's eyes follow my movements, terror evident in their depths. Good. Let him know fear.

"The things I imagined. They would make even Alex uncomfortable. And he's quite creative, as you've discovered."

My grandfather's chest rises and falls in shallow, rapid breaths. The heart monitor beside him registers his increasing distress with quickening beeps.

"You're afraid," I observe, leaning closer.

His lips move again, forming words I can barely make out: "Family...blood..."

Something ugly and fierce rises in me, a tide of rage I've kept carefully contained for months. I straighten up, turning away from the pathetic creature on the bed. My eyes lock with Alex's, those icy blue depths that have witnessed humanity's worst and somehow remained steady.

"I want to end this. I want him gone."

Alex studies me, his expression unreadable. "Are you certain?"

"Yes." I step closer to him, drawn by some magnetic pull I've felt since the day he pulled me from that hellhole. "Show me how to kill him. How to make it permanent this time."

Alex moves toward me with fluid grace, closing the distance until we're standing mere inches apart. His towering frame blocks out the harsh fluorescent lights. He's so close that I can feel the heat radiating from his body. If I rose up on my toes, just slightly, our lips would meet.

"There are many ways," he considers. "Quick or slow. Painful or merciful. The choice is yours." His hand rises, hovering near my face without touching, always so careful with me. "What do you want, Luca? Revenge? Justice? Release?"

"Revenge," I smile. "I want revenge."

# Epilogue

## VESPER - 1 YEAR LATER

THE HEAT of Oscar's mouth between my thighs makes me forget I'm supposed to be reviewing the quarterly reports from our Boston operations. My fingers dig into the edge of the mahogany desk, body arching as his tongue finds that rhythm that makes my toes curl.

"Fuck," I breathe, one hand tangling in his hair, guiding him closer. "Right there."

His blue eyes flick up to meet mine, dancing with mischief as he doubles down on his efforts. Even on his knees, Oz exudes that same calculated control that first drew me to him. Every stroke of his tongue is deliberate, crafted to push me to the edge without letting me fall.

The mansion is blissfully quiet for once. Matteo is down for his afternoon nap with Talon standing guard, and Z has taken the security team through their paces on the grounds. These stolen moments have become precious currency in our new life.

"Someone could walk in." I make no effort to stop him. If anything, my thighs tighten around his shoulders, keeping him exactly where I need him.

Oscar's laugh vibrates against my core, sending fresh shivers up my spine. He pulls back just enough to speak, his breath hot against my sensitive skin. "That's half the thrill, solnishko. Besides, I locked the door."

"Like a locked door has stopped Z or Talon. They're both professional locksmiths at this point."

His mouth returns to its exquisite torture, and I let my head fall back, surrendering to the pleasure building inside me. The quarterly reports scatter across the desk, forgotten as Oscar slides two fingers inside me, curling them.

"God, I've missed this," I gasp, my free hand knocking a pen holder to the floor with a clatter that neither of us acknowledges. "Missed you."

Oscar has been gone for five days, handling a situation at our West Coast operations. Five days without his steady presence, his methodical touch that knows exactly how to take me apart.

The pressure builds, my thighs trembling as I hover on the precipice. Oscar senses it, he always does, and slows his pace deliberately, drawing me back from the edge with maddening expertise.

"Don't you dare," I warn.

He lifts his head. "Patience, solnishko. We have time."

"I don't want patience," I growl, using my grip to guide him back. "I want to come on your tongue before someone interrupts us."

His smile is wicked as he lowers his head again, giving me exactly what I demanded. The rhythm shifts—faster, rougher—his fingers working in sync with his mouth until the tension finally shatters. My back arches off the desk as pleasure rips through me, raw and consuming, Oscar's name tumbling from my lips like a prayer, a curse, a benediction all at once.

He stays with me through it, easing me down from the heights with gentler strokes until I collapse boneless in my chair, my chest heaving over my large belly. The twins are expecting in two months' time. Oscar rises with fluid grace, wiping his mouth with the back of his hand before leaning in to capture my lips in a kiss that tastes of me.

"Welcome home," I mutter against his mouth, feeling his smile.

"If that's my welcome, I should leave more often," he teases, helping me straighten my skirt.

I catch his wrist, pulling him closer. "Don't you dare. It's going to take all of us when these two arrive." My fingers swirl over my swollen belly.

"Never for long, solnishko. You know that."

The bulge in his tailored pants hasn't escaped my notice. I reach for his belt, but he catches my hand, pressing a kiss to my palm.

"Later," he promises, his voice rough with restraint. "Z is probably already suspicious about why I rushed straight to your office instead of debriefing him first."

As if summoned by his name, three sharp knocks sound at the door, followed by Z's unmistakable voice. "If you two are done fucking on the desk, we have a situation."

"Your timing is impeccable as always, brother," he calls out, straightening his tie.

I smooth my skirt, trying to regain some semblance of professional composure.

Oz walks over to the door, unlocking it. Z pushes the door open, his silver eyes taking in the scene with a knowing smirk—the scattered papers, my flushed cheeks, Oscar's slightly rumpled appearance. He leans against the door-frame, crossing his tattooed arms over his chest.

"Nice to see you too, brother," Z drawls, his observance lingering on Oscar before shifting to me. "Though I was hoping for an actual briefing on the San Francisco situation before you debriefed our queen."

"I was getting to that. Priorities, brother." Oscar replies smoothly. He moves away from the door and perches on the edge of my desk with casual elegance. "You and Talon have had her to yourselves for nearly a week. I think I should be given a little grace."

I roll my eyes at their banter, but there's no real annoyance behind it. This is our normal, the easy teasing, the casual intimacy that's grown between all of us since we forged our strange family out of blood and chaos.

"What's the situation?" I ask, getting back to business as I shuffle the scattered reports into a semblance of order.

Z's expression shifts, playfulness giving way to the focused intensity that makes him so lethal in the field. "We got a hit on one of the trackers we planted in Mikhail's network. A facility in northern Manitoba."

My heart rate picks up, and it has nothing to do with the afterglow of pleasure still warming my blood. "Manitoba? That's—"

"Remote. Isolated. Perfect for hiding his victims," Oscar finishes, already reaching for his tablet to pull up the information. His post-coital relaxation vanishes, replaced by the strategic mind that's helped us dismantle my grandfather's empire piece by piece.

After my grandfather's downfall, we've spent the last year tracking down his facilities. Shutting them down one by one and reuniting his victims with their families. He destroyed lives for his family legacy. Our new future will be one of unification and peace, so long as I am the head of the family. We deserve that much now that his reign of tyranny is over. We are nearly there with two facilities left to locate.

"How solid is the intel?" I push myself up straighter, instinctively placing a protective hand over my belly where our twins grow. Every facility we've found has been a new fresh horror.

"Solid enough that Talon's already prepping the jet," Z answers, pushing away from the doorframe to approach my desk. He slides a tablet toward me, its screen displaying satellite imagery of what appears to be a compound nestled among dense forest. "Remote location, heavy security, power consumption consistent with medical equipment. All the hallmarks of Mikhail's operations."

I study the images. "How many people are we looking at?"

"Thermal imaging suggests approximately twenty staff, and..." Z hesitates. "At least a dozen potential captives."

My stomach tightens, and not from the twins shifting inside me. A dozen lives. A dozen families torn apart by my grandfather's obsession with genetic manipulation and power.

"When can we move?" I ask, already knowing the answer won't satisfy me.

Oscar's hand settles on my shoulder, gentle but firm. "We move. You stay."

I turn to face him, ready to argue, but Z cuts in before I can start.

"You're seven months pregnant with twins, Vesper," he says, his tone brooking no argument. "This isn't negotiable."

"I don't need to be on the ground team," I counter, though I know it's a losing battle. "I can coordinate from the jet, stay in Canadian airspace—"

"No," both men say simultaneously, their rare unity on this matter telling me exactly how seriously they're taking this. Oscar's fingers press slightly into my shoulder, a gentle reminder of promises made.

"We agreed," he says quietly, his tone softer but no less

determined. "No field operations during the third trimester. The risk is too high."

I exhale slowly, frustration warring with the logic I can't refute. These children inside me, our future, deserve protection above all else. Still, the thought of sending my family into danger while I remain behind feels like swallowing glass.

"Fine," I concede, though my tone makes it clear I'm far from happy about it. "But I want real-time updates. Full surveillance feeds to my secure tablet. Are you all going?"

Z's lips quirk into a half-smile. "Already arranged, moya koroleva. Talon's staying behind. He insisted."

Of course he did. Talon—my shield, my conscience, my steadfast protector—would have anticipated my reaction. In the year since we claimed my son and dismantled the Petrov empire, he's become attuned to my needs in ways that sometimes unnerves me.

"I also want a few bags of ketchup chips. For the babies, of course."

Z's eyebrows shoot up. "Ketchup chips? Those Canadian abominations?"

"The babies want what they want," I shrug, fighting to keep my expression neutral. "And they want ketchup chips."

"I'll add it to the supply list," Oscar says, his thumb absently stroking the nape of my neck. "Along with the all dressed ones you demolished last week."

"Don't forget the dill pickle ones, too," I add, unable to hide my smile as Z's face contorts with exaggerated disgust.

"Your pregnancy cravings are a crime against humanity," Z declares, pulling out his phone to make the note anyway. "Talon's still traumatized from the peanut butter and sardine sandwiches."

"Says the man who eats gas station sushi at three in the morning," I counter, shifting in my chair as one of the twins delivers a particularly enthusiastic kick to my ribs. "Oof."

Oscar's hand immediately moves to my belly, his expression softening as he feels the movement beneath his palm. "Active today?"

"They're practicing their kickboxing," I mutter, placing my hand over his. "I swear they're more active when they hear your voice."

Z's phone buzzes, interrupting the moment. His expression shifts as he reads the message, all traces of humor vanishing. "Talon said the jet is ready. Wheels up in ninety minutes."

My throat tightens as reality sets in. They're leaving, again, while I stay behind. I nod, pushing aside the instinctive protest rising in my chest.

"Ninety minutes, you say?" I repeat.

"Absolutely not," Oscar says firmly, his hand still resting on my belly.

Z shakes his head, a mixture of amusement and exasperation crossing his features. "We're not having a quickie before wheels up, Vesper."

"I wasn't—" I start to protest.

"Yes, you were," Z counters. "I know that look. It's the

same one you gave me in the weapons room last week before you asked me to bend you over the—"

"That's enough," I cut him off, though I can't help the smile tugging at my lips. "Fine. You caught me. But can you blame me? You're both leaving, and these pregnancy hormones are driving me insane." It's hard enough to find alone time while running our empire and raising Matteo. The twins will make it that much harder. If they think I am bad now, they'll be in for a rude awakening after the birth of our twins. Alone time will be a slam, bam, thank you ma'am in between diaper changes and feedings.

Oscar's thumb traces small circles on my neck, his touch both soothing and maddening. "We'll be back before you know it, solnishko. And then you can have your wicked way with both of us."

"Promise?" I ask, hating the vulnerability that creeps into my voice.

"Have we ever broken a promise to you?"

"Only when you promised to let me come with you on missions while pregnant," I remind them, arching an eyebrow.

Z's laugh is low and warm as he leans down, pressing his lips to mine in a kiss that's both tender and possessive. I taste Oscar on his tongue and smile against his mouth, loving how they share everything, including me.

"That wasn't a promise. That was a negotiation tactic."

"One that failed spectacularly," Oscar adds, his fingers still tracing patterns on my neck. "Some battles even you can't win, solnishko."

I sigh, leaning back in my chair. "I hate being left behind."

"We know." Z's expression softens as he drops to one knee beside me, his hand joining Oscar's on my rounded belly. "But these little warriors need their mother to be safe. And we need to know you're protected."

As if responding to their father's voice, one of the twins delivers a sharp kick against Z's palm. His face lights up with wonder. rare, unguarded moment from a man who wears his reputation like armor.

"See? Even they agree," he says, grinning up at me.

"Traitors." My hand covers his, holding it against the place where our children grow. "Just...be careful. Both of you. I need you to come back."

Oscar leans down, pressing his lips to my forehead. "Always, solnishko. We have too much to live for now."

"The children need their fathers," I say, my voice catching slightly. "All of them."

Z rises to his feet. "Talon will keep you busy while we're gone. You both could use a little alone time. And we'll be back before these little ones can miss us."

I nod, swallowing the lump in my throat. This is our life now, the delicate balance between the family we've built and the mission we've undertaken to dismantle my grandfather's legacy of pain. Each facility we shut down brings us closer to the peace we've fought so hard to achieve.

"Go," I tell them, summoning the strength that's carried me through worse than this. "Go free those people. Bring them home."

Oscar's hand squeezes my shoulder one last time before he straightens, already shifting into mission mode. "I'll download the latest intel to your secure tablet. You'll have eyes on everything except the ground operation."

"I want comms access, too," I insist. "I need to hear your voices."

Z's expression softens. "Done. But no backseat driving when we're in the field."

"I make no promises," I reply, the ghost of a smile touching my lips.

Oscar heads out first, tossing me a wink as he grabs his jacket from the hook by the door.

"Try not to miss me too much," he teases, already halfway into the hallway.

"Not if you remember the chips," I shoot back, grinning.

He disappears around the corner, the sound of his voice still echoing faintly—rich, familiar, and warm.

Zaire lingers. He always does. Always the last to leave, like even a few steps away from me costs him something. He walks to the door in slow, deliberate strides, then pauses in the frame.

"I love you, *moya koroleva*."

The words land in that quiet, sacred place he always seems to reach without trying. He offers me a small smile—rare and real—before stepping out and pulling the door closed behind him.

I'm alone in the soft hum of silence, still seated in my desk chair, surrounded by half-finished reports and the lingering scent of the life we've built. I lean back and rest both hands on the swell of my belly. The twins shift beneath my palms, like they heard the voices fading down the hall and wanted to answer.

"Two of your fathers are already impossible," I murmur, brushing gentle circles over the curve of my belly. "And the third?" A smile tugs at my lips. "He's going to relish having two more girls to spoil."

None of them know yet.

It's a secret I've kept for myself. One perfect truth tucked away in the quiet corners of my heart—twin girls. Two strong, wild little hearts beating beneath mine. And not a single one of their fathers' suspects.

A soft breath escapes me, half amusement, half awe, as I picture the chaos to come. Zaire, blindsided the first time one of them outsmarts him. Oscar, pretending to grumble while being utterly wrapped around their fingers. And Talon? He won't even pretend. He'll spoil them relentlessly and call it good parenting.

God help them when these girls figure out the kind of power they're born into.

I shift, bracing one hand on the edge of the desk as I rise, the other still cradling my belly.

"Let's go see what your other father is up to," I murmur. "Oz and Z didn't want to play, but Talon will."

The pint of ice cream waits for me in the little freezer Talon had installed in my office by the cabinet. I grab a pint and a spoon from the container on top of the freezer, then head for the door, my steps slow but sure. The reports can wait. The world can wait. The lights in my office flicker gently as I step into the hall, leaving behind the chaos, the strategy, the past. Heading toward the only thing that matters now.

Because after everything we endured—every betrayal that cut too deep, every scar we thought we'd never stop carrying, every truth that shattered the ground beneath our feet—only one thing remains unshakable.

Family. Not the one we were born into, but the one we bled for. Fought for. Chose.

We didn't just survive *all the darkest truths*.

We rose from them.

And in the ashes, we built something fierce. Something real.

Something that finally feels like home.

**Want more from the world of the Second Sons?**

Dive into the darkness with *All The Sins We Inherit*—a brand new MM duet that takes you deeper into the shadows.

**Join Luca and Alex.**

Their story begins here.

**Pre-Order Now:** https://books2read.com/AllTheSinsWe Inherit

Have you ever wondered what would've happened if Alex didn't push Vesper away in that basement?

If she took control instead—demanded what she wanted and refused to let him hide behind restraint? This is that moment. Uncut. Unforgiving. Unforgettable.

Download the deleted scene and get a glimpse of what it really feels like to be wanted by Alex... and to want him just as fiercely in return.

Download Now: https://BookHip.com/CMTKGBM

# Acknowledgements

**(aka: The Part Where I Cry, Roast My Friends, and Try Not to Thank My Houseplants)**

First, to my husband Glen — my real-life hero who survived a massive heart attack, the loss of his job, *and* his mom's open-heart surgery... all while I was in the corner muttering, "just one more chapter." You didn't just survive life's chaos — you survived *me writing a book during it.* That deserves a medal, a vacation, and probably a therapist. I love you more than caffeine, and that's saying something.

To Cass and Mads — you absolute gremlins of encouragement. You cheered me on like deranged cheerleaders possessed by literary demons, demanded updates with the intensity of FBI interrogators, and suffered through more unfinished snippets than any humans should be legally exposed to. Sorry for the mental whiplash. On second thought... *I regret nothing.*

Alicia and Rae — my "This Book Is Driving Me Crazy" hotline operators. You gently talked me off ledges, slashed my overthinking with machetes of logic, and reminded me (again and again) that *no, this didn't need to become a trilogy,* I just needed to write the damn book. You're the reason this didn't end as a 500-page document titled *"WHY GOD WHY"*.

To the readers, influencers, and fellow chaos gremlins who've supported this story over the past *ten freaking years* — thank you for screaming, swooning, crying, meme-ing, and surviving every update, delay, and existential spiral right along with me. You made this wild ride worth every panic edit and caffeine overdose. Your support kept this book alive when I was ready to throw it (and my laptop) into a volcano.

We made it. Somehow. Probably through a pact with demons and sheer spite.

This book is for you. 

# About Avelyn

Meet Avelyn Paige, the creative genius behind thrilling romantic suspense and heart-pounding motorcycle club and mafia romance novels that have conquered the Wall Street Journal and USA TODAY bestseller lists. Nestled in a cozy corner of Indiana, she shares her quaint abode with her hubby and a lively bunch of five furballs.

By day, Avelyn transforms into a cancer research superhero, battling in the realm of science. But when the lab coat comes off, the writing cap goes on, and she dives into a world of passion, intrigue, and leather-clad rebels. An unabashed bookworm from the get-go, Avelyn decided to weave her own tales after a plot twist in her life – losing her dad in 2015. Since then, she's been on a wild ride through imagination and hasn't hit the brakes!

# Join Avelyn's Reader Group: Avelyn's Angels

**The Bastard Boilers MC**

Property of Azrael

Property of Fox


**Voodoo City Queens MC**

Devil's Queen


**Second Sons Duet**

All The Pretty Little Lies

All The Darkest Truths